First Meet Foul

JAQUELINE SNOWE

PUBLISHED 2023
Published by: Jaqueline Snowe
Copyright 2023, Jaqueline Snowe
Cover Design: StarChildDesigns
Editing: Katherine McIntyre
Formatting: Jennifer Laslie

This is a work of fiction. The characters, incidents, dialogue, and description
are of the author's imagination and are not to be constructed as real. Any
resemblance to actual events or persons, living or dead, is completely
coincidental.

Doug and Armano McGann

I can't describe how much our group chat means to me. From Thiccolas Cage to Oh My Gus to Furbies and to competitive juggling to dog face to B Frais. Thanks for being in my life. Figured dedicating a book to you was better than trying for an awkward hug?

Also, don't read this book. Thanks.

FIRST MEET FOUL

Lorelei Romano thought junior year would be spent living with her best friend, having the best season of her life on the girls' soccer team and enjoying time with her boyfriend. Instead, she was suddenly single and stuck living with her brother in the football house across the hall from the grumpiest football player on campus. The tight end might be easy on the eyes with his tree-trunk thighs and gorgeous thick hair, but the guy hates her on sight.

Luca Monroe doesn't have time for feelings in his plan to get to the NFL to financially take care of his grandma. He had a rough life and can't afford to veer off track—no matter how much his teammate's sister tempts him. She's a weakness he refuses to indulge, so keeping his distance is the only solution. He'd never betray his quarterback like that, and plus, every second of his day is focused on football.

But when Lorelei ends up in a fight for an internship with the guy who broke her heart, she teams up with Luca to wow her professor. The project brings the two together, and with that, their chemistry implodes. They agree to a friends-with-benefits arrangement. The rules are simple: no feelings and no one ever finds out.

Despite their own rules, feelings get involved. Lorelei refuses to be kept secret, and Luca always puts the football team first. However, when she walks away, Luca's on defense. He either risks it all for the girl who's become his everything or miss a chance of scoring real love.

.

CHAPTER
ONE

Lorelei

I'd never actively thought about committing a crime, but Mrs. Henrietta Whittaker had me contemplating it.

"What do you mean you're *selling* the complex?"

"Ms. Romano, the letter you received explained it clearly. As did the email and posters I've hung all over the building." She pushed her gray hair behind her ears and huffed. "Stop making a fuss. It's not my fault you failed to realize the severity."

"The building is on *campus.*"

She blinked. "I know where it's located, thank you for stating the obvious."

"You're giving us a month's notice to find another place? In September? When most of campus's housing is booked?"

She eyed me up and down, her gaze narrowing on my duffel bag with the Central State Soccer logo. After pushing away from her computer chair, she used one finger to adjust her glasses. "There is nothing more to add to this conversation. It's

1

being sold. You have thirty days. Now excuse me, I need to do anything but repeat the same conversation with you."

Mrs. Whittaker turned her back on me, dismissing me in the rudest way possible. I clenched my fists, my left eye twitching as images rushed through my mind. *Me stealing her car. Me spray painting on her computer. Me shaving off her eyebrow.*

It'd feel good as hell to see her pointy face all red and pouty, then she'd understand how much she ruined my day. Hell, *year.* My vision board contained images of this exact building, with the ivy and exposed brick and a coffee shop on the first floor. I'd be far away from Eric—the ex who broke my heart. My goal was to hang with Mackenzie and focus on earning the internship in marketing. I'd have to beat out everyone else in my marketing class, Eric included, and this place had the perfect café on the bottom floor where I planned to work.

Only… not so much anymore.

So not only did I have to worry about my soccer season, keep up with my grades, impress my professor to get the internship, and try not to show Eric how much he hurt me because the ass signed up for my same class, but I also had to find a place to live in thirty days.

A scream built inside me, and I did the only thing I knew to deal with stress: run.

After dropping my duffel in my room, I put in my earbuds and set off for a jog. My feet hit the pavement in dull thuds, the sneaker to cement sound a consistent rhythm that matched my music. I jogged along the quad, near Greek Row and most the houses the athletes lived at, and that was when it hit me. The solution of all solutions. My saving grace. My holy grail.

See? This was why I ran. It solved shit. It kept me in shape and let my mind settle down to think, and wham, bam, thank you ma'am, I wasn't gonna be sleeping in the library…probably.

There were perks to having your twin brother attend the same school *and* be the starting quarterback, like not getting a parking ticket because they never knew what Romano they were dealing with. The name had weight, and even though I liked to think I held my own as a scholarship recipient for soccer, I knew it was my brother's reputation. Dean Romano was the face of the football team, and he wasn't completely hideous.

There were definite cons of having him here, like my so-called friends using me to get closer to him, to being recognized if we went anywhere as a family, to his face being all over campus. But right now, there was a huge-ass perk sitting in front of me.

My brother is down a roommate.

It felt wrong to be happy one of his teammates had injured his leg and moved back home for the semester, but that left an empty room that I wanted to claim. I adjusted my route to head toward the football house, hope blooming in my chest like my favorite appetizer—the blooming onion.

Sweat covered my neck and chest as the September humidity clung to the air, and my dark curly hair went in every direction. I hummed to myself as I stood in front of an old-bricked building. A large porch with a couch led to a blue front door with a football painting on it. I rolled my eyes. Could my brother live in a more obvious house?

I paused my dance mix playlist and sent him a text. *You up? I'm outside.*

It was ten on a Monday, and the guy lived and breathed football, so if he wasn't home, he'd be at the gym or at the field watching tape. I *needed* him to be home though. The thought of not having a place to stay made my skin crawl and my stomach heave.

It derailed my plans, and I stuck to my plans. They were my commandments, and Eric had thrown the first wrench in them. Now the apartment? I was one distraction away from losing it.

Dean: what do you want?

Lorelei: fame and fortune

Dean: go away

Lorelei: this is serious

Dean: five minutes

I raised my fist in a cheer just as the front door swung open.

"That was mighty fast, Deansie Boy. Thought about breaking in tbh," I said in my most cheerful voice.

The door closed, revealing the person who opened it. It was not Dean. Not at all. It was Luca Monroe, the guy whose first word to me was *ugh* two years ago. My eyes widened, and I slammed my mouth shut as the giant, grumpy, and wee-bit-too-handsome tight end stared daggers at me.

Not small daggers either. Big ones. Like swords.

He wore black jeans and orange chucks as well as a white polo with a football logo on the chest. The fabric pulled tight across his pecs, but I made sure to not notice. Luca might be *hot* and a mystery and talented on the field, but he and I were enemies. Not full-on fight to the death enemies but more the "go out of his way to make my life hell" kind. Like, he always used *my* machine at the gym when I went to run or how he'd interrupt me every time I talked or how he insulted me to his friends.

It was...fine.

My stomach tied up in knots at seeing his dark expression, but I refused to cower. Luca Monroe disliked me for some reason, and that had never mattered until this very second.

Because if I was going to beg my brother for the spare room, then that meant sharing this house with Luca. *Sonofabeezy.*

"Why hello there, handsome." I flashed a smile, clasping my hands behind my back to hide my nerves. I loved complimenting him because it threw him off his grump game. The best defense against a jerk? Surprise. "You look wonderful —swell I'd even say."

He blinked. "Why are you here?"

"To rob you?" I tilted my head to the side, enjoying the evident irritation on his face. His brows furrowed, and his lips were pressed in a thin line. Yes, I might've enjoyed annoying him. It was better than fretting over what I'd done for him to dislike me. I still could see the cringe on his face and the *ugh* sound he'd made when I held out my hand and introduced myself freshmen year.

His jaw tensed before he sighed. He reminded me of my rude uncle who thought the world's purpose was to make him angry. Luca had big anger energy. Ragergey.

"Dean's busy." His clipped voice was as pleasant as metal cleats on tile.

"He texted me he'll be here in a few minutes. Can I go inside?"

"No. You can wait here." He crossed his arms, his gaze remaining on my face.

Luca had dark brown eyes that were the same shade as his hair. Luscious, wavy hair that kinda had me jealous. I had no doubt he could use any product he wanted and make his locks look perfect.

Not like my feral curls.

He eyed my hair, and I instantly ran my fingers through it, self-conscious that the wild curls were even more extra. The wind gave me more wisps, but I scolded myself for caring. It was Luca *ugh* Monroe.

"Nah, I think I'll head inside." I stepped toward the entrance, but he held out an arm, like he planned to block me. "You for real, bro?"

"I'd prefer you don't go in there.'

"And I'd prefer that female athletes were paid the same as men, but we don't all get what we want, do we?"

He pinched the bridge of his nose, mumbling something before heading down the stairs in two large steps. The guy had thick thighs, that was for sure. If he wasn't always so rude to me, I'd think him handsome.

Sigh. I needed a place to live more than I needed to stay away from Luca. If I remembered correctly, there were five bedrooms in the house on two separate floors. Maybe I'd have the room farthest away from Luca so we'd never have to see each other.

My stomach fluttered with the fact that Dean could say no, that they'd found another roommate, or it had flooded or *something.* My confrontation with Luca rattled me, and I paced the porch until Dean finally walked out.

Of *course* he'd just woken up.

"What is it?" He yawned and ran a hand through his messy hair. "You said it was serious, and I have someone waiting for me."

"Gross." I made a blech sound. "Better get to the point then, huh?" I laughed, my nerves escaping.

Dean narrowed his eyes and sighed. "Please, Lo, spit it out."

"I need to live here."

"What? No." He coughed into his fist. "It's the football house."

"Technically, accurately speaking, soccer is more football than your football, so if there was some unwritten rule, this wouldn't break it." I faked a smile as my stomach rolled with

6

unease. "Dean, someone sold my building. I have thirty days to find a room, and unless I want a place miles off campus, this is my only hope."

"Christ." He rubbed his palms over his eyes, yawning loud enough to wake a sleeping bear. Death by bear seemed better than no place to stay. But I wasn't desperate…yet.

Dean might act like I was the dramatic one, but he had his moments. I put my hands together in full begging mode. "I'll cook dinner? Bake cookies? Hide in the closet?"

He rubbed his palms over his eyes, groaning like an eighty-year-old man. "The guys won't like it."

"You're the quarterback. They listen to you," I fired back. Worry didn't look good on me. I never cried. I refused to, but my eyes prickled, and the feeling of losing control gripped me head to toe. I'd spiral. I had been since Eric dumped me two months ago. "I'll pay, obviously. I'm an athlete, so I won't mess around. And I can be a bro. I'm easy." I hopped from one foot to the other, like the dance proved how laid-back I was.

"You, are *not* easy." He glared at me. "You blow fuses, leave your shit everywhere, have way too many bottles of crap in the bathroom." He stared off toward campus, scratching the back of his neck. "You'd have to share a bathroom with two guys."

"I've shared one with you most of my life. Not a problem." Inside, I screamed. My brother was gross. Most athletes were gross. But I'd weather the storm if I could live here. "Just a semester. Let me get through the season and then I'll move."

"Goddamn it, Lo. They will hate this."

"Why? What would be so bad about having another roommate who happens to be your sister?"

"I don't know. We play hard, party hard."

"Great. I'll buy beer for you."

He pinched his nose so hard a red spot formed on either side. "Can I talk to them about it?"

I pulled on the end of my ponytail. "I mean, sure, but Mom's calling me later to chat about when her and Dad are coming down for a game, and you know she'll suggest the same solution when I tell her."

Dean's gaze sharpened.

I had him.

See, the thing about big Italian families was that our mother ruled the house. Her and my dad were relationship goals, but no one wanted to disappoint Celestina Fogliano Romano. Dean was a mama's boy through and through, and if she asked him to do something, he'd do it.

Why didn't I realize that sooner?

He gritted his teeth before nodding. "Fine. *Fine.* Let me talk to the guys."

"You're the best!" I jumped into him, throwing my arms around his shoulders. "Thank you, Dean. You won't even know I'm here!"

"Get off me, you smell." He shoved me away but not with real force. "I have a good thing going with the guys, the team, so please don't blow this for me."

"Of course. Duh!"

"No hooking up either, you *or* your friends," he said, his voice becoming stronger. "We can't afford the distraction. Plus, you're my sister, so, this is nonnegotiable."

"Okay, first, *ew footballers.* And second, when have I ever interfered with football for you? I would never. I understand what I means to you." My voice lowered, an odd, emotional ball in the back of my throat making an unwanted appearance. Dean had almost lost his football career because of an accident in high school. A dumb car crash where he wasn't wearing a seatbelt. It had rocked our whole family, and he'd come so far.

"I know, Lo." He swallowed, his mouth forming half a smile. "You can hang just fine but none of your…girl nights here, okay? No team sleepovers."

"Uh, you're missing out. Face masks? Food? Movies? It'd actually do you well to relax a little and replenish your body's nutrients instead of partying them away." I shrugged. "But fine, I will listen to your demands.'

He snorted. "Give me the next week to talk to them about it."

"But I can, for sure?"

"Probably. I need to ask them though. One semester. No bullshit."

"You're my favorite twin." I grinned, opening my arms like I was gonna hug him again.

He held up a hand, shaking his head. "No more hugs. Leave my porch, and I'll call you when you're good to come over here."

"Thank you, thank you, thank you. I'll make sure to tell mom what a *santo* you are. *Santo* Dean." I kissed my fingers and saluted the air. "I'll start packing my bags!"

He rolled his eyes before returning to the house. My brother might be the face of the football team and a major player on and off the field, but he was a good guy. There hadn't been a single time in my life I couldn't count on him, and a wave of gratitude washed over me.

I wouldn't be homeless or sleeping on friends' couches during my junior year season. I'd have a place with a bed, where I could introvert all by my lonesome and relax. My grades wouldn't drop because of stress, and I could keep my stats up.

Sure, this plan made me share a roof with Luca Monroe, but I could deal with it. I shifted plans all the time during a game, so why would life be any different? Life was about being flexible, changing course when something got in your way. You adjusted to the opponent, and right now, the opponents were Mrs. Whittaker, Luca Monroe, and everyone else in my marketing class.

I stretched for a few seconds, eyed my new home, and smiled.

Hope you're ready for me, football boys.

CHAPTER
TWO

Luca

I leaned back in the chair at the student union, crumpling a wrapper of gum and tossing it into the red trash bin. Voices carried around me, not loud enough to distract me from my own thoughts.

I had failed. Well, not completely but the plan I wrote for myself wasn't working. I was unfocused. My mind raced through every scenario that could go wrong—I flunked out of college, I lost my starting spot and my chance to show my worth for an NFL team, my grandma became sick, and I couldn't take care of my family.

The same cyclical thoughts always hit me when I felt off-balanced, and it didn't happen often. I refused to let it, but seeing *her* this morning had thrown me off my game. Lorelei Romano defined beauty to me. From her gorgeous curly hair to the large brown eyes to her always sun-kissed skin and muscles. She was my weakness in every sense of the word. My pulse pounded when she was around, and my clothes felt too tight on my body.

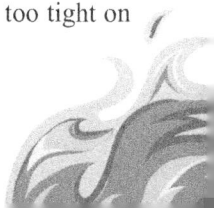

The first time I saw her, my throat had closed, and my skin heated, and I forgot how to speak. She'd worn tight black running shorts and a cutoff shirt, her face clear of any makeup, and she stole my breath as she smiled. Like, the air stopped flowing to my heart because she took my ability to function. She was a goddess, and in those few seconds of seeing her, I dropped every plan I had and wanted to learn her name, her favorite color, and the sounds she made when she stretched in the morning.

That's Dean Romano's sister, Lorelei. She's on the soccer team.

And just like that, the fantasy burst because I never, *ever* fooled around with a teammate's sister. It was rule number one and a law I followed at all costs.

Two years later, she had the same effect on me, and I hated it.

Not only was she my quarterback's twin sister, but she also threatened the carefully crafted regime I created for myself. Girls got in the way of my goal. Well, not random hookups. Those took the edge off and kept me sane. Girls with emotions and messy feelings and attachments were an absolute nope. Been there, almost lost my football career because of it. A high school girlfriend thought it'd be fun to sleep with my teammates, trying to get us to fight because she was bored. That kinda shit stays with you.

The one woman in my life who deserved the world depended on me to play my ass off and make it to the NFL. *Nothing* would stop me from making that dream a reality, and that meant shoving thoughts of Lorelei in her running gear and sweaty stomach out of my head, regardless of the temptation.

"You shouldn't be this tense, Monroe." Xavier Smith clapped a hand on my shoulder before sitting down next to me in the student union. "Ladies, looking fine today," he purred.

"Do you ever turn it off?" I asked, half amused, half annoyed by him. Most of the guys on the team fell into that category. We played our hearts out, but no one else had the same desperation I did, and sometimes that overwhelmed me. My grandma's health and future depended on my success. There was no opportunity to fail because if I did… I winced. I had to succeed. Did I miss the shit I used to do for fun? Of fucking course. I wished I could go to car shows and admire the wheels I'd buy later in life. I loved tinkering with them. The free time was now watching game film.

"Nah, why would I want to?" He winked at a few ladies taking photos of us a few tables over. "You played great Friday, and didn't Leslie find you this weekend for some fun?"

"Yes," I said. I pulled up the assignments on my laptop that I had to do now since the game and film was done for the weekend. Mondays and Tuesdays were the days I did most of my homework and prepared for the week, but I'd already slacked this morning because my grandma wanted to FaceTime.

I loved her more than words. She'd raised me. She wanted to come to a football game this year, but getting her here wasn't cheap. She'd need a driver, a hotel, and a way to attend the game. All those things cost money, and my monthly allowance didn't have room for extras. *Not with the rising costs of her nursing home.*

"Leslie's hot, man. You seeing her again?" Xavier leaned onto his elbows, taking a huge bite of a sub sandwich. A little mustard got on his chin, and he wiped it with the back of his hand.

Disgusting.

"No." I adjusted the collar of my shirt, the fabric suddenly too snug.

"Ah, that's right, my player. One and done for Monroe." He

snickered and hit my shoulder. "I should follow your lead sometime. It works well for you."

"Be my guest."

I put headphones in, blasting my focus playlist, and hoped Xavier got the hint. I liked the union over the library because the quiet and stillness there freaked me out. I preferred controlled chaos, and even though it meant people would recognize me and annoy me, it was better than the tranquility. The silence reminded me too much of the year my parents realized they didn't like having a child. I'd spent a lot of time by myself in their house. No thank you. I loved noise—it made me feel less alone.

My courses were about sports management, and I was already in the hole the first month of school. Between the season and classroom, it'd be a miracle to get by with Cs.

My phone buzzed on the table, and my gut tightened. *Is my grandma okay?* I snatched it fast and sighed at Dean's name popping up.

Dean: gotta talk to you all about something. Might've found a new roommate.

Callum: fuck yeah when?

Oliver: fam meeting tonight?

Family meeting. My eye twitched. I appreciated the sentiment from Oliver, but most of his self-prescribed *family meetings* ended with two of us horsing around or making a bet or getting into trouble. They were entertaining at least. I couldn't walk away from a bet even though I knew it'd never end well for me.

Luca: I'm busy until six.

Dean: six it is then.

Having a new roommate would fill the void since Gage, our other teammate, had gotten injured and had to move back home for a few months. His room sat unused, a twin bed and an empty dresser shoved into a corner. It'd be nice to have a little extra income for us to split, but mainly, I wanted a roommate who would leave us alone.

If they were an athlete, all the better. They'd understand how tough it was and the dedication it took. Dean wouldn't suggest someone unless they'd fit in. I knew that. Relaxing into my chair, I silenced my phone so I could jump into my homework. I'd worry about the roommate later, when I had the mental capacity.

At two minutes before six, the four of us sat at the kitchen table Callum's mom had found for us and refinished. The school's logo sat in the center, and each chair was either orange or blue. It always smelled like paint, but I liked it. The thought was kind. Oliver grabbed a sports drink for us and sat at the head of the table, his glasses perched on his nose and his blond hair in a manbun.

He had the most style out of all of us, that was for sure. Callum came next with his loud personality and swagger. Dean was more like me, focused and football everything. He had the face for a QB and the attitude to handle the stress. These guys were the closest things I had to brothers and the only people who knew the truth of my situation. They understood my desperation and determination and that anything that got in the way of that would be removed.

"This feels too formal." Callum frowned at Dean. "A full fam meeting? What's going on?"

Dean squeezed the back of his neck, his face getting red as his attention flicked to me for a beat. "Look, this isn't ideal, but it needs to happen. Please support me on this."

"Anything, bro." Oliver adjusted his hair and leaned onto his elbows. Nothing flustered Oliver, ever, and it made me strangely jealous. I'd love to not stress about every *single* thing all the time and just exist. Watch horror movies and buy random shit online. Not worry about my grandma's health or her finances or the fact I was one injury away from losing the financial security our family needed. I'd love my biggest issue to be how I did my hair that morning.

"It's my sister." Dean swallowed hard. He stared at the table and blew out a long breath.

My lungs froze, Lorelei's face flashing in my mind. She hadn't seemed hurt when I'd run into her earlier. Was she injured? Sick? In a car accident? I scooted closer, every muscle tightened and ready to spring into action. We could help drop stuff off or bring her food or—

"She needs a place to stay for one semester. And by that, I mean she wants to live here."

"Lolo?" Oliver asked, his face lighting up in a grin. "Living in *this* house?"

"Yes, but don't say it like that." Dean leveled his gaze and growled. "She has always and will always be off-fucking-limits."

The other two commented something, but the sound was distorted, like my mind couldn't understand their words. It remained on the fact Dean's sister was a walking wet dream. Lorelei Romano, here, in this house, near me was unacceptable. I couldn't... she'd... I closed my eyes, my ears ringing as panic washed over me. I couldn't afford to be distracted, and she defined the term. My pulse raced so hard my fingers throbbed.

The conversation came back to me, their voices returning as I inhaled.

"She won't care about the hookups or parties?"

"Nah, she's laid-back and is always working out. We'll

hardly see her." Dean frowned at me, his head tilting to the side. "Luca, you've been quiet. Is this okay? I know you're strict about who comes here during the week."

I met his eyes, different scenarios running through my head. Me receiving a bad grade because she played music too loud or me not sleeping well because of girl drama and the lack of sleep causing me to get injured. Me getting caught up in her spell and forgetting why I was here. Me breaking my control and ruining my relationship with Dean, thus, destroying my NFL chances. Been there, done that, and Lorelei might be the most beautiful distraction on earth, but she couldn't be *mine*. "Truthfully, I'd prefer she not live here."

Dean winced and ran both hands through his shaggy hair. "Why? I can talk to her to make sure she doesn't interfere with your study schedules or workout regime. She agreed she won't have her friends over, no partying, nothing." Dean's frown grew as he stared me down. His eyes pleaded with me, and the same large brown eyes he shared with Lorelei filled with regret.

Shit. How could I explain this to him without revealing my strange, selfish thoughts? Not one of them made sense. *Oh, I'm attracted to your sister and don't want to tempt myself* or *She's my weakness.* My reasons made me sound irrational. I ran a hand over my jaw, hoping to buy myself a few seconds to come up with a brilliant, very reasonable explanation. "Girls complicate things."

Dean laughed. "No shit, but this is my sister we're talking about. Not some cleat-chasing chick."

Callum and Oliver snorted, and the weight of their stares hit me right in the chest. My face burned, and I scooted back in the chair, uncomfortable as hell. "I understand, but she could complicate our dynamic."

Dean ran a hand over his face with a loud groan. "I know. Fuck, I do. But what am I gonna tell her? Sorry you gotta live on someone's couch when we have an empty bed? We can write up a contract with the rules. Whatever you need, Luca. She won't bother you. I'll make sure of it. She... it's the start of her junior season. Some guy broke her heart, and she's been down about it. This year is important to her and to know she doesn't have a place to live? Could *you* imagine not having a bed during the season?"

My throat tightened with all the words I didn't say. *Who broke her heart?* Where did he live? What idiot of a human had hurt her? I willed my spiraling pulse to right itself and cracked the knuckles of my left hand.

Objectively, taking *her* out of the picture, it would suck ass to not have a home while the season went on. Everyone needed a spot to be themselves, decompress, reflect on a game however they preferred. I didn't have siblings, but my teammates were my brothers, and the thought of them having an empty room and not giving it to me because of some asshole and his own issues...

"Okay," I barked out.

Dean's entire body relaxed, the light returning to his eyes. Guilt clawed down my chest—I'd made him stress. All the dude wanted was to take care of his twin sister, and my uptight ass had almost prevented him.

"What do you think? A contract? We can list the rules?" Dean cleared his throat and glanced at each of us, but his gaze returned to me. "Would that help?"

"I don't care at all." Ollie shrugged. "Girls smell nice."

"Okay, you're not *smelling* my sister."

He smirked and arched a brow. "Obviously, but it's a known fact girls smell better."

"Eh, Lo is an athlete. She works out most the time, has this gym bag that has never been washed... she's... wait, why are we talking about this?" Dean groaned and hit the table. "Again,

Lo is my sister. There's a rule about that in the team handbook somewhere."

Callum raised a hand, earning an eyeroll from me. The dude was too much.

"I vote no contract. If she causes issues, we'll handle it with you." He eyed Dean. "My sister is my favorite person in the world, and if she needed a place to stay, I'd make it happen with or without your approval."

I hid my wince.

"Thanks for understanding." Dean blew out a breath and met my eyes. "You sure you're good?"

I nodded. What choice did I have?

It meant I'd have to keep my distance. Despite all the reasons I wanted to learn everything about her, I couldn't. Dean said she was off-limits, and I couldn't afford distractions. I couldn't betray him, our leader on the field. My football future meant everything, and regardless of Lorelei's full lips and gorgeous hair, it wasn't worth even the slightest risk.

CHAPTER
THREE

Lorelei

Nothing caused my body to hum alive more than competition. It wasn't just on the field, either. My favorite professor, Mrs. Gravestone, had mentioned the opportunity for a few students to have a kick-ass internship next summer to those who earned it, and it had become my sole identity.

I loved marketing and how words and images could cause reactions in people. Soccer had never been my end goal. It was my entire life, and I loved it, but I didn't have the same dreams like some girls on the team who dreamed to play for the US Women's team or even the Olympics. Me? I wanted to join a marketing firm. Would I work for the US Women's team? Without question, but my passion was with words and creative ways to get people thinking.

In order to show my professor I was the right choice for the internship, I had to pick a solid project, and she'd already turned down my initial two ideas. They were too basic.

There was also the fun little element that Eric was in the

same class as me, who *also* wanted the internship, so in my mind, getting it over him meant I won the breakup. Silly but not untrue. I sighed, rubbing my temples as I stared at the requirements for our semester-long project.

Mack slid her Gardettos across the library table, a large pile of the brown ones staring at me. "For you, Lolo. You have your stress sounds."

"Angel." I grabbed five of the beautiful salty snacks and crunched into them. "The spice combination is lethal. Like, how can something be this addictive?"

"Magic." She laughed and adjusted the end of her French braid. My former roommate, best friend, and teammate pulled out another bag of my favorite food from her purse.

That had me on edge. She brought gifts when she had bad news. Like the time she'd cancelled our friend trip to Lake Michigan because her boyfriend surprised her in town or the weekend she baked me cupcakes when she lost my favorite pair of earrings. Mack with snacks equated to bad news.

My muscles tensed, preparing for the worst.

"What's going on? Are you breaking up with me?" I forced a laugh, refusing to let the absolute flurry of butterflies in my stomach take over. "Mackenzie Marie, tell me right now."

She swallowed and placed the flats of her hands on the table. "I found somewhere to live, but its only for one person, and I'm so sorry, but I couldn't find a place with two, and I hate this so much."

"Oh." I exhaled, replaying her jumbled words over. "That's... hey, don't feel bad. My brother said I could *probably* stay with him."

She closed her eyes and sighed. "You don't hate me? We planned on living together junior year for years. It was gonna be me and you, girl, partying and having fun and decorating after our vision boards."

"Not even a little bit." I squeezed her hand. "I mean, if my brother doesn't let me crash with him, I might use your couch or something, but I'm hoping his ingrained guilt forces him to let me live there."

"Couch, floor, anything you want." Her teeth came down over her bottom lip as her attention moved toward the entrance of the library. "Great."

"Hm?" I craned my neck and knew the object of her sarcastic comment. *The football players.* Dean told me how strict their coach was about study tables and ensuring their team GPA was stellar. I loved how most of the guys took studies *and* football seriously. With all the injuries, it never made sense to bank on just athletic ability. Hell, look at Gage, the reason I might have a room to stay in.

But Mack's annoyance made sense. Whenever any football or hockey player went anywhere on campus, they were recognized. They might've had good intentions to study, use the library for any solid reason, but they caused a scene each and every time. A part of me thought they did it on purpose, to get fawned over and flirted with. It'd be a nice ego boost. Dean loved attention. Even as a kid, he ate it up, so being a quarterback was the natural move for him.

"We can move to a table farther back?" I spoke to her but kept my attention on the guys. Dean, Callum, Oliver, and Luca didn't just walk, they strutted. My brother's teammates and friends were decent guys. Sure, most of them partied hard, but they were kind in their shenanigans. If you wanted a good time, they were the guys to hang with but never more than that—a temporary night of fun. Not that I had any interest in that. I was *done* with athletes. Forever.

"No, it's fine." She rubbed her lips together and twirled a blonde curl that escaped her braid. Her cheeks reddened, and I was about to ask her why she had that blush creeping up her face, but Dean walked in our direction.

My pulse raced, my stomach getting a different kind of butterfly explosion—hope. *Please let me live with you. Please. Please.* I'd texted him last night asking when I could move in, but he'd responded with *we're discussing it.*

Discussing *what?* My possible homelessness? Had it been a fun dinner topic with the bros?

He hadn't texted me again, which was fine, but I needed an answer soon or I had to come up with another plan of desperation. I could...check online for places off campus. Yeah, I could do that. It would suck because I didn't have a car, but it wouldn't be impossible.

His face, similar yet different than mine, seemed neutral. No smile, nor hint of anger. Just, blank. His game face.

I hated that I couldn't read my own twin. It wasn't like the movies where we could send messages through our minds. If anything, us being twins made us too similar to communicate sometimes. I crossed one leg over the other, then sat straighter. No matter what he said, I'd take his answer with pride and dignity. Then, I'd call our mom and cry.

"Hello, Dean." I smiled, looking totally chill and not like I was freaking out inside. I pushed my hair behind my ears, some curls getting stuck on the large hoop earrings I wore. "How are you? Well? I'm jazzy for a Tuesday."

"Stop being weird." He snorted and stared at Mack for a second, then back to me. My teammate did not acknowledge him.

"Me? Weird? Never." My voice rose an octave, and I felt more than witnessed his teammates staring at me. My skin tingled from the attention. My brother liked being in the spotlight, but me? Nah. Only when I was on the field and in my jersey. The uniform was armor of sorts, protecting me.

"Look." He rubbed the back of his neck. "You can live with us, but there are con—"

"Yes! Ohmygod." I jumped from the chair, throwing my arms in the air and spinning in a circle. "I could cry. I won't, but I could!" I did a jig dance before flying at my brother in a hug. He caught me with a grunt. "Thank you, Dean!"

"Okay, chill." He patted my back awkwardly and gently shoved me away. "There are concerns we need to talk about."

"Of course, yes, I totally understand! Anything! Need me to promise an oath? Get something notarized? I'll do it." My smile stretched across my face, the gesture so large that my cheeks hurt. "You're saving my life, you know. I acted super chill about it, but I was a mess inside. A hot mess express."

He rolled his eyes, his own mouth curving up on the side. "So dramatic."

"Normal dramatic," I corrected.

He held out a fist, and I bumped it before he stepped back. I hadn't been kidding about almost wanting to cry. With the news that Mack had found a place already and this huge project my professor needed from me, my nerves were fried. Having a home until the holidays eased my worry. I took a breath and made sure to meet Oliver, Callum, and Luca's eyes. "Thank you, all of you. I know this isn't what you wanted, but I promise you won't even notice I'm there."

"Dean said you could cook." Callum arched a brow. "Feels like this is an easy thing to negotiate. If we let you move in, you feed us."

"I can cook for you," I blurted out. "Not on game nights but other nights, yes. I mean, I probably can't buy all the food—"

"She's not *feeding* us. We have a rotation."

Everyone stared at Luca, his aggressive tone out of place for this conversation. I swallowed and played with the string from my sweatshirt. I couldn't tell if he was mad at me, the world, or chefs. His usual grumpiness seemed more somehow. Luca's brown eyes narrowed at Dean, then he flicked his gaze to me for one second.

So much emotion swirled behind his eyes, but none of it felt kind.

"We'll put her in the rotation then, that's fair." Oliver smiled at me, easing the tension growing inside my chest. His hair was in a bun and had an orange tie around it. Cute.

"Luca created a schedule where we cook one night a week. Game days don't count obviously, but I can add you to the schedule." Dean tapped the edge of the table twice. "I'll leave you and Mackenzie alone. We came here to study, but I figured I'd tell you the news since I saw you."

"How long were you gonna make me sweat?" I asked, a little annoyed he hadn't texted me this last night. "Did you decide five seconds ago?"

"Take the win, Lo." Dean's tone grew louder, irritation lacing it. "The room is available now, so just let me know when you're coming."

"This Saturday work?"

He nodded, and with that, he headed toward the back of the library. Oliver and Callum grinned at us. Callum saluted me with two fingers, and I repeated the motion back. Luca though…he'd already walked away without so much as a look. The nerves in my stomach sank to my feet.

"I cannot believe you're living with *them*." Mack stared at me wide-eyed. "Luca might actually hate you."

"So, I'm not making this gross sensation up?" I rubbed my chest, picking up one of the strings and chewing the tip. "I don't know what I did, but every time I've talked to him, I feel *so* small and bad, like I did something."

"Yeah, I felt secondhand daggers from him." She shivered.

"I'm glad your brother didn't tell you to piss off. Mine would have for sure."

Mack's brother, Jonathon, was a piece of work. Dean might be a playboy and like being the center of attention, but he was kind. Not all siblings were like that, I'd learned, and that kinda sucked. He was my friend and twin, and him not being in my life seemed so strange. I scrunched my nose in a shrug. "Yeah, Dean is better than Jon in that sense."

"How are you gonna survive this, Lo? They party at that house."

"Yes, but *only* on weekends. Dean is strict about that." I didn't mind a party or two. Plus, it wasn't like they'd want me going. I'd hide in my room. Listen to music or watch a movie, or hell, I'd stay at the library. "I can handle the parties, and maybe I can even partake in some fun in this post-Eric world."

She nodded. "And Callum and Oliver's...flirtations?"

"Are you blushing, my best friend?" I laughed and leaned onto my elbows. "Oh my god you are."

"I'm... okay, yes. Callum... hell, even your brother makes me blush. They are hot. I don't know if it's the jersey or the swagger or Dean's face, but it makes me stumble on my words."

I cringed. "You have a thing for Dean? We've been friends for three years and you're mentioning this *now?*"

"Not a thing. Not a thing at all. No, no. I like my guys quiet and soft and gentle." She blinked a lot and lowered her voice. "You know how you get flustered around firefighters?"

"Okay, don't throw my weakness in my face. I can't help it! It's the uniform, the sexiness, the strength. I—"

"It's the same for me, but mine is football players." She blew out a breath, shook her head and stared off into the distance. "Trust me, I would never... consider one in that way. I just get nervous and stutter and think they're hot."

27

"Then it's a good thing you're not the one moving in, Mackenzie Marie." I snorted. "You'd just be a walking horndog living with them."

She laughed, and her blush crept down her neck. "I really, really would."

"Good thing I don't find them attractive at all." The lie wasn't untrue for the most part. Guys like Oliver and Callum were like Dean, flirty and charming. It was the players like Luca who got under my skin. But there was no reason to talk that out or bring my unwarranted attraction to him up. I had a living space now, and my goal was to stay as far away from him as I could. Athletes were on my never list, and I had too much to worry about other than my love life. Eric's abrupt dismissal of me messed with my confidence and taught me that I couldn't settle for being someone's third or fourth priority.

"Now, let's silence notifications for an hour and see how much we can get done, hm?" I turned off all alerts on my laptop. "Then, we can go run."

"How am I supposed to move my shit if my teammates can't come with me?" I asked my idiot brother, hands on my hips and my hair going every possible direction. Instead of running in the cool morning weather, I was moving into the football house. The place that had *parties* on weekends, but I wasn't allowed to let my teammates help me move.

"This is dumb," I yelled, annoyed already. "Are you going to help me?"

"Can't. Gotta head to practice. Coach wants me in to watch film from last night."

"So, I don't have a car, and I can't call my friends, so I have to carry all my shit, by myself, a mile to get here."

Dean winced, running a hand through his hair, and nodded. "I'm sorry."

"No, you're fucking not. Is this revenge of some sort?"

He glanced at his watch and muttered a curse. "I gotta go now, sorry, Lo."

That was unhelpful.

The gratitude I had earlier in the week melted into annoyance at the hurdles in my way of moving in. I also had a game the next day and needed to prepare for it. Football wasn't the be-all and end-all, and seriously, why couldn't I have someone help me?

"Damnit!" I kicked my bag of workout clothes on the porch. I had a key and a brief description of my room.

Top floor, empty room on the right.

Dean was not gaining any points in my book today. None at all.

I hoisted one bag over each shoulder and went inside. It had been awhile since being here. Parties were not my scene, and the smell of lemon surprised me. It was clean? And nice?

Interesting.

A living room was to the left, a hallway straight ahead, and stairs to the right. One staircase went up, and the other went down. The wood floor had seen better days, but there was a rug? That seemed risky. A rug in a college house was just asking for beer to be spilled.

Top floor.

I adjusted the straps of my bag and headed upstairs. Wait, were there three stories? Damn. My brother was a real dick for not helping me. My legs could be sore before the game tomorrow if I had to do all this lifting myself. A dull headache formed as I went up to the third floor, and I sighed. There were two rooms on the left, one on the right, and a bathroom.

Oh snap. I'd forgotten about our shared bathroom. Fine. It'd be fine.

My face heated as I passed the door on the right. The made bed and movie posters on the wall clearly showed it was Callum's room. That meant one of the other rooms was mine.

Both doors were shut, which... again, unfucking helpful, Dean. My eye twitched as I thought about telling our mom. She'd have words, no doubt, but I never played that card unless I had to. It was getting close though. I figured the room nearest to the end would be mine. It was tucked in the corner and at an angle. I straightened my posture, my back hurting from carrying two large bags, and twisted the handle. "Home, here I come!" I sang to myself.

Two things happened at once.

An angry, loud voice shouted, "What the *fuck*?"

Then, moaning sounds carried to my ears. Loud, sexy, throaty moans that meant...

My gaze snapped to the large, naked Luca on the bed. He wore nothing. No pants, no shirt. Just, nude. His thick thighs spread out, each one like a tree trunk on the dark blue bedsheets. A laptop sat on the bed next to him, images of two people fucking. Moans came from the device as my heart leapt in my throat. His fingers gripped his dick, moving up and down.

"Get the fuck outta here," he growled, his tone dangerously low. "Leave. Now."

My mind and feet didn't agree, and I blinked, my face white-hot as I backed up too fast. I smacked my head against the doorframe. "Shit. Shit. I saw nothing. Nothing!" I practically cried, my face stinging as the headache was fully formed.

I smacked my hands over my eyes and stumbled over the duffel bag I'd dropped. *Oh my god.* If I thought Luca hated me before, he would murder me now. "I'm sorry, I'm sorry, I'm not staring at your dick. Or the porn. Shit, didn't mean to say that. Just, uh, pause your playtime. I'm—"

Someone lifted me off the ground. Not someone, Luca. It had to be him. But how had he done that if he was busy? I wasn't sure, but next thing I knew, my ass was in the hallway, my duffel bags next to me, and the door to *not* my room slammed in my face.

My lungs heaved for breath, the reality of what had happened knocking the wind out of me. I'd just walked in on the guy who hated me as he…masturbated. I needed to melt into the wooden floor and live there forever.

How could I face him when he'd want to kill me? I lay there, cursing Dean and hating this situation all over again. *Be grateful you have a place.*

Fuck my conscience.

This sucked.

What if he leaves soon and sees you on the ground?

That got my ass in gear. I heaved the bags into the *other* room across the hall and shut the door fast. There was a bed, a dresser, and a built-in desk, and oof. Not a great move-in day. Not at all.

I unzipped my duffel, hoping to unpack my clothes when Luca's door opened. I froze, regretting not locking my door and waited. Would he come in here, yell at me? Demand I move out? My throat constricted in worry as the loud footsteps stopped outside my room. *Shit.*

I held my breath, refusing to make a sound, and after what felt like ten hours passed, the shadows moved on, and Luca thundered down the stairs. I fell onto the bed, sans-sheet, and threw my arm over my face. Why was the memory of him gripping his cock so hot? My face skin prickled at the image ingrained in my memory, his tight, corded muscles moving in his arm, the sweat on his forehead. Not a good start for me. Not even a little bit. I had to make it up to Luca, or I was confident my ass would be on the front porch.

CHAPTER
FOUR

Luca

My feet pounded against the pavement, sweat dripping down my face and onto my shirt. I needed the release. I couldn't fucking believe *she* walked in on me like that. My body heated, and I slowed down, taking a huge swig of water before wiping my forehead with the edge of my shirt.

Lorelei had seen me jacking off. I wasn't doing anything wrong; I knew that, but god, I couldn't imagine a worse thing to happen. She'd stood there with her wide eyes and lips forming the perfect little "oh" as my dick was in my fist.

She had no idea her face came to mind as I stroked myself. Why would she? My stomach rolled with embarrassment and something like regret. I'd thought getting off would ease the tension of knowing she'd sleep across the hall from me, but it only amped me up.

She'd tripped over the bags, and my heart leapt in my throat at seeing her fall. Without thinking, I'd wrapped a sheet around myself and tossed her out of my room. It had been the only way.

I adjusted my headphones and searched for a heavy rock playlist to finish my run when a familiar head of hair caught my attention for a second time that day. Those gorgeous curls pulled me in every time. My new roommate walked on the other side of the road with two large bags on her arms.

Her red face was set in determination, and the muscles in her arms and legs flexed, like the bags weighed more than her. My jaw tensed. Where was Dean? Why wasn't he with her? Why were her bags bigger than her?

I watched her, hoping someone trailed behind her with help. Her parents, maybe? A minute went by, her curls escaping her ponytail more and more. She was delightful with those wild curls. I enjoyed how they bounced and went every direction, like they had a stubborn mind of their own. My fingers twitched with the urge to touch one, to feel the texture of her hair.

Seeing them now though had me frowning. It was warm outside, really humid, and seriously, why was Dean making her do this alone?

Oh, film. I rubbed my temples and made up my mind. I'd help her. It was the right thing to do. I paused the run on my watch, checked to ensure no cars were on the road, and crossed the street to her. The subtle scent of fall teased the air, the familiar smell reminding me of bonfires and corn mazes and haunted houses. Despite my strict football schedule, I loved Halloween. When I finally made enough money to help my grandma out, I'd go wild for the holiday. I'd buy the entire Halloween store for myself to decorate the nursing home, my home, all of it.

That went on my list of dreams and wishes, along with buying a nice car, getting a shoe subscription, and expanding my wardrobe. Not until I met my goals though.

Nearing her side of the street, I prepared myself for her large brown eyes. They gutted me every time she looked my way. Irritation and curiosity always lingered in her stare, but would it be different now that she'd seen me with my hand around my cock? It had me on edge, the flush of her cheeks and the pulse racing at the base of her neck. I *liked* that she saw me.

Ten feet, seven, five…my heart fluttered against my ribs at being near her, my skin tightening at the thought of the last time I'd seen her, just an hour ago.

"Fucking Dean," she mumbled. Her arms flexed as she adjusted a red strap on her shoulder.

"Let me help," I said, my voice scratchy and low. I'd forgotten to carry a water with me on this run, and my throat desperately needed moisture.

She froze, slowly tilted her head to the side, and when her gaze landed on me, her entire face reddened.

Was she thinking about earlier? I self-consciously ran a hand through my hair, regretting coming over here already. Those large, doe-eyes with long lashes blinked at me. Then again. She swallowed, and her gaze dropped to my waist and *shit.* Was she staring at my dick?

Clearing my throat, I tried again. "I can carry those for you. You seem to be struggling."

She narrowed her beautiful eyes and gripped the strap tighter. "You calling me weak? I realize I'm not a meathead beef stick like you footballers, but I can hold my own. I am *fine.*" She turned her back to me and kept on moving.

She wore a tank top that showed off her back muscles, and they were divine. Sweat glistened on her tanned skin, and wait —did she think I'd insulted her? I hadn't, had I? Self-doubt crept in, and I jogged to catch up to her. "I know you're strong, but these bags are big. Let me take one."

Lorelei's cheek twitched before she set the large black one down. "Thank you."

Relief flooded my veins. I scooped up the bag, and soon enough, we walked side by side on the sidewalk. The house was still a good ten minutes away, and I hadn't thought this part out. The walking time. Did I chat with her? Ignore her? Ask about... anything that didn't revolve around this morning?

It made no sense that my mind turned into this indecisive mess around her. I flirted with women of all ages, charmed most of them when I wanted to, but Lorelei Romano? I became speechless. It was like someone had tackled me head-on.

One minute turned into two, then three, and we were almost halfway to the house. I could survive this, then finish my run and study the rest of the afternoon. The guys would want to party tonight since we won against Indiana, and I could enjoy myself for a few hours. Hell, I needed to get laid to work through this tension.

"You played well last night."

"Hm?" I was still thinking about sex while looking at Lorelei's face, and my stomach swooped. That would *never* happen. Dean would kill me, she'd distract me from football, and my plans would deteriorate. My mantra would help me survive this. I forgot to soften my voice when I said, "*You* watch football?"

"Mm, don't know why you have that tone but yes. I do. My brother is on the team, and I actually support him? Sorry if that's weird for you." She rolled her eyes, scoffing before staring at the sidewalk. "Look, Luca—"

I sucked in a breath, loving how my name sounded in her sultry, deep voice. She made the U sound longer, like she held it an extra beat, and I wanted to hear her repeat it. "Yes?"

"I'm sorry. For earlier. I should've knocked or something."

"Oh." My face heated. She wanted to talk about this

morning.

"I won't say anything. It's no biggie. Wait, I'm not saying *you're* not big, I meant—" She closed her eyes and shook her head. "I didn't see anything. Well, a little but not the whole thing."

"Oh my god." My lungs burned from forgetting to breathe. "Lo—"

"It's normal to masturbate. I'm not judging. I would never judge. Hell, everyone does it. Or if they don't, they're really unhappy. I bet those uptight people who complain the sky is blue never do. You can tell." She spoke fast, blurring the words together.

My brain stuck on *everyone does it.* Meaning… her. God, it was hot. I needed water. To go swimming. Yeah. I'd go to the rec center and swim to cool down. She kept rambling off facts about fucking masturbating, and I thought about dropping her bag and running away. This was too much.

"We can have a code or something, like, we put a sock on the door if one of us needs time to ourselves."

"What?" I gasped. A code? "I don't… no. I don't ever need to know that." I gulped, picturing her *doing that* to herself making me sweat buckets. "Instead, we just leave each other the hell alone. Always."

I couldn't risk looking at her. Dean assured me her temporary living with us wouldn't cause too much distraction, but she wasn't even moved in, and she was messing with my mind. I knew it wasn't her fault, rationally. I wasn't a dick.

But man, I had to get it together. She was Dean's goddamn sister.

The rest of the walk was in silence, thankfully, and I practically threw her bag on the front porch before putting my headphones back in my ears. "Wait until your brother is back, then have him help you."

"Right. Uh, thanks."

Her voice seemed small, defeated, and I snuck a quick glance at her. A blush covered her cheeks and neck, and her dark eyebrows were furrowed together, like she was upset. Had I...upset her? The same magnetic feeling I always had toward her pulled me in, drawing me to ask a follow-up question. My tone might've been harsh earlier, but talking about *that* stuff distracted me. It wasn't like I was a—

"I know you hate me, but I promise you won't even remember I'm here. I'll make sure you never see or hear me."

She hoisted the bags and disappeared behind the front door before I could get a word out. She thought I hated her. That was simply not true.

My mouth parted as I tried to think of an explanation that would appease her, but my phone buzzed before I could. *Grandma.*

"Hello?" I answered, my focus shifting instantly. My jaw tightened. "Are you okay, Grandma?"

"I'm seventy-four years old, Luca. Chill out."

My shoulders sagged in relief, and I smiled. "So, you're fine?"

"Define the word *fine*. Am I alive? Yes. Am I single? Also, yes. I want to go on the old lady bus trip, but you and Val won't let me."

"Because it's reckless," I said, my relief shifting to annoyance. "We've had this chat before, and you know it's silly."

"Silly for me to have fun? Play poker? How am I the more fun one this relationship, Luca Monroe?"

"Because you're immature," I teased.

"Ugh." She sighed, and the sound made me laugh. My grandma was a piece of work but the strongest, best person I knew. She'd taken me in and raised me as if I were her own son, and I owed her the world. She'd driven me to every practice and game and never let me feel unloved for a second.

"Is the new place going okay though?" I hated that I hadn't been able to visit since the season started. I couldn't miss practice during the week, and the three-hour drive was just a hair too long to do for one day. She was on a fixed income and wasn't able to save a penny with the price of the home.

This was why this year mattered so much. I could graduate early and head to the NFL. I'd get the signing bonus and make sure she was set for the rest of our lives. It was the only way to pay her back for *everything.*

"Eh, it's, fine." Her voice hitched, her telltale sign she fibbed.

"What happened?"

"Nothing happened, Luca Loo. I'm healthy and well and in an intense group of women who play rummy twice a week. I schooled Agatha last week for twenty dollars and a joint. Not as much fun as a trip to a casino, but it'll do."

"Grandma." I itched the back of my head. She always did this, lied and distracted me with something she knew would make me ask more questions. "Cut the bullshit."

"Okay killer, watch the language. I'm not some punk you talk shit to on the field."

My lips curled up at her spunk. "Hypocrite."

"You're too perceptive. I hate it."

"You raised me."

"Yeah, yeah, don't remind me." She sighed, and I pictured her running her hand over her face. The silence lasted a few more seconds before she cleared her throat.

"They treat me like I'm a child, like I'm incapable of making a decision for myself. I'm still me and rational most of the time. I lived through too much to be made to feel small, and it grates on me."

My pulse raced in my ears, and my stomach dropped in an aggressive, angry way. My hands tightened into fists, and I wanted to punch the pillar to my right. Making my *grandma* feel small? "Who? What's their name?"

"It's not a specific person, hon. It's their mentality. Like old people are a burden to them."

"You're not a burden. Just," I said, cursing. "This is my final year. Then I'll get that bonus and get you out of there. Wherever you want. The beach, Vegas, New York. I'm not kidding, Grandma, I'm moving your stubborn ass out of there."

She sniffed, and my heart ached. Tears were my weakness. My breath deepened, and anxiety billowed under my skin, matching me itch. My brain went into *fix it at all costs* mode. "I can send more money somehow—"

"Hush. You hush. I sniffed because I have allergies."

"No, you don't."

"For both our sakes, let's say that's it. I hate that you have to take care of me, Luca."

"Why? You're the reason I'm here, playing football. You're the reason I'm alive."

The door opened and closed, and I whipped around to find Lorelei standing there, wide-eyed and lips parted. My grandma spoke again, but all I could think about was how much had she heard? Would she judge me? Ask questions? Laugh?

I opened my mouth to say anything, but she took off, ducking her head and jumping off the porch and onto the sidewalk. Her departure should've pleased me, but instead, an uncomfortable lump formed in my gut.

"You hear what I said, Luca?"

Shit. Perfect example why staying away from Lorelei was a must—I could never say or do the right thing. Guilt ate at me from her thinking I hated her, but I didn't have time to rectify it. Football would always come first.

CHAPTER
FIVE

Lorelei

The three words best used to describe me were dedicated, movie-obsessed, and superstitious. Not like a cute little *make a wish on a yellow light* person. More of a… I wouldn't wash my socks if I kept playing well or my sports bra. I'd do the same pre-game ritual every time or I convinced myself I'd have a bad game. I'd make sure to take the same walk to the field, listen to the same four songs, and wear my hair the same.

I took no chances in messing up the universe. If that meant my socks smelled a little but my stats kept getting better, then that was a small price to pay. Did I also kiss my lucky penny I found when I was seven at the zoo? Sure did. Everything was set, except I needed to grab a snack before our game at 1.

Protein and hydration were key.

Despite playing soccer for fifteen years, the pre-game nerves never went away. I could feel my pulse all the way to my toes, and the adrenaline… I might be a junkie for it. The rush? The way my senses went into overdrive? I craved it.

I felt similar about horror movies in October, but that was different.

Mack: I hate Angela's face.

I snickered at Mack's text. Her ex-boyfriend from high school had cheated on her with one of the players we faced later, and yeah, don't let anyone tell you *men's* soccer was rougher. The women's game was filthy, and Mack might have a sweet face, but she'd leave a body on the field if she could.

Lo: Channel that anger bb.

Mack: It's been three years, but I'm still so pissed.

Lo: Anger doesn't have a time limit.

My ponytail sat high, the same elastic band fraying on the edge. It was my lucky one, and if it broke... no, I couldn't think like that. Coach wanted us there hours early to talk strategy and make sure we were warmed up, mentally and physically.

I rolled my shoulders back a few times, a little stiffness on my leg arm from carrying those bags yesterday. Annoyed, I scoffed as I went through my bags to find some Tylenol. I would only take one to help, then after the game I'd ice and see our trainer. But where the hell was the medicine?

After a five-minute search of my stuff, I sighed. Someone else in the house would have to have some, but the thought of leaving my room sent a different kind of trepidation through me.

I didn't want to run into Luca. At all.

Be brave, you little chicken. I chewed the center of my lip before saying screw it. I was a grown, strong woman, and yes, Luca made me nervous with his scowl and intimidating glare, but I'd run away from him. Yeah, great plan.

I could stare down a girl bigger than me on the field, so a grumpy uptight tight end would not make me cower.

With one final breath, I cracked my bedroom door open and relaxed. His door was cracked and his room empty. He was gone. I did a little jig of excitement just as Callum came up the stairs.

"Oh, hi there," I said, flashing him a grin.

"What did I just witness? You filming a TikTok?" He chuckled and tossed something into his room before joining me. "You gotta get one of those ring lights and a stand, Lolo."

My brows went up. "Lolo?"

"Shit. Is that... Dean always calls you that, so that's how I picture you in my head. What do you prefer to be called?"

"Lolo is for people I'm close to, usually. Lo for my teammates." The tingling of a blush started at my head and spread down to my fingers. "Lo is good. Lo is mature. Lolo makes me seem like I'm six years old again."

"I hate when people call me Cally boy for the same reason. Like, I'm six four and grown, do I look like a *Cally boy?*"

Laughing, I shut my bedroom door. "Hey, do you have any Tylenol? I know I have some, but it's become lost in the move. I have a game in a few hours and need to get rid of this damn tenderness in my left shoulder."

He frowned. "Yeah, downstairs. I'll show you."

I followed him down the two flights of stairs. I always liked his easygoing vibe and soft eyes. We weren't friends or anything, but every time I talked to him the last two years, he'd been kind. Even now, he didn't glare at me for moving into their house.

"We have a cabinet in the kitchen with this shit. Tape, meds, a brace or two. It's a little drugstore area."

"Ah, perfect."

He opened it, shuffled around some bottles, and pulled out a white one. "There you go, Lo."

"See, better. Don't feel young anymore." I grinned, taking the meds from him. "Thank you."

"Sure thing." He ran a hand through his messy hair and eyed my arm. "Are you sore near your neck?"

"Yeah, right here." I pointed to the spot just above my collarbone. Callum frowned and stepped closer. He smelled like sweat and laundry, and while it wasn't a pleasant combination, it wasn't bad. It reminded me of Dean and football camp growing up. "Why do you ask?"

"Want help?"

"What do you mean?"

"Give me your arm." He jutted his chin toward my shoulder and held my bicep with one hand. His other hand came down on my collarbone, and he gently pressed his fingers on the tender muscle. "My trainer showed me this a few weeks ago. You'll obviously need to work with your team's trainer, but if I massage this—"

"Oh my lord," I groaned, closing my eyes. "Yes, this feels *ugnnn.*"

"*What* are you doing?" An angry voice penetrated the air, the tone I knew belonged to my dear, wonderful new housemate. "Remember the rules."

The temperate chilled, and I fought the urge to cringe. *Luca.* The protein bar I ate earlier churned in my gut, like I was guilty of something. But what? I'd done nothing wrong but exist.

"Lo has a knot in her shoulder. I'm helping her out before her game," Callum said, his voice hesitant. His gaze flicked from Luca to mine, a line forming between his eyebrows. He didn't say anything more, but the question lingered in the air.

Why had Luca yelled at us?

Also, what *rules?* What had Dean done?

The giant grump didn't respond, but his retreating footsteps indicated his anger. I exhaled, letting out a nervous laugh. "He hates me if you can't tell. Probably yelled because he doesn't want my gross germs on you."

I wanted to ask about the *rule* comment but refrained. I was pretty sure it involved Dean, and I already had a list of reasons to discuss with him later. This could be added on.

"Mm, not sure if that's true." He pressed my muscle three more seconds before releasing. "That looser?"

I moved my left arm in a circle, over my head and behind my back. "Oh yes. Much better."

He looked smug, his chest puffed out and victory dancing in his eyes. "Good. Glad to assist."

"Thank you. I could play with the pain but can't risk pulling anything."

Callum ran a hand over his jawline, his gaze moving toward the back of the kitchen where Luca had stormed out. "Luca is… intense. I'm sure he doesn't *hate* you, but this is just a blip in his routine, and he never strays from it."

"Dude, he really dislikes me." My face warmed thinking about what transpired in just two days. "It's fine. I can… handle it."

Callum didn't look pleased, and my stomach dropped. I didn't want this to *be a thing.* I preferred no drama. That was Dean's ask—zero drama, no messing with the guys. Easy to follow. Yet not even a full twenty-four hours in and there was the flicker of some. "For real, don't worry."

"You sure?"

I nodded, hard.

"All right." He stared at me for a second longer before flashing a playful, way-too-flirty grin. The switch was incredible. One second, he'd been concerned and friendly, then bam, oozing charm.

"Okay, none of that. Stop it right now." I flicked between his eyebrows, earning a laugh out of him.

"Dayum, Dean mentioned you were off-limits, but I like a challenge."

"Off-limits?" Ugh. I rolled my eyes. "I prefer guys who don't smell like sweat and wear tighter pants than I do. That's a hard hell no."

"Fuck off, Lo." He chuckled, just as Dean and Oliver walked into the kitchen. Callum nodded before walking toward them. He helped take one of the grocery bags from my brother.

"Lo? Y'all friendly already?" Dean asked, his gaze hardening at me. "What did I tell you?"

"Jesus, Dean." I groaned and flipped him off.

"We agreed you'd stay out of our way."

"And we promised to always be friends when we were six, and you've already done three things wrong today," I fired back.

He scoffed. "Pretty sure letting you live here trumps all those."

"You didn't help me move, and it injured my arm. You didn't show me my room, and you obviously gave some speech about rules to the house. Am I not allowed to even *speak* to anyone else?"

He frowned. "You're hurt?"

"Yes, because I dragged my shit over a mile without a car or help." I rolled my arm again, unashamed that this went down in front of Oliver and Callum. Dean and I beefing happened with or without an audience. They would need to get used to it.

"I had film." He sorted the groceries and placed two boxes of cereal in the front of the cabinet. "I'm sorry, Lo, really. I hate that you hurt yourself."

"Fine, accepted. But the rest? Am I allowed to be friendly with anyone or do I have to keep to my room like a little silent mouse?"

"You're never quiet. Ever." He laughed, shaking a box of cereal at me. "I got you your favorite cereal, by the way. You're welcome."

"I hate all of you." My lips twitched, but I refused to smile.

"I didn't do anything!" Oliver held up his hands. "Leave me out of it."

I winked as I left them in the kitchen, partially amused and annoyed at the entirety of the football house. Luca's anger and disgust at me combined with Dean's dumb rules…it made a girl want to have a wild night. Not that I could do it here. No. I'd have to hang out at Mack's or Tessa's—another one of my favorite teammates. She played goalie and had the coolest red hair. It gave me envy, and I tended to appreciate my wild locks most days.

Rotating my left arm in a circle, I headed up the stairs to grab my duffel and head to the field. My playlist was ready to go, and yes, I listened to the songs in the same order every single time, no changes.

"Lorelei."

Shit. My heart leapt in my throat at the deep growl of a voice. I spun, hand to my chest, as I studied in Luca leaning against his doorway. His broad shoulders took up most of the door and the crossed arms…the lean… my mouth dried up at the cords in his forearms. Oh my lanta, he was *intimidating* with those dark eyes and strong brows and wicked jawline. "Um," I said, swallowing to get rid of the raspy voice. "Yes?"

"Here." He held out a blue thing with gel. It took my brain a hot second to note it was an icepack. It was the size of his hand. Did he want to give it to me? Was this… why was he holding it in the middle of the hallway?

My lips parted, but nothing came out. Instead of being a normal human, I was afraid to say the wrong thing. The angry tone from earlier, from yesterday, all came back to me, and I didn't have the emotional energy to worry about him today. Not on a game day. "I gotta go."

He frowned and stepped toward me, pushing off the frame.

47

His clean, soapy, and leather scent surrounded me, and I stopped breathing. He smelled nice. Whatever. No big deal. Candles smelled nice too, but they didn't make my heart beat twice as fast.

"This will help your neck before your game. Alternating between ice and heat, along with massages, will keep it loose. Use it."

"Right." I took the ice pack, not meeting his eyes and instead focusing on his calves. They were twice the size of my arms, and I was proud of my muscles. "Thanks, I guess."

"This is Dean's fault."

"Hm?" I glanced at him, his statement confusing me. His jaw went tight, and his eyes narrowed like he was mad at me. I just didn't get it. "I know me living here is Dean's fault, but I can't do anything about it now, all right? Fuck."

"No, I meant your arm." He cleared his throat, his face paling. "He should've helped you move your stuff in knowing you had a game today."

"Oh." I slammed my lips together, embarrassed that I'd yelled at him for another reason. The concern and softness of his tone distracted me. I'd never heard him speak all even and kind to me before. It was strange.

"Do you need more help, or did you get everything?"

"Are you offering?" The question slipped out without thinking about it because why would the guy who hated me even ask that question? "Wait, of course not. That makes zero sense."

He blinked, his lips turning down in a grimace before I had enough. I pressed the ice onto my skin, double-checked that my phone was in my bag, and took off. "I need to head to my game."

I felt his stare on me as I jogged down the hall. It wasn't

until I was on the first step down that I heard a quiet "Good luck."

I shook my head, hoping to clear the confusing Luca-inspired cobwebs. He unsettled me, and I didn't have space to worry about him or my brother or my temporary roommates. I had to focus on kicking ass at the game.

CHAPTER
SIX

Luca

During the season, my schedule was tight and rigid. Every day, except game days, started with strength and conditioning from six to eight. Then, I'd shower, eat, and get to my classes. Those would go by fast and in a blur, then it'd be film, getting taped and prepped for practice, then practice until six. Then showering, training, dinner. Then, it'd end with study halls before I'd head back to the house to rest.

Monday's film was on improving plays from the previous game, and Tuesday's would be on the upcoming team we'd face. I loved the repetition and cyclical part of being a D1 athlete. It wasn't cut for everyone, that was for sure, but I took pride in earning every cent of my scholarship. I worked my ass off to be here and would remain at the top of my game.

But fuck, I was tired today. It was only nine, and I dragged my feet upstairs, hoping to binge-watch a show and pass out. Callum was with friends, which, I didn't know how that guy functioned. He had to be a vampire. It was the only explanation on how he had endless energy but never slept.

Without meaning to, my attention drifted to Lorelei's door. She'd left it open a crack, and her voice carried through it.

"Are you *sure* he's there?"

"I swear, Lo. I never blocked him for this reason. And he's posting from the courtyard. We can go somewhere else."

Lorelei groaned, a loud and unattractive grunt. "No, fuck. We promised we'd have our Monday Meet-Ups since we don't live together anymore. This sucks."

"We can meet at the place on Green Street instead."

"But they don't have the stamp card to get the free T-shirt. You know my ass is motivated by a free T-shirt. There's nothing I wouldn't do for one."

"Except see your ex."

"Mack Marie, shut your whore mouth. Uncalled for," Lorelei said.

Her friend responded with a laugh. "Have you talked to him recently?"

"I see him twice a week in our marketing class, but I've avoided eye contact and conversation." Her voice came out all defeated and sad. My chest tightened with the stark contrast to the happy, sunshine woman I knew. How dare her shitbag ex cause her any sadness?

"I'm not hung up on him you know, but seeing him out… was he with someone?" Lorelei asked.

Her friend clicked her tongue. "Yes."

"Of course, he is. *Baseball will always come first, babe,* my ass. God." Lorelei groaned again, this time with less attitude. "I want to make him regret what he did."

"Wear the outfit that he likes, and let's go. Fuck him. Sure, he might be great in bed, but we're not missing a chance to get another stamp. You've wanted the *I rode the rail* T-shirt since freshmen year. We never change our goals for stupid boys."

"You're the best wingwoman. Okay. I'm doing this. I'm having a drink and looking good."

"Atta girl."

Then fabric rustled, and soft footsteps thudded on the floor, snapping me back to reality. *I'm eavesdropping like a creep.* The thought of getting caught had me darting into my room and slamming the door. I leaned against it, my pulse pounding. Did she know I was there? That I'd heard her?

She wanted to make some guy jealous, the guy who dumped her? Was Eric a fucking idiot?

The urge to find him on campus startled me.

I ran my hands over my face, the impulse to ask questions stopping me from my plan. Mondays were for binge-watching a show and relaxing. Reflecting on the previous game. Not... plotting to kill Eric.

The familiar creak of her door had me sitting up straighter. Was she leaving? Going out? Was she wearing a sexy outfit?

God! Why did I *care*?

Annoyed at myself, I pushed off the door just as Callum walked upstairs.

"Damn, Romano. Where you heading dressed like that?"

Dressed like what?

I gritted my teeth, my headphones frozen in my hand. I should just put on my show, ignore her, him, everyone.

"Meeting up with my girl Mack on Madison Street Bar. Monday night madness where you can—"

"Yeah, drink the rail. I've been. Have the T-shirt."

"You have it? Damn, that's my goal, man."

"You can have mine, Lo."

"Nah, I'm earning that shit myself. One beer at a time."

He snorted before saying, "Want some company as you head there? I could use a drink."

"Are you allowed to hang out with me? Will Dean ground you? I'm off-limits, remember?"

They laughed together.

A vein would surely pop in my forehead. Callum was so damn *much* all the time.

"You're funny. For real, I can at least walk you there. Dean can kiss my ass."

Eric is at Madison's. The guy she wants to make regret breaking up with her in a sexy outfit.

Would she use *Callum* do to that? The thought nauseated me. I tossed my headphones onto my bed, twisted the handle, and stood in the hallway. They both stared back, and my skin heated. Had it been *that* long since I went out on a Monday?

"What up, Monroe?" Callum leaned closer and held out a fist.

I hit it with my own, but my attention zeroed in on Lorelei's outfit. High-waisted jeans and a tight and I mean *tight* black lace tank top that showed off her muscles. Her hair was down, curls going everywhere, and her lips were bright red.

My skin heated with how sexy she looked.

"Want to get a beer? I'm walking her to Madison's but could use a drink. Didn't love going over my mistake from last Friday ten fucking times today. A brew would help that."

"You lost focus," I said. "It happens."

"Not to you though." He rolled his eyes, dropping the subject. "Let me change my shirt first then we can go."

He headed into his room, leaving Lorelei and I alone in the hall. She chewed on her top lip, her cheeks dusted in pink as she shifted her weight from one foot to the other. Her crossed arms pushed up her chest, and I let my gaze drop to her cleavage for one second before returning to her face.

If she noticed, she didn't give anything away. She stared right back at me, her eyes swirling with questions. I opened my mouth to say something, to explain why I needed to come with or that Eric was a dick or that I didn't *hate* her. I could've said any of those things, but I refrained and kept my trap shut.

"Let's hit it." Callum returned, smelling like his expensive cologne and a new shirt. "You can tell me about who you're meeting there."

"Are you going to talk to Eric?" I asked.

Lorelei whipped her head around, and her eyes narrowed. "What?"

"Your voice carries."

She winced and adjusted the ends of her curled hair. "Well, that's... good to know."

"Who's Eric? Do we like him, hate him? Are we banging him?" Callum asked, breaking the tension.

Lorelei laughed and sped up so they were shoulder to shoulder. I was the odd one out, walking behind and watching her smile at him. I hated the way my muscles tensed at seeing her joy directed at him and not me. Which... made no sense because I didn't have time to deal with it.

Yet here you are going to a bar on a Monday?

"We hate him," Lorelei said.

"Noted." Callum snorted. "Get that, Luca? We are not team Eric."

"Never was," I mumbled. Lorelei glanced back at me, frowning.

My skin flushed, but I kept my game face on. The evening air cooled from the unusually sunny day, and I sighed in contentment. I loved fall. Not only was it football weather, but it meant it was winter soon, and some people hated the cold but not me. Sweaters and sweats were my uniform.

Cicadas buzzed, and a mildewy, leafy smell surrounded us. It was bewitching.

"Wait." Lorelei pulled me from the momentary daydream "Are you guys... should you even be with me?"

"What do you mean?" Callum tilted his head to the side.

"Dean made it sound like I can't acknowledge y'all exist. I'm not trying to get kicked out my first week here, you know?" Her gaze flittered to mine, lingering for a moment before she sighed in defeat. "Seriously, stay home. I'm okay."

"I'm fine walking you to a bar, Lo. I'm not trying to make out with you. Now Dean might have something to say about that," Callum said with a smile.

Lorelei hit his shoulder. "You flirt too much."

"I can't stop it. It's a gift." He put his arm around her, and she leaned into it

I ground my teeth together, wanting to punch my teammate in the face. He was always like this, but did he need to be with *her?* "That's Dean's sister."

"For fuck's sake," Lorelei yelled. Anger flashed in her eyes, all of it directed right at me. "This is dumb." She shoved Callum's arm off her.

"Babe, I'm going to the bar with or without you. Is Luca making you nervous? I understand he's intense, but he can hang back." Callum sent me a look.

Her attention moved toward me, her fingers constantly pushing her hair behind her ears. *She's worried.*

I felt as small as an ant. Callum didn't make her react this way. I did.

While I was aware my issues with having her around were my own, she didn't need to feel the brunt of it. Owning up to my shit had been ingrained in me from day one of living with my grandma, and I knew what I had to do.

"Lorelei—" I started.

"Oh my god it's McGregor and Monroe!"

A group of women on the other side of the sidewalk spotted

us, their excited voices carrying through the air. This wasn't unusual, but the timing sucked. Their outburst ruined the moment I was trying to apologize. They ran across the street in a fit of giggles as Lorelei snorted. "Oh Jesus. Well, I'm not waiting for this, no offense."

"Hold on, Romano, it'll be quick." Callum flashed his grin and put his arm around me. "This is the life, man. Fans. Beautiful ones. Gorgeous, curvy ones."

I tensed but knew what game to play. Our Coach taught us the importance of public image but not ruining a future before you had one. Callum flirted a little too much and too often, but I wasn't judging. He had more charisma in one hand than I did in my entire body. He took the lead, same as Dean, and let Oliver and me ride the coattails. I preferred it that way honestly.

He spoke with the fans, taking selfies as I went along with it. I attracted fans too and put up with the hugs and smiles, but it wasn't the part I was excited about when I thought about being in the NFL. I was financially motivated but also wanted to give back. I had so many coaches take the time to get to know me beyond the dumbass punk with attitude. I hated everything in my teenage years, trying to figure out the world. Coaches molded me, gave me a chance when they could've let me suffer and fall through the cracks. Without them, I had no idea where I'd be. Certainly not at Central State, playing football with a future in the NFL.

The thought of starting a nonprofit to help other kids who might not have the money or family support would be a dream come true. The sexy women who were always game for a one-night stand was an added bonus too. They were uncomplicated and didn't require more than an hour of my attention.

So again, why am I out on a Monday?

Callum and the girls talked about our next home game, and Lorelei's figure was a block away already. Damn. This could be my chance to talk to her alone. I slid away from the girl nearest me and jogged up to Lorelei, her florally scent so damn delicious I forced myself not to inhale. "Wait a sec."

She turned, and her brows about disappeared into her hairline. "Yes?"

"I'm sorry."

She blinked, licked her bottom lip and nodded. "Love an apology but for what, exactly?"

She continued walking, and I gently placed my fingers on her elbow, pulling her back. Even her skin was soft, and I had a hard time letting go. She sucked in a breath and crossed her arms over her chest. I waited for her to look at me, and when she did, the words I planned to say jumbled together. She was a knockout. The streetlights hit her face in a way that showcased her huge brown eyes, her birthmark under the left one, her full lips, and her rosy cheeks, and my stomach swooped.

While I knew I had to stay away from her because she could ruin me, I could be nice about it. I didn't want to be the reason Lorelei Romano was nervous and uncomfortable in the house—and not just because she was Dean's sister.

It was the right thing to do.

I held her gaze, speaking gently and with intention. "I don't hate you, and I'm aware I've made you feel unwelcome. I don't want that, and I'm sorry."

She nodded. "You have."

"I don't have time for… " I started, hating how it made me sound like an asshole. I could be better. "I excel with routine, and having you move into the house messed with that."

"What about my ass offends you, exactly? You hook up with girls all the time." She shrugged, but the tips of her cheeks pinkened.

Is she thinking about her walking in on me that day?
Damn. *Focus.*

"Those are one and done."

"So what? You think I'm gonna try and seduce you and ruin your routine? That's never going to happen. I am *done* with athletes. No more dating or sleeping with them. Plus, hello, Dean would kill me if I messed with the team vibe." She rolled her eyes and laughed yet not with real humor. "I need a soft, quiet man who is feral in bed and doesn't know what a sport is. Nerd in the streets, a freak in the sheets. A kind man without coordination."

I frowned, her words causing my stomach to clench with unease. The thought of her and some guy with a calculator didn't connect in my head. I asked before I could stop myself. "Because of Eric?"

"Ah, yes, that's right, you little eavesdropper." She poked my arm with her finger, laugh lines forming around her large eyes. "I guess it's only fair. I walked in on you watching porn, and you listen to my conversation about my dirtbag ex."

I cleared my throat, my skin heating.

"Don't worry, Luca," she said, her singsong voice filled with amusement. "I won't tell anyone you're into busty brunettes."

Choking on my own saliva, I hit my chest as Callum joined us. He patted my back. "Dude, you all right?"

"Yeah, just talking about porn got him nervous."

"Ha!" Callum cackled. "It's amazing how he still gets bashful. The guy sleeps around."

"And you...don't?" she fired back.

"I mean, psh." He rolled his eyes. "I've committed more to a girl than he ever has. He's a one and done and never look at me again. A real heartbreaker. A real playa."

"Okay, chill." Lorelei shook her head, the two of them sharing a goofy look.

Their little banter annoyed me. Were they friends? Why

were they so chummy and smiley at each other? Also—he painted me in bad light. It mattered, for some goddamn reason, what Lorelei thought of me.

"I'm not an asshole about it," I grunted out.

"Never said you were, bro." Callum slid me a look, his brows arched. "Just saying you sleep around and yet you still blush sometimes."

"Adorable," Lorelei said, her focus on the sky and not me. We walked fast to the bar right across the street. Lorelei froze and sucked in a breath. "Okay, this was a dumb idea. Why did I let Mack convince me this was a good plan? My stomach is in shambles."

"We hate Eric, right?" Callum said.

"Yes. I felt bold after talking to Mack, but now I'm nervous. It's trivial to make him regret breaking up with me. Like, how would this work?"

"Oh, I have an idea," Callum purred. He put an arm around her shoulders and *nope.* Not him. If she needed someone to do *this* with, I wanted it to be me.

"Let go of her," I blurted out, ignoring how my ears turned red. "I'll do it."

Callum's smile grew, and his eyes beamed with victory… like he knew what he was doing.

Lorelei looked up at me, her eyes swirling with mystery. "Do what?"

"Make him regret hurting you."

CHAPTER
SEVEN

Lorelei

A thrill went through me at Luca's words. Swallowing hard, I tried to read his face, his jaw set in determination. I imagined, for a hot second, that his bedroom face *and* game face were the same. Strong, set eyebrows, tense muscles, mouth slightly parted. *Mm.*

Focus.

"You, Luca grumpy Monroe, want to help *me?*"

"Yes." His eyes flashed with victory.

"Why?"

"Yeah, great q." Callum stared at his roommate, his lips almost curling up into a smile.

Luca rocked back on his heels, his gaze never leaving my face. "For starters, to apologize for being an ass about everything. But secondly, the best revenge is to feign indifference. What better way to do that than to pretend to be interested in me?"

"Mm, yes, I do like that plan." I pursed my lips, eyeing

Luca up and down. *Not much pretending there.* "I guess you'll do."

"You guess, huh?" he replied, his eyes lighting up. "Wow."

"Game plan." Callum pulled me from the weird, semi-truce Luca and I had. There didn't seem to be hate spilling from his eyes, which was a nice change, but I still didn't quite understand his switch of heart. Would I deny this moment though? No. Would I question it the entire time? Yes.

Would I secretly enjoy being up close to him? Also, yes. The guy was hot, and I'd always thought so—ever since I met him freshmen year.

"Guys hate when something is off-limits. Especially athletes." Callum eyed the bar. "Obvi this guy doesn't play football or Dean would murder him. What sport?"

"Baseball."

"It's not even in season," Luca mumbled.

"So boring," Callum groaned. "Okay, we go in, Luca, keep your hand on her the entire time. Neck, shoulder, back, arm, tit."

"Um, maybe not the last one?" I said, my face flushing. I still didn't glance at Luca, which felt safer for some reason.

"Fine, boring. But Luca, you gotta play it up. If she's *your thing,* then act like it."

"This sounds weirdly possessive. I don't... like it?" I said, frowning and regretting this entire idea. "We should go back. I'll cancel with Mack."

"No." Luca stepped forward and picked up a piece of my hair. The sensation of his fingers twisting my long hair gave me shivers. He touched it for a few seconds before lifting my locks from one shoulder and smoothing them down the center of my back. It both tickled me *and* gave me goose bumps. My nipples tightened from his touch, and I crossed my arms to hide them.

He moved his large hand from the ends of my hair to the

base of my neck, gripping it to the point his finger almost wrapped all the way around it. Words escaped me. The feel of his rough hands on my skin, his soapy scent filling my nose, and the way he gently massaged into me? My stomach flip-flopped.

"I heard you talking to your friend. You're doing this. One drink," Luca said, his voice low and soft.

Every nerve was on edge, either from knowing I'd see Eric or from the fact Luca's hand was on me. My tongue swelled, if that was even a thing. Speaking became increasingly difficult from the adrenaline rush. I couldn't decide if I liked Luca's hand on me so much I wanted him to dip those long fingers down into my shirt or if I should slap him.

I was discombobulated.

"Come on, Lo." Callum nudged me, and that got me moving.

I wished for a lot of things in the short distance from where we stood to the bars front entrance. One, I wished I had a drink at the house before leaving. Two, I wished I'd seen Eric's red flags earlier. Three, I wished I understood why I was reacting so much to Luca's body being so close to mine. Sure, he was hot, but the dude wasn't for me in *any* way.

We crossed the street, a part of me watching the scene unfold like a movie. Me, sandwiched between two football guys, walking into a bar with my head held high. Eric sat at a high-top table with a girl perched on his lap. His arm was around her, his classic grin stretching across his face. He wore the hat I'd bought him, ugh, and twisted it backward. *My weakness.*

The DJ played some house tunes, and a few couples danced off to the side. The place was known for being low-key and for cheap drinks. It smelled like stale beer, weed, and cologne. Mack waited for us outside the entrance, her eyes as big as saucers once they landed on me and Luca. She arched a brow, and I subtly shook my head.

Questions later.

"Hey y'all," she said. She eyed Callum up and down. "Didn't realize the footballers were joining us? Is your brother coming too?"

"Just us, baby." Callum winked and put an arm around her.

Mack blushed but leaned closer to him. "I feel like I'm joining a conversation late, but I'm down for whatever is happening."

"Good girl," Callum cooed.

The four of us walked into the bar after showing our IDs to the security guard. My skin prickled with heat—either from the fact Eric was there with another girl or the fact Luca touched me so gently. For a large guy, his hands were soft on me.

"Hey," Luca said, his voice coming directly next to my ear. His lips brushed against my hair. "What do you want to drink?"

He placed both hands on my shoulders, pulling me tight against his chest. His warmth and strength surrounded me, and I gulped. Goose bumps exploded down both arms, and god, when was the last time I'd felt that?

Focus. Make Eric regret what he did. I let my gaze move slowly toward where he sat, but he still hadn't seen me. He once told me he could feel the air move when I walked into a room, but I was calling bullshit on that. Here I was, ten feet away, and he was face-first in a girl's neck.

Mack frowned at me over Callum's shoulder, her eyes worried. A few months ago, this sight would've gutted me. But it was relieving to *not* have a punch of jealousy go through me. If anything, it was more hurt that I thought we had something special, when we never really did.

"Whatcha want, girlies?" Callum slapped the bar and whistled at the bartender. "Love your hair, gorgeous."

She winked before shifting her gaze to me. "Wow, Monroe is blessing us with his presence tonight. Football fans will go wild to see you out."

Luca stiffened next to me, and his hand moved from my neck to my lower back. "Wanted to hang out with my girl here."

The bartender's attention moved to me, curious and assessing. "Your girl, huh?"

"For the night," I blurted out, regretting it instantly. "You know how he is."

"That I do." She licked the side of her lip, then studied Callum. Her nostrils flared. "I've already been with two guys on the team, can we make it three?"

"Doll, please." Callum smirked, leaning onto his forearms. "I don't want to embarrass my teammates with my superior skills."

Her gaze flicked back to Luca. "Eh, one knew what they were doing."

That's when it hit me. Luca had *slept* with the bartender. A gross, jealous-like feeling squeezed my chest, which it had no business doing because, um, hello, it was Luca Monroe? The grumpy guy who kinda hated me but was making it up to me by helping me and confusing me? Also… hearing Luca call me *my girl* sent a flurry of *ohmygods* through me.

I was a hot mess express of emotions and feelings, and I hated it.

"Jesus, Tamara," Luca huffed.

"What? Your Monday night special doesn't seem to mind."

"Oh my god, do you *call* your hookups that?" I asked, laughter spilling out. "Luca, that is … wow."

Mack laughed, a bit hesitant. I could tell she was trying to gauge my feelings, and god, she was the best friend ever. I met her eyes, grinning.

"Tuesday night temptation, Wednesday wonder," Tamara

said, arching her brows. "The ladies know what we're getting with him. One night, that's it, but it's worth it."

"Good to know." I moved to stand next to Callum. "Four shots of whatever is closest to you."

"'Atta girl." She grabbed a bottle of rum and poured us shots. I felt more than heard Luca stand *right* behind me. His hips came up to the middle of my back, and his powerful thigh pressed into my side, his presence overwhelming me in a strange, wonderful way. For a hot second, I wondered about how he'd be in bed.

Attentive? Selfless? Focused? Heat rushed me head to thighs, and I cleared my throat. Eric hadn't been bad in bed, but he wasn't amazing, and based on how friendly Tamara was with him, Luca had to be *amazing.*

Callum leaned closer to me, his breath hitting my face. "Where is he?"

"Back right." I'd definitely seen him when we'd walked in, but Tamara distracted me enough that I hadn't looked back. I wasn't sure if he'd seen me. But now that the reason we were here dominated the conversation, my nerves returned full force. My fingers shook against the bar as I tapped them over and over.

"Dude with the hat and the girl?"

"Yes." I exhaled, thankful Tamara slid the glasses our way. Without waiting for the others, I took mine and downed it. The welcomed burn continued down my throat, and I wiggled my hips. *Shit.* I forgot Luca was *right* there, and with my movement, he stiffened. "Sorry."

"No, you're fine." He gripped my hip now, his other hand taking the shot. "Come on. Let's sit."

He squeezed my hip once then released me. He held out a hand, and I stared at it, blinking away any uncertainty. I had to sell this. I flashed him a smile and stared up at him. The same intense look I'd grown used to was there, his eyes narrowed and his jawline sharp as hell. I took his hand, and he interlocked our fingers. None of the weird, mitten-holding of hands. He *held* my hand, and for some reason, that was hot?

"Okay, lovers, what are we doing? Dancing? Darts?" Callum moved to the beat just as a group of girls spotted him. He groaned. "Walking temptations."

"You never turn it off, do you?" Mack asked.

"Never, baby." He gave Mack a heated look, running his hand over his jaw. He then smiled bashfully at me and winced. "Mom, can I go play with them? Please?"

"Oh my god," I said, laughing. "Yes."

"You'll be okay?" He flicked his eyes to Luca.

"What the fuck, man?" Luca asked.

"I was gonna come here with her without you, and you have your growly, grump face going on, so I wanna make sure she's comfortable." He held out a fist, and I bumped it. "Don't wait for me." He cupped his boobs. "There's a ninety percent chance I won't be coming home."

My lip quirked, and soon enough Callum strode off, leaving me, Mack, and Luca. My fingers were still interlocked with his large ones. "Should we—"

"Shit, he's staring *hard*." Mack narrowed her eyes, her grip on the table tightening. "Don't turn around, Lo."

"What's he doing?" I asked.

"Frowning at you two." Mack tapped the side of her lips. "Honestly, this is great, you flirting with Monroe. His reputation precedes him, and clearly Eric knows about him. His face is red."

This is so messed up. Why had I ever thought this was a good idea? Pretending to be over everything? Moving on? My stomach rolled with discomfort, and I let go of Luca's hand. The absence of the heat startled me.

"What's wrong? You tensed." Luca bent forward, a familiar frown on his face. He lowered his head so we were eye to eye. "Do I make you uncomfortable?"

"What? No." I brushed my hair over my ears, a huge rock forming in my gut. Eric was watching us! What did that mean? Was he still looking? God, why did I care? That made no sense. He'd treated me poorly at the end and hadn't communicated what I meant to him the entire time. "It's this situation."

Mack sighed. "Eric played her, bad. Lied about their relationship, said it was casual the whole time and nothing serious even though it was almost a year. Told her baseball was more important, and if she wanted to continue being a fuck buddy, he'd let her, but he couldn't do more."

"Jesus, Mack." I glared at her. "Laying all my business on the table."

"Forgive me for kinda wanting Grumpy McGee to beat his ass."

"No, he can't do that," I said, staring at Luca. His entire body stiffened, and his face had red splotches on it. "He can't risk getting injured for football. My brother would kill me if I caused him to get hurt."

"Dean should also beat Eric's ass."

"He doesn't know the whole story," I fired back.

Luca craned his neck to look over his shoulder, his jaw tensing. "Lorelei," he said.

He pronounced each syllable with intention and a deep, gruff voice that sent a burst of heat through me. I *liked* him saying my name like that. "Hm?"

"Eric looks like someone who doesn't know how to please a woman, and if I ever were to punch anyone in the face, it'd be him. He has my top spot." His dark stare met mine, the absolute seriousness of his words plastered on his face.

I nodded, my own face tingling with warmth. "Good to know."

"He's also on my punch in the face list, followed with that beezy from Indiana." Mack pounded a fist into her palm.

My lips twitched. "You'll carry a grudge until you die."

"Hell yes I will." Mack hit her fist on the table, her face paling as she looked over Luca's shoulder.

"Lo?"

Shit.

My ex appeared right next to us. Eric O'Shea, the face of the baseball team with his pitching arm. Blond hair swooped to the side and the charisma people would kill for. Heartbreak and anger fought for control, and I opened my mouth to say something, but no sound escaped. It had been a month since we were face to face, and my stomach bottomed out with nerves.

Luca wrapped his beefy arm around my shoulders and nuzzled me into his chest before positioning us to face Eric. Time slowed down as I stared at my ex. He looked good. Dark blue shirt and jeans, the damn hat I bought him, and no girl on his arm. There definitely had been one though. I saw her.

"The ex, right? Derrick?" Luca asked.

I wanted to laugh and thank him profusely. *Derrick.* Classic. My lips curved up even though my insides were a war zone. "Eric, but yes."

"Close enough." Luca left no room between our sides, our bodies pressed so tight together you couldn't fit a penny there.

Eric ran a hand over his mouth, his eyes bouncing back and forth between us. "Are you with Monroe?"

"She is, yes." Luca answered before I could, and I nudged his side.

"I can speak, you know."

"Right. I forgot." He playfully rolled his eyes, and my smile grew. I was aware, deep down, that this was an act, but I kinda liked this version of him. Goofy, territorial, decisive. Getting Eric to plan *anything* had been exhausting.

"But yes." I held Eric's gaze. "Luca and I are…what are we doing?"

"Besides fucking?"

Oh my god.

My face heated, and my thighs tensed. It was hot in the bar. Like, had their air broken suddenly or had they accidentally turned the furnace on? I laughed, nervously, and Luca's stoic face broke out in a huge smile. "God, don't be an ass."

He faked a wince. "Might be too late. Derrick might be upset."

"Eric, come on." I nudged my hip into his, and he did it right back. Eric cleared his throat, and I glanced at him.

His frown deepened, the familiar curve of his lips not quite as pleasing as it once had been. He cleared his throat and shifted his weight from left to right. "How long has this been going on?"

"Mm, it's recent." I shrugged. "We're keeping it casual. Sports will always come first. You know how that is."

"Now, what do you want? We're busy, and you interrupted for what?" Luca asked.

Eric took off the hat and ran his hand through his hair so it stuck up on the end. I used to *love* that gesture when he was nervous, but now it looked dumb. His jaw tensed as his attention shifted on me. "Lo, could we—"

"Eric, baby!"

A beautiful, leggy blonde walked up to him and threw herself at him. He caught her, and his cheeks pinkened.

"Can we go? I want to watch Ted Lasso again," she purred into his ear.

Ted fucking Lasso.

The show I made him watch with me. I felt like I was living

in an Olivia Rodrigo song, and I hated it. I'd begged this guy to watch the show with me, and he'd complain because he'd rather do anything else. He thought soccer was *boring*. But wow... not with this new girl. Eric paled as he rubbed the girl's back.

"Continue with your night, Eric." Ice laced my tone, and I bit my lip to prevent from saying anything else. Luca stepped closer to me, placing a hand on my shoulder and gently squeezing.

I needed that reminder to ground me, and damn, I liked it.

Eric nodded before walking away with the leggy blonde and I deflated. The anger swirled and billowed, like smoke coming from a grill, and I gritted my teeth. "That rat bastard."

"I hate him," Mack said. "Didn't he complain about soccer the entire time you were together?"

"Yes." I breathed hard, hoping to exhale all the negativity in my mind.

"Vent or fix?" Luca asked.

"What?" I snapped. His question made no sense.

"My grandma does this thing... do you want to vent right now about him? Or do you want a fix?"

"I'd love a fix for this." I tilted my head to each side, cracking my neck and wishing I did another shot at the bar. "But I'm angry. I had to *beg* him to watch Ted Lasso. Beg. Like, pout and he'd act like I was so irritating. He made me feel annoying." I rubbed my eyes, irritated that I'd put on mascara so I surely had racoon eyes.

Luca squeezed the back of his neck and stared hard at me. Indecision clouded his face before he held out his hand again. "I have an idea. Let's walk Mack home and then I want you to come with me."

CHAPTER
EIGHT

Luca

What am I doing?

Why aren't I studying?

Why am I not at home, in bed, doing my routine?

My brain shouted the questions at me, loudly, and there was only a moment's hesitation because Lorelei's crumpled face became more important. Fixing those frown lines and the worry behind her gaze, the deflating of her shoulders and slight lip trembling she couldn't hide from me.

How could the girl of my dreams be this sad from a prick like Eric?

The bar music thumped around us, and the smell of stale beer and fried food invaded my nostrils. It made me nauseous.

"Where are we going?" Lorelei asked, her voice small and unsure. Her fingers, intertwined with mine, tensed, and it was a reminder that we held hands. A part of me liked this, reminding me of a time back in high school where I allowed myself to have a girlfriend. It was fun to have a partner, someone to have your back. Plus, I enjoyed how small Lo's hand was in mine.

After the two of them got one of their cards signed for the drink to complete the twenty-drink requirement to earn the T-shirt, we walked Mack home. Her friend eyed me the entire time, but I knew what Lorelei needed.

Once we got to Mack's place, the two of them whispered and hugged. Mack glared at me for a beat before going inside. Now, it was just Lorelei and me. Without thinking, I held out my hand for her to take again, and she intertwined our fingers.

I could fix the ways I'd fouled up our initial meeting while helping her release some of the anger directed at that fuck face Eric.

A ripple of electricity danced along my skin up my forearm and to my neck, goose bumps bursting out from her touch. It was magnetic and bewitching. Wonderful and terrifying.

"We're going to a field."

"To murder me? Why would we go to a field?"

"Because." I shook my head, my face heating. *Because?* What a silly answer. It mollified her though. She remained quiet as we walked back toward the football house. A few people passed us on the path, nodding their head at me before glancing at Lorelei. There was curiosity in their gazes, but if Lorelei noticed, she gave nothing away.

I glanced at her, my attention stuck on her full, pillow lips currently pursed as her eyes stared into the distance. She had to be lost in thought, and I was dying to know about what.

Eric? Did she miss him?

Why do you care?

I cleared my throat, a sudden flicker of nerves twisting in my gut. What if Dean saw us holding hands? How could I possibly explain this for it to make sense? I let go of her, hating the cold left from the loss of her touch.

If he didn't know the full story about what Eric did, then I could tell him. That'd explain everything, why I held her hand and wanted to help her out. Yes. That was the perfect excuse. Relief settled the tension in my shoulders, and I almost smiled.

I could spend time with her right now and *not* feel guilty.

She sucked in a breath, crossed her arms, and narrowed her eyes, all while *not* looking at me.

She chewed her bottom lip, and I'd give anything to bite down on it and taste her.

No. Nothing more than one-night stands.

This had to be the last night I could do this, hang out with her and inhale her perfume and feel her skin on mine. It confused my goals and thoughts and tempted me to say fuck it to my entire plan just to kiss her.

But that was assuming she'd even want to *and* if I would risk everything with Dean. Regardless of the status of kissing her, I spent too much time worrying and thinking about her for this night to ever repeat itself, so if I only had tonight… then I planned on making it memorable.

We approached the house in silence, her soft footsteps the only noise she made. Her usual chatterbox self was buried inside her, and I wanted that back.

I gently put my hand at the base of her back, waiting for her to stare up at me. She did, and it was a sucker punch to the gut. Wide eyes, nose dusted with freckles, and an earnest, curious look on her face.

"Give me two minutes, I'll be right back."

"What are you doing?" She frowned.

"Grabbing something real quick." I jogged toward the front door, used my key to get in, and I found what I needed in the hall closet. It had been a while since any one of us had used it, but I knew it was the right move when I held out the soccer ball and bounced it on my knee.

"No," she said, her eyes widening. "What is this?"

"We're gonna have a shoot-off."

Competition flared in her gaze, and I knew I had her. Pride filled my chest as I dropped the ball to the ground and passed it to her. She stopped it, kicked it into the air so it landed on her knee, and smiled.

If she learned the power her smile had on me, she could get me to do anything in the world. Like betray Dean without question. My ears got hot as I stared at her white teeth and full grin, and I blinked. *She said something.*

"Hm?" I said, scratching the back of my neck.

"What are we playing for? What's the wager?" She kneed the ball into the air and juggled it, her smooth movements so ridiculously sexy.

"I hadn't thought that part out yet, just figured a girl like you would like a little competition to distract you."

"A girl like me, huh?" She arched a brow and whistled. "Careful with phrases like that, Luca. Could get you into trouble."

"What type of trouble?"

Oh my god. I couldn't help myself. Around her, my brain resorted to primal instincts.

She ran her teeth over her top lip, her eyes heating. "Not the fun kind."

"Oh, is there a fun kind of trouble?"

"We both know there is." She juggled the ball again, her strong legs distracting me from my original plan. "Now, where is this field?"

"Two blocks behind the house. Come on."

I shoved my hands in my pockets and quickened my pace. It'd be easier, probably, to stop thinking about her and the way she said trouble once we were on the field. She said the word like a flirtation, a challenge, and despite the reasons I couldn't get into *trouble,* I kinda wanted to. With her.

My quarterback's twin sister… my temporary roommate… a girl I could lose all my focus for… why did the things I wanted cause so much damage?

"If your plan was to distract me, you're doing a great job. Excellent even, if you wanted to annoy me just a bit too."

"Annoy you?"

Her footsteps shuffled behind me. "*A girl like you* could be taken a lot of different ways."

"We're both athletes. There are fewer things in the world that can help a busy mind than doing something active. I took a guess you were the same as me where the thought of competition excites you and dulls everything else in comparison."

"Damn, Monroe. Fair assessment." She laughed.

I loved the deep, throaty sound of her cackle. Full-bellied and loud. It echoed in the air, lingering and almost making me smile. The neighborhood was mostly student housing, grad students or athletes, but there was the occasional small family. It smelled like wet leaves—a very specific scent I associated with this park, and I breathed it in. I came here every once in a while to relieve stress, and it certainly wasn't a secret place, but sharing it with Lorelei seemed more personal than I realized.

We approached the park, and the streetlights hit the soccer goal perfectly. It illuminated the posts, and someone had recently cut the grass. I inhaled the scent and glanced back at Lorelei. "You want to kick or block first?"

"Depends on the wager." She juggled the ball again and ran ahead of me, weaving the soccer ball between her legs. Even in her outfit, she moved fast and smoothly. She stared at me, one thick brow arched. "I know I'm a better kicker than you, so I'd like to ask what's on the table before deciding if I take the lead first or second."

"Confident, huh? I played soccer too."

"Okay, bro. I've thrown a football before then." She rolled her eyes, tossing her hair over one shoulder in a sassy move.

Hated to admit I liked seeing this side of her.

"Fine. New game." My voice came out stern and grumpy, but Lorelei didn't seem to take offense.

She moved closer to me, the ball still in sync with her feet. "We just making shit up as we go, huh?"

"Yes, smartass." My lip quirked up.

She scrunched her nose, the mischievous glint highlighted in her eye by the streetlamps. She juked left, then right, then whizzed by me before gently kicking the ball into the goal. "Point for me."

"Mm, we hadn't started."

"Says you." She jogged backward, a winning smile stretching across her face. "Apparently, we can just make up rules. So, point to me."

"You're mouthy."

"A girl like me is mouthy? No. No way."

"And sarcastic." I walked up to her, watching the ball move back and forth. She kicked in between my legs, ran around my left side so her back pressed against my side, and zoomed by me. Her floral perfume was delicious, but it mixed a little bit with sweat. It was intoxicating.

"If I win," she said once I faced her again. "You stop being an asshole to me."

"What?" I snapped.

"Yeah, we can be cordial. Friends, even. Don't give my brother a hard time about me living in the house." She bounced it left to right, right to left. Then she rested the bottom of her foot on top of the ball.

"No." I shook my head, guilt eating me inside out. A painful swell of my gut made my jaw tense. "Not no, I meant—" I winced and fanned myself with the collar of my shirt. The weather had warmed. "I'll do that regardless."

Especially after seeing so many smiles tonight.

She narrowed her eyes in the same way my grandma did when she wanted more of an explanation. I ran a hand over my jaw twice before continuing. "I won't make Dean feel bad, and we can be *friendly* to each other."

"Be friendly is not the same as friends."

"Correct."

She pursed her lips, a coy smirk on her face. "So, you'll put up with me in a friendly sort of way, but we won't be hanging out?"

"Yes." It had to be that way. Didn't she see? She already took up too much time and energy and had me wanting more. Limiting my time around her was the only rational solution. The more I was around her, the more I wanted to break my rules.

"Got it, Monroe. I understand the assignment." She faked right, then did a wild move with her feet and was by me in a second. She scored again and stuck her tongue out at me. "Two to zip, baby."

"I'm letting you win so you're not thinking about Derrick Dick face."

"Ha! I love that one. Derrick Dick face. Hold on." She pulled her phone out of her pocket, her grin showing all her teeth. "Let me write—oh."

My muscles tightened. "Oh what?"

"He texted me." Her face paled, and she looked up with irritation swimming in her eyes. Her breathing increased, and her nostrils flared.

She didn't say with what, and my god, I needed to know.

Did he realize he was an idiot and want her back? Disappointment spread through my body. I didn't want that to happen. "What did he say?"

"*U look good. Wanna come over later?* He even spelled it with one dumb u and do I want to come over? Shit on a stick. Ugh." She kicked a patch of grass and groaned. "The guy broke my heart. Was I just a piece of ass?"

"You're not going, right?"

"No." She growled and kicked the ball hard. It soared down the entire park and rolled near the playground with three slides. "I wanted to make him jealous or have him regret what he did, and yeah, I know I look good, and pretending to flirt with you or whatever sparked something in him, but this hurts worse."

Distraction. She needs a distraction.

I shouted, "Loser vacuums the hallway." Then I sprinted toward the ball.

"Wait! Hey!"

My lungs expanded as I put everything I had into this sprint. A million thoughts went through my head, all about injuries and me acting out of character and what if I stepped on a rock and twisted my ankle? None of the thoughts stopped me though. I inhaled the cool air and checked over my left shoulder, and *holy shit.* Lorelei had caught up to me.

I couldn't let her win.

I moved my legs faster, harder, but she kept pace, and the soccer ball was right there. I just had to slow down and bend to get it. She did the same thing, and by some twist of fate, we reached for it at the same time.

"Not today, Monroe. Nope."

She *shoved* me out of the way, but I wrapped my arm around her waist and yanked her with me. Shielding her body, I landed on my back with her shoulders pressed against my chest.

Her hair fell over my face, her round ass pressed up against my waist, and her body was on top of me. It was a torture and a dream wrapped into one. My pulse pounded in my ears, toes, and fingertips.

"I cannot believe you did this!" she shouted.

It took my brain a few seconds to catch up.

She's laughing.

"You huge wombat." She snorted and rolled to the right, pushing herself off me. "You tackled me."

"No, you took me down." I pushed up onto my elbows, admiring the curls escaping her hair. It was a magical sort of chaos, and my fingers itched to touch them.

"You raced me like we were six years old."

"But it took your mind off that asshole, didn't it?"

She pulled her knees up to her chest, rested her chin onto her knees, and looked at me with a sad smile. She held my gaze, not saying anything, and the magnetic pull to her grew. I leaned forward, not even meaning to, and she squeezed my forearm. "I know our paths to *not* friends but *not* enemies wasn't traditional by any means, but I see what you did tonight." She took a shaky breath. "Thank you."

"You're welcome." I couldn't stop staring at her fingers on my arm. She brushed her thumb over my skin, rubbing it, and it was such a simple, sweet gesture that there was no reason to feel her touch from there to my toes. Clearing my throat, I focused on the green slide when I said, "What do you want as your reward?"

"Wait, for real for real?"

"You technically beat me." I flicked my attention to her, and the hope on her face solidified my answer. "You can pick anything."

She narrowed her eyes, a glint of malice brewing behind them. Would she make me clean the toilets? Sing to her? Girls were strange creatures, so I wasn't sure.

"We do friendly stuff like this every once in a while."

"That's what you want?" I gripped the back of my neck. She wanted to *hang out* with me? Why? "How many times?"

"Do you plan your hangouts, Monroe?" She smirked, then smacked her forehead. "Of course you do. Monday night special, Friday night get your freak on."

My muscles tensed, the urge to defend myself on the tip of my tongue. "I live by a tight schedule."

"No kidding." She stared up at the sky, sighing. "How about this? I'll make a punch card for our hangouts and send you a calendar invite."

"That seems extra."

"Monroe, I am extra." She flashed another grin, and all traces of the lingering sadness disappeared. Then, she yawned.

Her face was an open book, every thought and emotion displayed with her full lips and wide eyes and button nose.

"Come on. We're walking back." I stood and held out a hand to help her up. She took it, and the same tingling shot through my arm to my heart. I made another mental note—*don't touch her.*

I didn't regret volunteering to help her because Eric was a prick, but if a simple hand-holding had me flustered, I couldn't imagine what a kiss would do. *Like I would let that happen.*

Dean would murder me if I touched his sister in any way that wasn't friendly. I had a defense for us hanging out tonight —one he couldn't find a fault in. But if I *ever* acted on my deepest fantasy, it was game over for me. He could punch me, kick me out of the house, and ultimately, he could affect our relationship on the field.

Football had to come first, always, and distracting Lorelei for one night was a momentary blip of judgement. That was all. It wouldn't happen again. I'd find a way out of hanging with her... I had to.

CHAPTER
NINE

Lorelei

W ords mattered and were important. Messaging made a difference. Images set a tone and could either drive you away or pull you in, and it was clear as day that our school didn't quite value the girls' soccer team.

One of my marketing class's assignments was to study signs on campus and note the purpose. Did they succeed or fail? I eyed the large, blue and orange football billboards and signs and banners. They were all dark, intense, with the players' faces and their team motto: unfinished business. Intensity and unity and toughness shouted from the marketing.

Dean's dumb face looked over the campus, like he knew he led the entire student body when he threw a football across the field. Oliver and Callum were around too but not as much as Luca. The giant and grumpy tight end never smiled in his photos, and it somehow worked? Like this was the guy who blocked for his teammates or caught the ball from Dean.

Our field was only two streets away from the football

stadium, yet I didn't see more than one banner with girls' soccer. Did we bring in the same amount of money? No. But we deserved a marketing blast.

My professor had turned down my initial project idea—a marketing push for the girls' team. With the popularity of the US Women's team and increasing viewership, now was the time to get those young fans excited about girls' soccer. She said it was too easy for me since I was on the team and that a future in marketing meant promoting things I wasn't all-in on. She wanted me to *push myself.* Staying with soccer meant I was playing it safe.

The already familiar thud of footsteps alerted me Luca was home. It had been three days since *that* strange night, where he had been friendly but refused to accept that we were friends, and the momentary high had faded into confusion.

Blame it on my people-pleasing upbringing, but I hated knowing someone didn't like me. I was a people pleaser, enjoyed being liked. Who didn't? So, knowing there was someone who lived across the hall who just didn't want to be friends? It bothered me like a hole in the bottom of my sock. I could ignore it for a bit, but I knew it was there, growing and being a pain.

"Is she okay? In pain? I can't... I can be there Saturday, but I have a—"

I sat up. Luca's voice was pained, hoarse. My door was clearly open, but he didn't seem to notice or care that I could hear. Who was in pain? Who wasn't okay?

He stalked into his room, shut the door, and kept talking to whoever was on the phone. I couldn't make out the exact words, but the unease and hard syllables broke through. *He's worried.*

I could pretend I didn't listen to this. Focus on coming up with a new marketing plan to pitch to my professor. Not only did I need a theme, a purpose, but creating a proposal would take time. Lots of time. However, that excuse wasn't enough to keep me in my room. I could rewatch all of Ted Lasso and imagine my life with Roy Kent. I could… *be the better person.*

Luca had helped me out Monday. I could offer to support right now as one of our hangouts. I smoothed my crew neck sweatshirt and made sure there weren't any crumbs on my tight black shorts. My hair sat in two buns on the top of my head, the rest of it down, but *why am I worrying about how I look?*

Mr. *we'll never be friends* shouldn't care what I'm wearing. Nope. Not one bit.

My palms sweated as I stared at the opening in my door, eyeing his very shut bedroom that wasn't inviting. What did I say?

Oh, hello there, are you okay? Do you need help?

I snorted. Our situation wasn't traditional. I'd walked in on him yanking one, and he'd overheard my plans to make my ex regret ever hurting me. This tension was nothing compared to those situations, yet it felt like a lot. More personal, somehow. Butterfly wings flittered in my stomach as I tiptoed toward his door. It seemed like he'd hung up. There were no more angry sounds. My poor lip hurt from the anxious nibbling, and I exhaled. This was silly! Being nervous was ridiculous! I faced down enemies on the field without breaking a sweat and yet this boy had me anxious? Unacceptable. My mother didn't raise me to let grumpy attractive men make me worried.

Moving my hand to knock on the door, I got about an inch away from the wood before the door flew open.

"Oh, hi, hey hello!" I jumped back, clutching my chest. My heart felt like a jackhammer against my ribs.

"Lorelei." His jaw tightened, and his brown eyes narrowed, like he was angry at me. "What are *you* doing?"

"Uh, well, funny you should ask." I let out an awkward

chuckle, which wasn't funny at all. My usual confidence disappeared around him. Instead, I became a dork, unsure of myself. It was his eyebrows. "Are you alright?"

"Why wouldn't I be?" He crossed his thick arms and leaned against the wall. His dark brows furrowed, and there was no amount of *friendly* on his face. His muscles were all tensed on his arms, his dang jaw working back and forth.

He encapsulated the perfect description of the word *anger*.

"Our walls are thin, remember?" I tilted my head to the side, making my eyes go big.

"Your point."

Okay, so he was doubling down on this mad situation. I mimicked his stance on my own door, eyed him up and down, and repeated my question. "Are you alright? You sounded upset on the phone."

He huffed. "I'm not upset."

"Monroe." I pinched my nose, irritation dancing along my neck and making it heat. *Why did I think this was a good idea?* Might as well follow through. "Stop being a pain in the ass for no reason. What's going on?"

"None of your business." He scowled and went back into his room, blocking me out from whatever was going on in his mind. That was his prerogative, which fine. Fine by me.

But it stung a little to have him shut me out like that, like Monday hadn't happened between us at all. Lesson learned. I'd let grumpy Monroe suffer in peace. Plus, he was rude. I went through every memory I had of him, and in ninety percent of them, he'd been like this with me. One night was a fluke, so it was foolish to think things were different. *Come on, Lo. Be smarter.*

My marketing plan called my attention again, and I glared at Luca's door, flipping him off for good measure. *Take that, grump face.* As I turned, a creak caught my attention, and Luca returned, his face unreadable, almost like he was lost.

No frown lines, no softness, no anger. Just… blank. It made me want to do a dance or sing or be goofy just to see him smile.

He held up both hands in the air, like a shrug, before sighing. "I'm sorry, Lorelei. I shouldn't have been upset with you. You did nothing wrong. You were making sure I was all right, which was nice of you."

I arched a brow, my pulse spiking at the intensity on his face. An apology—either good or bad—was still an apology, and the features on my face relaxed. He didn't exactly seem approachable or wanting to have a heartfelt convo about what made him happy or sad, so I responded with a mere "Fine."

He ran a hand over his face, letting out a garbled groan. He parted his lips, closed them, then stared down the hallway. "It's… I don't talk about her a lot."

I nodded, desperate to know who the *her* was in the sentence, but the uncertainty on his face was evident. He seemed at war with himself. Should he or shouldn't he tell me? He adjusted the sleeve on his left forearm, rolling it up before he faced me again. The line disappeared between his eyebrows, and his eyes softened.

"It's my grandma."

I dug my toes into the ground, my muscles tensing with worry. "Is she okay?"

"Physically? Yes. She's stable now, just unable to live alone." A slight smile formed on his lips as he stared beyond my shoulder. "The woman's attitude is relentless, and she's feistier than ever. Almost a pain in the ass, actually. It's just… the facility she lives in isn't great."

"What do you mean?" I tilted my head to the side.

"They are technically fine, but the place is falling apart. My grandma is tough and refuses to complain. She once broke her foot and told people it was a *slight* inconvenience." He laughed, quick and short. Like a clap of thunder. "She also told me ginger ale cures every sickness, so I know she's full of shit sometimes."

"She sounds awesome." A flicker of a smile danced on my lips.

"She is the best. Strongest person I know. She raised me. I —" He paused, his gaze narrowing on me. "Not a lot of people know this."

"If you're insinuating I'm gonna share your family shit with people, then you hang out with terrible humans. Family stuff isn't gossip. Plus, hello? My brother is a quarterback. You don't think I understand how shit spreads? When people find out I'm his twin, they try to use me to get to *him*. He hates it. I'd never do that."

"Right. Of course. You understand it." He sighed, his features softening. "I don't trust easily."

"That's quite clear, Monroe." I smiled. "So, back to your badass grandma, the place is falling apart?"

"Yeah. Unclean water from the faucet, missing tiles, a smoke alarm that kinda hangs. They clean it, but its old, unkempt. It's a public place and all I can afford, so she doesn't have much of a choice, and I hate it."

"Wait, *you're* paying for it?"

He froze, his gaze sharpening on me like he was a hunter and I was prey. A shiver went through me. I recrossed my arms, the hair on the back of my neck standing on end.

"*That* is none of your business."

And we're back this this again. I rubbed my temples, my temper rising.

"Okay, look, what do you think my endgame is here, bro? You helped me out Monday night, and I heard you upset because our walls are thin. You worried about me finding out an iota about you, which makes you a normal person? I can go back to thinking you're a grump after this. Just answer me. Why are you paying for it? Those places are expensive. My grandpa is in one, and it's a ton of money. Our parents talk about it all the time, but it's my dad's dad, so of course they'll help."

His left cheek twitched as he eyed me up and down. There… might've been heat in that gaze, but I couldn't be sure. Either way, I cleared my throat and wished I wore more than loose sports shorts. They showed a lot of skin and bruises. He eventually met my face, and his tongue wet the center of his bottom lip. I swore I felt that little movement between my thighs. Which, *what?* Luca was hot, yes, but like, from afar. Not like I wanted that tongue on me. He was… hm, this was interesting.

"So, tell me," I demanded, needing to move my head away from thoughts like those. I didn't want to have Dean kill me *or* subject myself to heartbreak. It was a lose-lose here despite the bolt of attraction.

He ran a large hand through his hair, messing it up. "There's no one else to do it. Just me."

"Then she's lucky to have you, and I'm sure she's grateful."

"I know she is. I just—" He sighed, and his shoulders slumped. "I wish I could do more for her, but I can't."

"I'm sure what you're doing is more than enough."

"No," he snapped. "I'm putting her in a place that's not top quality, and I can't do a damn thing about it. People just don't seem to care about the older community. Like, once people turn a certain age does society stop giving a shit? This woman raised me after my parents *dropped me off* at her house. She deserves the world, and the public doesn't care about the facility. It pisses me off. Sure, they'll donate to animal shelters, which, of fucking course that's important, but no one sees a nursing home

89

and goes *oh, I should donate money.* They assume someone has family to take care of them, but if I don't get drafted after this year? I don't know what I'm gonna do. She has *no one else.*"

"Luca," I said, but it was too late. He went back into his room and shut the door. My heart felt heavy and sad and broken for him. That was so much responsibility for a twenty-one-year-old to live with. Dean's biggest duty was showering and throwing a football well. He didn't have half the emotional weight Luca did, and wow. Luca cared for his grandma, not just like he loved her but financially.

Hell, my biggest worry was earning an internship and getting over a heartbreak. Both seemed frivolous compared to Luca's struggles.

My mind raced as I went back into my room, my potential project ideas from the brainstorm staring up at me. What if... hm. He said the public didn't care about nursing homes...He wasn't one to want hugs, but I could come up with something.

A way to help him out *while* kicking ass at my project.

CHAPTER
TEN

Luca

Game day.

My senses went into overdrive on game days. The air smelled thicker, like bonfires and homecoming and turf and sweat and locker rooms. The wind came through my window, providing a brief moment of peace before I started my routine. Game days weren't to be fucked with. It was my golden rule. I stretched my arms over my head, moving right to left, then left to right.

After I stretched, I'd eat and shower. No classes on Fridays except some online course that I could catch up on this weekend. Game days were for getting in the right headspace. The day I couldn't have a single distraction.

Knock, knock.

Who would be at my door? I bolted up, damn well knowing Callum wouldn't knock, he'd yell instead. That meant... Lorelei. It was eight. Too early for people to knock on another's door, but what if she needed something? I ran a hand over my face before twisting the handle open.

"Hi, good morning, look, I have an idea." She walked right on by me, smelling like springtime. My just-awake brain couldn't move beyond her outfit. She wore tight running pants and a half-shirt thing. It was black with some cutouts that showed skin, and was there a glint of sweat on her neck? Her curls escaped around her ears and the base of her head and *shit*. She'd definitely said something.

She stared up at me with wide eyes and joy. Okay, she was happy about something. It couldn't have been me because I turned into a jerk around her. My skin heated in embarrassment, and I cleared my throat. "Today is game day, so my mind was elsewhere. Could you repeat that?"

"I want my marketing project to be about what you told me." She held a pad of paper against her chest, a bright orange pen hanging from the spiral. I finally dragged my gaze from her body to her mouth, and her full lips curved up on the sides. I had the strongest urge to rub the tip of my thumb against her bottom one, just to see how soft it was.

Focus. Marketing project. "What part, exactly?"

"How the public doesn't care about nursing homes. You're so right! They don't have the cute photos or social media that animal shelters do. Some have a Facebook page, and that's about it, but that's old now. Like, my grandma has one, but she's not gonna donate unless she's going there, you know? I want to focus on this facility and do a marketing plan as a way to help them spread the word."

"Wait." My mind raced. It was tunnel vision most of the time, either on football or working out or a quick release with a willing female. But then she walked in, and I couldn't stop thinking about her skin and the gleam of moisture I wanted to lick up. She was talking about my grandma, assisting her, the facility. Hope shotgunned through my body, the same exhilarating feeling I got when I ran through the tunnel and onto the field. "You'll help?"

"Yes. Luca, yes. See, I'd been struggling with what to pick as my final project. My professor is big on real world, not jumping-through-the-hoops types of assignments, and I wanted to focus on soccer at first, but since I'm on the team, it was a no-go. This is perfect, right? I can put all my attention on it, build out a plan for them, and track the data and results." She scrunched her nose and batted her eyelashes. "Please? Can I do this?"

I wanted to fucking kiss her, and I didn't trust my voice. Instead of speaking the absolute firework of joy exploding through my head, I nodded.

"Yes!" She fisted the air and wiggled around in a circle. "This feels good. Better than good. Plus, it'll help you and your grandma out. Do you think she'd be okay being on camera? I'd love to focus on a handful of residents and tell their story."

I shrugged, working my jaw back and forth to do something with the adrenaline. Why hadn't I thought of something like this? I could've posted or gotten social media… instead, I blamed it as a distraction and refused to get a single profile.

Her smile faltered. "I won't do anything without your permission, I promise. You have my freaking word. I would… no, I'll even type a contract? Maybe get it notarized? Okay, I have no idea how to do that, but I'll do whatever you need."

"I want to get it notarized," I teased, my lips curving up.

She sighed, closing her eyes and nodding. "Alright, I will look it up and have something done… today. Well, you're busy all day. Tomorrow? No, they are closed. I can—"

"Lo, it's fine." *Shit.* I called her *Lo.* "Lorelei, I was teasing you. I love this idea. I can't believe I never thought of it."

"Well, champ." She hit my shoulder softly with her free hand. "You've been a little busy bulking up and taking care of her. This is my jam. Social media, marketing, and soccer are my three pillars of life. I think this will be fantastic and fun! Totally out of my element. Plus! Oh!" She jumped in the air. "What if I… yes! Let me write this down."

She sat on my bed, pulling the paper up to her chest where she took the cap of her pen off with her teeth. She clicked her tongue against the little orange piece as she scribbled on the paper. I couldn't have imagined a more perfect picture—her sitting there, next to my pillow, her scent filling up my room as the sunlight hit her skin.

My body tightened with need. What if—

"Game day, brooooo!" Callum walked into the room, hitting the top of the door frame. "Oh, shit. Lolo, you sleeping with this guy?"

The thoughts of her spread on my pillow assaulted my mind, the absolute ravaging need to touch her making me fist my hands. *She's Dean's sister.*

"What? No. Never," I barked out a little too loudly. My tongue swelled, and moisture dripped down my back. Callum couldn't possibly know my deepest, darkest fantasies about her. He'd kill me. So would Dean. "She barged in here on her own. I didn't ask her to."

"Message received, Monroe," she said, her tone slightly colder than what it had been before. She stood, her cheeks bright red, and she gave us a tight smile. "I'll work on this plan, and we can chat Monday."

She ducked her head and walked by me, avoiding my gaze and making me feel two inches tall. I'd offended her. *Idiot.*

"You heading to the breakfast?" Callum plopped on my desk chair and had his phone in his hands.

"Right. The team." I pulled the ends of my hair, staring at Lorelei's door. Her blush and quick departure had been because of my mouth. A rock formed in my gut, but I couldn't do a damn thing about it. Not until tomorrow, maybe, but usually Saturdays were for post-game. I couldn't afford to let her sneak in there, especially after how much she'd been appearing in my thoughts lately.

"Wanna leave?"

"Sure, yeah." I forced myself to let Lorelei go for now. Football would always and forever come first, and even though I rarely upset women, I seemed to offend her the most. It wasn't her fault either, and that didn't sit right with me. If my grandma had any idea, she'd smack me in the head.

Lorelei wants to help me.

The ball of anxiety in my stomach lingered, even as Callum and I headed to a team breakfast. It put me on edge. Callum didn't mention her at all, and I wasn't sure if it was intentional or not, but it made me think even more about the look on her face. Like, my words had upset her?

Why would she be upset? Unless she *wanted* me to be into her? No?

Fuck. Focus, Monroe.

We arrived at the stadium about an hour after the other players. All one hundred and five guys dressed, but the starters arrived later. I loved how the younger players looked at us as we walked in, the hunger in their eyes to be where we were at. The equipment mangers washed and placed everything we needed in our locker, and seeing the photo of my grandma grounded me.

I played for her.

Lorelei wants to help her.

"The vibe is good tonight. You ready, Romano?" one of the other juniors asked Dean.

Hearing his name reminded me yet again, I had no business thinking about his sister so damn much. I put my jersey over my pads in the same order I always did. Then, I made sure I had socks and gloves.

We broke out into position groups to do our own warm-ups. Then, we headed back into the locker room to finish gearing up. My favorite though was when we went out onto the field to do our team warm-up. The music pounded throughout the stadium, the lights shining down on us. Cheerleaders chanted, and the band got ready, and *this* was the best feeling in the world.

Football would always come first, I knew that. But I didn't have to leave behind a trail of asshole behavior. I'd play my heart out, then fix the situation with Lorelei because despite zoning in on the game, her offer to help my grandma kept returning.

"Let's go!"

Oliver and Callum hollered as we left the stadium. Everyone's spirits were high. We'd kicked another big ten school's ass, and it felt fucking good. We won by fourteen points, and with every win came the reward.

I stopped worrying about my grandma and routine and plans and let myself go wild only on games we won. That meant tonight? I could drink, fuck, and pass out.

"The houses on Lincoln are where the parties are at. These girls sent the address. Wanna head there?" Oliver asked. "The other guys are starting two houses down, then we can meet up."

"I'm in." Dean shrugged, his attention on a group of girls standing off to the side. "Hold on a minute. Your QB needs to show his fans some love."

"Fuck off, man." Callum groaned. "I hate when he talks about himself in the third person."

"All QBs need an ego though," Oliver said. "It's a fact. They need something to protect their head when they get sacked."

"I heard that." Dean flipped us off before spinning around and approaching the girls.

"Wasn't trying to be sneaky."

I laughed, my mood fantastic. I'd played great. Best stats I had in a while, and my grandma texted me that everyone at the facility had watched it. Plus, now that the game was over, I could find Lorelei and thank her before going wild. "I'm gonna run to the house real quick—"

"Is that Lorelei?" Callum asked, his gaze narrowing across the street. "Is she talking with guys from Indiana? That is… hell no. Dean? Get your sister right now."

Dean snarled, changing direction to beeline toward his sister.

The streetlights illuminated her hair and face, and my heart stuttered. She wore short cutoff black shorts, an orange long sleeved shirt, and Chucks. Her hair was down and curly and everywhere, and some guy in a red and white T-shirt had his arm around her.

Something dark and green and gross slid through me. I hated him. He was an Indiana fan and touching her? Dean should be furious! He should fight him!

"Lo!" Dean cupped his hands around his mouth and yelled. "What the fuck are you doing?"

She was mid-laugh when she found us, and her smile grew. "Hey, great game!"

"What trash is this?" Dean snarled.

"Yeah, why are you consorting with an animal like an Indiana fan?" Callum asked, crossing his arms and trying to look tough.

97

The guy's eyes widened, and he blinked, then dropped his arm and stepped back. "I'm out. I'll catch y'all later."

"Bye," Lorelei said, then looped her arm with a pretty blonde girl I'd seen around a few times. "You guys suck."

"Why? Because I'm stepping in and protecting you from our enemy?" Dean asked. "You cannot be with a guy from Indiana."

"I forbid it," Callum said, his eyes going crazy.

Dean snorted, putting a hand on Callum's shoulder. "No football guys. Ever. Even Cally agrees.'

Lorelei rolled her eyes, and the blonde snickered. "You cockblocked me," she said.

"*What*?" I barked before I could stop myself. Cockblocked, as in she wanted his dick. My blood boiled. "Is this about your ex?"

She sighed, resting her head on her friend's shoulder. "No, it's not about him, and I'm messing with you guys. I played on a travel team with his sister, and we met up to watch the game. Y'all need to chill."

"Unacceptable. Dean wouldn't allow this," Callum said.

Lorelei glared at him before arching one brow at her brother. "*Dean* can try and stop me."

"I can't believe you live with these animals," the blonde said, her eyes bouncing from each of us for a few seconds. "My couch is open if you can survive the crooked springs."

"They're… fine. I ignore them when they annoy me." She shrugged. "Anyway, you guys go party your faces off. You played great." She held out a hand and fist-bumped Oliver, Callum, Dean, then held hers up for me to do the same. I swore her expression shifted when she got to me, and the ball of unease from earlier grew.

I gently touched my knuckles against hers before saying, "Hey, could I—"

Fans swarmed us. Girls and alumni and guys dressed in jerseys and hoodies walked around the corner and screamed. Their catcalls and cheers were met with an echo of celebrations as the night's victory hung in the air. The infectious energy from the game usually carried on through the rest of the night. We never had to pay for drinks, and fans would take pictures, hugs, and the women wanted to hook up. Our coach trained us to always remember we were the face of the team. That meant showing respect and thanking them for support.

Despite being introverted, I could turn it on when I had to because it was about meeting my goal—getting drafted and earning a high payout. Because *money* motivated me, I could play the game.

"Luca, oh my god I love you!" A girl clapped her hands, and soon enough four more were around me. Callum and Oliver posed for photos, and Dean, well, he was living the life.

"Lo," I said, disliking how she'd backed away from me. I searched for her hair, but ten fans turned to more and then a small crowd formed. I hated missing my chance, but it was my night to go wild, and I'd just search for her later.

It'd be great to let loose and find a way to relieve this sexual tension I had toward her because I couldn't do that to Dean. Not ever. Lorelei would never be more than a dream, and even if she was more… she was a lifer. All I could offer was a one-Friday-night stand.

CHAPTER
ELEVEN

Lorelei

Having the large-ass house to myself should've been a blessing. No boys to bother me or to worry about running into—well, one grumpy one to be specific. Instead of enjoying the silence, each sound freaked me out. It was an old creaky house that moved with the wind. Pipes creaked, and the windows rattled with any light breeze. Plus, it was after midnight, and people were rowdy outside. Not a typical disorderly crowd either. The guys had played incredibly at the game, and people thought the party was at the house—which it was not. It was me, alone in my room, a little worried. I chewed at the hangnail on my thumb, wincing when I tasted blood.

The constant knocks on the door and crowd gathering outside freaked me out. I double-checked the lock before sprinting upstairs to hide in my room, but like… if someone got in, I didn't have anything to fight with. *Stop being silly. I won't need to fight.*

Mack offered for me to sleep on her couch, but with the

game on Sunday, I couldn't risk having any pain from an uncomfortable sleep. I needed to stay in top shape, and that meant my bed here. We split an Uber to our places around midnight because we needed sleep, but now it was one a.m., and I regretted being alone.

Thud. I sat up straighter, my pulse pounding through my body.

Okay, that was... an owl hitting a window? A car door?

Thud, thud, thud.

That sounded like footsteps. But were they outside or on the stairs? *Shit.* My breath caught in my throat as the thuds grew louder.

Thud, thud, thud, thud.

Okay, someone was in the hallway. Callum? Luca? I hid under my covers like a coward and held my breath, desperate for a sign it was one of the guys. I never heard keys in the front door or the timbre of one of their voices, so had someone broken in?

Fuck.

Think, Lorelei, think!

I had hairspray, which burned like hell if it got in your eye. With the grace of a cat, I slid out of bed, not making a sound, and reached onto the dresser for the hairspray. My water bottle was heavy too. I could hit the person in the head hard then run. *Surprise attack!*

Speed was my friend, and yes, a sudden burst through the door would throw them off and then I could escape. God, I was too young to die. I had things to do, and this person clearly had nefarious ideas. Why else would they break into a football house at this hour? My legs shook, my fingers trembling with fear. My heart beat so hard it sounded like gongs in my ear. I squeezed my toes into my socks.

Unless it's a girl...

Did I act or wait or sprint or—

Shadows appeared under my door. The person stood outside it, and my body shuddered with fear. My ears rang, and I panted, trying my best not to make a sound, when—*"Shit."*

Luca! I knew that voice.

I dove for the handle, opened the door with my hairspray locked and loaded, and met the very intoxicated and buzzed Luca Monroe. He stumbled and fell backward, landing against the other wall as he laughed. "Oh, Lorelei."

"It's you." I sighed in relief, closing my eyes and willing my heart to settle. My ribcage ached.

"Of course? Who else would be here?" He glanced down the hallway, pulling his knees to his chest and spreading his legs wide. He leaned his elbows onto his knees before his gaze darkened. "Were you expecting some guy?"

"No." I swallowed, the adrenaline coursing through my body.

"Then why do you look… why do you have a bottle in your hand?"

"Oh." My face flushed. "It's nothing."

"I love your blush." He smiled and closed his eyes. "You're adorable, Lo. Your cheeks get all pink, and it makes your freckles stand out."

"Okay, you're trashed." I cackled, uncomfortable with how nice he was being. He called me adorable *and* called me Lo. His absolute insistence of not sleeping with me that morning had embarrassed me earlier, so this had to be because of his buzz. Even if I didn't care that much, a total dismissal like that offended the ego and pride a wee bit. I rubbed my lips together, my pulse finally evening out. "Drink some water and go to bed."

"Is that hair spray? Were you doing your hair?" He frowned, hard, like the thought of me doing my hair hurt him.

"No. It was my weapon. Only weapon at that." I shrugged. "Not my best moment."

"A weapon?" The lines around his eyes deepened, the signature scowl returning and causing all his features to tighten. He was gorgeous with a frown or a smile. It was so unfair.

"I was freaked out, alright? I was in the house alone, and people were outside and pounding on the door looking for a party." I ran a hand over my hair, the slight tremble giving my nerves away. "I thought, well, it doesn't matter. It's you."

"You assumed someone had broken in." He paled, and his eyes widened. "Oh my god. You thought I broke in."

"I guess, yeah."

"Lorelei, I'm so sorry." He gripped his hair and groaned, rocking side to side. "I hate that you were scared. I didn't even think about you at the house! Well, not true. I thought about you most of the night and about the things I need to say to you, but this is the first time someone was at the house when we were out after a game." He pushed up to his feet, groaning. Then he swallowed hard. "You're okay. I'm here. I won't let it happen again."

He seemed so flustered and genuine that I couldn't stop the smile from forming. "You gonna drag me to the next party then?"

"I'll stay back if you're here." He stared at me with wide eyes, like he was trying to send a secret message. It was not received, and my skin prickled from his attention.

"You don't have to do that." I waved a hand in the hair. "It's fine."

"Nope. Not fine. Opposite of fine. Poor? Ineffective? Not well?" He closed his eyes and scratched his forehead. "Not good."

"Okay, grumpy-pants, you're funny when you're drunk."

"Yes well, it's my one night off. I can go wild and be free, and I accidentally did a few shots of stuff. I never do shots, but you were on my mind, so I stressed out and needed the release. Your fault, really."

The back of my neck heated. "You getting drunk is *my* fault?" My voice raised an octave, and the same, sudden rush of adrenaline coursed through me, a flicker of curiosity, a dangerous feeling of tell-me-more mixed in. Why was I on his mind?

"I couldn't stop thinking about you."

"Wait." I shook my head, clearing what I thought I heard him say. *Thinking about me?* No way. That made no sense. Why would he think about *me?* "Come again?"

"Look, Lo," he said, his voice soft and gentle. He dragged his attention from my feet to my face before continuing. "I can't afford to stray from my plan, and you are the most tempting. Like, so fucking tempting. And to even think about it would be… terrible for me and unfair to Dean too."

"You're not making sense." I stepped closer, his magnetic tone pulling me toward him. *What's unfair to Dean?* I had no idea what he was saying, but I wanted to hear him speak all kind to me again. I liked it a lot. "I'm tempting? We're back to you not wanting me to live in the house because I could ruin your routine?"

"This morning." He ran his hands over his face, rubbing his eyes and letting out a loud groan. "I saw your face."

"You're talking in circles right now, and I want to understand, but I'm tired." The reference to the morning caught me off-guard. First, he said he thought about me a lot, then that I was a distraction but also acted like he'd rather sleep with a rat than be caught dead with me.

"You're right. I'm sorry." He took a big step toward me, cupping my face with his large hands. His rough skin caressed my cheeks, his fingers gently grazing underneath my eyes. He tilted his face down so our mouths were a foot apart, and I froze.

My body erupted in goose bumps and heat, my stomach swooping from his touch. He smelled like alcohol and pine trees, along with sweat and leather, and I forgot everything.

How to speak, breath, move, what my favorite sport was or why we stood in the hallway with his hands on my face.

"Un," I mumbled, not really saying a word. "Um what—"

"I'd be lucky to sleep with you. The luckiest. You're... I can't even..." He closed his eyes, struggling to get words out.

My pea-brain was repeating the words *I'd be lucky to sleep with you* over and over and over like what did that even mean? Should I be mad or happy about this? Confused, sure, but *what?* "Luca."

"You're gorgeous. I think, possibly, when I said what I did this morning in front of Callum, you thought that I didn't think you were the most beautiful thing on this green earth. You are, by the way. Like, perfection. Stunning. Like, if I didn't have to worry about my grandma or football or Dean, I'd be doing whatever I could to score a date with you. You're a goddess, Lorelei, and it bothered me all damn day to know you probably thought the opposite." His breath hit my face, and he lowered his hands, stepping back and nodding to himself. "I needed to tell you that. I can't get my words right with you."

"Whoa." I blinked, a lot.

"So, we're good now?" He tilted his head to the side, like a cute little dog.

"Good?" I laughed, utter chaos raging inside me like a pig loose during a state fair. "You say that to me and ask if we're good? Luca Monroe, that was quite a speech."

"I don't know if you're laughing because we are totally good or laughing out of anger. I know people do that sometimes."

"I'm confused, that's it. I thought… you look and speak to me like I'm incredibly annoying. Then you say I'm a goddess? How drunk are you?"

"Medium drunk, and you are a goddess." His mouth opened, and he sucked in a breath as he reached up and took a piece of my hair between his two fingers. "It's the hair, maybe. Or your eyes. Or lips. All of it."

"You think I'm hot."

"Yes, but Jesus Christ, I need to work on my compliments if you're still unsure of what I'm saying." He let go of my hair and stared down at me, his tongue wetting the center of his bottom lip. "I've thought you were the prettiest thing since I met you freshman year."

"*Freshman year?*" What… was I drunk? Was this a dream? The time he went *ugh* at me?

"Am I making this worse?"

"Luca." I held up a hand, my mind sprinting a marathon to comb though all his words. This was front page news. Huge. Massive. "I thought you disliked me. This is the opposite."

"Nothing will ever happen between us. I think… yes, that's why I kept my thoughts to myself. Until now. Damn shots of Patrón. I'm defriending Callum. Only choice here." He mumbled something else about our third hallmate before his eyes heated. "I will never act on this attraction. I can't. Football is my life. Dean… he'd kill me. Do you understand? No matter what happens, we will be nothing more than friends."

I nodded, not really having a choice. The intensity on his face and the way the air seemed to thicken around us had my heart crashing against my ribcage. Did I want to do something about this attraction? I didn't think so. Hell, he played football, and I was *done* with athletes and their bullshit. But that was before he made the best declaration of lust I had ever heard. The most Eric ever said was *mm you're hot.* Goddess? Shit. Almost had me forgetting my "no athlete" rule.

Say that! Reassure him. He seemed worried as hell with all the glaring and unblinking eyes. "I agree," I said, my cheeks blazing with heat. "I'll never be with an athlete again anyway. I want to come first and with you I never would."

His nostrils flared. "Right. Good. We agree."

"Yes."

"Excellent."

We stared, neither one of us moving as the awkwardness weighed me down. In the silence, I couldn't help but admire his strong nose and full lips. He'd shaved, and his clean jaw was sharp, flexed, and *what the hell am I doing?*

"Good night, Monroe."

"Yeah." He blinked, then turned so fast he almost ran into the wall before disappearing into his bedroom.

I stood there, frozen, lost in my own head at what had just happened. The confession, the newfound fact he thought I was gorgeous... *no.* I shook my head. I would never date a football dude, let alone someone on Dean's team. I'd learned that lesson the hard way, and just because Luca lit something up inside me, it didn't mean shit.

If anything, it solidified I had to protect myself even more. I would just end up getting hurt. Fool me once, shame on you, fool me twice... well, that'd be on me, and I didn't have time to be heartbroken again. I had an internship to score.

CHAPTER
TWELVE

Luca

All of us had our own custom cure for a hangover that we swore by, but there was no fucking way Dean's *spicy food* worked. Just smelling the greasy hashbrowns coated in hot sauce made my stomach churn.

Not as badly as it did when I thought about last night and what I'd said. *God.* Could I have been more ridiculous? I winced, my hungover mind replaying everything I'd said to Lorelei like a *most embarrassing moments* reel of my life. I called her a goddess! To her face! I rubbed my head and groaned.

"Drink this." Oliver pushed a red sports drink at me. "We need electrolytes, boys. Lots of them."

Red was the worst flavor, and I shoved it back.

"Coach will be pissed if we smell like beer." Dean chugged a water bottle, then crumpled it up before tossing it into a trash can. "But man, last night was *sick.*"

"Say less, man." Callum hadn't opened his eyes yet as he leaned back on the couch. Coach wanted us back at the field midmorning to reflect on the game, to make sure we iced or were tapped, and some of us would do a light workout if we needed to.

I would opt out of that today. My mind felt like a freight train and a tornado had a love child, and I blamed Callum for the damn shots. "Why did you insist on bringing the bottle of tequila?"

"Because it seemed like a good idea at the time. Obviously." He moaned, the sound like a dying animal, and it echoed in our living room. Dean was the only one capable of eating real food, and even he struggled to swallow it.

Oliver changed the channel to put on another college game from the west. I took some aspirin earlier and needed it to kick in ASAP. At this point, it was a waiting game until I felt human again. We stank, and a shimmer of shame coursed through me. Was all the partying and letting loose worth it to feel like this the next day? Maybe, maybe not, but it was the only time I could.

Soft thuds came from the stairs, and my breath caught in my throat. Unless one of the guys had a houseguest and forgot, that meant it was Lorelei.

She rounded the stairs, and a smile broke out across her face when she saw us. "Morning, boys. How we feeling? Ready for a run or want me to make mimosas?"

"Shut up, Lo," Dean groaned.

"God you all smell." She scrunched her nose and avoided looking at me. I knew because my gaze hadn't left her once. She wore a navy crewneck sweatshirt and loose shorts, and her legs were shiny. My fingers twitched. I wanted her, badly.

And now she knows it.

"Wasn't there some agreement when I let you live here about making us food?" Dean asked. He shoved his fork to the side of his plate and paled. "This tastes like vomit."

"I could've told you that." She walked up toward the back of the couch so she was about four feet from me, and I swore I could smell her lotion.

It reminded me of summer days, flowers, and sunshine. I closed my eyes, breathed it in, and when I opened them again, she stared at me. Her large doe eyes filled with heat for a second before she masked it.

Shit. That flicker of heat had my body sparking to life. What did that mean? That she wanted me too? It was one thing to see women attracted to me, but having it come from her made everyone pale in comparison. I was used to people wanting me for football fame, but with her? She didn't give a crap, and it was sexy as hell.

Her last name is also Romano.

Lorelei sneezed twice before saying, "I have an hour before I'm heading to the union for a bit to work on this project idea with Mack."

"Mack's meeting you there?" Dean asked, a bit more oomph to his voice. "Why not come here?"

"You for real?" Lorelei's eyes blazed. "You *insisted* I couldn't bring friends here or else because of your teammates." Her gaze flicked to me for a second. "That they would be too much of an annoyance."

"Dude, I didn't say that. I want females here. Mack, especially. Please," Callum said, the dude still keeping his eyes closed. "She's the blonde, yes?"

"Yes, but I'm going to stop you right there, Callum. Mack is off-limits from you." She narrowed her eyes and pointed her finger at him real aggressively. "I'll shave your eyebrow off while you sleep."

He peeked one eye open. "Bet."

Her face flashed with victory, and Oliver laughed.

"I mean, shit," Dean said, wincing. "I did say too many distractions were bad, didn't I?"

"Yeah, you were a real dingus about it," she fired back.

Dean said that because of me. God, he was a good friend. Gratitude washed over me, right before a flash of guilt for the thoughts I had about his sister. He knew what my life meant and that having people over here messed with my routine and plan. The fact he hadn't thrown me under the bus with it meant a lot, and my stomach tightened with unease. What would Lorelei think if she knew it was *me* that had almost prevented her from moving in?

Dean sacrificed having his sister be upset with him for me, and I was thinking about kissing her and how she'd taste.

Was I that much of a selfish asshole?

"I mean," I said, clearing my throat. "I'm okay with it. As long as everyone else is, yeah, that's cool. Your friend, Mack, can come here. To work on a project."

She chewed the side of her lip, eyeing each one of us. "While I appreciate all your *permission,* you're being weird. So, no." She flicked Dean's ear before heading into the kitchen.

With the open floor plan, I could still see her in the kitchen area without her knowing. Her shorts hugged her ass, and seriously, I couldn't believe what I'd done last night. Confessing to her? She had to think I was a fucking creep.

The whole point of telling her was to make her feel better and to get it off my chest, but now I felt worse? This was why feelings were dumb. I should be laughing and eating with the boys instead of wondering how I could come up with an excuse to walk into the kitchen with her.

Idiot. Food. "I need food."

Callum opened both eyes, smirking. "Thank god you have legs that can strut into the kitchen and hands to bring me back something."

"You're annoying." I was tempted to push his legs off the couch so he'd fall, but I didn't. Instead, I acted as naturally as possible as I stood up from the couch. Dean wasn't staring at me with questions. *Good.* I was being smooth.

"Ask for C Dubs," Dean said once I set foot in the kitchen.

"Wait, what?"

"C Dubs. She'll know."

I sighed. I had zero clue what the hell Dean said or what it meant, but I was glad he gave me something to do with my mouth because when she turned around and faced me, my brain turned into mush.

"Hey." She licked the side of her lip as a slight blush crept up her cheeks. "Good morning."

"C Dubs," I blurted out.

"Fucking Dean." She sucked her teeth before setting a banana on the counter. She laughed, whether to herself or me, I wasn't sure.

She grabbed flour and syrup and baking soda. She then bent low and opened the bottom cabinets. Watching her work all around me was intoxicating, how she mumbled to herself and moved so fast between items. "Is there a waffle maker?"

"Um, why?"

Crouched down, she glanced over her shoulder and stared up at me. "C Dubs. Chicken and waffles. Lolo's chicken and waffles. It's a dumb nickname Dean's called me since we were in junior high, and I owe him one."

"You owe him… waffles?"

"Yes." She glared beyond me, sneering. "It's this weird language we have that honestly makes us sound nuts, so I'm not gonna get into it. But we each get one use of it a year, and mine involves waffles."

"So, you're going to make him chicken and waffles, no questions asked?"

"Not chicken. Waffles, yes. It's the sibling rule we swore an oath to." She shrugged and clapped. "Ah ha, there it is. I knew you were in here, you sexy grill." She pulled out a large waffle iron and twirled it. "Oh, Dean?" she shouted.

"What?"

"Are you sure you're turning in your C Dub card?"

"Yes. I'm desperate."

"Okay, you're done for the year." Lorelei sighed and met my eyes. Amusement danced on her face, and she smiled. "Honestly, I'm glad he's using it. He's held it over my head all damn year, and I just knew he'd bring it out when I really couldn't do it."

"Having a sibling must be strange," I said, an unfamiliar longing taking hold of me. I loved my grandma and my teammates, but this language and understanding between Dean and Lorelei fascinated me.

"It's the best and worst. Dean is honestly a great guy." She found measuring cups and pointed her chin toward the fridge. "Could you get some butter out for me?"

"Sure." I brought her the ingredients, enjoying watching her more and more. She hummed to herself and moved like she listened to a beat in her own mind. I wanted to learn more about this language, the reason she was so happy, and to ensure her and I were okay. "So, listen—"

"You hungry?" she asked. She pulled out eggs and texted someone on her phone. "Mack's coming over."

"Waffles?" I asked.

"Yeah? You want some?" She met my eyes but quickly looked away. "Oliver, Callum, you want some too?"

"You're a fucking dream, Lo," Callum yelled back.

My eye twitched. Callum had gotten real chummy with her, and while I knew he did that with *everyone,* I hated it. She seemed so relaxed around him, and I wanted to earn those smiles myself.

She laughed, and it was a twinkle of sorts. "Keep it in your pants, McHenry, I don't fuck with athletes."

"Goddamn you don't, not footballers at least." Dean chimed in. "No one in this house ever."

She rolled her eyes before smiling at me. "Anyway, you want some?"

I nodded. I wasn't hungry yet, but if I said no, I'd probably have to leave the kitchen, and I didn't mind being here. It was better than feeling like shit on the couch. Plus, I still had to bring up the previous night. I coughed into my fist, my entire body on fire. "Was last night as bad as I'm imagining it in my head?"

She reached for a spatula to mix the mix and eggs in a bowl, and she paused. Tilting her head to the side, she stared at me with her eyes simmering. "When you said I was a goddess?"

"Shit." I closed my eyes. "Yes. That."

She laughed, and something soft landed on my arm. "I'm flattered, honestly. Thank you. No one has ever said such nice things about me, and it flustered me a little to be truthful, but it's totally fine. To even things out, I think you're fine as hell."

She squeezed my forearm and let go, way too soon. "It's great that we're on the same page though. We'll never be more than friends. And like, yeah, sometimes I want to stuff my face with all the fudge in the world. I am a slut for chocolate, but that doesn't mean it's good for me or that I'll actually stuff my face with it. My mouth might water, but I'm not gonna shove it in my mouth."

She's talking about chocolate. The food. Not you.

My lips fell open, and she smacked her forehead. "Oh my god, I realize how that sounded. I'm not comparing you to chocolate. Well, I guess I am, but in a metaphor way. Not physical? God, this is the worst! I'm making it worse! Tell me to stop talking!" She threw her hands in the air and looked so ridiculous I laughed.

I laughed *hard.*

"Are you drunk?" I teased.

Her blush covered her face, but this time, she giggled too. "No! But wow, what a pair we are. We're competing for first place in the worst award ceremony ever: the most awkward."

I snickered. "Thank you for making *me* feel better about me. I didn't compare you to chocolate at least."

"Ugh." She hit my hand with the spatula. "No waffles for you."

"Oh, come on, I think I get some since I did call you a goddess."

She growled. "You get one goddess comment a week, that is it. Yes, a great compliment that goes to my head, and I kinda like this confidence boost, but you cannot, in good measure, use that to convince me because it'll work."

"You're a little conundrum." I grinned down at her, my insides fucking floating from how much I enjoyed this conversation. "You're sending me mixed signals here, Lo."

Her eyes heated at the use of her nickname, and I made a mental note about it. It was filed away with the other inappropriate things I enjoyed about her.

"I'm cancelling this topic and moving on."

"You can't just *cancel* a topic."

"Yes, I can and will." She straightened her shoulders as she poured the batter into the grill. "Your grandma, where are we on the notarized situation?"

"I trust you," I said, damn well feeling it in my bones. She might terrify me because of the power she held over me, but my gut told me to trust her. Yeah, I knew she'd never do anything to hurt my grandma or me. The only person who could get *hurt* was myself if I let myself focus on her and not football.

She nodded. "I appreciate that. I'll still type up something formal so you have it just in case. Mack's gonna help me come up with my plan, then I'd like to run it by you. I can also email it to you if you don't have time. I know you're regimented."

"Give me your phone," I said, holding out my hand. "I'll text you so you have my number. Tell me when it's ready, and I'll find an open spot."

"Perfect." She handed her phone to me, our fingers brushing for a second. "I'm really excited about this, Monroe. I have a million ideas."

"Can't wait to hear them." I meant it too. Her face lit up, and knowing that her ex was in her class and that her having the best project would stick it to him but also help my grandma was really a win-win.

I leaned against the wall, arms crossed, and watched as she made waffle after waffle. It wasn't an uncomfortable silence, not like last night. This one was pleasant. She'd ask me to grab something, and I did, and we found an easy rhythm of working together. In a weird way, being with her reminded me a lot of my grandma. The woman was stubborn and found joy in the simplest things, like going in the car wash or sweeping to an old record. Lorelei seemed like the person who would enjoy small things, the quiet moments.

"Alright, you heathens, waffles are done." She stacked three of them on each plate, smothered them with butter and syrup, and set silverware to the side. Dean appeared first, his eyes as wide as the plates.

"Worth it. Thank you. I'm dying inside."

"You're welcome."

"Thanks, Lo." Oliver licked his lips as he grabbed his plate. Callum followed, moving twice as slow with his lazy gait.

Instead of grabbing his plate, he walked up to Lorelei and put an arm around her. "You're an angel. Your face, your cooking. Your—"

"Knock that shit off right now, McHenry," Dean warned.

"I'm complimenting your twin sister." Callum rolled his eyes before winking at Lorelei. "Thank you."

"None of you get used to this shit. Dean called C Dubs, which he gets once a year, and since I'll be long gone by January, this won't happen again."

Long gone by January? Hearing those words were like a punch to the gut.

"What if I threatened you'll be kicked out?" Dean asked, shoving a huge bite into his mouth so it came out muffled. "Blackmail you into food."

"I'll get Mom involved."

"The fuck you will."

Lorelei laughed and handed me a plate. "Eat, Monroe. You need some carbs to soak up that alcohol."

"Right, thanks." I took it from her, a previous comment she made coming back and changing my mood. *I'll be long gone by then.*

She'd only been here a week, and her presence felt like part of the house already. Man, I needed to get it together. As we ate waffles and Lorelei and Dean gave each other shit the entire time, I made a plan. I had to avoid being at the house as much as possible because around her, my focus crumbled. She made me want to say screw my rules, which were to *never* get involved.

CHAPTER
THIRTEEN

Lorelei

My left cheek twitched at watching Eric lean close to the girl on his right. She giggled, and he said something smooth, probably, and ugh. Why was I watching them? What good would it do? He didn't have my heart anymore. I didn't have many regrets in my life, but picking *this class* with Eric when we'd first started hooking up was a dumb choice. The fact we both wanted the internship too added another layer of emotions in there. Seeing him chat with Mrs. Gravestone last week and watching her laugh with him, sent a flurry of anger through me. He was charming as hell, but that didn't mean he'd earned the spot… probably.

I wanted it *more*. Plain and simple.

This wasn't a box to check for me though. I loved the power of words and how an image could tell a story. Marketing was what I was meant to do, and Eric had taken away some of that passion. That was frankly quite unfuckingacceptable. The internship would be mine, and I'd earn it. I wouldn't charm or flirt my way into it, no. I'd work hard and do a damn good job to show Mrs. Gravestone this was who I was—someone who got knocked down but pulled herself up and tried even harder. I was that way on the field, so why couldn't I be like that in real life too? I was even more determined to help Luca's grandmother. It lit a fire in me. Excitement buzzed through me.

Building my inner confidence up, I stood tall and made my way down the stairs. It was a small lecture hall of about seventy people, and we met here two days a week and in a small group on Thursdays. *Thankfully,* she had two rounds, and Eric wasn't in my small group.

"Mrs. Gravestone?" I asked, refusing to look at Eric who stood only a few feet from us. He said he sat in front to pay attention, but I knew it was because he liked *getting* attention. It was different.

"Yes, Ms..."

"Romano." My face heated. *She doesn't know my name.*

"Ah, yes. Ms. Romano." She smiled. "What can I do for you?"

It was hard to tell when people had that flash of recognition when they heard my last name. Was she a football fan? Did she know my brother? Maybe. Did she remember my last name from the syllabus? Unsure. Either way, it bothered me. I wanted to be known for *me,* but it was hard having a quarterback for a twin.

I'll make myself memorable.

"I'd like to chat about the new direction for my project." My voice came out louder than normal, stronger.

"You had the..." She paused and glanced at her notebook. "Girls' soccer team. Hm. Yes, we vetoed that being too easy and convenient for you."

I felt more than saw Eric's gaze against my back, and I put on my game face. "My new proposal will be ready Friday."

"In three days." Her eyes flashed.

My gut tightened. "Is that okay?"

"This class is not some BS place where you read and reflect. You learn. You experience. Priorities change daily in the business world. You could have a ten-page detailed plan with color coordinating tabs, and your boss could change their mind that morning. Being able to shift and produce under pressure is part of the job. So yes. Do it. Adjust. Impress me."

"I will." I grinned hard and spun in a circle of victory. That internship was mine, baby. I'd impress her, help Luca's grandma, *and* stick it to Eric. It really was a trifecta of wins. Butterflies exploded in my stomach, some of it nerves but mainly excitement. Eric eyed me with unease, his lips flattening as I did a little wiggle. Feeling ballsy, I flipped him off with a smile.

He blinked before a shadow of a grin crossed his face. Usually, I'd analyze the shit out of that reaction. Did he miss me or was he plotting my demise? The guy had messed me up so much I couldn't be sure, but it didn't plague me as much as it did before. But Luca's words came back to me, how he thought I was a goddess. His compliments warmed me more than anything Eric ever said, and my face heated. Luca didn't say a lot, but when he did, the words packed a damn punch. Like how he spoke about his grandma? How thankful he was for her and determined to care for her? Eric complained about his family all the time, something that had always bothered me.

I had a new goal and mission, and I couldn't wait to get started on it.

Now I just had to corner Luca and get his approval because he had straight up disappeared from the house. After Saturday morning, I never saw him. I heard him, sure, with his loud footsteps, but he'd always be in his room or leaving.

I wasn't paranoid, that would be too extreme, but a part of me, a little bit, thought he might be avoiding me? Which, I understood. But the hot and cold, friends but not friends, *let me know when the outline is ready* but never answering my texts was getting annoying. I *could* move ahead without his stamp of approval, but that felt gross. This involved *his* life.

I sat in the back of the lecture hall and texted him immediately.

Lo: Hey, I got permission to move forward with the new marketing idea. Can we please meet to go over it? I have until Friday, and I don't want to lose three night's sleep if you hate it.

Lo: If you changed your mind, that's okay. Just, tell me. You kinda ghosted me?

Lo: Not like, for real ghosted, but I haven't seen you in real life in days. Just a thumbs up is enough approval. Or even a ghost emoji if you're feeling frisky.

There. That would be sufficient. He'd either accept or not.

Luca: Where are you

Yes! He engaged! I smiled like a fool at my phone.

Lo: In class, but I'm free in forty minutes. You on the quad?

Luca: What hall

Lo: Follet

Luca: see you in forty minutes

Okay, short and to the point, but hey, this was perfect. I'd go over the plan I made with Mack and earn his approval. Then, it was go time.

Class dragged on because I was so excited to get started. Usually, I loved Mrs. Gravestone's lectures, but there was an undercurrent of nerves living under my skin. A minor, miniscule part of me looked forward to seeing Luca. It had been days since we chatted, and I wanted to make sure we were okay.

And to see if the attraction was in your head.

Yes, also a little of that, brain. Knock it off.

I got up from my seat and shouldered my bag just as Eric approached me. I sucked in a breath, hating the immediate rush of heat to my face.

"Hi, Lorelei."

"Hello." I kept it professional because I was a goddamn mature adult. My head remained high and my posture straight as I walked toward the exit. "How are you?"

"Okay, are you even able to look at me?" he asked.

"Whatever for?"

My pulse raced, and I wanted to run. I'd never understood where I was with him, what I meant. He'd push me away, pull me close. Promise me one thing, then take it back. I hated feeling insecure because it made me think I was irrational, when Eric didn't have his shit together and was toxic.

I marched through the exit doors, the fresh air hitting my face, and I breathed it in, welcoming to slight smell of fall. Like burning leaves and bonfires. The leaves changed from green to red across campus, and it was a sight. "The leaves are so pretty," I said.

"What's your new idea?" he said, not getting the hint I was ignoring him.

That made me snap my gaze to his. "You're asking me what my project is? For real? Why would I tell you?"

He shrugged. "I want to know. You were gung ho about girls' soccer and how it's better than men's and shit. It was all you talked about honestly. A little bit too much."

"Whoa, okay, do *not* start that with me." My temper flared, the fire dancing along my spine daring me to do dangerous things, like *punch* his throat dangerous. I sneered at him. "My project is *my* business."

"You used to be so easy to be around." He ran a hand over his face. "Now you're even more—"

"More *what* Eric?" I shouted. I hadn't meant to, but my emotions got the best of me like usual. I was loud and competitive and messy, and *fuck* Eric for making me feel bad about it. "I'm more *what?*"

"Lorelei," a deep, strong voice said.

My stomach swooped at finding Luca standing off to the right wearing navy joggers and a tight long-sleeved shirt. His hair blew in the wind, and he stared daggers at Eric with his dark brown eyes. He looked as intimidating as he was on the field and even hotter than in my imagination. That clenched jaw, stern face, biceps flirting with how far they could stretch his shirt... he painted a hot-ass picture.

"Is Derrick bothering you?" Luca stepped closer to me.

My lips quirked up, and I beamed at him. That comment had to bug the shit out of Eric. "Nope. Want to grab a coffee with me?"

"Yes." He spoke to me, but his attention remained on Eric. He tensed his jaw before raising his arm and tucking me underneath it.

His warmth spread through me, and he smelled like laundry and apples. I tried not to breathe him in, because that would be weird, but man, Luca smelled good. He steered us away from the entrance to the lecture hall and down the stairs. I couldn't be sure, but it seemed like he held me tighter against him the more distance we put between Eric and us.

He led us to a bench right underneath a tree with changing leaves. This was *the* bench I'd always dreamed about. It sat perfectly center of the quad, right in front of the largest, prettiest tree on campus, and it belonged in a love story. I sighed, stared up at the leaves, and smiled. "This is the most romantic spot."

"Yeah? How so?"

"The placement. Plus, the leaves changing over from summer to fall? Simply gorgeous." I made the chef's kiss gesture with my fingers. Luca's gaze softened at me before he studied the area.

"You're right."

"Damn right I am." I plopped down and moved my bag to rest on my knees. He remained standing, his brows furrowed as he stared at me. "What?"

He shook his head. "Nothing."

"Mm, you have something on your mind. I can tell." I pulled out my notebook and pen and grinned up at him. Maybe it was the high of getting permission on the project idea or the fact he one-upped Eric with the wrong name, but I was feeling very warm and fuzzy toward Luca Monroe. Warm enough to wonder what he'd feel like to hug. His broad shoulders and large chest would feel nice, I was sure. My face heated, a stark contrast to the anger Eric caused me.

This was different.

Luca ran a hand over his hair, messing up the ends up a bit. "I don't understand why you were with that guy and in the same class."

"We had fun, and I had a different idea of what we were. Joining the same class seemed great last spring, and since we're both marketing majors, being in some classes together is inevitable. The hard part is that we're competing for an internship." My heart skipped a beat. "I want it so badly I can taste it. It keeps me up at night."

He snorted. "I relate to that sentiment. That's how I feel about getting drafted." He pointed to the spot next to me. "Can I sit?"

"Of course, please." I patted the metal bench and smiled. "Appreciate you asking though."

He lowered himself, his massive body almost touching mine. He wasn't even sitting like a dude with wide legs, and his body took up over half of it. He leaned back and put his arm on the edge, his fingers just inches from my shoulder. I wore a sweatshirt and yet seeing his hand dangle so close had my stomach swooping. God, this was bad. I had to get it together.

He eyed his watch. "What's your plan? I have twenty minutes."

"Right. Duh." *Stop talking about leaves and shit.* "I'll hurry to get you out of here."

He didn't respond, and I scrunched my face. This was going well. "Okay, I'd like to visit the facility and ask about what socials they have. Are they on all medias? Do they have a newsletter created for family members or the public? Who manages outreach? Do they have a website for volunteers or just the main one with information? It's outdated and could use some upgrades. Are they tracking usage? I would need those answers first before getting to work. I'd also—"

"I'm visiting her Sunday. Want to come with?" He kept his attention straight ahead.

My stomach dropped. "I have a game on Sunday. I can't. What about Saturday?"

"I use that day for post-game stuff."

"Monday?" I could probably miss an afternoon class and weights if I explained it to coach. "Well, maybe not."

"Sundays are the only day I can."

My shoulders slumped, and the bench seemed colder. "Damn. Okay. I can... hm. I can call them. Maybe borrow someone else's car." I went through the mental list of everyone who had a car, and *Eric* was at the top. Ugh.

Luca leaned back, his shoulder leaning against mine as he

faced me. His jaw was tight again, and his eyes flashed with *something,* but it disappeared fast. "It takes a few hours to get there."

"Yeah, I know. I looked it up." I pulled at the end of my ponytail with frustration. "Would your grandma take a FaceTime or Zoom call? I could interview her that way, but that wouldn't be good for the video pieces I wanted to do. I thought it'd be amazing to film the residents with fun facts about them. Like they were alive before we had TVs. That is wild. I could do TikToks with them about life back then." I flipped to the third page of my notes. "There could be a buddy system paired up with the high school nearby—like senior and seniors!"

"That's a great idea." Luca sighed, and his right knee bounced. "You'd need to be there in person for a lot of this, wouldn't you?"

"I'm thinking so, which… that doesn't work with our sports schedules."

He grunted, and the momentary high deflated. I was a popped tire. A balloon with a hole. A hose with a leak. I closed my eyes and leaned back, unintentionally resting my head on his arm. He stiffened but didn't move.

"Okay," he said.

It jolted me from my pity-party. I peeked one eye open. "Okay… what?"

"We'll go this Saturday."

Hope burst through me like the crowd rushing in for Black Friday sales. It knocked over every emotion I had, taking the lead. "You for real? What about your coach?"

His nostrils flared. "It's not… it was my own routines getting in the way, not his. I'll be fine."

"Oh, Luca." My heart felt like someone squeezed it with two hands. This was almost unbelievable, him sacrificing his time for me. "Are you sure? I know you're intense and focused.

This wouldn't... I can find another way. My parents could let me borrow their car! Yes, that's it."

He shook his head. "No, I can take a few hours off. Plus, my grandma has been pestering me to see her."

"I can be quick. The quickest. I'll email everyone in advance so we can be in and out." I spoke too fast, too loud because the excitement came back on steroids. "Gah! This is gonna be awesome. I could just hug you right now!"

He let out a tight laugh and removed his arm from the back of the bench. "Want to leave around two? That lets me finish post-game film and a light workout."

"Yes!" I jumped from the bench and spun in a circle. "You won't regret this, Monroe. Not one bit."

CHAPTER
FOURTEEN

Luca

Why the fuck had I gotten a haircut and shave for this? It wasn't a date. It was a few hours in a car with Lorelei Romano to visit my grandma. That was it. Nothing more. Yet, I felt like I had to clean up. Look nice. I found my newest jeans and showered. No big deal.

"Ready?" Lorelei knocked on my doorframe as I put on a football hoodie. That felt more casual, like friends hanging out. Because that was what we were.

"Almost." I chewed the inside of my cheek as I grabbed my wallet, keys, and froze. Had I put on deodorant? I couldn't remember, but I didn't want to smell. "I need thirty seconds. I'll meet you downstairs."

"Sounds good! Don't worry, I made car snacks." She laughed and left my room, thankfully.

I quickly applied deodorant and sighed. This wasn't anything, and I had no reason to be nervous. Like, what the fuck? I'd stared down some of the biggest fucking dudes against a Michigan team last night and yet a car ride with her had me sweating. Maybe the sweatshirt was too much. I took it off and would just toss it in the back of the truck. Why did I have to confess my attraction to her in such an obnoxious way the other night? Like, she didn't just know I thought she was hot. I told her she was a goddess, like I was a total idiot.

My usual Saturday night involved homework to keep my grades up and watching more film of the game and finding areas of weakness. Then I'd create my own workout plan for the next week. Instead, I'd be in the car with Lorelei and visiting my grandma. I could handle it.

Liar.

I met Lorelei downstairs, and while she chatted with Dean about the project, I admired her from afar. She dressed in workout pants and black running shoes and a long extra-large football sweatshirt. She wore her hair down and wore an orange headband thing, and she defined perfection. If someone asked me to draw the perfect woman for me, down to the outfit, it was this right here. Her.

My throat tightened, and I fisted my hand. She was Dean's sister. My quarterback. My brother. I *felt* his gaze on me, and I quickly averted my attention from his sister to the ceiling. Running my hand over my jaw, I mumbled, "There's a crack up there."

"What are you saying?" Lorelei asked.

"What? Nothing." *Fuck.* My face burned.

Dean stared as his phone, not me, thankfully.

There was a reason I'd stayed away from her all week and yet, here I was, making more time for us to be together. It was torture, and she glanced up and smiled at me. "I made puppy chow!"

"Leave half of it with me since I let you live here." Dean grabbed a handful, but she smacked his hand. "Come on, Lo. This is crack."

"You can have whatever Luca doesn't eat. He's doing me a huge favor." She snatched the bag from her brother and grinned at me. "It's a rule in our house. *Car rides longer than thirty minutes require snacks.* It's like one of our family's guiding principles."

"One time, we drove to Florida and went through how many bags of chips?" Dean said.

"Disgusting. You were an animal then."

"Okay, princess, you weren't?"

"Not as bad as you!"

"I was a growing teenage boy. I drank a gallon of milk a day. Clearly, the calories didn't stay." He admired his arms, and Lorelei rolled her eyes.

"You disgust me."

"How's finding another place to live going?"

"How's being the uglier twin going?" she fired back.

I was utterly charmed. I loved how she gave her brother shit and never backed down. The image of her worry at being around her ex returned, and I hoped to never see that expression on her face. I liked her like this: loud and tough and witty.

Dean cackled and took a handful of the dessert and left to the living room. He hit my shoulder. "Can't imagine a better person to keep her safe."

"Right." I nodded at him. The dude had no idea what was going on in my head or he wouldn't allow this. He'd punch me in the face or make me move out. The thoughts I had about his sister were not healthy, that was for sure.

"Okay so are you a playlist kinda guy or a podcast guy? Wait, you're a silence type, aren't you? That's a little serial killer for me, but it'll be fine." She clutched her laptop and water bottle, the bag of snacks hanging from her shoulder. I held out my hand.

"I'll carry that."

"You just want some. I knew it. Luca Monroe has a weakness for sweet things."

"You have no idea," I mumbled.

She laughed, but clearly, she didn't get the meaning.

We loaded her stuff into my truck and headed onto the interstate toward the facility three hours away. We'd get there by four, and she had an hour or so of interviews set up before we'd have dinner with my grandma. No girl had ever met my grandma before. Not even when I dated someone for a year in high school. Lorelei would be the first.

"I teased you, but you didn't answer. Are you a music guy or a podcast guy?"

"I'm pretty sure you said silence as an option too," I teased and snuck a glance at her.

She scrunched her nose and shrugged, not looking the least bit ashamed. "Sure did. Who else drives three hours in *silence?*"

"I like true crime podcasts, actually."

"Interesting turn of events." She gaped. "Not… Sports Facts 101 or Football for the Ages?"

"Both of those sounds terrible." I set the cruise control, and my lips twitched. "Sports Facts 101? What would that even mean?"

"I don't know. Like, who invented football? Why was the ball brown? Why is there only like ten minutes of action the entire game yet fans go wild for it?"

"I'm sensing some attitude around football over there."

"You're so bright," she deadpanned.

I laughed. God, she was amusing. "You think soccer is more fun?"

"Oodles more fun. I say that without an ounce of bias."

I snorted and let myself study her for a second. She had a small smile, her eyes twinkling with joy, and my chest tightened. The sun hit her hair and lit up her face, and damn, she was pretty. "I've never been to a game before."

"*What*." She glared at me. "That is unacceptable."

"I know. I've never deviated from my plans, and Sundays are for—"

"Yeah, yeah, yeah, some routine you have. I understand you, but dude, you can't talk shit about something you've never seen! Soccer players are so much fun and aggressive. Like, people assume football is rough, which yes, with the concussions and injuries it is, but girls' soccer? It is a different kind of vicious. No pads, no helmets, just the drive and grit to win at all costs."

"Yeah, I saw a bit of this when we tied at our shoot-out."

"Hey, I would've won if we kept going!"

"You're fun to play cards with, I bet," I teased.

She growled, and I smiled again. With her, smiles came easier and easier. I wasn't thinking about the ways I could fail and let my grandma down. Instead, I was playing calendar Tetris on how I could attend one of her games. Dean went to every other game or so, and it'd be easy to tag along with him. He always invited us, and Callum went from time to time.

Just thinking about Callum made me roll my eyes. He'd flirt with her, probably.

"No need to roll your eyes at me. I understand I'm a lot to deal with."

"What? No. I was thinking about something else." I frowned at her. "You're not a lot…to deal with."

"Thanks, I am, but it's okay." Her voice lost a little zest, and that wouldn't do.

"No, you're not. You're you, and that's…I like how competitive you are."

"Well, thank you, Monroe." She hummed. "Now tell me

your favorite memory of your grandma. I want to get a backstory on this incredible woman I'm about to meet."

"Ah well." I cleared my throat. I wanted to spend more time on telling her she was perfect, but that probably crossed the friends-only line I kept drawing in permanent marker. "She loves pranks to the point it's maddening. Most of them are terrible, but every once in a while, she gets you really good."

"Okay, I love her. I adore this woman. What type of pranks?"

"Cans with stuff popping out, hiding balloons in closet, switching up furniture in the room when you leave. My favorite memory though was when I was eight and really sad because it was my birthday. Being the kid without a mom and dad was hard, so she wanted me to be surprised. She invited my entire elementary school class to a park that night and filled water balloons. She declared war on the kids, and we just went bananas. She'd saved up for weeks and called off a shift at the restaurant to fill up those balloons. It was just the biggest gesture ever. So, when we were done, she told me she couldn't afford any presents, and I didn't care. The balloons were enough, but when we got back to our apartment, she'd bought me football posters of my favorite players. It was…" I trailed off, the story reminding me why I fought so hard for a future. "Amazing."

Lorelei sniffed, and my gut tightened.

"Are you crying?"

"Yes." She laughed and sniffed again. "That is quite a story, my goodness. What an icon of a woman."

"She is. That's why I focus so much. There is no margin for error."

"I get it." She whimpered.

I slid her a look.

"I am a crier. I show emotions for everything. Good, bad,

great. Like, I cry when I'm angry and happy and sad. It's annoying. And, when I win or lose, tears come too. It's just a part of my personality at this point."

She sounded defensive, but I didn't see the issue. "Okay then."

"I always say I got all the emotions, and Dean didn't get any. Something weird went on in the womb or something because the imbalance is not fair." She used the end of her sweatshirt to wipe under her eyes. "Ah man, my mascara! I can't be a raccoon when I meet her."

"Oh, she won't care."

"I care, Monroe. I have to seem put together."

"You look beautiful," I said, my face immediately warming up. "For this. Fine. I mean, you look fine."

"Settle down over there. You already told me I'm a goddess, so there's no going back."

"I do regret that," I grumbled.

"I know." She giggled and pulled down the mirror. Wiping her eyes, she let out something between a sigh and a snort. "Don't worry. I won't let it go to my head."

I playfully rolled my eyes. "So, what's on your agenda?"

"Ah! Well, so glad you asked." She crossed one leg over the over, her bare ankle on display.

It was just an inch or two between the end of her tight pants and her socks, but the tanned skin there seemed smooth. I wanted to drag my fingers over it, see if she liked being touched there. *Focus on the road.*

Fuck. Not hooking up with anyone the last two Fridays was getting to me. I was worked up. Really tense and it wasn't *her* fault I was so damn drawn to her. It put me in a miserable situation because did I want her? God, yes. But could I do that? No. Never.

"I have a meeting set up with the owner, Patrick. He'll

provide an overview of their marketing efforts, but when they had to fire people, the marketing specialist was the first to go five years ago. They are quite behind in terms of presence and seem really excited about this idea. Depending on how that goes, I'll talk to their outreach director. Then, I'm chowing down with you and your grandma, and I'll ask all sorts of embarrassing questions about you. I'm very persuasive and usually get my way when I want something."

"No, my grandma won't spill anything. She's a vault. She wouldn't do that to me.

"Mm, we'll see. Remember, I'm competitive at *everything.*"

I arched a brow and got her to smile at me again. I loved seeing her grin. It made me feel normal, like I was just some guy hanging out with a girl who liked me for *me* and not a ticket to the NFL. I enjoyed my time with those women, for sure, but it filled a basic need and nothing more. Weird, how it had never bothered me until this second. I scratched my chest, ignoring the buildup of pressure and handed Lorelei my phone. "You can choose the episode. It's called *Lost Killers.*"

"How nice of you, allowing me to pick. And trusting me with your phone! An honor. The things I could do right now."

I sighed, mentally going through anything embarrassing on the device. Nothing came to mind. "You're a handful, Lorelei."

"I'm aware." She crossed the other leg now, hiding her ankle to my disappointment. "Ah, the lost sister? This seems dark."

"It is."

"Wait, you've already heard this one? Let's do another. What about… the neighbor?"

"What's the summary?"

"A man leaves his house one day and never comes home, leaving a wife and a child alone. Four years go by, and they declare him dead but then one day he shows up like nothing happened without any memory."

"Shit." My eyes widened. "Sick."

"Look, I love Halloween. It's my favorite holiday, and I even love horror films. But those are fiction. Not. Real. This stuff freaks me out."

"Oh, we don't have to—I'm sorry. Here, put something else on." I reached for the phone, but she slapped my hand. "What?"

"You're driving, but no, now I have to listen. Where did he go? What happened? Like, I need answers now. That's one of my flaws. Like some people can stop reading a book at some point because they don't like it. I can't do that. I'm a finisher. I finish things all the way through, regardless of if it's a good use of time. Wow," she said, sitting back. "This explains a lot about me."

"Nothing like true crime to have a mini-identity crisis."

"Ha." She snickered. "You're more fun that I thought. I like it."

My ears heated. "Thanks, I think?"

"Yeah, you're welcome. But yeah, we gotta listen to it now, and I'm preparing you, it's probably going to become my whole personality afterward."

"I don't even know what that means."

"It's okay, you don't have to." She tucked her knees up to her chest and closed her eyes. "I'm hitting play."

"And you're closing your eyes because….?"

"Preparing myself. Focus on the road, Monroe."

"Yes, ma'am." I fought a grin as the familiar narrator's voice filled my truck and the intro keys thudded. It was a chilling effect—on purpose, I was certain—and Lorelei's face scrunched together in a wince. "You okay?"

"Yup. Hate the music, that's all. My pulse is pounding."

"For real, come on, let's stop it."

"Luca." She opened her eyes, her large brown ones boring into me. "I *need* to listen now that I read the premise. If we don't finish on the trip, then I will at home by myself, and that would be worse."

At one point, Lorelei gasped and stared wide-eyed out the window. Her face paled. I paused the interview with the guy himself. "Hey, you okay? Have a snack?"

"My food." She shook her head. "I forgot I brought the snacks. Here, eat puppy chow."

"I'm fine, but you seem pale. Are you scared?"

"What if...your grandma disappeared for years without reason? I can't... what happened to him? It is terrifying! What! Like, my mind is spiraling right now." She rubbed her temples. "I'm thinking time travel, right? I mean what else..." She shivered. "What do you think? I need every thought you have."

"Honestly? I don't have any." I shrugged. "Digesting it, I guess."

"Oh my god," she yelled. "You don't have a million things going on in your head at all times? Like, what if the truck veered off to the right or what if I ran out of snacks or had to go to the bathroom, but there wasn't a place to stop for miles or if a deer ran out, and we hit it or if we got a flat tire?"

I sucked in a breath. "Jesus, Lo, why are you thinking all that?"

"If I knew, I'd stop it." She rested her head back, closing her eyes. "And throw in my suspicion about time travel."

I snorted. "Well, if this helps, the tires were rotated this summer and are in great condition, but if we veered, it's just open plains, so you'll be okay. I have a spare in the back and learned how to change a flat, so no big deal. If you need to stop, there is a gas station in twenty minutes. And I try to keep an eye out for deer. My grandma hit one once, and I scared the shit out of us."

She exhaled. "Okay, those plans sound great."

"I'm good at reacting to plays. Way better at reacting than thinking ahead."

"Interesting as you're on offense."

"I know." I sighed. "But I stand by it. I react to the team, to Dean, to the opposition. I become what the team needs. I guess I'm that way in life too. I don't think about what's going to happen, I wait for the event to occur, then respond."

"I wish I was that way, damn. I worry so much all the time before things happen, and most of the time, they never do. It's an exhausting use of my mind."

"You're not—" Shit!

A fucking deer ran out in the road, and I veered right. The tires screeched, and we lurched forward. I stuck my right arm out, shoving my hand against Lorelei's chest. Then we spun out.

CHAPTER
FIFTEEN

Lorelei

My heart about fell through my ass. I gripped the side of the truck like my literal life depended on it, and something heavy shoved against my chest. The seatbelt tightened and dug into my neck, and the sound. Ugh. The high-pitched squeal would forever be stuck in my mind, replaying over and over. We spun in a full circle, and a loud horn blared in the distance. *Oh my god, another truck.*

I closed my eyes, the terror of dying seizing me.

The pressure on my chest deepened as the heavy roar of the truck grew louder. We lurched forward, then slowed. The wind knocked out of me, and I couldn't move. My limbs grew twice their size, the heaviness of the almost-crash making each breath difficult. The narrator's voice carried on, talking about cults, when suddenly, the truck stopped.

"*Fuck*, Lo, I'm so sorry." Metal clicked, and a door opened. Then, the cool air was blowing on my face, and Luca was right there next to me.

He undid my seatbelt and ran his hand over my neck,

collarbone, and chest as his gaze darted between my face and chest. "Are you hurt?"

I shook my head, my entire body trembling from fear. The adrenaline rush was unlike anything I'd ever experienced. Each breath pulled tight in my throat and lungs, my toes and fingers throbbing from my pulse.

"Fuck." His face fell, and he moved his hands over my arms and down my sides. "You're okay. You're good. No injuries."

"A-are you?" I croaked out. His face paled, his eyes somehow darker.

"I'm fine. It's you I'm worried about." He cupped my face and waited until my gaze met his. "I might've hurt you when I reached out."

He dropped his attention to my chest. My skin prickled as he stared at me, and at the mention of it, a dull ache formed over my breastbone. I cringed.

"I might've bruised you." He pressed his lips together, squeezing his eyes shut. "I'm so sorry."

"Why did you do that?" I asked.

"To protect you. I didn't even think, I just did it." He rested his forehead against mine, his breath hitting my face as he shuddered.

My skin tinged for a different reason this time. The heightened emotions from the almost-accident, the way he'd *protected* me. In the middle of a potential accident, he'd reached over to *me,* ensuring I was safe. That was amazing. "Luca," I whispered.

His breathing deepened, and his fingers dug into my face as he exhaled. I was too afraid to move. Something warm and hot grew in my gut, a bolt of lust overtaking all rational thoughts. I tilted my head up slightly, just a hair, and our lips were a centimeter apart. It would take no effort at all to close the distance, and my god, I wanted to. But I held back, out of fear, worry, I wasn't sure.

"I'm sorry," he said, the movement of the words causing his lips to touch mine. He wasn't kissing me, but holy shit. Electricity sparked through my skin, getting into my veins and spreading like fire.

My stomach fluttered with butterflies, and I squeezed my thighs together. "It's not your fault," I said. My lips grazed his too, and I craved to close the distance, bite his lower full one, to suck it into my mouth.

I wanted to feel his hands dig into my body as I kissed him.

Every part of my body tuned to his: the way he smelled like sweat and laundry, the way his breath hit my face and smelled like mint, the feel of his hands on me and the way his fingers shook. "Are you okay?" I whispered. I wanted to make sure he was but also needed an excuse to talk because that meant our lips grazed again.

It was the sexiest, non-kiss I'd ever had.

He released a huge sigh, pulled back, and nodded. His eyes swirled with worry and heat. He kept gripping my face as he stared at my mouth, his tongue wetting his bottom lip. His nostrils flared as he moved his thumb toward my lip. He pressed into it as he groaned. "You are—"

"You guys alright?" a voice called.

Luca *flew* off me like I'd caught fire. I hated the absence of his heat and strength. If the dude waited two seconds, we would've kissed.

Luca darted out of the passenger side door and waved a hand in the air. "We're good, just shaken up."

"Need anything?" the same cheery voice said.

Luca stared at me the lingering heat sizzling between us. He arched a brow, and I shook my head.

"No, we're okay, thank you," he called out but held my

gaze. Even though there was a good ten feet between our bodies, there was an undeniable pull between us.

I still felt the whisper of his lips against mine, and I rubbed my lips together, wishing I could prolong that moment. Luca had protected me and was so gentle and worried that it confused me into thinking that *maybe* we should explore being more than friends.

The second the thought crossed my mind, a cold dose of reality hit me. He played football, and that was his only priority. I knew better than to get involved with a guy who told me over and over we'd never be anything. Even if I had a crush and wanted to kiss the hell out of him, that was still an entanglement I didn't need. This project, my team, the season, finding a new place…. Those were my priority. Not exploring the wild attraction I had for this intense guy.

But imagine how he'd be in bed.

I cleared my throat as Luca stared up into the sky, pinching the bridge of his nose. He looked in pain, and my chest tightened. "You didn't hurt yourself, did you Luca? Your arm is okay?"

He snapped his gaze to me. "I'm fine. Need a minute, that's all."

Was his tone chillier than before? I pulled my legs up to my chest again, hugging myself and closing my eyes. Eric made me feel too much and like an annoyance all the time, that I'd never come first or second to him. Luca made me feel the opposite, which was wonderful even if it never became more than friends. It showed me that I wasn't wild or needy—it proved to me Eric really was a dick.

Boots on gravel crunched, and Luca walked up to my side of the truck, his eyes troubled and filled with disgust. I braced myself for the usual hot and cold from him. The sting of him being mean or telling me, for the millionth time, that football would come first. "I—"

"I know. Football comes first. I remember. No need to drive it home." I focused on the dashboard and a speck of dust on the top right.

"That wasn't… I'm not… hey," he said softly. He ran a hand over my hair, gripping the back of my head, tilting it so I could face him.

The warmth on his face combined with the softness of his eyes, and I about melted. Luca was *gorgeous*. "What?" I asked, a little breathless.

"I love your hair." He smiled, the gesture taking up his entire face. He sighed as he ran his fingers through it.

"Oh."

"It's perfect." He narrowed his eyes, his smirk growing. "You're becoming a real problem, Lo."

"Wait, what? You're all over the place right now, and I have no idea what to do." My stomach did a flip-flop, and my heart backflipped. Was he teasing me or threatening me? With those gooey eyes, it couldn't be a threat. I was seventy percent sure. "You have a strange look on your face, Monroe."

"You keep finding ways to entice me." He chewed the side of his lip, drawing nearer to me.

"Yes, that's my goal. To entice you. My whole purpose in life," I fired back, absolutely out of control with my emotions and hormones.

"See? Even now, with your sassy attitude, you are a temptation." He closed his eyes. "One I can't afford but goddamn, I want to so badly."

"Want to what, Luca?"

He shuddered. "I like my name on your lips. It makes me want to break my rules, and I just…can't."

"I'm not asking you to, you know?" I said, placing my hands over his. "Being into each other is one thing, but doing anything about it? That's up to us. I'm not *trying* to distract you in any way."

"I know that, and I'm sorry if it came out like I blamed you."

"It didn't. I understand what you meant, but we should probably stop touching like this if we aren't going to do anything about it. I understand why it's a terrible idea, but when you touch me," I said, gulping, "I'd agree to about anything."

His eyes flared, and his jaw tensed. He stared at me hard, indecision clear on his face before he stepped back and muttered, "*Fuck*."

Without his touch, I cooled down and could think more clearly. This was for the best. He knew it too, and after a few seconds of him staring off into the distance, he nodded to himself before getting back into the truck. He started it, gripped the wheel hard, and focused straight ahead. "You get your seatbelt on?"

"Yup." I clicked it. "All good over here."

"Great. Perfect."

After a minute of tense silence, he was back on the highway, and we were en route to his grandma's. The almost-accident and almost-kiss felt like four hours, but it was only about fifteen minutes. An intense, emotional roller coaster of a quarter hour. It was a bit unfair, if I was honest. Why did I have to have this magnetic pull to someone who was off-limits in so many ways to me?

I snorted, focusing on the farms in the fields as we drove by.

"What was that for?"

"Why do we have to be into each other when we are completely wrong for each other? Why couldn't I be into a nice unathletic boy? Someone who can kiss me without worrying about the future? A guy who doesn't play on a sports team with my brother? The list of what who not to go for is like three bullet points, and you meet all of them."

Luca cleared his throat. "Why do you think an unathletic guy is right for you?"

"Because I know what it feels like to be put second or third all the time. My parents are great, but football is sexier. Dean's career was more important always. One could say it was because of money, but it doesn't take away the fact that I came in second. Then, the first guy I really fell for made me feel like an annoyance whenever I wanted to hang out. Baseball always came first, and I understood that because hello! I'm a fucking athlete too, but it was *not the same* because I was a girl. And with you, ugh, you look like you'd give me the best time in the bedroom ever, but I cannot go through feeling like second place again. And I don't blame you—you need to put football first. Your grandma deserves that from you, so please don't take that the wrong way, but wow, I'm talking a lot. I'll shut up now."

Luca didn't respond, which was probably for the best. I'd gone on a mini rant from his question, and now my face heated in embarrassment. This was *not* how I'd envisioned this trip to visit his grandma. I thought we'd talk about the facility and life and her—not about why we could never give in to our attraction.

With the silence, I refocused myself on the goal: the project. The data backing up my success. The yellow brick road of what I was doing and how it would work or not. That was the thing I loved about Mrs. Gravestone's class was that every campaign provided data, and even if it didn't succeed, you learned what hit and what didn't. It was about experimenting, like what time of day was best to post based on the end-user? Was it Wednesdays at three or Fridays at four?

Yes. This is better. Thinking about school shoved Luca

thoughts into the back part of my mind where they should stay, untouched, forever. I locked my mental box. I tossed the key out the window, never to be found again.

Avoiding thinking about Luca in that capacity would be the *only* way to stay safe.

CHAPTER
SIXTEEN

Luca

"You seem distracted. Why? Tell me everything and don't leave a detail out because I'll know."

My grandma hit me with one of her knitting needles, and I snorted. "Maybe the last guy was right, you are a threat."

"Can it, Luca Maron Monroe. Is it this girl you brought for a *project?*" She eyed the door, her impatient gaze almost cheering me up. She'd hit it spot on. Lorelei was the reason for my unfocused thoughts.

"It's nothing. We're here for you." I forced a smile and hated the way her eyes narrowed. She was a damn hawk for knowledge, hunting and flying around until she found her prey, and right now that was me.

"You have never, since you were fourteen, brought a girl to me. Forgive me for having questions, but I'm a bored old woman stuck in this prison, so I need drama. More than hearing about the latest wave of STDs going around this place. Or that Gwen accused Henry of stealing, when we all know Gwen is forgetful as shit and left her necklace at Peter's place when they hooked up. This place is a brothel, Luca." She rolled her eyes and sighed.

I laughed for real this time. "Your dramatics have only increased in age."

"It's a cycle of life, dear. At some point, you stop caring. I reached that a decade ago, and I'm going senile. Its rude to point it out."

I squeezed her arm. "Is everyone treating you well here? You eating regularly and able to do what you need?"

"Do *not* tell me you came down here to fret. I want to see my grandson and live through you. Tell me about the last party. Did you play a drinking game? Did people cheer for you?"

"Why can't you be normal?" I teased.

"Missed that boat years ago, Luca. Now, who is Lorelei?"

I scratched the back of my neck, wincing at her beady eyes. I knew her. She wouldn't let this go no matter how hard I avoided it. "She's the quarterback's sister. Dean—"

"Romano, yes. I know him. Good arm, good instincts. Have a bet going on with Patricia next door that he'll kick her precious alum's ass up north. Put fifty bucks on it."

"Should you be gambling?"

"Should you be questioning the elderly? Death is on my door, and I do as a please." She adjusted her gray messy bun and pouted. "You want to deny me joy?"

"Jesus." I barked out a laugh. "I should be living vicariously through you. You have way more fun than me."

Her face fell just as a familiar floral scent entered the room. "Hello, hello!" Lorelei said, knocking on the frame. I'd left the door cracked, and she pushed through.

A sudden blast of nerves fluttered in my gut, like pre-game jitters. What if my grandma hated her? Or what if she said something that offended Lorelei? I really wanted these two to get along for some dumb reason I refused to dive into. "Uh, Grandma, this is—"

"Hi, you rascal!" Lorelei walked up to my grandma and held out her hand. "It is an honor to meet you. You have quite the reputation around here, and I am here for it. The bathroom bandit, the party planner, and the dessert diva? You are who I want to be when I grow up."

"Keep her. I love this girl." My grandma beamed at her. "I earned those titles the hard way."

"Has Luca told you anything about my project?"

"No. He refuses to indulge me of anything interesting, instead worrying about me. It's cute but annoying."

"Sounds about right." They snickered like old friends, and something warm as honey formed in my chest.

"So, are you dating him?"

"Ha, no." Lorelei flashed her eyes at me for a beat before smiling. "I don't date athletes."

"Anymore," I added, giving her a pointed glare. "You have in the past."

"Correct. I'm sick of someone always putting me last, and with Luca, football is his life. So negative, we are not dating."

My grandma sighed and looked at me with so much disappointment my toes curled into my boots.

"I can't afford any distractions."

"Luca, son, come on." My grandma closed her eyes. "I'm not getting any younger. If anything, your singlehood is killing me slowly. I need to know you have someone in your corner or I'll wither away here with worry."

"Can we chill with the theatrics today? My lord, woman."

Her lips twitched. "Fine, fine. Now, Lorelei, what is this project about?"

Lorelei's eyes lit up, and she plopped down on one of the chairs next to my grandma's couch. "I'm running a marketing campaign for this facility in hopes of getting donations and more people to help out. I spoke with Patrick? I think, yes, Patrick, the owner of the place, and he didn't really seem to care. He's letting *the youth* run wild with the idea and if it helps, then great."

"Patrick is a stick in the mud."

"I got similar vibes."

"One year, I spiked the punch at the Halloween party, and he lost it. Refused to drink any, but many would argue it was our most successful year."

"Obviously." Lorelei laughed and a had a twinkle in her eye. She seemed to enjoy herself, and it was silly of me to think these two wouldn't get along. They were similar spirits, a little mouthy and ballsy.

"What does this campaign have to do with me though?"

"Great question. I'd love to do a profile of some of the residents, put your face, your story, your vibrant personality out there. You're not just," Lorelei paused, waved her hands in the air as she frowned. "What's the right word?"

"Old farts?"

"Yes." She giggled at my grandma's answer. "You're not old farts hiding away and counting down until death. You're people with personalities and hobbies and goals and incredible lives. I want others to know that too."

"Hm, it won't be for some charity thing? They won't see my face and be like 'oh, that poor old biddy needs funds?'"

My entire body tightened with unease. I gripped the edge of my chair, about ready to say to hell with this. If my grandma felt upset in any way, the plan was off. I hated seeing her show even a flash of vulnerability in front of Lorelei. She was the strongest human I knew, and if this caused her an ounce of pain, it was done. How Lorelei answered made all the difference. I needed her to have a good excuse, something to make sense of it.

"This absolutely not about charity." Lorelei set her notepad down and met my grandma's gaze. Her large brown eyes filled with determination as she said, "That will not happen. Not for a second. You have my word."

"I trust you, dear."

"You don't even know her," I fired back, still on edge of seeing my grandma display an iota of weakness.

"You wouldn't even bring her here if you didn't feel the same." She patted my hand, her lips curving into a smile. "You annoy me with how much you take care of me, Luca, so yeah, I trust her because you trust her."

Lorelei wore a huge grin, the top of her cheeks pinkening. I *hated* that my grandma was right. Crossing my arms, I leaned back into the chair and shrugged. My grandma took that as a sign to continue, and she clapped.

"What do you need from me?"

"Your life story. The weirdest, best moments of your life. What would you want young people to know? Your name is Nanette, right? I'd love a *Nanette's Knowledge* or *Nanette's Nuggets* of wisdom or something." Lorelei bit the end of her pen and arched an eyebrow. "Thoughts?"

"Hate the name, love the concept." My grandma studied her bookshelf where hundreds of thrillers and romances sat. She lived on books and always mentioned how she read every book the facility had.

"Books!" I shouted, making them jump. "Could one of your pushes be to get more books donations here?"

"Oh, of course." Lorelei wrote so fast there was no way it was legible. "Books, oh, we could get a local author, maybe? I love this. Yes."

"My grandma is an avid reader and has gone through

everything they have. I've tried getting her an e-reader, but she fusses over the cost."

"I can take the bus to the library every other week. I am fine doing that."

"The bus broke down two months ago, Grandma. You haven't gone since June." My tone came out firm. "This place could use donations to get it back to full capacity. That's what Lorelei wants to do."

"But why?"

"Because I'm one of those passionate Gen Z kids, and whatever I do has to have meaning. I want to help show who lives here and how the power of words can make a difference." She shrugged and flashed a goofy grin at my grandma. "Plus, my ex is in the same class as me, and we're going for the same internship, so I gotta show I'm better than him."

My grandma's face lit up. "Yes, this is the drama I'm needing. So, your ex, he's in your class? That's horrible."

"I know." Lorelei sat back, rolling her eyes. "We thought it was cute last spring, but now I hate it. He wanted to *focus on* baseball a week before school started, and *it's not even* baseball season. I'm a fucking athlete—forgive my language, but since I'm a female… he said it's not the same. It's harder for *men.*"

"Oh, honey." His grandma clicked her tongue. "We'll beat him. I'll do whatever you need. I dated a guy once, back in the eighties, who told me the only thing I was good for was opening my legs."

"Grandma, Jesus." I put my hands over my ears, my stomach rolling. "What are you doing?"

"Hush. Now, Lorelei, I slapped him in the face and found out the next week he'd be working in the same building I was in. I'd been promoted to executive assistant, and you know what I did for years?"

"I cannot wait to find out."

Seeing them get along caused a weird, warm sensation in my chest. My grandma was the most important person in my life, and watching Lorelei bond with her made me think about what-if scenarios. Like what if we dated? My grandma obviously liked her. Or what if we were—no. I had no business thinking about these fantasies.

"Spat in his coffee every single morning. Do I regret it? Not for a second. If anything, I wished I'd done more. So, how's that for a nugget? When men say stupid things, you don't get even, you take the lead."

"God, you're an idol." Lorelei wrote a bunch of notes down, and I couldn't help but admire her long neck and gorgeous hair. We had been *so close* to kissing, and seeing her chat with my grandma, who was sharing a story I had never heard before?

My damn heart pounded in my chest with a continuous *break your rule, break your rule, break your rule.*

It was getting harder and harder to not say to hell with it. Lorelei Romano would be my undoing.

CHAPTER
SEVENTEEN

Lorelei

The thrill of the project combined with playing some of the best games of soccer in my career put me on a high of sorts. My professor loved the outline I'd sent her and the beginning notes of who I'd spoken to.

I officially had the social passwords for the older home facility—Heath's Lodge—and created an account for the social media accounts they were missing. Young people weren't on the same socials as older folks, and that was okay, but after reading a quick study about Gen Z, we wanted to feel purpose and would be more likely to donate time or resources to give back. I wanted to target that age group.

The manager of the place, Tim, had contacted me this morning to see if I could come back this Saturday. A current of heat and excitement ran through me at the thought of driving there with Luca again. Things had been…interesting since our almost kiss. He hadn't avoided me like the week before, but he kept his distance.

I caught him staring at me hard a few times, but when I met

his gaze, he'd blink and return to some mundane task in his room. He was meticulous, but instead of making fun of him like I would've before, it made sense now. After seeing the place and meeting his grandma, I understood his direct focus and mission.

Heath's had seen better days, and Tim hadn't flat out said they were going under but hinted at it. The cost of everything had gone up—from food to facilities to paying wages—yet the residents there were on a set income. If he raised prices, those people wouldn't have anywhere to go.

I made it a personal mission to help this place. They deserved to be comfortable and to enjoy the last chapters of their life. Patrick could be an asshole and raise prices, but he didn't because he knew what it'd mean to the residents. I'd focused on soccer my entire life, making it my whole purpose, but this felt different. It sparked something deep in me, and I liked it.

I wasn't *Dean's twin sister* or *the soccer girl* or *Eric's sidepiece.* I was a marketing consultant for an older home facility.

The only minor hitch in my plan was getting Luca to drive me up again. Mack said she could get her parents to let me borrow their car, which I would do, but I wanted to talk to Luca first.

Only problem was—it was game day, and they were leaving for the game in Ohio in an hour. They'd be back tomorrow morning, hungover if they won, pissed if they lost, and that meant my window narrowed down each second I delayed.

Groaning, I pushed up from my bed and stretched my legs. I was tight. I'd stretched and iced, but my ankle felt tender. Brushing it off, I twisted my left foot in a circle, then the other way before opening my door and staring at Luca's room. Despite the progress we'd made, his room felt intimidating.

Kind of like him with the always-shut door and silence on the other side.

If it weren't for that fun memory of me walking in on him watching porn, I'd never guess he was human. *Shit. Why did I think of that?* Now I pictured him stroking himself, his face set in determination, and my skin prickled with heat. Our almost kiss had lingered in my mind all damn week, a flurry of what-ifs followed by hell-nos. He was heartbreak and hormones. I knew how it would end.

Sure, could I enjoy the middle? Probably. Yes. Fuck yes, I would. God, I shivered just thinking about him blasting me with his intense eyes and strong jaw. The roughness of his skin from stubble coming in. If he ran that scruff along my thighs, *yum.* Something hot and steamy coursed through me, making my cheeks flush. *Shit.* Get it together. I raised my hand and knocked, my heartbeat an erratic rhythm.

Thirty seconds, forty…

He might've left, but I'd listened for him. I would've heard him sneak out of the room with his heavy footsteps. No one his height could sneak around. Too much muscle and bones to be quiet. Disappointment settled deep in my gut. The thought of seeing him had more of an impact than I cared to admit. We'd barely spoken all week, just casual hellos, and now I wouldn't see him today *or* tomorrow…There was no reason to be this disheartened about it.

My brain already formulated the next steps of calling Mack and ordering an Uber to pick up her parents' car when the handle twisted. Hope burst through me, like a bird escaping out of a cage.

"Lorelei." His gaze swept up and down my body, lingering on my bare toes for a second. His nostrils flared, and I dug my feet into the floor. I'd painted my toenails orange and black for my favorite month of the year and instantly felt silly for attempting to design a pumpkin on my big toe. It was a large orange circle and terribly done.

"Hi, hey," I said, biting down on my top lip. Here he was and I'd forgotten words. It wasn't my fault though. He didn't wear a shirt, and sweat beaded on his forehead, his chest moving faster than normal. "Were you... are you... porn again?"

"What?" He blinked. "No, I was doing crunches." He coughed into his fist, red painting the upper part of his cheeks.

There was something magical about seeing a blush cover Luca's face. It made me think of naughty things. Inappropriate, lusty, and dirty thoughts. Why was he blushing? Was he hiding something? God, I wanted to know. I tapped my toe over the frame of his room and grinned. "You are lying, Luca Monroe. You're blushing, and that tells me I caught you doing something."

He cleared his throat, and when I glanced up at him again, his brown eyes were almost black. A simmering volcano of heat reflected back at me. His lips parted, and he licked his full bottom one, but before he said anything, he shut his eyes and stepped back. That small movement was a cold splash of water on my libido.

Stop setting yourself up to be rejected.

"Did you need something?" he asked, an edge to his voice. If I wasn't so stung by the huge step away from me, I'd notice the higher pitch of his tone.

"Yes." I straightened and crossed my arms behind my back, resting them against my lower spine. "I've been emailing and chatting with Tim all week, and I need to go back to Heath's Lodge tomorrow. I was—"

"No." He worked his jaw back and forth, rubbing his hand over his chin.

"Didn't appreciate being interrupted or having you say no

that fast." I faked a smile, not losing my bravado. Romanos were built with nerves of steel. "If you're not able to go up there, could I possibly borrow your truck? I'll pay for gas, obviously. Tim wants me there to interview some residents, and I had so much fun last time. I could say hi to your grandma too if you can't go."

"You can't do it over a Zoom call?"

"Have you met the clientele there? For real? No one has the patience to show them how to join a *dang Zoom* call." I laughed. "Even Tim, who was super kind, couldn't do that."

His lips quirked up on one side. "My grandma learned how to text and use gifs, and it's been downhill from there."

"Exactly. Now, I know you're busy and probably not able to tag along," I paused, as Callum walked out of his room in low-riding shorts. He'd clearly just woken up and nodded at us as he went into the bathroom. "Can I borrow your truck?"

Luca lost the blush, which saddened me, but he shook his head. "It's big, and if you don't have practice with it, it could be too difficult."

I tried one more time. "And there's nothing I could do to convince you to come with me? We could make a deal of sorts?" I lowered my voice and widened my eyes, hoping my goofy face was the tipping point. It had to be more difficult to say no to a silly face. It was science.

He pressed his lips together tight as his brow wrinkled. It seemed like he *wanted* to say yes but couldn't. "I don't think I can."

Defeat. It sucked. "Okay," I said, my stomach twisting. I still had to find a way up there though. "I'll manage. Good luck tonight."

"Did I hear you need a ride?" Callum yawned, rubbing his eyes as he exited the bathroom.

"Yes. Why? Can I borrow your car?" And I was back, baby!

"Whatever you need. I'll do it. Chores. Food. A lap dance. Okay, I take that part back. I'm shit at dancing."

Callum laughed. "Mm, that could be fun though."

"My mouth ran away from me. It happens in desperation."

"Fine," Luca growled, pulling my attention back to him. "Callum's car is a piece of shit, and mine is safer."

"Fine as in I can borrow yours?"

"I'll take you." He ran a hand over his face and sighed. "What time?"

I couldn't believe the turn of events, and a small, weird part of me wondered if he was jealous? Did the thought of me driving with Callum bother him? No. There was no way. He didn't get involved, ever, and that seemed involved-y-ish. I snuck a glance at Callum, and he winked at me before going back to his room.

I felt played but didn't care enough to figure out why. I had a ride, and Luca was coming with. Spending time with him seemed precious and rare, something to never hope for but moments to cherish. I jumped in the air and let out a little cheer. "Yes! One? Does that work for you?"

"We get back around noon."

"Okay, two then?"

"No, one is fine." Luca sighed and studied my toes again. He seemed angry, annoyed even. He'd agreed to this after saying no, so it couldn't have been my fault for the mood shift.

"Will you be too tired? I can drive if you want to use the time to study or watch film or sleep off the hangover. Tonight is your wild night, right?" My stomach twisted about him going out and having fun, hooking up with another woman.

His silence ate at me. He stared too much and said too little. It made my desperate need to fill the quiet come out even stronger.

"I'll be fine."

"No partying tonight? No hookups?" I asked, fake laughing. "Thought Fridays were your get-out-of-guilt-free cards. Where you can let loose and be a normal person."

Luca's eye twitched. "No hookups. Not tonight."

Ask why. Ask it. Do it.

I opened my mouth but chickened out. I had zero reason to feel sick with worry thinking about him with someone else. It made sense for him to hook up with someone out of town. That was his favorite flavor—one and done. No feelings, just pleasure. My mouth dried up. Luca deserved to have fun, even if it wasn't with me. "You should! Yeah, you should have the best sex ever tonight. Go to pound town."

Oh my god. What is wrong with me?

Everything, apparently.

Amusement danced on his face, his gorgeous smile teasing me. "Pound town? Really?"

"I… regret saying that." My face flushed. "Not my best moment."

He smiled for real this time, two dimples popping out on either side of his chiseled face. I wanted to poke each one, just to feel how deep they went. The smile felt like the best prize, and I grinned, giddy for no damn reason.

"You are ridiculous," he said, but there was warmth in his tone. "The most ridiculous."

"I'm aware." I bowed because my god, all normality had disappeared. The dimples short-circuited my brain, and I couldn't quite unplug and plug myself back in. "Well, have fun tonight. Be wild. Safe. Fun. All the things. I'll see you tomorrow."

Without a backward glance, I went into my room and leaned against the shut door. The familiar, breathless feeling of a crush knocked the wind out of me, and that wouldn't do. I'd been down this road before, and just because a hot guy flashed dimples at me, it didn't change a thing. Not a one.

No one would ever call me ill-prepared. After last weekend, I knew the zing between us would flare in the truck, so I took matters into my own hands. Literally. I wouldn't be so pent up if I got off before being around Luca for hours. They weren't due home for another hour—the perfect amount of time to get my vibrator.

I only felt secure enough to use it when no one was home. I could lock my door and turn music on loudly, but the dull vibration sound carried, and it would be the worst if Callum or Luca heard it. That meant taking advantage when they weren't home.

I lay on my bed, naked, and put on The Weeknd. His voice was the absolute sexiest, and all I had to do was picture Luca and *oh yeah.* Hot tingles of pleasure danced along my skin, swooping deep in my gut. It had been a while since I'd gotten off, and my body could tell. I was tense as hell, and I applied some lube before sliding the vibrator inside. Groaning, I turned the clit stimulator on and *fuck.* "God, yes." I angled it perfectly as I arched my hips and fucked myself.

Sweat beaded on my skin as I rocked against my bed, the pressure absolutely lethal. My clit swelled, and my muscles tightened as an orgasm closed in. Without permission, my mind went to Luca and that day I walked in on him.

His hand had fisted around his cock, his heavy and large one. His face had been tight in concentration as he stroked himself. God, his hands were huge, and his dark eyes lit up with pleasure. I wanted to see his face like that in real time, his jaw working left to right as he moaned.

What would I do to see Luca lose control? I shuddered as the pleasure built up into a symphony. "Yes!" I shouted, closing my eyes as the music dulled at the roar in my ears. I wanted Luca to suck on my tits and put his strong mouth between my thighs. "*Luca,*" I shouted as the orgasm was so close. I thrashed on my bed, using my free hand to pinch my nipples as the tingles exploded

"You okay?" A deep voice penetrated the air.

I gasped, absolutely frozen at the sight. Luca stood, in my room, mouth parted and his eyes wide. I couldn't stop the orgasm though. It came fast and aggressive, and I bit my lips, groaning as I came *hard.*

I panted, and not once did I look away from Luca. He watched, his chest heaving and his dark eyes absolutely feral. Instead of feeling shame or embarrassment, him watching got me hotter. Needier. I thrust the vibrator with my other hand.

His nostrils flared, and he panted as he watched me. And watch me he did. He swallowed so hard it sounded like thunder as his eyes roamed over my chest. He licked his lips, then stared between my thighs. The vibrator hummed, and I rocked up and down, spreading my legs wider.

He blinked and stepped back, running into my dresser in a loud crash.

"Stay," I demanded, his presence alone sending my body into overdrive. Goose bumps broke out over my skin, my body fully sweaty now. I pulled my nipple hard, loving how a vein popped out on Luca's forehead.

He seemed intoxicated from me, and I drank up the power. I moaned loudly as I shuddered, and the combination of the dildo and vibrator along with his stare undid me.

"Yes, *yes.*" I arched my back, slamming my head into the

pillow as a second orgasm hit me. "God, I wish this was your mouth, Luca."

He growled. A deep, guttural sound escaped him as I rode out my orgasm. My ears rang, like the time I went to a concert and couldn't hear correctly for a few days. Sweat dropped down my chest, pooling between my breasts, and I reached down to turn off the device. Two orgasms were good for me. Three would knock me out, and I needed a little energy to deal with the aftermath of this because I knew there would be some.

Pushing up onto my elbows, a sliver of worry danced down my spine. Luca still stood there, but instead of lust, anger radiated from him. His sweats tightened against his bulge though, so he could pretend to be unaffected, but I saw the truth.

"I..." he trailed off, his gravely low voice sending a shiver down my spine.

I played offense as well as defense, and I noted the second his guard went up. His eyes shuttered, and he fisted his hands at his sides. If I didn't say something, he'd push me even further away. Even back out of driving me.

"Now we're even." I arched a brow, hoping my flushed face wasn't showing vulnerability. I slid the dildo out of me and stood up, loving how he sucked in a deep breath at my nudity. I grabbed a silk robe from the closet and covered myself. "I saw you, and you saw me."

"You said my name."

"I know." I walked up to him, my legs shaking from the impact of the orgasms. He might not have given them to me, but he'd helped. "I wanted to get my horniness out of my system before we left together."

He breathed like he sprinted up the stairs, and he hadn't moved a single body part since he fell against the dresser. The guy was a statue. Except for his eyes, those gave the flurry of emotions away.

"You moaned *my* name," he said, each syllable drawn out in his deep growly voice.

"We established that, yes." I crossed my arms, the post-orgasm glow fading as Luca remained there, unmoving with his tone sharpening. "This isn't new, Luca. We've admitted we're attracted to each other."

His jaw clenched.

"We can't... I can't..." He gulped, running a hand over his face as he let out a huge groan. "I'm sorry I walked in on you. This was wrong."

I arched my brows, something ugly plucking down the back of my spine. "Wrong? What do you mean by *wrong?*"

"I stayed. I should've left. You're... Dean's sister."

Anger flared. "I know who I am, thank you. Not sure what my family has to do with the fact you watched me get off, but whatever." I shook my head and gripped the tie of my robe to do something with my fingers. "I should get dressed before we drive together, and honestly, you should do something about that." I jutted my chin to the press of his cock against his sweats.

He cleared his throat, not bothering to hide his reaction. "Lorelei—"

Footsteps thudded outside my room; a familiar whistle sounded. "Monroe, you stole my sweatshirt by accident."

Dean.

Luca's eyes turned so wide they were like two large olive pizzas at this point. I pointed behind the door, and Luca quietly fit there. Since the door was already cracked, Dean would surely ask me if I saw Luca.

My pulse hammered against my ribs, and it was like Dean's presence doused me with freezing cold water. *What was I doing?* Teasing Luca like that? My skin heated, and my stomach twisted with regret. I'd crossed a line...but he did too. He'd stayed and watched.

"Monroe?" Dean was right outside my door, tapping the doorframe.

I moved toward my frame, putting me six inches away from Luca's body. He stood rigid, panicked, and a part of me felt bad for him. He cared about the team so much, and this might've jeopardized that even a little bit.

"I haven't heard him."

"Ah, damn." Dean faced me, his frown growing. "Okay, I'll text him or something."

"Nice stats last night," I said. Did I stream the game? Yes. Was it for my brother? No. School spirit? Also no. It was to watch Luca.

"Thanks, Lo." He sighed and walked to the stairs. "Hey," he said, not quite turning around. "I'm glad you and Luca are becoming friends. I never expected that to happen, but it makes sense."

"Oh?" A warm and gooey feeling enclosed around my heart. "Why do you say that?"

I swore Luca tensed even more next to me.

"He doesn't let a lot of people in, and we're protective of him. His family life... well, he has to work twice as hard. He's been smiling more since you moved in, which trust me, I don't get it because you generally suck as a human, but what I'm trying to say is thank you."

My breath faltered. *Act chill.* "There was an insult in there too."

"I can't be nice to you. It's in the sibling handbook to compliment and insult at the same time."

I snorted. "Right, duh. Chapter seventeen."

Dean laughed and hit the top of the staircase banister before heading down. Once he disappeared from view, I stepped back into my room and felt Luca's penetrating stare.

He didn't say a word before marching past me, making sure our bodies didn't touch at all. "We leave in an hour."

He shut his door, but Dean's words repeated in my head. *He's been smiling more.* I loved that, and even though I wanted to kiss him more than my next breath—I couldn't. I refused to be put second again, and Luca would only break my heart.

CHAPTER
EIGHTEEN

Luca

There were core memories that would live with me forever. The first time I played on a football field, the first Christmas with my grandma, and seeing Lorelei touch herself while saying *my* name.

I shuddered, unable to think about anything else. I was a man obsessed. Yet, every time I let myself finish the sentence of *what-if,* the memory of Dean almost catching us smacked me in the head. But even as I'd stood there, holding my breath out of fear he'd know I hid behind the door, all I could look at was Lorelei. The flush of her face, the smoothness of her neck, the way the silk robe clung to her curves. The indent of her calf muscles and even the Halloween colors on her toenails. No woman had ever, in my life, had a grip on me like this.

She loved her brother, which in a weird way made me like her even more. She was kind and so damn smart and strong, and *this isn't helping.* I adjusted my grip on the wheel and wet my lips. An hour into the trip to visit my grandma, and we'd barely spoken. It wasn't a painful silence. I'd lived through those. This one was more comfortable. It was clear we avoided chatting since I'd stayed in her room and saw her naked.

I should've jacked off before this.

I cleared my throat, my cock swelling as the images of her dark pink nipples and full, heavy breasts plastered across my eyelids. My mouth watered. Needing some air, I asked, "Care if I crack the windows?"

"Not at all. I love the smell of fall in the air." She smiled but didn't look at me. I'd watched her out of the side of my eye the entire time, studying her like a playbook. She crossed one leg over the other, the same lush curve of her lips acting like she had an inside joke with herself.

I wanted to know the punchline so badly. What had her so happy?

"Thank you, Luca, for driving and coming with me this afternoon. I know this takes away from our routine. Two weekends in a row too! I really appreciate it." Her voice grew soft, and it fell over me like my favorite song.

Shit. I hadn't thought about my routines once since I got back from the game. What did that even mean? My usual films and post-game rituals never happened, and that hadn't crossed my mind until *now.* A surge of panic shot through me as loud as a lightning bolt. I'd planned to watch tape, but I heard her say my name, and well, her naked body was why I hadn't gotten anything done.

I sighed, and she tensed. *Oh no.* I'd taken too long to answer, and I worried her. "I'm glad I could help."

"I'll find another way to get here next time. It doesn't have to be every weekend, you know? But kicking off the project requires face time." The frown lines left, and her usual grin replaced them.

It was wild how her smirk calmed me down. The world wasn't right if Lorelei Romano wasn't smiling. It was law. "If

172

you know what weekends, give me a week's heads-up or so, and I'll see if I can move my routine around."

"Really?" Her face lit up.

"Yeah." My neck got hot, and I ran my fingers through my hair. "My grandma always wants me to visit more, and I enjoy spending time with you."

"Wow, Luca, that was the nicest thing you've ever said to me." She laughed. "Well, besides the goddess comment."

"Today only confirmed that statement," I said, my voice low.

"Ah." She faced the window, hiding her reaction from me. She twirled a silver ring around her thumb three times before she eyed me. "I'm surprised I'm not more embarrassed. I've never done *anything* like that before with anyone."

"Meaning?" My muscles went rigid, ready to pounce. Those words threatened my entire future because it made me want to devour her, to say hell with my plans.

"I've never let someone watch me do that. But with you…"

"With me, *what?*" I barked out, my voice raspy and deep.

"It felt normal. Hot. I really liked it. That's what makes this zing between us so complicated. We clearly are into each other, but we know nothing will happen. Maybe it's the forbidden, off-limits thing that makes it so naughty?"

She had to stop talking about this and using words like forbidden and naughty. My cock was so damn hard it could drive the car itself. Yet, it was clear she wanted to talk this out, and I could grant her that. "Maybe it's that, yeah."

She chewed her top lip and stared out the window again. "I didn't ruin our friendship, right? I've enjoyed getting to know you, and I respect the hell out of you. Dare I say I even like you? If I broke that in any way—"

"You didn't."

"Are you sure?"

"Lorelei, I'm positive."

"Okay, phew. I feel like we could really be good friends, you know? I mean, I've never been this into a friend or let them watch me come, but like, this is a new experience? We should probably veto any of that stuff again. Right?"

No. I'd die to see you like that again.

"Mm."

"I know I'm talking too much and rambling, but I think I'm nervous about where we stand. Your words are reassuring, but your body language isn't, which I'm not putting this on you. You react how you need to, but oh my god, stop talking, Lorelei," she mumbled.

"Tell me about your plan when we get there," I said softly. I knew her pretty well now, and distraction was key when she went on a tangent. Plus, I loved hearing the enthusiasm in her voice. "What's on the agenda today, and can I help in any way?"

"Ah! Well, Tim set up fifteen-minute interviews with eight residents, and I'm going to film them for sound bites. Then, I have some photos to take, and I want to get the vibe. Make aesthetics for posts and then I'll work on the newsletter. I asked him yesterday if he could get a group of residents to do some glamour shots, but it was short notice. I'll play it by ear there."

"What are you going to actually do with the footage?"

"Social posts about who represents Heath's Lodge. There's a nearby high school to the facility, and I sent them an email to maybe partner up for a senior-to-senior prom. Students always need volunteer hours, so why not have a high school kid repaint the building for free? They'll save money instead of hiring out. I think the crux of my plan is to facilitate making connections."

"You seem happy."

"I am. Oodles so." She beamed at me. "This came from you

too. So, when I kick Eric's ass and get the internship at the end of this year, I'll make you the biggest cake as a thank you."

I thought of a million other things I'd like to have as a thank you but kept those in my head. I'd successfully moved us away from horny topics, and it was safer to maintain distance. Even if my dick and head weren't on the same page.

She stared at me with an expectant look on her face, like she waited for my response. I smiled. "I'll never say no to a cake."

"Noted."

With the shift away from tension, the rest of the drive consisted of her talking through her ideas. She'd start a sentence one way, and midway through, it shifted another direction. Her contagious energy had me second-guessing leaving school after this year for the NFL. She had a vision for her career, and this project would lead to an internship, then a job.

I played football. Sure, every game was a tryout for the NFL. People always watched, and I knew conversations were already happening. I *liked* the sport because what it provided for me—a secure future for my family, a stable income, a way to never worry about money again. Yet there wasn't a chance to decide if I loved it in the same way Lorelei loved marketing.

It made my gut twist in a way it hadn't in a long time. Without football, I was *no one,* and I'd made damn sure it was the only path forward.

"I *might* need you to film some things for me. I want to do the half-heart challenge with residents, where you hold your fingers like this." She curved her fingers and thumb into half a heart. "And you see what the other person does."

"Interesting."

"It's a thing that happens online. I imagine you are very much *not* online."

"Correct." Guys talked about shit all the time, but I refused to get distracted. My teammates were my closest friends, and I saw them every single day. Why would I need another avenue to talk to them?

"Anyway, can you film for me?"

"Yeah."

"Great. I have a good feeling about this idea."

"Viral, you say?"

"We have twenty thousand views within two hours. Those are solid numbers for me." Lorelei grinned and showed her phone to my grandma. "I put a specific link in the bio that tracks clicks, and we have thousands of them. Even if ten of those people donate to the account I set up—" Lorelei's eyes widened "—it'll be amazing."

"Youths are fascinating. In my day, we wrote notes. Took turns on the phone. Luca, my boy, you need to help set me up with social medias. If it's this easy to be connected, I can see if my high school crush is single. Maybe he's widowed."

"Grandma," I blurted out, my face reddening. "That's not polite."

"Hush. I stopped giving a shit about being polite three decades ago. Now, Lorelei, tell me more about viral."

"It means the algorithm decided to push certain content. Since we created the video within the app *and* it's the first one we did, it's pushing our video to find our audience." Lorelei beamed and wore her pride like a badge.

I was impressed. Following her around with her phone, I'd watched as residents of all ages and demeanors reacted to her half-heart. My favorite was a grumpy old man by the name of Colin who pretended to take the beer from her hand, crack it open, and pretend to chug it. He even smiled at the end.

"So, if I were to… do one of your videos, millions of people could see me?"

"Not if you're uncomfortable," I said, making sure that was clear. "We agreed you'd do nothing that you don't want to."

"Yes, Luca. Thank you for bringing it up *again.*" Lorelei narrowed her eyes at me, a flash of hurt behind her brown eyes. "Nanette, everything you do is up to you. I have enough content for the next four weeks. If you want your face displayed, great. If not, also great."

"Oh, I want to show my face." She spun in a circle, her all-black outfit sparkling in the light. "Do you see me? I look good."

"That I agree with one hundred percent." Lorelei laughed. "Okay, with some red lipstick we could do a love-advice gig, where you provide answers to questions. Or you could talk through lessons in love. Or dating. Or, to hell with that, teach life lessons."

My grandma's face lit up as her eyes flashed with humor. Seeing her this happy made the difference. Yes, I realized Lorelei was part of the reason. I chose not to analyze it. My grandma had been so quiet about living here, and now her energy was contagious.

"I have an idea." She spoke to Lorelei, not me. It was like I wasn't in the room anymore. It was weird to be replaced, but it wasn't unpleasant. If Lorelei ended up being another person to bring my grandma joy, then I was thrilled.

"I'm here for it." Lorelei leaned forward.

"Nanette's News." She pursed her lips and clapped. "Like how to not get your car stolen or how to attract the right kind of man. *Person.* Not just men, sorry that was insensitive of me."

"Nanette's News, yes. *Yes.*" Lorelei grinned so wide she

showed all her teeth. "I love it. We can do a bit every week. I can't come down here that often, but you can send me videos any time, and we can make it work."

"I can have my boy—friend. My friend help me." My grandma's gaze flicked to me, her cheeks pink. "Sebastian is great with the camera."

"Who is Sebastian, and why is the first time I'm hearing this name?"

Was he after her money? She didn't have much. But she had some jewels that she refused to sell. Unless he wanted more...

"None of your goddamn concern."

"Grandma!"

"You don't mention your love life, so I don't talk about mine." She arched a brow, challenging me with so much attitude, it amazed me.

The thought of aging always depressed me because football was a young person's sport. But her attitude and refusal to fall back into the shadows gave me hope. She wasn't alone here, biding her time until I could visit. She had a life. Things she did that I had no idea about. I might not have football forever... so what would I have then? Friendship with my teammates, sure, but was that it? I used to enjoy collecting baseball cards and going to car shows to dream about owning a fast one. But once I realized the only way out of this life was football, everything else fell to the side.

How fucking sad.

"To his credit, Nanette, he doesn't have a love life to speak about except his one wild night out a week."

"Lo," I said, exasperated. "Why?"

"What?" She winked at me. "Tell me I'm wrong."

"Luca, you cannot live like a nun!"

"Oh, he's not," Lorelei said, smirking. "He just prefers dating football more than anything else."

I eyed my watch. It was already seven, and the drive would take long. "It's time to head back."

"Aw, look what we did, scared him off," my grandma said, pretending to sulk. "I'm sorry. I'll behave."

"No, you won't." I stood and pulled her into my arms in a big hug. She wrapped her small arms around me and squeezed me twice. It was her thing. She smelled like the same perfume she'd worn for my entire life. "You're a pain in the butt."

"So are you."

"Please, could you two settle down with the sentiments? I'm getting emotional."

I met Lorelei's gaze, and she wore the same, goofy grin she had all day. I glared at her, but she just stuck out her tongue. God. This girl.

"Make sure he has fun, okay, Lorelei? Please? I'll make you famous with my Life Lessons, but in return, Luca needs fun."

"I'll try, ma'am, but he's as stubborn as they come."

My grandma eyed me up and down. "Yes, I know. Now, drive home safely. And please, visit me again soon."

It was the soon that gutted me. She'd never tell me she missed me because she knew I'd feel bad, but seeing her laugh with Lorelei and smile so much...she never laughed with me. She loved seeing me, but Lorelei had something about her. I knew it. Hell, she'd pulled me into her like a damn magnet.

"I'll be back even if this guy can't get away from the field." Lorelei hugged my grandma, and when my grandma met my eyes, she mouthed *I like her.*

I sighed. I did too, and that was the problem. I couldn't afford to like her. A brief image of her spread out on her bed returned in my mind, and I shoved it away.

Lorelei and I had to remain friends. Not only for my sake, but for my grandma's. It would never last, and if I got involved with her... it would hurt my grandma when it ended.

CHAPTER
NINETEEN

Lorelei

I broke a personal record, scoring three times in our game the next day. There was a fire lit inside me, fueling me to play harder, go harder. Maybe I was on edge because of the lusty thoughts I had all night for Luca, replaying when he watched me yesterday. Or the fact I adored his grandma, and every time I saw them together, my chest ached with a need I couldn't explain. The third culprit for my unmatched energy was the fact my ex had liked my social posts? He was either spying on me to gain insight on the project or... what? Missing me? Not likely. Regardless of why, my adrenaline remained high, and I took advantage on the field.

I ran faster, pushed myself further, and my footwork was top-notch.

"Romano," my coach said, pulling me in for a half-hug. She smelled like sweat and fresh-cut grass. "You rocked it today."

"Thanks." I grinned hard. Coach Ramirez was tough as nails and rarely smiled but knew her shit. A compliment from her was amazing. "I felt good. Focused."

"Keep it up. Whatever it is, do it Thursday. We're facing my cousin, and god, if I have to hear her brag about beating us during the holidays, I'll cut off my ears."

"Sure thing, Coach." I snorted at the grumpy expression on her face. We played a Missouri school Thursday at their home stadium, and I wanted the win too. I was on par to have the best season of my career, yet I couldn't let that get to me. If I thought about it, I'd overthink everything I did on the field. Being a successful athlete was almost all mental. Yes, you needed the physical skills and talents and practice to make repetition permanent, but the mental stamina and headspace were equally as important. No one really talked about that—it was just expected for us to deal with it. Coach Ramirez looked into having a part-time psychologist work with the girls, which I loved. It wasn't the norm though. Plus, Ted Lasso honed in on the mental strength players needed, which was the right direction.

What if there was a marketing campaign about mental health of athletes? What if the Women's National Soccer team needed a marketing specialist?

I shoved the thought away as we headed into the locker room. For girls who dreamed of having a soccer career, the USWST was endgame. Possibly play in the Olympics or World Cup. For me though, that wasn't it. I loved the game and was grateful I could pay for school with it, but continuing after college didn't excite me like it used to. My entire life had been soccer or Dean's career. All my memories revolved around a sport. My first Christmas I could remember, I'd gotten a soccer ball. Every holiday after had a travel team or indoor soccer or intramurals. The future without it seemed a different kind of fun, one where I could be whoever I wanted without the crutch of being Dean's twin sister or a soccer player.

There was a countdown on my athletic career, and for some

reason, that made me play better. Coach always said leave everything on the field, and that was what I planned to do.

"Girl, let me touch you." Mack approached me and put her arm around my neck. Her braids plastered to her face, a few loose strands blowing in the wind. "I need your sauce."

"No sauce." I hugged her back, our sweat combining. We laughed for a bit before letting go. She too was a scholarship recipient, but instead of planning a future career, she wanted to play for the US. It was all she'd dreamt about.

"You dominated today. Kind of annoying, actually. Like, I like when you pass to me so I get the goal. Your girl needs the stats."

"Should've made more goals then," I fired back.

Mack rolled her eyes, but there was a warmth to her words when she said, "Great game, girl. I gotta ask though…"

"Ask what?"

"You play that way cause Luca is here?"

My pulse sped up, roaring in my ears. "Wait, he's *here*? At the game?"

She nodded, a spark entering her eyes. I didn't like that spark. It meant she knew things but *what* things? I hadn't mentioned yesterday, our moment. I told no one. It was a secret I'd take to the grave, but *why* had she looked at me like that?

I coughed into my fist as heat spread to my fingers. "I didn't realize he came."

"Him and your brother. They caused a scene because of you know, football players." Her tone held a hint of annoyance as the sparkle shifted to something else.

"Of course they did." I chewed the side of my lip, a million questions going through my head. Why had Luca come today, after we'd essentially agreed nothing ever happen between us? Unless Dean forced him to attend, but Luca didn't do anything he didn't want to.

He wants to come then.

A bright, pleasant feeling grew in my chest at the thought.

As we showered and listened to our post-game chat with Coach Ramirez, I couldn't quite focus. The post-game high was a real thing, and I couldn't sit still. My left leg bounced up and down, my gut twisting with anticipation of some sort. I wanted to do something, anything really, to rid of this energy. Could be something easy like a long walk or even a small workout for a release. Deep down though, I'd admit I wanted to do something rash, something…wild.

Like Luca.

My face flushed, and I took another long swig of water. I knew better than to let a guy distract me after what happened with Eric, but the temptation was there. Even more so after Luca watched me touch myself. That combined with the brief whisper of his lips against mine last weekend caused a tornado of butterflies in my stomach. I couldn't recall if I'd felt that with Eric. I knew I was into him and liked our chemistry, but this vibe with Luca was more intense.

"Great game, Lorelei," Mally Higgins said. She was a sophomore on the team and rarely complimented me. She intimidated me on every level, looks, muscles, and skills even though I was a year older.

Age didn't equate power though. That was a lesson I learned playing for Coach Ramirez.

"Thank you." I swallowed and flashed a smile. "You too. You had what… thirty saves today?"

"Thirty-five." She flashed a smile. "And thank you. Tell your brother Higgs said to fuck off. He'll know what I mean."

She added gel to her hair and slicked one side of it back, and ugh, she looked so cool. The coolest. I stared and she caught me in the mirror, and I made an awkward smile.

"You're such a dork." Mack snorted. "Stop staring at her."

"She's so cool though. Like, I know she's a sophomore, but I want her swag. The badassery that radiates around her. If we were walking in a crowd, people would move out of her way. Me? People push me around."

"Cause you're short."

Mack shoved the doors open to exit the locker room, and the familiar smell of grass and cleaner filled the air. I breathed it in deep, the same electric bubble of *something* circulating under my skin. I could lie to myself, but it was the fact I was about to see Luca again. So soon too. After we got home last night, he'd walked me to my room and immediately shut his door. If life repeated itself, I didn't expect to see him for at least a week.

How fun, our routine was for us to cross the line and then avoid each other. Healthy. Super fucking normal.

"But what did she mean about your brother?" Mack said, drawing my attention back to her. A slight blush crept down her face and neck.

See, the thing about Mack was, she tried really hard to hide her crush on my brother. She heard me complain about the girls who used me to get to him, the fake attempts at friendship just to try to hit on Dean. I appreciated her effort to never be one of those girls, but she was shit at hiding the truth

"*Fuck off, he'll know what it means?* I mean, it's pretty clear." I laughed as my gaze landed on Dean and Luca. They headed toward us, and Luca's dark eyes narrowed as he glanced down my body. My skin prickled from his perusal, and I was glad I put on my favorite jeans. They provided an extra layer of armor. For what? I didn't know, but I needed it.

"Are they—" her question was interrupted by Dean holding up his hands in a double high-five. Our tradition.

"Fivesies." He grinned hard at me as we did our handshake. It was three hits, elbow, elbow, one kick and a double clap. We both laughed by the end, and I snuck a glance at Luca, who stared unblinking at me. There might've been warmth in his gaze, but it disappeared as quickly as it came.

"Y'all know how lame you look, right?" Mack said, amusement filling her tone.

"By lame you mean awesome?" I fired back. "I'm sorry you don't have an annoying twin who was your best friend growing up."

"We weren't best friends," Dean said. "We tolerated each other."

"Are you saying we weren't close? What the hell?" I punched his arm. He swatted my hand. "Why are you at the game then?"

"School spirit."

"Liar." I shook my head and took my time eyeing Luca's outfit. Tight, fitted black jeans, a thermal with a hood, and his fresh, clean scent that reminded me of him. Now *why* had he come to the game? "You also feeling spirited? Why are you at the game? Sundays are for... color-coding your socks, I thought?"

His lips quirked up but not enough for a smile. "Figured I could support my quarterback's sister."

"That's a weird sentence." Mack scrunched her nose, her frown growing as she stared at Luca. Her apprehension matched my own confusion at seeing Luca here, studying me.

A part of me was thrilled. He came to a game! But the reason why was unclear, and I wanted to know. More like, I needed to know. I couldn't get him out of my head. Was I stuck in his too?

"I dragged him along. The poor guy was neck deep into a book, and I saved him from that torture." Dean stared at Mack for a beat too long then asked me, "You heading back to the house or hanging with your teammates?"

"Speaking of teammates. Higgs wanted me to pass the message *fuck off* to you."

Dean cackled. "That girl. She's funny."

"Funny?" Mack said, her brows drawing together. "How do you—doesn't matter." She shook her head, her voice betraying a little too much curiosity.

I wasn't exactly sure what to do about her crush besides nothing. It was her life and her choices. Did I think Dean was ready for a relationship? Absolutely not. He was as polite as an ogre.

But moments like this, where she wanted to ask so desperately, I could help her out. "Yeah, why the hell do you know Mally well enough to get cussed out?"

Dean ran a hand through his hair and laughed. "We fight over a parking spot outside Phoenix Hall. It's an ongoing war, nothing more than that."

"Strange." I shrugged and adjusted the bag from my right to my left shoulder. In doing the motion, a familiar head of blond hair came into view, and my body went rigid. He wore a Central State soccer sweatshirt with *my number* on the chest. I knew that shirt. I'd *made* that shirt.

Why was *Eric* here? What the actual hell? Luca rocked me off my game, but Eric flattened me.

My lips parted, and my skin flushed. My stomach soured, and I knew the second Mack saw him because she looped her arm through mine.

"What's wrong?" Luca asked, his growly voice pulling my attention. "Lorelei—"

"What's happening?" Dean's frantic energy matched the unease in my gut as he also narrowed his eyes at me. "Lo, you paled."

Luca frowned and glanced over his shoulder, his body tensing when he too saw the object of my discomfort. He fisted his hand at his side, and the only reason I even saw that was because I was too uncomfortable looking at Eric.

The thing about my ex was that I never could figure out his intentions. He'd make me feel important one week, then like dirt the next. He'd say he loved my attitude and fire and drive, then act embarrassed by me. It was unhealthy and inconsistent and even now—he had zero reason being at the game with my number. Did he think I'd forgive him for how he'd hurt me?

Eric approached us, his easy smile flashing. "Hey all, great game, Mack."

She rolled her eyes.

"Lo, can I talk to you for a second?" The smile fell, and worry laced his eyes. "Please? It won't take long."

My jaw tensed, and I hated that I nodded.

"You don't have to," Luca said, his voice stern and almost angry. "You don't have to speak with him if you don't want to, Lorelei."

I met his stormy eyes, and my breath caught in my throat. His eyes were cloudy and angry. Tight lines formed around his mouth, and his left cheek twitched, yet my mind couldn't piece together why.

I hated the minor pull I still had to Eric, the curiosity to hear what he had to say. Did I want to be back with him? No. Did I still love him? No. Definitely not. But maybe my ego needed real closure or to know he regretted it. I nodded at Eric and moved past my brother and Luca.

Luca growled something under his breath, but I couldn't hear it. My focus was on Eric, the guy who made me want to never date again. I eyed his shirt and sneered. "You shouldn't wear that. It was a gift when we were together."

"It's the only soccer gear I had, and I realize what it looks like." He winced and gripped the back of his neck. "You played insane, Lo. Watching you on the field was like… I'm impressed."

"Thank you," I said, coolly. "It's clear this is the first time you've seen me play."

"Yeah, and I'm sorry for that." He sighed, his breath hitting my face, before he stared at my mouth. "I'm sorry for a lot of things, and I wish I had a good excuse. I don't. I fucked up. I miss us. I hate that we glare at each other in class, like I can't even talk to you anymore. We were friends first."

Irritation danced along my spine, flirting with the simmering anger I always got when I thought of him. A dull ache formed in the back of my eyes. "What do you want from me? I don't get this. We broke up because you're an asshole. You moved on—we both moved on."

"I want us to be friends. Talk about things. Like our projects in class—"

"Are you fucking joking?" I yelled, my seething anger turning my vision red. Did he *come to my game* to try and talk about our class project? The nerve. "Tell me right now before I—"

"Time to go, Lo." A strong voice was nearby, a voice I recognized, but I wanted to punch Eric in the face.

Someone put their hand on my shoulder, grounding me, and then the hand moved to my hip, drawing me into a large chest.

"Leave," Luca barked at Eric. "She played one of the best games of her career, and you're making it about *you*."

Luca nudged me in the other direction, his chest heaving like he'd sprinted down the field, and I let him lead me. It was easier than trying to think. If I allowed my mind take control, my fists would be in Eric's face.

I growled, my entire body overheated and angry and hyped up from the game. "I hate him."

"Hold it in, your coach is still here. Once we put some distance, you can let it loose, I promise."

I nodded, my emotions all over the place. Why was I suddenly thankful and happy that it was Luca who was with me right now?

CHAPTER
TWENTY

Luca

"I'm going to kill him."

"I'd suggest refraining from murder," I said.

"*Would* you? Would you suggest that? Helpful, Luca. Helpful." She shook her head, mumbling under her breath. We walked for ten minutes and were enough distance away from the stadium that it felt safe to let her unleash. I texted Dean I'd take her home. It was the two of us now, for better or worse.

"Want to talk about what happened?"

Please say yes.

After hearing her come to my name yesterday, then watching her on the field, which…. Fuck. She was divine. Her focus and muscles, the way her body moved and her hair going everywhere. Lorelei on a normal boring day was incredible, but seeing her on the field sparked a new longing for her. I wanted that passion, that spark just for myself. She was addictive, and despite the warning bells going off in my head that it was a bad idea, I couldn't stop being drawn to her. This electricity between us would destroy me if I didn't do something about it. That much was clear.

I knew after last night that this tension and attraction between us would bubble over. I came up with a terrible, disaster-promised plan, but it was the only thing I could do. I wouldn't be able to stop thinking about her or wanting her, so why not find a way to make it fit in my carefully crafted life?

If she'll be up for it.

But then her dumbass ex wanted to talk to her, wearing her number like he cared for her. And she went with him! My own irritation threatened to ruin the moment. She needed a friend, not a guy obsessed with her. Jealousy ate at me when Eric spoke to her but then she yelled, and I knew it was time to step in.

So yeah. I needed to know what he'd said.

"He missed us as friends and had the audacity to say he missed us talking in class! You damn well know he wanted to pry about my project since we're in competition for the internship. The bastard used my emotions to try and get information. I'm so pissed I could spit!" She growled and kicked the air.

I almost laughed but refrained. *Not the time.* "Why did you talk to him then if you knew he was a rat bastard?"

She stopped as we neared the front door, and I unlocked it, gesturing her in. She went in and tossed her bag against the hall closet, then stomped up the stairs. I followed because where else would I go? I wanted to orbit around her. I'd worship her like the sun if I had a different life, one where I could be a normal person. Once she got to the top floor, she spun around and pointed at my chest.

"I keep thinking he'll provide closure or a reason why everything happened the way it did. My poor heart needs an explanation, like what if there was a noble reason he played me that way? Or what if I misread the entire situation? Don't get me wrong, I don't have feelings for him anymore. Not like that. Do I have leftover hurt? Yes. But my foolish ass hoped, for the last time, that he'd share something meaningful."

"Mm."

She pinched the bridge of her nose, closing her eyes. "I sound dumb, don't I?"

"No." I shook my head. I had to touch her, show her that she was the opposite of dumb. She was incredible and trusting and kind. "Not foolish or dumb for hoping for an answer. It's not the same but… I can relate. People make decisions that don't make sense, and sometimes, there's a reason. Other times… there isn't, and it's hard to live without one."

She nodded, her eyes opening and swirling with emotion. She couldn't read my mind, but she had to understand how fast my heart beat near her or how I wanted to breathe her in. Her lotion smelled like peaches. And my mouth watered with hunger. "I never found out the reason my parents didn't want to raise me. They left me with my grandma one day and never came back."

"Luca." She squeezed her eyes shut, closing down the window into her soul. I was never a huge fan of brown, but her eyes were beautiful. So many different shades and hints of other colors.

She chewed her bottom lip as her face fell. "Your parents abandoning you is mountains worse than my dumb heartache. They aren't even comparable."

"When people you love treat you differently than how they should, it's all comparable." I shrugged, glad I could read her emotions again. "I never got an answer and probably never will, and it sucks. I choose to let that go because what I have with my grandma is a love and trust some people never get with their own families. Bad things happen, but that doesn't mean good isn't right around the corner."

She shuddered, a line forming between her eyebrows. She fisted her hands and groaned, loudly. She raised her arms over her head, walking away from me. I immediately felt the loss of her heat, her energy, and panic clawed up my throat. *Did I say something bad?*

"Where are you going? What's wrong?" I asked, hoping she didn't hear the desperation on my throat. I wanted to keep talking to her, standing by her. Maybe she needed space. While I hated it, I accepted she could need time alone. "Do you... did I upset you? I was trying to help."

She spun around, her eyes flashing with an unexpected heat. Her warm gaze moved from my feet, pausing around my chest and landing on my mouth. My lips tingled from her staring, my stomach tightening with lust. Lorelei wet her bottom lip, and the little gesture was a lightning bolt straight to my groin.

"When you say things like that, all I want to do is kiss you." She swallowed, hard as her cheeks flushed red.

Tell her the idea. Tell her. Do it.

Her chest heaved, and the softness of her mouth, the half a second I'd felt it in the car, drove me wild.

"Remind me why we can't... give in. Just a little bit. Reward ourselves. I need an escape, nothing more." She inched closer to me, her voice throaty and raspy. Her damn tongue licked the side of her mouth as her feet were an inch from mine. She gently touched my chest. Each tap on my shirt felt like a hammer. "Luca, you can't get emotionally invested for good, solid reasons, and I refuse to fall for anyone right now, let alone my brother's teammate. But this... thing between us, it doesn't have to be complicated. We can use each other. I saw the way you watched me yesterday. The way your cock pressed against your sweats. The way your hands tensed and the heat in your eyes grew. You want me too."

I swallowed the ball of emotion in my throat. My skin grew two sizes too small, and my lungs forgot their entire purpose for existing—breathing. I gasped for air as my pulse punched through my body. Was she… suggesting… what I wanted? Her fingers brushed over my pecs, dancing up toward my chin where she traced my jawline. To give in to this chemistry and get lost in her, but only one time. Then she'd be out of my system, and I could breathe again.

I forgot we were in the hallway, where any of my teammates could see us.

I forgot my rules.

I forgot everything except the fact she wanted me to be her escape. "Lorelei," I growled, gripping her fingers in my hand. If she kept touching me, I'd need her.

She laughed, softly, her minty breath hitting my face.

"I promise I won't catch feelings or do *anything* to ruin your plans. I just want to get rid of this energy and feeling, and you make me so… " She trailed off, her eyes heating up as she zeroed in on my mouth. "Tell me. Have you thought about how it would be between us?"

"Yes." My voice came out all gravelly, rough. *A million and a half different times in the most secret fantasies in the back of my mind.*

Victory flashed in her eyes. "Amazing, right?"

I nodded, my restraint seconds away from snapping. I squeezed her fingers in my fist, my last terrible attempt at stopping this. Once it began… my body vibrated. I wouldn't be the same. "You deserve more than what I can offer, Lorelei."

Anger flashed in her eyes, her lips curving into a wicked smile. "Are you making a decision for me? I'm sick of men doing that. Let *me* choose my own path, and I'm telling you—I want *you*. Right now."

My cock swelled, and my gut tightened. Every muscle went rigid, ready to pounce on her. She wanted to use me, and I wanted to get lost in her. I moved closer so our chests touched, and I stared down at her. I gripped the base of her neck, dipping my thumb into the apex of her throat. Her pulse skyrocketed. *Yes, that's my girl. I'm not the only one combusting inside.*

"One time," I said, digging my nail into her skin in warning and a promise. "We do this *one time.*"

"Once," she repeated, breathless.

"No feelings."

"None," she whispered.

"Doesn't mean anything." I tightened my hold on her, lowering my mouth so our lips were an inch apart. "This changes nothing."

"Nothing." She gripped my shirt hard, her hands trembling. Her eyes turned to molten liquid and heat. The air intensified, each breath a sharp crash in the silence. I licked my lips, overcome with joy that this was happening. Every cell in my body was on edge. My toes dug into my shoes, and my jaw twitched as I fought the aggressive urge to claim her.

I wasn't an animal. I was attentive in bed, but with her, I wanted to lick every part of her body until she couldn't move. I wanted to erase every memory she had of Eric with my tongue alone. I wanted to bite her skin and mark her. In all the thoughts of what I wanted to do, dreamt about doing, trying to say these things completely immobilized me.

My desire for Lorelei Romano overtook rational thought.

"Make the move, Luca. I need you to make the first move." She pulled me hard against her so there was nothing between our bodies. I towered over her, my hand still at her throat and her face tilted up toward mine.

"Shh," I said, the control essentially disappearing. I shoved her against the wall and bent low, dragging my nose along her jaw and breathing her in. Peaches and vanilla and soap. The best combination in the world.

I licked the spot behind her ear, pulling on the lobe with my teeth. Her head fell forward, resting on my shoulder as I said, "Don't rush me, Lorelei. It's not every day I get to live out my fantasy of fucking you. I'm going slow, and you're going to let me."

"Luca," she moaned, the sound a shot of adrenaline. I wanted that sound on repeat, her pleasure and surprise mixing with my name. I'd heard women shout my name at games, but those calls had *nothing* on her throaty voice.

I nipped her neck, letting my other hand move from her throat over her chest. Her chest heaved, and the large curve of her breasts was perfect. *God.* I felt like a kid in a candy store, where I wanted everything all together at once.

Focus. Make it good for her.

Goose bumps broke out over her neck from my lips, and I loved that. Testing the move out again, I sucked the spot right where her shoulder met her neck, and she trembled. "You like this?"

"I-I do now." She groaned and let out a tiny whimper.

"Good answer." I kissed up her neck, over her jaw until I was half an inch from her lips. The absolutely chokehold this girl had on me... she had no idea. I had permission, from her and my own rules, to kiss her, but the thought of doing it stilled me. This was *my* girl. The one of my dreams.

I had to kiss her right.

My entire body hummed with anticipation, and I carefully, with the most control I had ever shown in my life, kissed *around* her mouth. I teased the side of her lips. "Lo—"

"Stop fucking around, Monroe," she growled. "If you don't kiss me in—"

I kissed her.

I slammed my lips against hers, a current exploding throughout my body. I felt that kiss deep in my chest, all the way to my cock and through my toes. Her lips were the softest, most luscious things I had ever felt. She tasted like cherries and smelled like peaches, and when she parted those pillow lips, I darted my tongue inside to taste her.

Fuck me. She kissed hard and fast and wild, like we only had ten seconds left on earth and we'd both agreed to die by kissing. Our teeth clashed together, and the animalistic sounds escaping me were unfamiliar.

I wanted to eat her alive.

"Luca," she moaned. "*Fuck.*"

I answered by picked her up and slamming her back against the wall. I wrapped her legs around me, grinding my aching cock into her. She whimpered again, her hands moving toward my hair. I sucked her tongue, the taste of her mouth my undoing.

Everything she did enticed me, and I wanted it all. I rocked into her, the gesture making her breathe harder. She pulled my hair to the point it stung, but I didn't care. I was touching her. Her neck, her hips, her curves. I craved skin.

Sliding my hand under her shirt, her warm body met mine, and my knees almost buckled.

"Shit," she said, pulling back. "Put me down. I'm too heavy."

"What?" I blinked, entranced by her existing alone. Her cheeks were red and her lips swollen and wet from my mouth. Her hair was *everywhere,* and I needed to run my hands through it.

"Luca, *set me down.*"

"No." I blinked and made the decision. Instead letting go of her, I brought us both to her bedroom. I kicked the door shut before walking us to her bed. "You're not too heavy."

"Yes, I am. I can't injure you."

I tossed her on the bed, my pulse hammering my skull. She pushed up onto her elbows and stared at me, concern on her face. I didn't like the worry lines, so I lay over her, framing her face in between my arms. "The truth? I touched your skin, and my knees gave out. You undo me, all from your skin."

Her lips parted, and I used that to kiss her again, this time more slowly. I felt every stroke of her tongue, the need for her to be in control. I let her, instead grinding against her.

We were both completely clothed and yet this was the most turned on I had ever been in my entire life. Would I survive more?

She writhed beneath me, and I finally, after years of thinking about it, tugged the tie out of her hair. Her curls were soft, and *fuck.* I shuddered and broke the kiss.

"What? What is it?" she asked.

"Look at you." I stared down at her, wishing I could take a fucking photo. "You're… gorgeous. Perfection." I worked my jaw, the aggressive urge to take her almost too much. "Lo, you're a dream."

"You're not so bad yourself, Monroe," she said, smiling. "Now please, *touch me.* I'm dying."

"Yes, ma'am." I grinned, for real, before guiding her to sit up. I ran my hands along her stomach a few times, enjoying her sounds, before lifting the shirt over her head. Her perfectly creamy skin greeted me, and I cupped her breasts in her black bra. They were so heavy, larger than my hands, and I pinched her nipples through the fabric.

My mouth watered, and my cock strained against my jeans.

I bent down and ran my nose between the valley of her

199

breasts, feeling the weight of them on either side of my face and holy shit. She dragged her fingers over my scalp, and I tugged one of the cups down, finally taking her perfectly pink and pebbled nipple into my mouth. I sucked, and she thrashed on the bed.

"Yes, *shit,*" she said, arching her back to have me suck deeper. "Wow."

I flicked the tip with my tongue, then bit down gently enough so it wouldn't hurt. Every gesture caused a different reaction from her. "You like this?"

"*Yes.*"

I moved to the other one, doing the same thing for a few minutes. Then, I pushed her breasts together, kneading and squeezing until I could almost suck both at the same time. I could die with my face here and be all right with it.

"I could lick these for hours," I said, drawing one in harder than before. She whimpered, and I stopped, reaching behind her back to undo the clasp. It took a few tries, then it was on the floor. Nothing on her chest. "Lay back, baby, I want to see what else you enjoy."

"Shirt off," she demanded, almost caveman-like with her words. "Skin."

Laughing, I grabbed the hem near the back of my neck and had it removed in seconds. She reached out and dug her hands into my shoulders, pecs, abs, then she let out a strangled sound. "You. Sexy. Fuck."

"You'll get a turn, Lo. Right now, let me have mine. I beg you."

CHAPTER
TWENTY-ONE

Lorelei

I'd been doing sex wrong. No one told me it could be *like this.*

My soul left my body when Luca ran his tongue down my stomach, pausing only for a second as he slid his fingers into the waistband of my pants and practically ripped them off. I didn't have time to worry about any insecurities. With him, I floated.

"Jesus Christ," he mumbled, nipping the inside of my thigh. He was on his knees, my legs spread wide as he stared at my pussy with wolf-like eyes—the same gaze I saw him have on the field.

He was *in* the intensity zone I'd fantasized about. Goose bumps broke out over my body, neck to my toes, as he gently blew on my legs. "What are you… doing?" I panted, seconds away from bursting into flames.

"Whatever you let me." He used two fingers to spread me farther, then I about arched my back off the bed and took flight when he flattened his tongue against me. He hummed as he lapped my clit, the vibration of his deep tones traveling from his mouth to my core.

I gripped my sheets in my hands, needing to hold on as pleasure built up in aggressive, earth-shattering waves. My pulse wasn't just a beat but a bass drum, setting the tone to my release. "Luca, *Luca,*" I breathed, the pace a little too fast. "I'm going to—"

"I *need* you to," he said, his lips rubbing against my sensitive skin. "Come in my mouth, fall apart, show me all of you *right now.*"

He slid one finger inside me, curling it before adding a second as he returned his tongue to my clit. Sweat pooled on my skin as he used his other free hand to cover my stomach, holding me down. I writhed around, thrashing as I fought for the orgasm, but he didn't let me move. His strength made everything hotter.

"I'm… it's…" I panted, throwing my head back and rocking my hips into his face. He sucked harder and stroked faster and *hell motherfucking yes.* Blinding pleasure, a current of energy purely made to feel like ecstasy, burst like a firework from my core to my fingernails. I couldn't breathe as my orgasm gripped me, lighting me up and sending every cell on my skin to tingle.

Luca ate me the entire time, licking and stroking and coaxing me to destroy his face. It was so much I felt drunk. Like it was a parallel life, not real. As the pleasure subsided, I opened my eyes to find him staring at me, his brown gaze filled with warmth and hunger.

He released his hold on my pussy and grinned at me, his lips wet with my juices and my skin flushed. He didn't let me stay in that space long. He crawled back over my body, nipping my nipple before smiling down at me. "So much better than watching you do it to yourself."

"Agreed," I said, my voice raspy. "Holy shit, Luca."

"This is just the beginning. Please tell me you understand." He licked the center of my chest, then my neck up to my ear. "If we're doing this one time, then I'm getting every part of you."

I nodded, the tickle of his scruff along my neck sending a flicker of warmth to my core. Which was wild. I needed time to settle down between orgasms, but with him, my body had never felt more awake, more open to try anything. Instead of alarming me, I *loved* it. The forbidden aspect, knowing it would only be one time, added another layer of naughtiness to it, and I bit into Luca's shoulder. He stilled, then stared down at me.

"What was that for?"

"You're not the only one who likes to use their teeth."

He shuddered, and I used the moment of weakness to roll him onto his back, leaving me naked and straddling his *still in pants* waist. But god, the view? His stomach muscles were carved and hard. I traced them along his happy trail up to his belly button. Nothing but a strong core and smooth skin. I lowered myself to tease him with little licks along his ribs, pecs, and when I swirled his nipple, he gripped my ass.

"Oh, you like this?" I baited him, biting down on his pebbled tip. He grunted and squeezed my ass in his large hands. I'd have a bruise, but what a badge to earn "You do."

"I like you touching me anywhere, doing any damn thing." He moved one hand to the back of my head, guiding me to his mouth. "Kiss me. I need your mouth again."

What a command. I obliged, happily, as I brought my mouth to his, the musky taste of myself on his lips. It was hot, knowing he'd eaten me so deliciously before, and my skin heated as our kiss grew longer and messier. He ground against my bare pussy, the front of his pants showing evidence of my arousal, but I didn't care.

This was the hottest night of my entire life, and I wanted

him to have that too. I broke apart our mouths and grinned as I scooted down his body and *finally* yanked off his pants. He gasped when I gripped his firm, thick cock in between my hands and *damn.* He was big and sturdy and hard as hell. "Show me how you stroke yourself," I said, my voice all throaty and honestly kinda sexy.

I liked this version of myself, unworried about what this meant because it was already discussed. He looked at me like I hung the sun and gave me the best orgasm of my life. Enjoying sex without the mental stuff was incredible.

Luca's jaw tensed as I stroked him up and down a few times. He covered my hands with one of his and adjusted my grip. Then, he set the pace. "I thought about this when I get off. What it'd feel like to have your hands around my dick."

"Did you envision it feeling like this?" I went hard, then slow, loving the way the pulse at the base of his neck went haywire.

"*God* yes. This is better."

"What if I did… this?" I winked before getting onto my knees and taking him in my mouth. He about dove off the bed, and the sound that escaped his throat? Incredible. He was undone, and I did that to him. The popular, gorgeous, grumpy football guy was putty in my hands.

Power like that was dangerous.

I sucked the tip of his head, then throated him all the way back. I gagged, and my eyes watered, but I took him deeper. I hollowed out my cheeks, swirling my tongue once before moving my neck, and Luca gripped my hair, hard.

He grunted and groaned and said my name over and over as I continued sucking him. Something about him made me want to do dirty, filthy little things to have them remain in his mind forever. I cupped his balls and let my finger flirt with his taint, wanting him to feel even an ounce of the pleasure I had.

I was wet as hell, my clit swelling with need as I destroyed Luca's ability to speak. He mumbled as his thighs turned to granite. My jaw ached, and my neck hurt, but I kept going. I wanted to make every fantasy come true, and even as my eyes watered, I powered through.

"Lo, stop," he begged, his hands pulling my hair.

I stilled and stared up at him. It was surreal, our gazes meeting as his cock twitched in my mouth. "Hm?"

"I'm not coming like this." He shook his head. "I want your ass in the air, your hair wrapped around my hand, and my cock so far inside you, you'll feel me tomorrow."

I stared, releasing him as my mouth fell open. No one, in my entire life, had said anything like that to me, and I *loved* it.

"Understood, Lorelei?" He pulled me up onto his lap, his rigid cock hitting his stomach as I straddled his thighs. He refused to let me look away, the intense eye contact making this more extreme, more intimate. "I'll make you feel good."

I trembled, and he used his thumb to swirl around my clit. We stared at each other, our bodies sweaty and breaths heavy. I groaned and bit my lip as he applied more pressure. "Luca," I said, not quite sure what I wanted or needed. It was almost too much to have him stare at me as he played with me.

His cheek twitched as he licked his lips, staring down at my pussy. We both watched his thumb on me, moving in a slow circle in a perfect rhythm. "I need you nice and wet to take me."

I moaned. He was so direct and to the point, his words fucking sexy. "Condoms in the drawer."

Without stopping the pressure on my clit, he reached into the nightstand table and pulled out a foil packet.

"Open it. My hands are busy."

I nodded, gasping for air as my gut ached. With just his thumb, he revved me up like he knew my own secrets. "I'm… I'm…"

205

"Focus, Lorelei. You're not coming again unless it's on my cock." He slid a finger inside me again, arching a brow. "Put the condom on me while I stretch you."

This had to be a form of torture, trying to focus on tearing the tiny packet. Who made condoms this small? Why wasn't it working? My ears rang, and my pussy tightened around his fingers, the smells of sex lingering in the air. It was so hot, and he used his fingers so well. I just needed more pressure to come again.

I rocked my hips, but he stilled.

"Lorelei, don't make me stop."

I whined, unable to form words, and he smiled. "What?" I asked.

"Love that little sound you made, like the thought of me not touching your pussy has you whimper."

I *finally* slid the condom on his cock, and he stiffened, his eyes flashing with heat before he lifted me and repositioned me so the head was right at my opening. My body ached with need, with how much I wanted him.

"You ready for me, Lo? Use your words. Be clear."

I rested my forehead against his, breathing him in. "Yes."

He thrust into me, and *oh, baby.*

"Take your time fitting me, I need this to feel good for you." He kissed me, softly, and the opposition of how dirty he talked with the moment of sweetness about did me in.

He allowed me set the pace, rocking my hips and finding the right angle to take him deep. He gripped my hips, letting out a little groan every time I clenched around him. After a minute of staring, he snapped and grabbed the back of my head and dragged my mouth to his.

He kissed me *hard,* and as our tongues stroked and slid against each other, my heart hammered against my ribcage to the point I might bruise. Every thrust lit me up, hitting my g-spot so perfectly that all other sex was ruined for me.

My nipples tightened with need, and it was like he read my body. Gripping my hair in his hand, he tilted my head back, forcing my chest out to him, and he sucked my nipple into his mouth so hard it stung.

But as soon as it hurt, he stilled and licked it nice and sweet.

Fucking Luca Monroe was just like that—I knew it'd hurt a little, but fuck, it was sweet as hell and totally worth it. We rocked together, our bodies in sync as my second orgasm built. My muscles went rigid as friction grew.

"You." He thrust, licked my chest. "Are." He thrust again, biting my earlobe. "Perfect."

The pain from his teeth set me off, and I lost it. Gripping his shoulders, I whined, the moan escaping out of me unlike one I had ever made. "Luca, I'm so close!" I cried, resting my forehead against his as my vision blurred. It was unreal, magical, and Luca slid out of me and placed me on my stomach.

I readjusted so my ass was in the air, reaching my hand between my thighs to ease the pain.

"No, your pleasure is mine."

He eased back into me, gripping my hair again as he used his other hand to reach around my waist and play with my clit. He matched his fingers to the pace he thrust into me, and it didn't take long before I exploded. My face was buried into the sheet, my cries dulled by the fabric, but Luca's… no, his were feral, wild, *loud.*

He tugged my hair, groaning so wonderfully out of control he fell on top of me. His weight knocked the breath out of me, but what a way to go.

I could feel the erratic, powerful beat of his heart as his

chest pressed against my back. His breath tickled my ear as he panted and damn…that was…

"Give me ten minutes."

Wait. "What?" I asked, my voice hardly recognizable.

"We said tonight, yes? That was it?"

"Yes, but…?"

"Then we get *all night.*" He rolled off me, laying on his side and propping up his head on his hand. His biceps looked huge, like the size of my face this up close.

He smelled delicious like this, sweaty and hints of laundry and wood. I wanted to breathe him in for a little while longer and take a fat nap, but he trailed his finger down my spine, a lazy grin spreading across his face. "Fine, you look sleepy. I'll give you thirty minutes to rest. But I want you naked like this. There's too much to admire."

I snorted, rolling onto my back and staring up at my ceiling fan. My hair was in disarray, tangled and in every direction. I surely had bruises or hickeys on my skin, and my face had to be bright red. "Admire is a strong word."

"I mean it."

He tilted my face toward him, his touch so damn delicate and gentle that my stomach swooped. Filthy and aggressive Luca was one thing. Soft and kind and gentle Luca was dangerous for more reasons that I cared to admit.

"Please tell me sex for you isn't always like this." His voice dipped low, like he too grappled with how life altering that was.

I shook my head, grinning. "Not even once."

"Okay, good." He chuckled. "That was something."

"Yes."

"And we get to do it until sun-up? Because then I have to get back to…"

"Hey." I inched closer to him. "No talk of tomorrow. We know what we agreed to." I kissed his nose. "Thirty-minute power nap, then we find a way to sneak into the shower together."

"Atta girl. I knew you were worth breaking at least one rule for."

"Just one?" I giggled, giving him my back as he tugged me against his chest. He kissed my neck as his cock wedged itself perfectly between my ass.

"You know you're trouble. Now focus. Thirty minutes are on the clock. Then it's game time."

CHAPTER
TWENTY-TWO

Luca

"Luca," a soft, sweet voice whispered. "You big lump. Get up."

"Hm?"

"Your alarm is going off for the third time, and you're using me like your personal blanket." Her voice held more rasp, and it warmed me inside out.

Sleep clogged my mind, but the feeling of peace radiated through me. There weren't a million what-ifs sprinting through my head, causing anxiety to riddle my every move. Instead, I was happy. I blinked, becoming more aware, and my face pressed into Lorelei's neck. I inhaled, her sweaty and sleepy scent absolutely delicious. She ran her fingers through my hair and down my upper back, and images of the night before came at me hard.

Her face as she moaned. The sound of my name on her lips. Her body. Fuck, her muscles and way she moved. How well we fit together. I groaned and tugged her harder against me. "Shh."

"Luca." Lorelei laughed and pushed my chest away.

I did *not* like that.

I growled against her skin, a startling weight pressing on my heart. I didn't want to leave. I didn't want to break this connection and end the night. She was so warm and perfect and sexy. My entire life was all focus, zero play, and I wanted to hang onto the reprieve so damn badly. Even the usual guilt that came with thinking about Dean dulled when she was in my reach.

She yawned before glancing at her watch. "It's 6:15. Don't you have to be at the gym in twenty minutes?"

I did the quickest math since times tables in elementary school. I could remain in this happy bubble for three more minutes and still get there without being late. Three more minutes of perfection before my life went back to my schedule. "I'll make it," I said, my lips grazing the spot beneath her ear. "Let me enjoy this until I have to leave."

She sighed, a happy contented sound. Her sleep voice and intoxicating scent had a hold on me, somehow wiping all the perseverance I had away. One night with her and I wanted to burn my entire rule book and dance around while flames engulfed it.

She wiggled against me and shifted her weight so her face was right in front of mine. She stared at me, her brown eyes filled with sleep and warmth. Would she ever look at me like that again?

When I left her bed... that was it. That was our deal. And no matter the reasons the compromise made sense; it didn't make it any easier.

"Last night was wild, huh?" she whispered, a hint of vulnerability in her voice.

I nodded.

"Totally worth it though." She smiled and quickly kissed

my mouth. "I've never done a one-night-only passion affair before. I'm a fan."

"Plan on doing this again, Lorelei? With someone else?" I asked, before my brain could tell me to shut the hell up.

Irritation flashed on her face, and the loss of her warmth filled me with dread. A soul crushing, panic-induced dread.

She wet her bottom lip and scooted away from me. She rolled off her bed, her spine and perfect ass on display before she pulled on a purple fuzzy robe from her desk chair. When she faced me, her face was back to normal, but that felt... worse. I wanted her reaction, her fire.

"This was special, Luca." She hugged herself. "It meant something to me, but *I am not* trying to break our deal. We both know the stakes, so I'm walking away satisfied, happy, and without a single regret. I'm going to shower, so please, let yourself out when you're ready."

She squeezed my calf on her way to the door, leaving me alone in her bed with her perfume lingering on the sheets. She said the right things that I wanted to hear—it was special, she enjoyed it, wasn't trying to distract me from my goal, but my heart still felt battered, and I had no idea what to do about it. Plus, my dumb ass had made a comment in jealousy before I thought it through. *If* she wanted to bring a different guy back here every night, she could. She had every right, and I couldn't do a damn thing about it. I'd have to invest in better headphones to ensure I didn't hear anything because the thought of listening to her moan out someone else's name would cause a vessel in my forehead to pop.

Groaning, I pushed out of her bed and quickly put on my pants. This wasn't even a breakup, yet it felt like one. A huge one, at that. I ran my hand over my face, rubbing my eyes until I saw stars. My stomach sank, and instead of feeling relieved at finally being with her, I felt worse.

God, I needed to knock this shit off. We had a huge game this weekend. We'd be on ESPN when we played Iowa, and this big of a game meant more eyes on our team. More exposure never hurt, and there were a million things I could be doing to get prepared. Instead, I was in my quarterback's sister's room, pining for her.

Enough.

I snuck out of her room with the intention of being friendly to her the next time I saw her and that was that. We'd be friends who got it out of our system. We'd laugh and remember the time together. Nothing more.

Nodding to myself, I rushed through my routine to get to the gym on time. The guys I usually did rounds with were already there. Timothy, Shawn, Lawrence, and Preston made up most of the O-line. They were built like houses, and Shawn was having a hell of a year.

"Monroe, you look like you might think about maybe smiling," Timothy said, hitting me in the shoulder. "Did you break curfew or something?"

Lorelei's face flashed in my head, her grin and wild hair, and I shoved it away with the mental strength of an ox. "Shut up."

His smile grew as he moved onto another machine. He was a senior on the team and the backbone of the O-line. Always the life of the party, he never let anything bother him, and most of the time, I found that annoying, but now I wished I had that talent. To not *worry*.

If I could push the worries away, then maybe I'd find a world in which Lorelei and I could explore this chemistry a little longer. Where I could take care of my grandma, get into the NFL with a fat check, *and* treat Lorelei with the attention she deserved. Right now? All I could offer was a few hours a week. Two tops. The rest was all taken up by football.

"Dude, what the fuck?" Lawrence snapped, pulling me back from my mind. I'd stopped spotting him, and he struggled with the bar.

"Sorry." My face heated, my jaw tensing at my mess up. I helped him right the bar after he bench-pressed. He glared at me, annoyance written over his face. "I fucked up, man."

"Where's your head at?" He shook his long dreads, concern replacing his brief irritation. "You're the rock. The consistent one. I can't have you clowning over something that doesn't matter."

I swallowed. "No, you're right. I was distracted. It won't happen again."

"No sweat, just threw me off to see *the* Luca Monroe not breathing football. I'd prefer if it wasn't when you were spotting me, but hey, we're all good." He hit my chest with his towel. "Breakfast is on you today."

"Of course." My eye twitched, the mental math of how much breakfast would cost stressing me out. I'd gotten takeout more than normal since hanging with Lorelei since we drove to my grandma's place, and I could feel the impact to my savings.

The realization that I could've hurt Lawrence because Lorelei was in my head kicked my ass into gear. I felt terrible, justified in my concentration. She had no place dominating my thoughts and focus, and I had to do whatever I could to get her out of there.

My shoulders ached, and I couldn't stop yawning. My usual seven hours of sleep was stilted last night so I could get my fill of my quarterback's sister, and the prickles of tiredness crept in as I walked back into our house after eight. I liked Monday nights to prepare for the week, schedule out my time, and watch film before sleeping.

I just wasn't sure I'd be able to get everything I needed to get done. There was no ounce of regret, but I had to make up for lost time. After brewing a cup of coffee, something I never did this late, I set my stuff out at the secondhand table Callum's sister gave us. I liked the faded blue.

My laptop sat to the left, my textbooks and planner to the right, and I put on some upbeat music and got to work. First, I set out what was due this week for school. I wasn't a whiz, but I grades weren't difficult for me. The problem was my grandma kept going on about me getting a degree—something she never had—but it wasn't likely to happen if I went to the NFL. I could always go back to school, yet the lingering weight of indecision hung over me like a Midwestern storm cloud. My degree was business administration, but I didn't have plans to do anything with it. It was a title to put on a degree.

If I had a different life, would I stay here another year?

I never let myself think about it because *my* choice didn't matter. After scheduling my assignments, I listed what tests were next and then it was film. My vision clouded, and I rested my forehead on the table, just for a second. It'd be worthless to watch film if I wasn't focused, and *man* it felt good to close my eyes.

"Luca?"

A soft hand rubbed my neck, then moved down my back.

"Hey, wake up. This can't be comfortable." The same, gentle voice grew closer. Peaches and vanilla filled the air, and my skin tingled. *Lorelei.*

I bolted up, my pulse racing. Lorelei jumped back, her eyes wide. "What... did I fall asleep?"

She grinned and jutted her chin at my forehead. "Judging by the huge red spot on your forehead, yes." She reached out and touched it, her face softening. "Aw, how cute. You passed out at your table."

"I didn't choose to," I said, immediately hating myself. Obviously, I hadn't planned that. I sighed, rubbed my face and stared at her again. The reason I was tired in the first place. She wore her hair in a bun and tight running pants, a shirt that missed the bottom half. Her stomach was on display, and *god,* my blood heated.

Why did the world's prettiest, made-for-me woman have to meet me *right now?* Two years from now? I could do this. But now… it was impossible.

"You seem busy," she said, her voice small as she glanced at the table. "But I figured I'd wake you. I don't want your muscles tense for the game Friday."

"We play Iowa." I rolled my shoulders, hating that she stood so far away. I liked having her hand on me.

"Dean's been talking about it all day. If I didn't have a game on Sunday, I'd try to come watch with my parents, but I'll have to stream it on TV."

The thought of her alone, in this house, had me on edge. While we hadn't had a party yet, some people knew she was here. No one would be an idiot to mess with her, but seeing her fear that one Friday night unleashed a beast inside me. "Mackenzie, your friend. She should come stay over."

"Ah, and break the no-friend rule?" She arched a brow, crossing her arms and popping one hip out. It was such a sassy stance, and I wanted her to boss me around. She could ask me to get on the ground and be her chair and I would.

"Let that go." I rolled my eyes, my lips twitching.

She grinned, hard, and made a fist. "*Yes.* I got a Luca smile. Feels like a touchdown."

"You're an idiot," I said without heat. My lips curved up even more as we stared at each other. Was she too, thinking about last night? I wanted to lick her entire body, tasting every flavor she offered. My cock stirred the more I thought about her naked, and she cleared her throat.

"I'll see if I can stay at her place. I really didn't enjoy being here alone last time. Too big of a house, too many sounds." She stretched her arms over her head, already walking backward. "I'll let you get back to your thing."

"Wait," I said, not knowing what I wanted to say except I wanted more time with her. It was already eleven, and I hadn't done any of the things I needed to, but Lorelei made my soul feel lighter.

Her fiery attitude and smiles were enticing, and I was addicted.

I pointed to the chair next to me, awkward as fuck. "Study with me."

She rubbed her lips together before a wrinkle formed between her eyes. "Luca, you should sleep."

"I didn't get through everything. I need to watch film and take notes, then review them tomorrow. If I don't—"

She shut my laptop and held out her hand. She wore a silver ring on her thumb with a tiny green gem. I wanted to know what it meant, who gave it to her? Did she like jewelry? I wasn't sure, since she rarely wore it.

"Come on. No more tonight."

"What are you..." I trailed off, my throat tightening. Her fingers were so soft as she tugged me away from the chair. "Are we...?"

"No." She laughed, staring at my hand for a beat before letting go. "I'm being a good roommate and putting you to bed." She looked around us and whispered, "Alone."

She nudged me up the stairs, and we ascended in sync, not saying anything but also not walking far enough away so our arms kept touching. There were so many things I wanted to ask but refrained. She was being a friend.

"Now, I'm going to tuck you in your room and make sure you don't sneak out. All your shit can wait until morning, understand me?"

I nodded, absolutely entranced with her.

Honestly, I couldn't recall the last time a girl cared enough about me to make sure I went to bed. They wanted me for my body, for a few orgasms, or a way to say they slept with someone on the football team. They'd tell me how hot I was or how good I was on the field but this? God, it was different.

We arrived to my room, and she gently pushed me inside at the base of my back. She walked backward to her door, her eyes dancing with fire. "I mean it, Monroe. Go to sleep."

"Can I brush my teeth at least?"

She narrowed her eyes. "Okay, smartass. Yes. Be quick, two minutes is standard so not a second longer."

"You're fucking cute." I smiled, so hard, my cheeks hurt. "*Two minutes is standard?*"

"My uncle is a dentist, and I listen. I have great teeth, and don't think complimenting me will help your case." She pointed at me.

I held up my hands before running into the bathroom and brushing my teeth as quickly as possible. It might not have been two minutes, but I used the bathroom fast too. When I walked out, she stood there, lips pursed, and I was pretty sure she owned me at that point.

"You had ten seconds before I went in there and kidnapped you. Now, in your bed."

"Are you tucking me in?" I teased. I tossed my shirt onto my chair and sat on the side of my bed. She remained at the door, her cheeks redder than before as a serious expression crossed her face. It made my muscles rigid. "What is it?"

"You're always taking care of everyone else, and I want to make sure you take care of you." She walked in, no, it was more like a glide. She chewed the side of her lip as she pulled up my blanket and covered me.

She legit tucked me into my bed. I was charmed as fuck.

"Friday is important for you, so please, get rest." She cupped my face, her fingers grazing my jaw, and I sighed.

"Lo—" I said, my voice lost.

She nodded but didn't say anything as she retreated from my room. The unsaid words weighed a million pounds. It would just hurt to say empty promises or say things that wouldn't matter. It was like she read my mind and fled before we did something we'd regret.

She gave me a small, sad smile before shutting my door, leaving me alone with her scent and lingering touch on my skin.

I could lie to myself and pretend I didn't have feelings for her all I wanted, but that woman was so far under my skin I couldn't see a way to escape her, and that didn't terrify me as much as it should've.

Lorelei

"**Y**ou *slept with him?*" Mack's mouth hung open, a bit of salsa on the side of her face. "Luca Monroe. The guy we thought hated you?"

My face heated as I nodded. "That's the one."

"Wow."

"It was…unreal." I blew out a long breath, fanning myself with my hand. It was Friday night, and while I had seen Mack every day, I couldn't quite tell her. Maybe it was easier now because the guys were at their game, off campus and away from overhearing?

"Why the fuck did you not tell me immediately? What's the point of our friendship then, ma'am? This is top-tier shit." She wiped her mouth with a napkin, her posture straight. Where I was messy and loud, she was clean and respectful. Unless she had a few drinks. Two Modelo Mack was fun.

I stared her down, the words almost spilling out. *Oh, like you don't share your massive crush on my brother?* I wouldn't do that to her. Instead, I sipped my water and went with the truth. "I thought I'd be over it, and it'd be no big deal. Something to share anecdotally."

"But that's not the case?"

"Nope. Not at all." My face flushed, and the uncomfortable pang grew in my chest. It was strange to know I was setting myself up for heartbreak, *again,* and there wasn't anything I could do about it. Not until I moved out of that damn house and stopped smelling him or seeing him or hearing his voice or watching his muscles ripple under his shirt. Hm, that was a great point. I should be looking for places to move into. I made a mental note to research apartments the next morning. "We both can't get involved with each other and agreed it'd be a one-night thing, but Mackenzie, it was wild."

Amusement danced on her face. "Better than Eric?"

I about spat out my drink. "Different universe than Eric."

"Atta girl. Proud of you." She held up her vitamin water and cheered my bottle. "How daring of you, Lorelei Romano. Having a filthy, sexy one-night stand was something we aspired to do freshman year."

"Oh, god, we had that dumb list, didn't we?" Groaning, I pictured one drunken night and a lot of promises. "Didn't I dance on a bar or something?"

"Sure did. Where I wanted to streak on campus and kiss three strangers in one night." Mack laughed, pink covering her cheeks. "Maybe not *three,* but the thought of kissing someone in a crowded room, not knowing their name seems fun."

I nodded, just because that *did not* sound as appealing as it would've pre-Luca. This was new territory for me; caring about someone when I knew I shouldn't and refusing to cut off all communication with him because he needed a buddy. Yes, the team was great, and my brother would give Luca the shirt off his back, but emotionally? Nah, there was no way they realized how much Luca carried around with him, the worry always lurking underneath his massive shoulders.

It didn't matter how many times he looked at me like I hung the moon, he couldn't afford the distraction, and I couldn't afford the pain.

Mack scrolled her phone as I finished my dinner, her knee bouncing up and down and causing the table to rock. "Mack Attack, what's going on?"

"We should go out." She set her phone down, a frown line between her eyes. "Let's hit up the bars, dance, kiss strangers."

I narrowed my eyes, trying to read her. "I thought we were going to watch the game?"

"Yes, but let's go out and watch. Meet people, flirt."

I did have a nervous energy all day, the thought of going back to the house alone unsettling me. Mack agreed she'd come too, but it was just so damn empty without the guys there. Plus, if they played well, they'd be partying it up all night, and I knew Luca would let loose.

Did I wish he would let loose here? With me? Yes. My *god* yes. But it wouldn't happen, and thinking about him hooking up made my stomach twist. *He did get jealous though....* No. Not helpful. We couldn't be jealous of others when we were nothing.

"I'm in. Let's do it."

We texted Alejandra and GraceLynn, who reached out to Alicia and Gloria, and soon enough, ten girls from the team showed up at the football house to get ready and *shit.* My brother was gonna kill me.

Thirty minutes turned into an hour, then another. I was three drinks in, and we glammified the place. It smelled like perfume and hairspray, and makeup lined the bathroom countertops. Music blasted from someone's portable speaker, and *damn this is fun.*

"Why don't we have a soccer house?" I shouted.

Everyone cheered, and a lazy smile overtook my face. This was the life. The girls and I hanging out. Sure, the guys would be furious at me, but they were away doing football shit, so I could do my team shit. I'd have to clean like hell in the morning, but Mack would help me. I'd force her since this was her idea.

"It's already game time! We should go!" Mack yelled, pausing the music. "The Lazy Palm is like, a whole mile. We can't be late!

By some miracle, I got everyone out of the damn house and locked the door. I triple-checked to make sure every hair product was unplugged and took pictures of them. I knew, even in my tipsy state, I would forget that I did things right. *Look at me being smart.*

I took a selfie of the front door with the key in my hand and stuck out my tongue.

"What are you doing?" Ale asked, her dark black hair twisted into two buns. She was so cool. I loved her. She also cursed in Spanish all the time, and it was sexy.

"Reminding myself I locked the door." I zipped the key in my small bag, and boom, I was ready to watch the game and cheer for the guys.

"Smart." She looped her arm through mine. "It's amazing you live in the football house. Are they shirtless and sweaty?"

"Oh, I want the deets." GraceLynn went on my other side. "They are so hot it's unfair. Callum. Dean. Luca. God, that man is fine."

"Oh damn. Oliver is a bit too much for me, but that boy is fine too." Ale put a hand on her forehead, being dramatic as hell.

"Who has the best chest?" GraceLynn asked. "Please say Callum. I love him."

"Luca." I didn't miss a beat. His pecs and muscles near his neck were *chef's kiss.* Plus, I knew if I licked that area, he'd jerk in response and release a deep growl. "Luca has the best chest."

"Makes sense. He's thickest. Real meaty." Ale said, making me howl in laughter. "I gotta say Dean is my flavor though."

"You like Dean?" Mack asked, turning all the way from her spot in front of us and eyeing Ale, her cheek twitching.

Ale laughed. "I mean, no offense to Lorelei here, but I like the swagger of him, yeah. His ass is nice, and his arms are thick enough to bite. If he needed an outlet some night, you send him my way, Lo. You got it?"

"End of this discussion forever." I gagged, making a real scene of it. "Y'all are buying me my first drink. I earned it."

We laughed and yelled as we walked into the sports bar near the party street on campus. There were already a lot of people there watching the game, but we looked great. The baseball team was there and invited us in with open arms. Obviously, I did a quick scan of the group, no familiar face of Eric in sight, and I relaxed.

Spending the night anywhere near him was the last thing I wanted. And a flicker of unease crept in at the notiong of getting photographed with him. Not that it mattered, but it made me feel guilty for reasons that didn't make sense. I owed no one a damn thing!

"Loooooo!" A cheery voice pulled me from my thoughts. Cooper Birmingham, one of the pitchers, pulled me into a hug. "It's amazing to see you, girl."

"You too." I squeezed him back, my stomach hollowing out in embarrassment. It was strange to be around him again after not seeing him for months. I'd hung with him and Eric all the time—like, four times a week, and when Eric did what he did, I lost his friendship. Did he think I was pathetic? Or did he feel bad for me?

I hated that I cared.

"It's been a minute, but let me tell you, Eric is a dumbass." He cupped my chin, his face serious. "I'm sorry it ended the way it did."

"Thanks, Cooper."

"Now, come sit. We can share school spirit." He put an arm around my shoulders, and we walked toward the large booth for ten people. Ale and Mack sat too, sandwiched between other players.

College athletes were a different breed. They were the only other group of people who understood the dedication, the energy, the sacrifices it took to be a D1 athlete. Hanging with them was easier. Cooper poured me a beer from one of their pitchers, and I let myself relax. I needed the liquid courage to watch Luca play and not worry about him.

The game started with a bang, our team running the ball all the way for a touchdown. The bar exploded in cheers, beer was spilled, and man, my blood was pumping. My brain had a booze fog, and by the third quarter, I convinced myself I wasn't falling for Luca Monroe.

Watching him play was intoxicating in a way beer wasn't. The 88 on his jersey was easy to spot with his length and thickness. Him being a tight end just made sense. He had a mean streak and played the O linemen and receiver positions well. He was a utility player, excelled at what the team needed from him. He commanded the field, or maybe that was my crush sneaking out. I loved someone who dominated their field. It didn't matter if it was cards or golf or painting for a sport. When people put the time and energy into something, it was sexy.

"Scoot in, scoot in!" a dude yelled. I laid my head on

someone's shoulder, smiling and closing my eyes as someone snapped a pic. I wore the jersey I bought freshman year. I didn't care whose number it was, just didn't want it being my brother's.

But now, I realized it was Oliver's. How fun! I took a selfie with the number and sent it to the *roommate* chat.

Lo: Just realized the jersey I've had since freshmen year was yours! Go Ollie!

Content with the text, I pocketed my phone and watched the rest of the game. We won, by a lot, dominating our rival, and damn, Luca played the game of his life.

Pride filled me like a helium balloon for a kid's birthday party. I beamed at the TV, tired and tipsy and happy. This was how I'd envisioned life in college. Doing shit with my teammates, living life to the fullest, and supporting a vision. That was the thing about me that drove my family nuts. I loved being a part of something bigger than myself. Being on a team —we had a mission to win a championship. All athletes were here to bring pride to ourselves and our school.

Luca understood.

In my sloppy haze, I fumbled with my phone, desperate to tell him how proud I was. He had to hear it! From someone!

Lo: I'm prude of yot. You playhed so erll.

My phone buzzed, and I yelped.

Luca calling.

Shit. They *just* won the game. How was he calling me? An accident, maybe?

I stared, confused as to why he'd call that I forgot to answer. Oops! I giggled, just as he tried again, and I picked up, determined to not forget. "Hello there, champion."

"Are you drunk?" he asked, no hello or anything.

Music blared around us, and people shouted. I tried moving past Cooper, but he was mid-convo arguing about the best cereal. "It's Reese's Puffs, idiots," I said, nudging him. "Hey Coop, can I get by you?"

"Sure thing, Lo." He picked me up by my hips and set me down, not even glancing at me before arguing with Ale about breakfast foods.

What a hoot.

"Lorelei, where the fuck are you?"

"At a bar. With my friends." I ducked through the crowd until I went to the patio. "Luca Monroe, how are you calling me? You just won! Dare I say played the greatest game of your life?"

"Who are you with?"

"Good sir, let's talk football. Shouldn't that be the sexiest thing ever?" I giggled and twirled my hair like an idiot with an ill-timed crush. His irritated voice was raspy and rough and then it hit me. "Why are you angry? Did you get hurt? Oh, Luca."

"Have you been drinking?"

"I mean, I've had a few drinks, but Luca, sweetie, why are you yelling at me? Did something happen? I wanted to tell you I'm so proud of you. Watching you tonight was unreal, the way you move and command the field. Dean is lucky to have you on his side, that's the truth."

"I—" he paused, the deafening silence like a punch to the gut. "You're proud of me?"

"Goofily so. Is that a word? Goofily? It sounds goofy. Ha!" I cackled. "How are you calling me right now?"

"I have a phone. It's this invention—"

"Luca Monroe, you're doing a joke. I am *here* for this!" I shouted, laughing again as warmth spread through my veins. "Why did you call me though? You should be doing body shots off a model or streaking through Iowa right now."

"I hate seeing Oliver's jersey on you."

"You called to tell me that," I deadpanned. "Liar."

"Is Mack coming over tonight? I don't want you alone at the house and... truthfully," he said, sighing. "I was worried about you."

"Aw, how cute." I scrunched my nose and twirled in a circle.

"Your text had typos, and your face was red in the photo. It's clear you're drunk."

The warmth cooled and my smile fell. "Ah, so not cute. You called to yell at me."

"You need to be careful and smart," he snapped.

"Because I'm not?" Maybe it was my beer-filled mind, but I wasn't quite sure how this conversation had me switching from smiling and giddy to angry. "Enjoy your night. You deserve to have fun, but I'm not going to do this."

I hung up, irritated as hell. He could've ignored my text entirely and left me on my merry way, but now I was pissed. *Careful and smart.* I wasn't some helpless idiot party girl. We had a friend code and never left anywhere alone.

My phone buzzed again, Luca's name appearing, and I debated not answering it. He didn't deserve me too, but I did anyway. "What, Luca?"

"I want to renegotiate our deal."

"Wait...what?"

"You heard me. One night with you wasn't enough. When I get back, you and I are having another conversation."

He hung up before I could respond.

CHAPTER
TWENTY-FOUR

Luca

W hile the rest of the guys woke up hungover, I awoke ready for battle. I'd nursed one beer the entire night and instead had imaginary conversations in my head about how the talk with Lorelei would go.

She might not be down for changing our deal because she said she'd never *date* an athlete, but this wasn't dating. I'd convince her or I'd do whatever I could to get her to agree to be exclusive friends with benefits. Sunday had changed the makeup of my DNA, and it was silly to credit *that night* for playing the best game of my entire life, but for a guy obsessed with stats, it was hard to disprove it. Letting myself go, having a little fun, made me more relaxed, which made my muscles less tense and made it easier to move.

So *technically,* sleeping with Lorelei was best for my future. *Okay, sure.*

It was how I rationalized it and let go of all the red lights flashing in my head as to why it was a terrible idea. It'd betray my QB, go against my own promise to myself, potentially hurt my grandma's future, and threaten to ruin my entire plan, but hey, it made me play better, so yeah, it was worth it.

Now she just had to agree. Plus, keeping it casual meant no one would get hurt. Not Lorelei, not me, nor my grandma who kept asking about her.

My knee bounced up and down on the bus ride back to campus, the nervous energy at seeing her overtaking my senses. God, the selfie she sent wearing my teammate's jersey with other guys around her... did the woman not know what that unleashed in me?

It made me want to bite her thighs so she knew I was there every time she took a step. Suck her neck so when she put her ponytail up, she'd see me there. Fuck her again, so any man in the future would have to work twice as hard to replace the memory of me.

Lorelei Romano had a hold on me, and I wasn't ready to let go.

I'd proudly avoided social media for years because it messed with my mental health too much, but I stared at my new account with zero followers and a placeholder profile picture. No one needed to know *sportsguy09809* was me, not even Lorelei—the one account I followed.

I scrolled through her posts, like an obsessed teenager. She went out last night looking gorgeous, in someone else's jersey. Photos of her and baseball players, beer, and *is that fucking Eric?*

My left cheek twitched. Had she hung out with her *ex* last night while I was out of town? My stomach hollowed at the thought. I closed the app, chewing my lip in annoyance. *This* was why I didn't get online. It pissed me off.

Sixty minutes until arrival. One hour until I could see her, ask about Eric, and beg her to renegotiate our deal. See, my plan was simple. I'd give myself two nights off a week, around both our sports schedules. It wasn't dating—that'd be a hell no. But friends with benefits. *Secret* ones. Exclusive ones—this one was important. It'd just be us, and no one would ever find out. Definitely not Dean. That was the first rule.

My phone buzzed with my grandma's name, and I answered instantly. "Is everything okay? Are you alright?"

"Luca, you cannot assume the worst every time I call you. I could be asking you a question about fireworks or thongs or that pretty girl you brought."

A strangled sound escaped my throat. "No thongs."

"You're no fun." She laughed. "I wanted to congratulate you. You played a hell of a game, honey. We were all hooting and hollering until Pete fell asleep. Then we pranked him, but I caught most of the game."

Smiling, I shook my head. "Thank you. Hopefully Pete is okay?"

"It was just a little thing, don't you worry. Now, are you coming up again with Lorelei soon? The manager told me today that we've had a few thousand dollars in donations come in already from some viral thing? I want to ask her questions about it."

Thousand dollars. I blinked. "Wait, really?"

"Don't you live with the girl? Luca, get your head out of your football helmet and smell the roses. I thought you'd be doing more fun stuff with her around."

"I am." I blushed. "I mean, I'm having fun."

"Okay, dear. Are you two coming up tonight?"

I sighed, rubbing the back of my neck. "I don't know. I'll have to ask her if she can."

"If not tonight, have her call me. Give her my number, would you?"

Something weird and painful wedged itself in my chest.

233

Lorelei had left a mark on my grandma, and for some reason, I worried my grandma would get hurt. That was unacceptable in any capacity. Frowning, I said, "Sure, but I can ask her anything you did."

I didn't plan on giving Lorelei my grandma's number.

"Okay, well, Beta is here with an onery look so I gotta go. Love you, Luca. Congrats again."

"You too."

I hung up, even more confused about the pressure and feelings growing in my chest. My body felt like a water hose with a kink in it, where these feelings were going to make me burst. I tended to repress them or avoid them, and I wasn't equipped to do much else.

I wanted to talk to Lorelei, and I put on a playlist to distract myself the rest of the drive.

Oliver, Callum, Dean, and I rode to the bus together, so we got in Callum's car to head back to the house. Oliver might've still been drunk with how he smelled, and Callum kept yawning.

Dean frowned at his phone, and if I wasn't so caught up in guilt about wanting his sister, I'd ask what was wrong. Asking meant opening up the door to more than football talk, and *football* talk was my comfort zone. Anything else was more difficult, and *god* why was Callum not driving yet?

"Want to get some food? Soak up last night's regrets?"

Dean shrugged. "I'm game."

"Ah, mate, no can do." Oliver leaned against the window, his eyes closed and his skin paled. "I have a routine that involves not eating and essential oils. Can you drop me off at the house?"

"Sure. Bro, you were insane last night." Callum *finally* started the fucking car, his amused eyes meeting mine in the mirror. "What about you, Luca? You joining hungover Ollie?"

"Drop me off, please."

Was I hungry? Yes. But for food? No.

The ride took less than ten minutes but seemed twice as long. Callum parked on the street with the front door, and I hopped out, got my bags from the trunk, and didn't wait for Oliver's slow ass to follow. My hyperfocus had pros and cons, determination being one of them. Opening the door, I immediately smelled Lorelei's lotion. *Thank god she's home.*

I bolted up the stairs two at a time, my pulse radiating throughout my body. Music came from her room, and the absolute joy I had at knowing she was here should've bothered me. No one should have this much of a hold on me, but she did, and that was the truth.

Her door remained opened as she danced in her room, her eyes closed and a half smile on her face. She swayed her hips, only wearing tight running shorts and a baggy long-sleeved shirt with a football logo on the corner.

A picture of her in Oliver's jersey flashed in my mind. I detoured from my plan for one second, dropping my bags off in my room and rummaging through my bottom drawer for one of *my* old football shirts. If she wanted to support our team, she'd be wearing mine.

With the navy shirt in hand, I gulped, suddenly numb with nerves. I'd already tasted her, yet this was more terrifying. More at risk to get distracted. I stood at my doorframe, watching her and thinking up what to say first. *I want to fuck you again* seemed too aggressive, where *I missed you* was too emotional.

She spun in a circle, a piece of paper in her hands when she opened her eyes and gasped. "Luca! You're back!"

A blush spread slowly from her face to her neck, and her wide brown eyes softened as I marched toward her. Oliver would be passed out, feeling like shit. Callum and Dean were gone. *This* was my moment.

"You wear this if you want to support our team." I handed her my shirt, letting our fingers brush as she took it.

She held it up, rubbing her lips together as her eyes sparkled. "And what is this?"

"Mine," I growled.

"Ah." She pursed her lips before smirking, her face lighting up with amusement. "You feeling jealous, Monroe?"

"I don't do jealous," I said, closing the distance between us until the back of her knees hit her bed. Her smell engulfed me, making my thoughts irrational, like how much I loved her hair and face and freckles. "So don't get ideas."

"Right. No ideas when you just growled *mine* like a dog."

God, the mouth on her. I held her lower back, pressing her so her chest crushed mine, and I used my other hand to cup her hair. Her lids fluttered when I massaged her head, and I sucked in a breath at how good she felt against me.

If this was more than friends with benefits, I'd say she was made for me.

I stared down at her, my heart in my throat with all the things I wanted to say.

I didn't get a chance. She grinned and ran a hand over my jaw. "You played *so* well last night, Monroe. I've always enjoyed watching you on the field, but now that I know a little about what's in here—" she paused, tapping my chest right above my heart. "You're amazing."

I let go of her head and tilted her chin, dragging my thumb over her smooth skin. "Let's talk about our deal."

"So you've said."

"I want more."

A wrinkle appeared between her eyebrows for a second, the concern on her face like a bucket of ice water.

"I'll be good to you," I said, desperate for that wrinkle to disappear. "I'll make you feel good."

She breathed harder. "I know you will, but what does *more* mean to you?"

"Two nights a week, you're mine. *Only* mine," I added. *That* part was important.

"So, the other five nights I can do whatever I want?" She arched a brow, a challenge on her face. "Whoever I want?"

"No." My eye twitched. "Exclusive friends with benefits. We're not *dating,* that would never happen," I added, to reassure her that she wouldn't be breaking her own rules.

A shadow crossed her face but only for a second before she licked her lips. That little gesture sent a flash of heat through my body.

It'd only been a few days since tasting her, and my control was slipping.

"I can't stop thinking about you, your mouth and body," I said, my voice shaking with need. I ran my fingers from her chin to her neck, over her collarbone and over her chest. "I played the best game of my entire fucking life, so it'd be foolish not to continue this."

She nodded, her eyes closing as I massaged her neck. I loved touching her. Any part of her, really. Contact with her calmed me down while also lighting me up. It was a lethal combination. She moaned when I found a knot, and I pressed a kiss to her temple. "Please say yes. I *need* you to say yes."

She sighed, pushing me gently enough for me to worry. The indecision on her face felt like I was falling through ice, slippery and terrified I'd get hurt.

"I'm a rational person, so I need to recap this, okay? You want us to be friends with benefits, exclusive ones, where we fool around twice a week. We will never date. And you want this so you can play better at your games?"

I nodded. "Yes, all of that." I gulped, my throat throbbing with pain.

"I'll think about it." She clicked her tongue and moved away from me, the loss of her body heat sending a chill through me.

Think about it? Panic clawed up my throat, gripping my voice box. "Tell me what's holding you back," I practically shouted at her.

"I have a lot to think about, Monroe, because all *your* reasons sound great to you. Besides making me *feel good,* and trust me, the sex was incredible, what's in this for me? If my brother finds out, he'll be furious, and I *need* to live here until the holidays. You've gone hot and cold on me before, so what if I get feelings and you cut me off? It'll hurt, and I just now got over the last guy. I know football will always come first for you because of your grandma, and I love that so much, but I need to think about me here."

"I'll do whatever you want, whatever you need. Please…"

She stood on her tiptoes and pressed her soft, perfect lips against mine way too quickly. The touch of her mouth on mine was a lightning bolt through my body, causing a current of electricity under my skin. I gripped her hips, holding her tight before she broke apart.

She gave me a sad, tiny smile. "How do we make sure we don't get feelings?"

"We just don't. We agree to the terms, and that's that. Neither one of us can afford feelings, and we're rational adults." Even as I said the words, an uncomfortable amount of pressure grew in my chest, causing my heart to beat twice as fast. I was so afraid she'd say no that an idea hit. *More time together.*

"My grandma wants us to visit her tonight. Are you free? Can I drive you up there and convince you to get dinner with us?"

She narrowed her eyes for a beat before she grinned, wide. "Are you using your sweet, wonderful grandma as bait for me to agree to this?"

"Sure am."

Laughing, she rested her forehead on my chest, her arms coming around my waist. "Playing dirty, I see."

"I can't express to you how desperate I am to have you again. There's nothing I wouldn't do, to be honest." The words were true, regardless of if it made me sound unhinged. "So, what do you say? We go visit my grandma, so you can work on your project, and I can spend the entire time convincing you to agree?"

"Fine. *Fine.*" She licked her lips, ran her hand through my hair and brought her mouth close to mine.

I tensed, waiting for her to close the distance and kiss me again, but instead, she took one hand and shoved my chest. She pushed so hard I backtracked out of her room and into the hallway. "Hey!"

"I'll be ready in an hour, Monroe. *Behave.*"

Then, she shut the door on me, and for some, dumb reason, that made me smile.

CHAPTER
TWENTY-FIVE

Lorelei

He smelled way too good, like soap and cologne. His hair was messy but also looked like he'd put effort into his appearance. He usually wore a sweatshirt, but instead, he had on a buttoned-up shirt with dark jeans that fit him well. If we were normal people, I'd say he dressed up like we were on a date. But I wasn't normal, and this was not a date. Not even a little bit of one.

I'd done the opposite. Dressed in a shapeless shirt with a jean jacket and ripped jeans, I could've been going to a punk rock concert. I even put on my high-tops and laced them. Seeing him looking nice made my stomach do a swoopy thing that annoyed me. I shouldn't care that he looked nice.

"I brought you some snacks, if you're hungry." He cleared his throat. "They're in the bag on the floor by your feet."

"Hm." I made a noncommittal noise, trying and failing to not analyze every single interaction. Was he being kind because he wanted us to have sex again? Or was he just nice? Was he trying to trick me?

Did I care?

The holdup to this *deal* was my heart. How much power would I give that finicky bitch when this massive, gorgeous man wanted to get me naked twice a week? Goose bumps broke out over my skin, the hairs on my neck tingling as memories from Sunday night washed over me.

Best sex of my entire life.

Mack and I joked about doing one-night stands freshmen year, and while she did it twice and hated it, I never could. Sex and feelings confused me. They were too intertwined in my head. My lust for Luca overtook my senses Monday night, but now? How could I separate the two?

I opened the bag, needing something to do with my fingers instead of pulling at my hangnails, and my throat tightened. Oreos and little portable packs of peanut butter sat there. *My favorite snack.* "What is this? How did you know?"

"I've seen you sneak those at the house." His voice warmed. "I made a quick trip to the store Thursday and thought I'd get those for you."

"Thursday? Not *today?*"

"Correct. Why? Is that… alright? Do you not like them?" he spoke faster, unsure of himself. "Damnit. I almost brought the Blueberry Cheerios but figured it wasn't breakfast, so I didn't know if you wanted those. I'm sorry."

That blip of uncertainty combined with the fact he'd done this *two days ago, n*ot today to bribe my heart but because he was nice. I needed to get over myself and stop overanalyzing everything. Sighing, I slammed my head against the headrest.

"Are you okay? Did I mess up? Shit. I was trying to be a good friend here."

"No, you are." I opened the cookies and took two out, biting the top half off and eating it. "I thought these were sex-bribing cookies."

"Mm, didn't know those were a thing, but they sound delicious." Humor laced his tone, and I snuck a glance at him. His lips were almost curved up in a smile, his jawline unfairly perfect. He gripped the wheel with his left hand, his right one resting on the console between us.

I felt my pulse in my toes, between my thighs, and in my neck when I stared at him. Every muscle on his body was hard-earned, and I knew how his skin tasted. My restraint at protecting myself slipped, just by looking at him.

"I can't get hurt again," I blurted out. "I *like* you as a person, Luca, and it might be smarter to not confuse our friendship with sex any more than it already is."

He nodded, working his jaw like he chewed food. Then, he sighed. "Excellent point, Ms. Romano, great concerns."

My mouth quirked. "Why do you sound like a gameshow host? I'm trying to be honest here, you dingbat."

He laughed, a full cackle that warmed me head to toe. "Dingbat, huh?"

"Yes." I fought my own smile. "This is serious."

"The most serious."

"Luca, oh my god, I'm going to hop out of this car if you don't knock it off."

He reached over with his right hand, placing his palm over my thigh and gripping my leg. Heat spread *everywhere* from his touch, and I sucked in a breath. My jeans were the only layer, but I might have been naked with how I reacted.

"I feel carefree around you, goofy. *Normal.* I can be myself with you without worrying about anything else, and selfishly, I want more of it, but I need rules, limitations to not mess everything up. You want to protect your heart, but I need to protect myself too," he said softly.

"Relationships shouldn't have stipulations," I said,

immediately regretting it. Relationship wasn't on the table at all, and I foolishly ducked my head, avoiding his stare.

"This isn't a *relationship*, Lorelei."

His tone wasn't mean, but it was direct. We hadn't agreed to a damn thing, and here I was, making it more than what it was. I crossed my arms and glanced out the window as my face heated in embarrassment.

Luca released a resigned sigh. "Lo, who cares about what we do with our rules? Do you enjoy spending time with me?"

"A little."

He growled and squeezed my leg tighter. "Little liar."

"Okay, yes."

"And have you thought about Sunday night often? I have, every second I can."

"Obviously." I squirmed in my seat. His fingers moved up my thigh, digging into the fabric like he was afraid to let go of me.

"You do something to me no one else does, and football will always come first, but I want you too. You know going in what this will be. No surprises. No lies, no games. Your ex was a dick, but I'll always be honest with you."

Sexually, not a relationship. I repeated in my head. I ran my hands through my hair, giving up on my resolve. There was no way I couldn't agree to this—to explore this chemistry for as long as I could? I'd be a fool not to, but I just *had* to build in layers of protection. This was similar to Eric, with baseball being his reason to dump me. Luca was not Eric. That was certain, but this still had *heartbreak* all over it. I nodded, more to myself than Luca, and smiled.

"If I were to agree to this, and that's an if, would we have a schedule? Like a quick bang on Monday and Saturdays?"

"Big fan of everything you said. The biggest, really." He laughed and gripped my thigh again, harder and in control.

My skin prickled with awareness and heat, any hang-ups I had completely gone. Licking my lips, I spread my legs a little farther apart.

Luca groaned and his grip tightened. It was a metaphor to how I felt around him—amazing, but with a little pain.

Maybe I was a masochist.

Chewing my lip, the flicker of resolve I still had shattered into a million horny pieces. "Fine. I'm *in*."

"Lorelei," he panted, his voice strained. "You're... in, in?"

"Yes. Let's do this," I said, not even fighting

A strangled, throaty sound left his mouth, a mix between pleasure and annoyance. I arched a brow, on the edge of my seat.

"You alright there, Monroe?"

"I'm contemplating what excuse I can give my grandma so we can turn around this second."

While my skin tightened with need, disappointing people, like his grandma, was not an option. I took his hand settled between my legs and intertwined our fingers, ignoring the blip of my heart at how natural this felt. "We will not let your grandma down. You can keep it together for a few more hours."

"I didn't expect you to agree this soon into the trip. I figured I'd convince you all afternoon. This was never part of the playbook."

"Ah, well, like any good athlete, you gotta adjust. I'm on the offense now, Monroe."

He slid a warm look my way, something like pride shining from his eyes. "I'm fucking glad we're on the same team, temporarily. This is gonna be fun."

Temporarily.

I blinked, giving myself one hot second to be hurt by that word, and pushed it away. I didn't get to be angry or upset when he spoke the truth. This was a more structured fling, nothing more. I forced a smile, attempting to let go of his hand, but he held on tighter. We remained that way the entire ride.

Watching Luca hug his grandma caused my already-confused feelings to morph into more complicated ones. There was something special about this tall, grumpy tight end showing affection for a petite woman with an attitude the size of a football field.

She patted his back for a few seconds before releasing him, and *what is she doing?* She walked *toward me,* her smiling face almost teasing me. "I'm so happy you're here, Lorelei."

I blinked back shock and tried to relax when her arms came around me. She smelled like old linen and lavender, and I squeezed her back. I wasn't expecting to hug Luca's grandma or have a rush of fondness for her. The woman was incredible, and for the second time that afternoon, a warning bell went off in my head that this was gonna hurt when it was over.

"I'm glad we were able to come up again," I said, pulling away and feeling Luca's gaze on my face. I didn't meet his gaze, too flustered and confused to, so I stared at the photos on her wall. There were photos of her and a young Luca, and even as a child, he'd been tall and had the same dark, mysterious eyes that gave nothing away.

"You've been the talk of the place, I tell ya. With the socials, we've had more money donated! They're working on replacing the ceiling tiles in the cafeteria. Isn't that great, Luca?" his grandma said, the excitement evident in her voice.

"That's good," he said, his tone flat.

"When I spoke to the manager earlier this week, he mentioned some news outlets covering the condition of this place." I squeezed the back of my neck, my face blanching with worry. "I know you've said you're okay with this, but if you're not, please let me know, and we can scrap everything."

"Honey, I am all in. Xavier and Jeffrey down the hall are thrilled to be getting their ugly mugs out in the world. Lupe is bragging to her family about how hip she is now." His grandma walked up to me and put a hand on my forearm. "I appreciate your concern, and I'm sure some of this is coming from Luca's overbearing protective streak, but we agreed to be a part of this."

The first real smile stretched across my face, and I nodded. "Well, in that case, do you have time to film more for posts?"

"Why do you think my hair looks this good? Yes. I'm ready!" She twirled, fluffed her hair, and grinned.

God she was a spitfire, and I adored her.

Laughing, I pulled up my notes on my phone.

Text from Eric.

I'd somehow missed that notification, and I swiped it away. I'd read it later.

"Okay, I want to revisit the advice portion. What can the youths learn from your generation?"

"I've been working on a bit with my gal Gertie." Luca's grandma had an ornery expression on her face, where her eyes sparkled and she seemed on the verge of laughing. "It's a winner."

"I'll follow your lead then."

His grandma pointed to the window. "We need to be in the parking lot for this one. Follow me."

She waltzed out of her unit, and I trailed her, but Luca gently gripped my elbow, stopping me. Even though there was a layer of fabric from his fingertips to my skin, I felt the warmth from his touch all the way to my toes.

"Hm?" I asked, a little breathless.

"You frowned. Is everything okay?"

"I'm great." I chuckled, trying not to breathe in his clean scent or think about what would happen when we got back to the house. His lips were *right there,* and his tongue wet the bottom one, sending a bolt of lust to my core.

"You had your concerned face though, where you get a little line here." He touched his pointer between my eyebrows, smoothing the skin. "What made you frown?"

"Honestly nothing." I shrugged. "I'm in a – oh, I know. I got a text from Eric."

"What did he want?" Luca growled.

"Oh, no idea. Didn't read it."

His left cheek twitched as his grandma said his name. "Luca, you can flirt with her later. I want to get this filmed before I forget my idea, so come on. I know you can move fast."

I smiled, charmed even more by this sassy-mouthed woman. Luca's eyebrows remained furrowed, the wrinkles along his forehead dented into his skin. He wore a frown well, hell, he wore nothing well too. Was I so horny for him that his frown was sexy?

Yikes on a bike. I needed to get it *together.*

"Okay, Nanette. I have my phone. Where are ya going?" I walked by Luca, ignoring the draw to him. Was it possible for his coat to be filled with magnets that scientifically pulled me to him? It'd make more sense and would let me sleep easier at night.

"Right here." His grandma stopped in front of a very weathered car. The old sedan had seen better days—*decades*— yet that didn't stop the beam from her face. "Are you ready? Count down and say action when the video is live, dear. I wanna be like the clock users."

I bit my lip, a snort coming out as Luca met my eyes. "She's my favorite," I whispered.

I queued up the camera and counted my fingers down to one. Go.

"Hey, kids. Want to know how to make sure your car is never stolen, robbed, or messed with? Nanette has the answer." His grandma clapped her hands and spun around twice. Then she grinned and pointed her thumb over her shoulder. "Here's how. Drive a piece of shit."

She jumped out of the way, and it took all my willpower to not drop the phone from laughing.

"Grandma!" Luca yelled, his voice amused. "What was *that?*"

"A little thing I like to call humor. Look it up sometime. It'd make you happier."

"This is… perfection." I saved the video, which I'd edit later. "Nanette. You are a gem to the world."

"As long as my string of exes see this, that's all I care about." She flipped her hair over her shoulder and slowly marched by us back into the building. "I don't need to be walked in. I saw how you looked at her, Luca. Take her home and use your bodies while you're still young."

CHAPTER
TWENTY-SIX

Luca

Light flurries fell from the sky, my headlights hitting them directly and making them look like cold little fireflies. I kept both hands on the wheel despite the aggressive urge to grip Lorelei's thigh the entire ride home. After the run-in with the deer, I wanted us safe.

Plus… there was no guarantee what I'd do once I touched her again.

"God, she is the best." Lorelei laughed against her fist, the trill of her amusement filling the silence in a fun twinkle. She snorted a few more times, her fingers moving over her phone fast before she stared up at me. "Dude, this video has thousands of likes already."

"You posted it?"

"Sure did. Added a viral song in the background, and a few filters that were trending, and hashtagged it up. She is a *hit.*" She leaned back in the seat, hugged the phone to her chest, and let out a squeal. "This is the most fun I have ever had."

"What is?" My chest got that funny feeling again, like the

time I downed too many cheese fries at three in the morning. Did she mean... me?

"This whole experience with your grandma and the adventures of getting up there. I know this will be difficult for you to relate to as football is your life, but soccer isn't who I am, just a part of me. I love it. I've always loved it. But there was no thought of playing beyond college. But marketing? Creating campaigns and meeting people? Doing good? This fulfills a part of me I didn't know I had. I wake up excited to try new things and explore ideas. I know this is for an internship, but I think... this helped me figure out what I want to do in my life."

"And what is that, Lo?"

"I want to do promotions with genuine, real people for good causes. No fake bullshit, no lying, no politicians. Yikes." She cringed and made a gagging sound. "Anything but them."

"So, you found your next steps."

"Yes. I didn't know they were missing, per se, but they weren't solid, and it feels... settled. Good. Calming, in a way. You have football and the NFL, and Dean too plans to go pro, and even my girl Mack wants to stay in soccer, but this feels more *me.*"

I couldn't stop myself. I patted her thigh, squeezing above her knee in a way I hope conveyed my support. "Good on you."

"Yeah. *Good* on me." She smiled, her nose scrunched and her joy almost tangible around her. "Oh, and would you believe the audacity of this bitch?"

"Eric? What did he say?"

"Oh, I meant my brother, but shit. I forgot to read his text."

"Read it."

"That was a little aggressive with that tone, Monroe. A little bossy." She smirked, a twinkle catching her eye before I moved my hand up her thigh. "Oh, is this one of those things where you punish me?"

"Wait, what?" My mouth fell open. "Punish?"

"Did you ever play that game in high school? A dude would put his hands here and go up slowly if the girl didn't want to answer the question? Something like that? The guy who went the furthest won?"

I wanna play. "Um, did you ever play?"

"No. I never got a chance to because feelings—"

"Let's do this."

"You're driving."

"The snow let up, and I'll be safe, I promise." I cleared my throat, my cock already hardening at the thought of teasing her. "Be a good girl and slide your pants down, Lorelei."

Her breathing picked up, and she let out the tiniest little sigh as she did as I asked. I wanted to eat that sigh. "So how does this work? I ask a question, and if you don't answer, I move up your thigh?"

"Yes."

I glanced over at her. Her thighs were spread out, but her shirt covered her pussy, so I didn't know what color panties she had on. "What color panties are you wearing?"

"Is that a question?"

"Yes."

"I don't want to say."

Fuck. *Hot.* I slid my fingers up a few inches, my pulse racing like there were two seconds on the clock and the game came down to a field goal.

"What did Eric's text say?"

"You want to ask me *that* with your fingers an inch away of discovering if I'm wearing panties or not?"

"You're not…" I swallowed, hard. "You don't have any on?"

"I'm not answering that."

"Goddamn it, Lo." I moved my finger up more, my knuckles grazing the outside of her *bare* pussy. I sucked in a breath. "Dangerous. You are a dangerous woman."

She grinned at me. "Remember that."

I growled, quickly grazing her clit with my finger. She groaned and rocked against it, but I stopped. "The text. What did he say?"

"That he wants to talk, apologize."

There were no cars coming down the interstate, and thank god for that. It was nothing but us, my truck, and my headlights on the road, and I had half a mind to pull over and lick her entire body right now. The squirming, the roughness to her voice, the fact she didn't wear goddamn panties. She had me twisted up.

"And what did you respond back?"

She sucked in a breath, her hand coming down and gripping my forearm. "I don't want to answer."

"Mm are you keeping things from me, or are you greedy?"

"I don't want to answer."

"That's two moves I get, right?"

My cock physically hurt with how turned on I was. I ran my thumb over her clit before swirling it until she groaned. Then I stopped. "That was one."

"This game sucks."

"I'm quite fond of it."

She snickered as I dipped a finger into her, teasing, then pulled out.

"*Fuck.*" She hissed. "How far until we're home?"

"Fifteen minutes."

"I won't last that long, not like this."

"Yes you will, baby. I won't give you a choice." I then took the finger that was just inside her and sucked it in my mouth. *"Filthy."*

She shuddered and gasped my name.

"New rules." I returned my hand to her. "If you don't respond to my question, I take my fingers away. How about that?"

"Is this some sexy torture?"

"It is now. I want answers, Lo."

Adjusting my grip on the wheel with my other hand, I continued slowly teasing her while I prepared my question. "Why didn't you ever play this game?"

"Um." She squirmed against my finger. "Don't you stop, I'm answering."

"Can't hear you."

"Feelings and sex are… hard for me to separate."

"Mm, how so?" I pinched right where she needed it, and she threw her head back against the seat. Her throaty sounds were better than a sports highlight.

"I never… hooked up with someone I wasn't with."

"Why?" Did that mean she didn't want to continue this because we weren't together?

"Trust, I think."

"Do you trust me, Lorelei?" I went harder, faster, bringing her to the brink. She gripped the armrests, and her face twisted in pleasure. "Answer me."

"Yes, Luca. *Please.*"

I gave her what she needed, and she fell apart on my hand. Gripping my forearm, she bucked and moaned as my cock fucking throbbed. Pre-come spread through my pants, but I didn't care. Lorelei screamed out her orgasm in my car, next to me, on the road, and I couldn't imagine a sexier image to remain in my head forever.

I let her ride my hand, giving her what she required before she stilled. "You're fucking hot when you come on me."

"Your mouth, Luca. I swear to god." She laughed and rested her forehead on the window. Her breathing came out heavy, almost like mine, like the orgasm took everything from her. "You talk filthy like this on the field too?"

"No. Just to you."

"Well shit, you're making me feel special now." She pulled up her pants and adjusted them to look normal. Besides the slight heavy panting, no one would know I'd made her orgasm with just my fingers. Pride filled me.

"Good."

She snorted, the sound pleasant and familiar. "You can tell me I'm a good girl who comes on your fingers without issue, yet you're all one-word syllables everywhere else?"

"Forgive me, Lo, my cock is hard as a rock, and I want you to sit on my face the second we get home. All my words are used up."

She popped her lips, clapped her hands twice, and nodded. "Alrighty then. Drive faster."

"There's a fucking party?" Lorelei stared out the window, groaning as people flooded our front lawn. The living room door was wide open, groups spilling out. "Dean said he was having some people over. *People.* People is like ten max. This is…"

"More than ten, yeah." I ran my hand over my jaw, my muscles tensing. I wasn't against parties on nights off, but Dean usually let me know. Fuck. Did he and I missed it? I pulled my pocket from the charging spot and winced. Sure enough, there were texts from them an hour ago.

Dean: I need a distraction. Can we party tonight? I'll clean up tomorrow.

Oliver: I'm in.

Callum: If I ever say no, know I've been taken

Dean: Luca, that cool with you? I'll block off your hall.

"Are you alright with it?" Lorelei asked me, her voice small. "I can see if Dean will kick people out if it's too much. I know—"

"You're worried about me."

"Well yes. It's not a game night." She ran her teeth over her bottom lip, concern etching itself all over her face. Her nose wrinkled, and the line between her brows dipped. Her wild hair cascaded over her shoulders.

"I was worried about *you.*" I played with the ends of her hair, the same tight feeling in my chest expanding. I stretched well yesterday so there was no reason to be sore, but the sensation wasn't pleasant. Rubbing my hand over it, I cleared my throat. "Seeing you worry about me… it makes me want to kiss you."

And be with her despite football and Dean and my future.

"Yeah?" She arched a brow. "Then you better find me. In there. But be careful." She leaned over the console, nipped my bottom lip, and dove out of the car before I could stop her.

"Hey, Lo! Wait!"

She winked, and goddamn it, that little gesture should've been the final clue that I was so fucking fucked. I parked the truck in a daze, still horny from making her come but also dizzy with how much she cared about people. From her brother to her team to my grandma to me… her heart had to be ten times bigger than mine.

She couldn't separate feelings and sex because of trust. That meant she trusted *me*. That came with additional guilt because no matter what happened, I'd always pick football. She knew that. Accepted it. But what did she trust me with then? Her heart?

Stop using your excuses, idiot. I ignored the intrusive thought, damn well aware I was leaning on the football defense because it was easy. Letting her in meant I could get hurt again. I knew what I felt like to be left behind. Why the hell would I put myself in a position to give someone that power? My parents had crushed me. This was no different.

"She has that effect on people." Dean leaned against the back porch, his hands in his hoodie pocket. I jumped, not aware my teammate could see me.

What if I kissed his sister? In front of him?

For the first time in years, the thought of breaking my own code seemed like a good option. Would he really tackle me in front of everyone? No.

I studied his expression, my reactions based on his offense here. He didn't seem mad, curious almost. "What do you mean?"

"My sister." He smiled, shaking his head as he stared off toward the back alley where we stored the trash. "We give each other crap a lot, but she's one of my favorite people ever. There's nothing I wouldn't do for her."

"You're both lucky." I pocketed my hands, my stomach downright caving in on itself. Did he know? Was he guessing? Was this a warning?

"I feel that way about you too, you know." He rocked back on his heels, his gaze slicing into me.

"What are you trying to say?" Shit. Shit. I didn't want to hash this out even though I wanted Lo desperately. If we talked about this—that meant I had to be honest with her and try, something that terrified me. Giving someone the opportunity to hold my heart in their hands.

"I never thought I had to worry about *you.* Callum? Yes. Oliver? Sure. But Luca Monroe? Never." He ran a hand down his face, groaning. "Fuck."

Some people panicked in a fight or flight moment but never me. My gaze became heightened, my focus better. The sounds of cars miles away faded, and every hint of expression on his face was a clue. His eyes were a bit lazy, like he'd been drinking. He said he wanted a distraction, so he hosted a party on a night that wasn't a game.

Did he need a distraction from *this,* or was something else going on?

"What exactly do you think happened?"

"You and Lorelei?"

"Again, what do you think *happened?* You're insinuating shit and talking in circles, but you're not actually accusing me of anything. You told me recently you were glad she made me happy since we've been friends."

"You both got out of your car."

"Yeah, because we drove to see my grandma together, like we've done a handful of times for her project. She needs to kick her ex's ass, and she's helping out my family in the process." My pulse raced.

"Wait, what about this ex?"

I held up my hands. "You can't sit there and ask me questions about your sister when you clearly aren't in the right headspace. Something's wrong, I can feel it. If you wanna talk about it, I'm game. If not, that's okay too. What do you need?"

Dean closed his eyes and pulled the ends of his hair before meeting my eyes. "I want to play beer pong and not talk about a goddamn meaningful thing."

"Then that's what we'll do."

"You're the best type of person, Luca. I'm sorry I accused you of anything. God, I'm a dick. You'd never do that to me." Dean leaned in for a bro hug, and I swallowed down the lie and guilt.

He needed me. I just hoped Lorelei understood why I bailed on her for the night.

CHAPTER
TWENTY-SEVEN

Lorelei

W hen I said to come find me, I didn't think I'd be waiting over two hours? A dull ache throbbed in the base of my head, a sure sign of stress and overthinking. Had something happened from the conversation in the car to now, hours later where I lay waiting for him in my room?

Yawning, I didn't have many choices. His room was empty. A party raged on downstairs. Callum was definitely down there, so it was just me, alone on the third floor. I had zero desire to party, not with having a big game tomorrow. Even if things weren't in this strange *what are we doing* with Luca, I'd just hang out in my room and keep busy.

So that was what I'd do, or I'd obsess about the reasons why he never showed. He'd gone hot and cold on me before, and people rarely changed. That I knew. Frustrated, I redid my ponytail four times before accepting defeat. I should take a hot shower and work on more posts for Heath's Lodge.

Or respond to Eric's text…

I'd successfully avoided responding to him due to not having the mental capacity to worry about my project, Luca, *and* him all evening, so now that Luca had left me worked up, I could focus on my ex.

Eric: I owe you an explanation. One that makes sense. I'm so sorry about everything. Call me when you can.

One that makes sense. Closure. Did I even want it?

Yes. I was human. Needy about my emotions. Who wouldn't want to learn the reason why someone they trusted hurt them? Would an explanation take the hurt away? No. But would it settle my imagination?

Lo: I don't know, Eric. What good would it do?

Eric: Stop you from hating me.

Eric: Maybe... I hate knowing I disappointed you. So, can I call you?

Lo: Not tonight.

Eric: when?

Groaning, I tossed my phone on my nightstand and grabbed my robe. My well-intentioned brother put up cones and tape, *and* physical barriers that prevented anyone from going upstairs.

It was overkill to say the least, but it reassured me no one was gonna sneak up here when I was in the shower. I still couldn't believe Luca had done what he did in his car. And I'd let him! And it was freeing, hot, and *were we done?* This was new territory for me, this land of gray area.

Starting the water, I waited for it to get hot before hanging up the robe and getting in. The bathroom had two stalls for toilets and three showers on the other side. I figured it'd be disgusting sharing it with two dudes, but it wasn't bad. They took care of their things. Plus, having my own shower stall was perfect. I could line my products in a row, and no one yelled.

The steam calmed me down as I scrubbed my body and

hair, not caring that it wasn't a wash day. The heat beat against my neck and nerves, and I massaged the spot behind my neck and groaned.

That felt good.

I repeated the process when thuds alerted me. *Someone is in the bathroom.* Muscles tensed, eyes alert, I waited as the footsteps neared me and the curtain pulled back. "Ah!"

"Lo, it's me, hey," Luca said, his voice in a whisper. He was naked, completely, and now wet.

God he was large.

"What…" I started, my voice catching in my throat. My eyes prickled with the familiar sting. *No. Not now. Please.*

"*Look* at you." He dragged his thumb over my throat, stopping at the hollow. He gulped, his breathing hitched. "I'm so sorry I made you wait."

"What—"

He dropped to the ground, running his hand down my body, through my cleavage and over my belly before stopping. "Lorelei, let me make this up to you."

He used both hands to spread my thighs, the heat of the water combining with his cinnamon scent. He smelled like whiskey. Water collected on his lashes in an unfair way, elongating them and making him even more gorgeous. My heart hammered against my ribcage, like a feather in a tornado, spinning and hitting into everything in its path.

Luca looked at me like I mattered.

"Lean against the wall, put your pressure there," he commanded, wrapping a thigh around his shoulders. "Watch me put my tongue on you."

I shuddered, my skin practically lava at this point from his voice, the hot water, him. I did as he asked and waited before he teased me with his tongue. The sensation was like a jolt of electricity. "Luca," I panted. "I waited for you."

"I know, baby." He sucked my clit right into his mouth, his eyes never leaving mine as he made an obscenely sexy sound.

My eyes about rolled into my head from how turned on I was. Breathing became a challenge. I gripped his hair, digging my fingers into his scalp just to ground myself. I forgot about the text sitting for me, the party, the fact he'd left me for two hours. I just felt the moment, him. His tongue swirling against me, his teeth gentle nibbling, and he groaned into me like this pleased him just as much.

"Keep your eyes open as you come, Lorelei."

Jesus. His voice was so low and dirty and hot and *shit.* Someone was in the bathroom! Someone knocked over a can of something. My eyes widened, the water splashing into them as I tapped Luca's face. *Someone's here,* I mouthed.

"Then be quiet," he whispered.

He then slid his hand to my cheeks, spreading them and running a finger down the crack until he got to my pussy. I slammed my head against the wall, overcome with everything. His teammate could hear us, pull that curtain back and see us like this—Luca holding me on his shoulders as he ate me out.

It made him lick faster, like he wanted me to explode with someone in the room. I squirmed, my thighs tensing, my chest heaving, when he reached up and pinched my nipple, hard.

Not yet. Wait, he mouthed.

Despite that warning, he didn't let up. Even as the person did their business and washed their hands, Luca kept sucking me. His fingers moved inside me, thrusting and matching the pace of his tongue, and I was seconds away.

The door to the bathroom shut, and Luca released the hold on my clit. My protest died on my tongue as he sucked it again, sending me over the edge into a place I hadn't been before. The most explosive, hot, wild orgasm I'd ever had lit me up. I flung myself against the wall, my hands knocking over everything in their way to find some part of reality to hold onto. Afraid of being heard, I held in my moan as best I could.

"You're so fucking hot it's hard to breathe," Luca said, kissing up my body and taking a nipple into his mouth. "I need to suck every part of you like that. I want all your sounds. All your orgasms."

"Luca." I saw literal stars. My fingers were useless. My legs turned into jelly. I gasped to catch my breath, all while Luca grinned up at me with his eyes gleaming.

"You saying my name right off an orgasm might be my favorite thing." He stood to his full height, grabbed a bottle of shampoo, and squirted some onto his hands...while still supporting my weight as I collapsed onto him.

I closed my eyes, leaning toward him like a cat near catnip. He rubbed the shampoo over my scalp, digging it into my hair. "Gnn."

"What was that now?"

"Dead. Me."

He chuckled and moved me so the water rinsed over me. His massaging of my scalp was heaven, and the deep timbre of his voice was my own personal siren call.

"Your brother needed me."

That snapped me from my momentary bliss. "Is he alright?"

The only indication he heard my question was the tightening of his muscles near me. My face was so close to his bicep I *felt* the tension. "Luca."

"He's okay. Needed a friend tonight, and I didn't have a choice. I'm sorry if you were worried."

Of course. I'd been coming in second to Dean my entire life, and now the guy I was into did the same thing. My chest ached and my stomach hollowed. I was chosen second. I repeated the rules, hoping it'd ease the sting. *We're not in a real relationship, just hooking up. I chose this.*

That means I can end it before I get hurt. I forced the hurt down, focusing on this gorgeous guy in front of me.

He kissed my temple before taking my loofa and staring at my bodywashes. "Which one smells like peaches?

"The orange one."

He put some on the loofa and rubbed it all over my arms, neck, back, and ass. Then he did it to himself. I arched a brow.

"Every time you walk by me, I inhale your scent. Makes me feel animalistic. Like I want to bite you right here." He nipped the spot where my neck met my shoulder. "And here." He grazed his teeth at the base of my throat. "And definitely here." He teased my earlobe.

"Luca," I begged, unsure what for. It was all *too* much. The emotions, post-orgasm sensations, the confessions. Too many feelings happening for me. Yup.

"I told Dean I had to run upstairs for a bit, but I couldn't let you not have another orgasm." He tilted my chin up and smiled at me. "Or let you worry about where I was."

"Thanks," I mumbled. My face heated even more, but the hot water was an easy culprit. "So are you—"

He stared at me, so hopeful and happy, with his erection pressing against my stomach. He was hard and ready.

"Do you have to return?"

"Yes. But," he said, his smile growing. "He's sloshed so I can take my time."

"Good."

I needed to distract my heart by using my body. It'd help me get over being second place. I shut off the water, winking over my shoulder at Luca. "Did you get a towel?"

"Didn't think that far ahead honestly."

"Then we better run to my room."

In a mix of wet limbs and slippery floors, laughter, and a chorus of *oh shits* followed us from the stall, down the hall, toward my bedroom where we dove headfirst under the covers.

"Fuck, I'm cold!" Luca wrapped me against him. "I need your heat!"

"Be my human blanket!" I shouted back, laughing and never feeling so alive. I shivered, our skin was wet, and my hair was out of control. But damn, I felt good.

"That's not a strange thing to say at all," he teased, rolling over so he was on top of me. The movement caused my phone to fall onto the floor, and he reached for it. I held out my hand, but he frowned at the screen.

"My phone, Luca."

"You're gonna meet with Eric?" His voice changed, went deep and angry. "He's not worth your time, Lorelei."

"Hey." I cupped his face, forcing him to look at me. "I can't even think about him when you're all I see. Can we please not talk about *him,* not when I can feel your cock hardening against me?"

He sucked in a breath, heat returning to his gaze. "Say cock again."

"I want to ride your cock, Luca." I pushed up onto my elbows, my tits on full display.

Luca's gaze zeroed in on my nipples, his mouth parting before he leaned over and sucked one in his mouth, *hard.* It stung, but before the pain lasted, he soothed it with a warm, wet kiss. "Your body will kill me."

"Worse ways to go."

He laughed, and I motioned him to sit down, his cock rigid and his legs stretched out. Reaching for the condom, I ripped it open and bent down to wet his cock with my mouth in a few strokes.

"Jesus." He gripped the edge of the bed, his tree-trunk thighs coiling with tension. "Your goddamn lips."

I sucked him another minute before putting the condom on and straddled him. I rarely wanted to be on top. I always felt too big, too muscular, too much for guys, but with him? I was empowered. He stared at me with lust and adoration, and I slowly slid onto his cock. "God, you feel good Luca."

"I want to feel your muscles when you ride me. Grind hard, take me deep."

"I like when you boss me around," I whispered, doing as he said. He filled me so well I moaned. I felt powerful, sexy, free. He gripped my hips hard, his thumbs digging into my skin to the point I'd have bruises. The ends of his fingers were rough, calloused as he held onto me like his life depended on it. "*Yes,* Luca."

"Rock your hips and lean forward. I need those tits again."

I did as he said, and he sucked my nipple into his mouth in a wet, dirty kiss. The graze of his teeth on my sensitive flesh had me buck, and he hissed.

"Lorelei, *god.*"

His voice dropped an octave, the restraint he showed earlier completely gone. He slammed up into me harder, faster, more aggressively. Then our limbs were tangled in a frenzy. I rode him, my body dripping from the shower, and it made our legs slide together. He grunted, then stilled. "Flip over. I want your ass in my hands."

He lifted me off him like I weighed nothing and set me on the bed, demanding me to roll onto my stomach. *"Fuck."* Something wet touched my spine. Then *whoa.*

"Did you just bite my ass?"

"I had to." He grabbed my globes, burying his face between them for a second as he licked. "You make me lose my mind, Lo. You're so hot."

My heart raced, and a tingle of pleasure danced down my skin, all from his words. No one in my past had ever said these things to me or acted this way, like they couldn't get enough of me. Yes, my heart was bruised, but my body had never been so celebrated. I glanced at him from my spot on the bed, my ass in the air as he stared at it. "Do it again."

His gaze met mine, his eyes blazing. The look on his face made me whimper.

"Gladly."

He bit my other cheek this time, slowly, agonizingly. His fingers rested on my clit, swirling in a perfect rhythm, and once he released his teeth on me, he slid his cock back into me. "Yes, you're so tight. Arch that back baby."

He gripped my hair in one hand, and his other remained on my clit as he thrust over and over, each time making the air escape my lungs. I'd never felt destroyed before, but goddamn, he destroyed me for *anyone* else. I held onto the sheets as pressure grew, the flares of a third orgasm growing at the base of my spine.

"*Oh* yes, Luca."

"Say my name when you come."

Jesus. It didn't take much more. I changed the angle of my hips and *hell yes.* "Luca, yes!"

Stars exploded around my eyes, my hands felt numb, and my legs were like fireworks. I couldn't breathe, see, hear, do a thing as I rode out the pleasure. I was pretty sure I cried. My cheeks were wet. I even heard Luca let out a deep, sexy ass roar before he collapsed on top of me.

My face pounded with how fast my heart beat. Each breath took so much effort it sounded like I'd run up ten flights of stairs instead of just having sex. My body took a pounding and holy shit. "Luca."

"He's gone."

I snorted. "Luca, hon, what did you do to me?"

"I don't know." He rolled onto his back, his chest moving

up and down at the same pace as me. "My ears have a ringing sound. Is this normal?"

"That was—"

"Fucking phenomenal." He pushed up onto his side and gently ran his fingers over my face, resting on my collarbone. "You're incredible."

"No need to compliment, we already did it." My face heated, and I had the urge to pull the sheet up to my chest. His words made me feel exposed, bashful. Clearing my throat, I slid off the bed before his large hand stopped me. "What?"

"No." He pulled me against him, burying his nose against my neck. "I wanted one more hit of you."

"You're ridiculous."

His hair tickled my chin, and he smelled so damn good, like soap and whiskey. The reminder of his drinking dulled the mood, the silence after the post-sex glow all about my brother. Sighing, I massaged his head for a few seconds before pulling back. "You should head back before they notice you're gone."

"I know." He stared at me, his dark eyes unreadable. "Dean needs me."

"I understand." I frowned, *hating* that I didn't want him to leave. And the fact Dean had found another way to make me feel less important. The entire point of this was no feelings, just sex, yet some feels snuck in the moment. Football was Luca's priority, which meant Dean had to come before me, but god, it sucked. If we were really together, this shit wouldn't fly.

We're not together.

Make it casual. Be chill.

"What are you thinking? Your face changed?" Luca asked, his voice tight.

"Oh." Well damn. He could read me that easily? "I was wondering when our next, uh, time would be together."

He closed his eyes, and a huge smile stretched across his

face. His features transformed with a grin, and my breath caught in my throat for an entirely different reason. He was so serious and focused all the time, so what made him smile like this? Ice cream? Corny holiday movies? The first snowfall of the year? When the Bears made the playoffs? I wanted to know, damn it.

His smile lingered as his gaze moved from my eyes to my mouth, then back up. "Monday. Not sure I can go two days without this."

I rolled my eyes and shoved him. "Go."

He slid off the bed, his hand lingering on my ankle before he frowned. "Can I uh, borrow your sheet to run across the hall?"

"Sure."

"Thanks, Lo." He wrapped it around his waist before looking at me again. He gripped the back of his neck, a slight blush creeping up his cheeks.

What is he thinking about?

He tapped the doorway twice, his lips parting, but he didn't say anything. He went to his room, leaving me in alone with my spiraling thoughts. One thing was glaringly clear—I had feelings for Luca, and even though I knew we'd end in heartbreak, I couldn't stop them from growing.

CHAPTER
TWENTY-EIGHT

Luca

We were winning games. Upsetting higher-ranked teams. Coach ran around with half a smile compared to his usual frown, and things felt *nice.* It was unnerving for stuff to be going well. I knew life experiences enough to brace myself for something to crack the façade. Life wasn't nice and fun. It was hard and a grind. It was about sacrifice and hustling.

My muscles clenched, almost like they did when the car suddenly came to a stop, and I forced myself to breathe through the rush of panic. Life had been good the last three weeks, and I didn't trust it.

I kept up on my schoolwork, stuck to my routine besides a trip to see my grandma every other week, and fucked Lorelei. *Lorelei.* I scrubbed my hands over my face in the locker-room shower, forcing myself not to think about her. I'd get a hard-on, and that was the last thing I needed in here.

I quickly rinsed after a brutal practice. We were facing the number two ranked team this week, and with the stats I had, it meant even more exposure. Coach seemed to think I'd have no problem getting drafted this year. *Leaving school, earning the money needed for my grandma.*

Getting dressed, I added an extra thermal since the temperature had dropped the last week. It was gonna be a cold Halloween in a few days.

"Monroe." Dean nodded at me, his face more relaxed than that party a few weeks ago. He hadn't shared what exactly had bothered him, but he seemed lighter, happier.

The guilt that filled my veins around him had only grown the more I kept a huge secret from him. He had no idea I was sleeping with his sister, obsessed with her being closer to the truth. I knew it was past the point of acceptable deniability. I straight up hid this from him, the one thing he'd ever asked of me.

Lo is off-limits. For all of you.

I swallowed the uncomfortable ball of emotion in my throat and forced a neutral expression on my face as I responded, "What's up?"

"We need to talk. Not here."

Shit.

Was his jaw clenched in anger? Betrayal? Had he found out? Sweat beaded along my lip, and I wiped it away with the back of my sleeve. What did I say? How did I explain what happened?

The truth.

My grandma's wisdom snuck into my daily actions and deep down, even though I knew it'd hurt, me, him, our team, I'd own up to it. It was the only path forward. "Look—"

"Not here." His eyes flashed around the room, his cheeks reddening.

Double shit.

"Okay." I shouldered my duffel bag, double-checked that

my phone was in my pocket. *I'm delaying this conversation.* Reading other's movements was my strength. Were they favoring one side, did they move right and jerk left? I did the same on Dean, but he remained still as a statue, his hands shoved in his sweatshirt pocket. The dude excelled at poker, and this was no different.

He hadn't punched me in the face yet, so that was great.

We exited the locker room, a normal occurrence for a Wednesday night. We had special teams practice, and it was our last tough workout before game day that weekend. We nodded at our teammates before Dean led us south, like we'd walk back to our house.

"Are you leaving after this season?"

Wait. "Is that your… is this what we're talking about?"

He stopped and frowned. "Yes. Why what—no. Don't distract me. I know you need money for your grandma, but Lo told me how much money has come in with her project and… Luca. I want to play another year with you. I love playing with you, man, and our team is the best it's ever been. We could have another season like this. I hate asking you this because I know what it means for you."

"How much money… she hasn't told me." I swallowed, a prickle of annoyance at that fact. "What did she say?"

His shoulders lifted to his ears. "That they've made about twenty thousand dollars from donations alone and that schools and businesses partnered with them for repairs. Her work transformed that place. I even follow their accounts. Your grandma? Hilarious."

Three things struck me hard and fast. The first—I missed talking to Lorelei. With our new arrangement, we had crazy, amazing, life-altering sex that went on for hours. We'd pass out after, and she'd sneak away, or I would. Were we just a booty call now?

The second—if what he said was true, why hadn't she shared that with me? It hurt to learn it from Dean. Was she not comfortable telling me? Did my grandma know? I itched the back of my neck, my skin too hot and tight for the winter air.

The third—if this was true... was there a possibility of me staying one more year to get my degree and... enjoying life? Could this thing with Lorelei continue? Could I have another year playing with Dean and the guys?

"So, what do you think? You're more quiet than normal. I overstep here?"

"No." I rubbed my lips together, trying to nail down a response. "I honestly don't have an answer. I didn't know about the money. It might change the situation."

"I understand if it doesn't, but we could make a Bowl Championship this and next year. That'd be huge. We could leave a legacy here. *If* you wanted that."

I did. But a change of plans was hard for me. The goal had always been to leave after junior year, but lately, staying sounded better. *As long as my grandma is okay.*

"Look, you don't owe me a thing. You do what you need to, but as your friend, hell, brother, I wanted to bring it up. Call me selfish, but I like having your big grumpy ass around."

The guilt grew twice in size. I had to tell him. Or end it.

Both options were not ideal.

"I appreciate it, Dean," I croaked out, my voice giving away my inner turmoil.

He sighed, patted my back. "I know emotions stress you out, so I'll leave."

I didn't correct his assumption. I let him think that was why I was emotional, confused. He walked away but I remained, letting the wind whip across my face and numb me for a few seconds. The cold felt good. Wanted. Needed to knock sense into me. The cold could push away the anger brewing.

Of everything he'd said, the thing that bothered me the most was that Lorelei hadn't told me about the money. I thought everything was good between us, amazing even, but this seemed like a big deal? It meant her project was successful. It hurt. It more than hurt that she'd hid this from me. She wasn't cruel, so if she chose not to tell me, there was a reason. But what? My mind spiraled, my emotions ping-ponging more than I was used to dealing with.

Sweat broke out on my forehead, my heart racing with all the reasons why she might've kept it from me.

Shit. I'd been so caught up in the chemistry between us that I hadn't checked in about the project, her internship, Eric... *god.* Was I a complete asshole? Did she think I just wanted her for her body? I wanted her for her mind, smile, eyes, *and* body.

With a renewed energy to change this immediately, I hurried back to the house and stopped in my tracks. Lorelei sat on the couch, Callum a few feet to her right. She wore a hoodie that was too large for her and had the hood up and strings pulled tight so only a small part of her face showed.

"Oh fuck, oh shit, oh shit." She buried her face in her hands. "What's going on? Why is this happening?"

Callum laughed and hit her knee. "Just watch."

"But he's going to kill them!"

"It's called Slasher 300, what did you think would happen? Knitting hats?"

"I don't know! I wanted an adrenaline rush but not like this!" She stuffed her face into a pillow and Callum inched closer to her. She ducked her head against him, letting out a very high-pitched squeal.

Horror movies were my favorite. I loved Halloween. I watched all of them the week up to the holiday, and seeing her watch one with him caused a storm of anger through me. First, she told her brother about her project, then this? My head throbbed, and I fisted my hands at my sides.

I wanted to yell at her, demand an explanation. Was she intentionally angering me in a head game of sorts? Had I upset her, and she wanted revenge? I didn't appreciate that at all. Not with a big game Friday.

Fuck this.

I huffed, the sound drawing their attention.

"Hey, Luca," she said in her cheery, sing-song voice. "Oh, I like your sweatshirt."

Her gaze trailed me head to toe, but instead of the rush of heat like I normally got when she did that, uneasy, uncomfortable knots of tension formed in my shoulders.

"I'm leaving," I blurted out.

Don't look back. Marching upstairs, regret had my shoulders slouching. She wasn't shit to me, just a hookup buddy. I didn't do feelings, even ones like anger or jealousy.

She didn't want to talk to me? Fine. She could talk to everyone else for all I cared. I had football to worry about and my grandma! Yeah. I'd call her, remind myself of the goal. The endgame.

Scoffing, I rubbed my temples as I entered my room. I'd call my grandma and work out. Yes, that'd pass time until my mood improved.

It didn't.

I did a thirty-minute set in my room, but that only made me angrier. Not at Lorelei though but at myself. I'd done this. I put myself in this position. I had no one to be mad at but me.

A low whistle came from my door, Lorelei leaned against the doorframe as she wiggled her eyebrows. "Hey sexy."

"What do you want?"

Those dark brows rose three inches as she tilted her head. "Um, are you okay?"

"Fine."

"Oh, are you?" Her gaze tightened, and she crossed her arms.

She still wore her hood, and it made her so fucking cute I couldn't stand it.

I stared at her hard, my pulse racing through my veins. I had enough adrenaline to run a mile. I knew the rules, the consequences of developing feelings for her, yet they'd crept in, and I needed distance. "You here to fuck or what?"

"Wow, someone's being a butthole today." Her initial surprise molded to hurt. "I'm not here *to fuck,* but I wanted to share some awesome news. Clearly, *clearly* that's not happening."

She didn't give me a chance to respond before she was out the door, taking her peach lotion with her. It'd be way easier to stay mad if she didn't smell so damn good.

"Wait. What's the good news?"

Did she get the internship? Had something happened?

"No." She spun around, her finger in the air. "You don't behave like an asshole and get the good parts of my day. I asked if you were okay, to which you said *fine,* so you can sit with your attitude *alone.* Why don't you fuck your hand if you need it that badly?"

She let out a sigh, one that sounded like she was done with me. It was the same disgust she used when she talked about her ex. It was like a cold hand reached into my throat, fisted my heart, and yanked it out with the force of a linebacker.

"Lorelei." I jumped up, not caring that sweat dripped all over me. She shut her bedroom door, the click of the lock like a slap in the face. "Can we talk, please? I'm… sorry."

She flung it open, the movement making me lose balance. Her face gave nothing away, her skin bare and flush and perfect. She'd taken her hood off, and her hair was in braids, making me want to tug on them and pull her into my arms. How had this become so confusing? I was mad *at her,* but I was now apologizing.

"This is why I don't do this," I said, out loud and instead of my head. I froze, wishing I could take it back.

"Do *what*?"

"That's not how it sounded. I mean, Christ." I scrubbed my face. "I'm shit at this."

"I don't even know what *this* is but yes, you're the worst at it."

My lips twitched, and I wanted to kiss her. "You didn't tell me about the money my grandma's place earned, Dean did. And then." I swallowed. "You were watching a horror film with *Callum.*"

She played with the strings on her sweatshirt, blinking slowly. "I didn't intentionally keep anything from you about your grandma. I would never do that."

"Wait, I'm not saying you would. I know that." I gripped the back of my neck, sweating even more. This wasn't going well. "You love my grandma."

"Then what's the problem? These aren't reasons to be an asshole to me."

"You're right. They're not." I groaned, cracking my neck left and right. She stared at me, her large brown eyes gutting me with how sad she looked. "I like it when you tell me everything. The stuff with my grandma or watching a movie or sharing good news. Seeing you with Callum... I hated it."

"I do share stuff with you, but the only times we're together are at night, and obviously you know I enjoy our arrangement." Her cheeks reddened, and she ran her toe along the floorboard, her gaze tracking the movement. "You sound jealous."

"I might be." I wanted her to look at me.

Shit.

She did, and so much disappointment lined her face. "Luca, you're never here, and if you are, your door is shut. I'd love to hang out with you more, but that's... a relationship, and we don't do that."

Sadness echoed her voice, gripping me in the chest and stabbing me with a thousand papercuts. "Lo—"

"Round two?" Callum appeared at the top of the stairs, his face hopeful. "We're starting the next one. Dean's coming too, wants to relax. Oliver is making his dad's homemade popcorn recipe, so basically, it's a fucking party. You in, Monroe or nah? It's library night, yeah?"

Lorelei didn't glance at me as she headed toward Callum, and even her strut looked sad. That didn't seem like the walk of someone who intentionally was playing games with me. It seemed like I'd hurt her, and that gutted me.

My phone buzzed in my hand, pulling me from the mental turmoil.

Grandma: I love Lorelei. She sent me COOKIES. Why aren't you dating her?

I didn't have an answer because I didn't fucking know anymore.

CHAPTER
TWENTY-NINE

Lorelei

The good news didn't last long. Well, the news remained good, but my mood had been shit the last few days. We didn't have a game tonight, which would've been a fantastic distraction to the fact Mrs. G had lunches set up with Eric.

I accidentally stumbled upon them at a café near the football house. She laughed, because of course, Eric was charming when he wanted to be. Between seeing that and Luca's complete disappearance from the house, I was in a funk.

The fact two jocks were the reason for my mood annoyed me. How dare they make me feel less than wonderful? Fuck that. I adjusted my scarf and hat, walking faster toward home. It'd be a rom-com kind of day.

"Lo, wait a sec."

That voice.

Eric.

Fuck. Masking my face to indifference because we didn't care about him at all anymore, I turned toward him.

"I thought that was you. I'd know that hair anywhere." He laughed awkwardly and shoved his hands in his pockets. "I tried texting you."

"I know, and I didn't feel the need to respond anymore."

"Fair. That's entirely fair." He scanned me, his eyes softening. "You look good."

"I'm cold, what did you want?"

"Have a minute?"

"Not really."

"Please, I'll walk you back to your place."

"Then you can rush off to Mrs. G?"

"It's not what you think." He ushered his arm to the left, the opposite direction of the football house.

"I live there." I nodded east. "With the football guys."

He frowned. "Interesting."

"Walk fast."

"That, I can do."

We matched pace, the wind whipping our faces and I led us into the front room. No one was home, thankfully, not that it mattered. I didn't owe anyone a thing. I plopped down on the sofa, crossing my arms and legs. "Okay, so what's up?"

"My dad cheated on my mom. On… all of us. He had another family."

"Whoa." My stomach sank.

"Yeah." Eric gripped the back of his neck. "I found out this summer, and it's been really fucking hard. My mom had no idea, and well, I pushed everyone away. Was an asshole. I needed to pretend it didn't happen, and it's no excuse for doing what I did, but I hope you know that I did love you. I miss you. You were… are… an amazing friend. You would've been there for me, and I'm sorry for hurting you."

Blinking away emotion, I ran my hands through my hair,

unsure what to say. He'd dropped a lot on me. "Are you okay? Is your mom?"

"I'm seeing a therapist." He gave me a sheepish smile. "It's been helping, honestly. I'm so angry, and I need to figure it out. My mom is not—she's getting through it." He exhaled, his brows twisting together. "Mrs. Gravestone's someone my mom knew. She heard about what happened and wanted to check in on me."

"Oh."

"Yeah." He smiled again, adjusting his sweatshirt for a beat before meeting my eyes again. "She told me I'm out of the running for the internship now. She'd rather mentor or check in with me this way, and I'm alright with it. I know how much you want the spot at her company, and I hope you get it. I've told her how hard you work."

"Eric." I stood, needing to do something, and I opened my arms. The front door opened, and heavy footsteps followed, but Eric pushed up and wrapped his arms around me. He smelled like outside and leather, but instead of the rush I used to get, I had closure. Like ending a book. "I'm sorry your family is going through this. Thank you for telling me."

He squeezed me, running his hands up and down my back. "I'm sorry I hurt you."

We broke apart, and he cupped my chin. "I don't deserve a second chance, but—"

"Friends, Eric. We can be friends." I smiled, shoving his hand away. "Nothing more."

"Great." He sighed, rocked back on his heels and eyed the room. "Can't believe you live here."

"Won't be for much longer." I'd found a solid two bedroom place a few blocks from here last week, and Mack and I were gonna check it out soon.

He walked toward the door, staring at me hard. "Thank you. For listening, for not hating me."

"Eh, I did for a little bit."

He laughed and walked out. "I'll see you around, Lo."

I shut the door, exhaling in relief once he left. While I hated what he and his mom went through, it explained why he became a different person. It gave me that closure. And he wasn't in the running for the internship? Even better.

"I take it by the smile on your face that you're happy you talked to Derrick?" Luca asked, leaning against the doorway into the kitchen.

He wore a navy thermal and jeans along with a ski cap, and damn, he was handsome.

My stomach swooped in a very different way, and my skin tingled. We hadn't seen each other for more than a few minutes since our chat. It was better to put distance. He raised his brows, like he expected me to talk.

"I'm not happy, no, but I got the closure I needed."

"So that was a goodbye hug?"

"Yes."

"He didn't deserve it from you." He walked toward me, his jaw set in a hard line. Once he stopped in front of me, he ran his hand down my arm, ending with my fingers. He squeezed my hand once before letting go. "Are you okay?"

I expected a sarcastic comment or something, not for him to use a gentle voice and ask in such a kind way. My voice shook, so I cleared my throat. "I am. Yeah. That's...nice of you to ask."

"I care about you, Lorelei." His mouth lifted in a half-smile, his eyes blazing with heat and *tenderness?* It wouldn't be love, that was crazy. But something soft hid behind his eyes, making my own feelings double.

He cupped my face, running his thumb over my lip. "I

really fucking care about you. I don't know what to do about it. I tried to stay away the last few days—"

"I knew it." I shook his hand off, stepping back. "You can't—"

"Because I'm scared, alright?" He let out a humorless laugh. "We have too much to lose, too much to risk. I want things with you I haven't wanted before."

"Like what?" I asked, breathless. I craved that too, so badly. It had taken most of my energy to avoid thinking about the *almosts* with him. Honestly impressed myself with how much I managed to tune out. Like how my feelings were in dangerous territory, near the point of no return. I wanted his grandma to be mine, his smiles to belong to me, and to take care of him. For him to put me first.

But that wasn't a part of the deal. Our friends with secret benefits situation that I looked forward to and dreaded twice a week. Keeping it from Dean also hurt part of my soul. I didn't lie to my brother, my twin. I didn't share every detail of my life, but we knew the big things, and this was the biggest. *The fact I'm in love with Luca Monroe.*

Wait. Fuck. Love?

I winced, rubbing my temples as Luca gently touched my heart.

"To kiss you whenever I want, to see you every day, to not hide you. To introduce you to my grandma as someone more. To watch scary movies with you and let you borrow my sweatshirts when you hide. To have you wear my jersey with my name." His gaze softened, that gooey, tender expression reappearing.

It was the warmth that had my throat getting tight. All the things he stated, I wanted those too. But… that meant he had to change his stance.

"What are you suggesting then?"

He rubbed his lips together, his nostril flaring as he glanced over his shoulder. No one else was home, just us.

Swallowing hard, his throat bobbed, and his left cheek twitched. "We hang out more."

"Luca." I closed my eyes, a prickle of annoyance dancing across the back of my neck. "Say more."

"We have a relationship." His grip on my hips tightened. "If you're into it."

Holy shit. Hope slapped that irritation away, his suggestion not anything I'd dared wish for because I knew what was at stake.

"We'd have to talk to Dean."

The warmth left his eyes, and he sighed. "You know we can't do that, at least not in season. It'd have to be in secret until then. I'm probably leaving anyway to get drafted, so he wouldn't be my teammate anymore, so it wouldn't mess with our dynamics." He pulled on the end of my sweatshirt strings, his voice getting lower. "I want this with you, more than anything."

The hope fizzled, the emotional roller coaster of Luca Monroe one I wasn't tall enough to ride. He wanted to keep it secret to not ruin the team dynamics. Even with Eric's reasons, he'd left me because I wouldn't be a priority. I wouldn't be here either. The closure with Eric served two purposes. It helped explain his behavior, right or wrong, but it also reminded me what I wanted in a partner.

Someone to put me first. Someone willing to have hard conversations. Someone willing to fall together and go through tough parts as a team.

"No."

The hard, one-syllable word was louder than a glass shattering. Even saying it, my body recoiled, like it knew it would cause me pain. Luca blinked, his jaw tightening.

"Lorelei," he sighed. "What changed? Is it Eric?"

"Yes, but not that way." I stepped back, my eyes watering. "I want to be with you, Luca. I do. I'm starting to fall in—it doesn't matter." A tear fell, and I wiped it away.

"Whoa, why are you crying?" He reached for my face, his eyes tortured. "Lo, please."

"I can't be a secret. I can't be on the back burner until it's convenient for you." I sniffed again. "I'm not mad at you, Luca, I understand why football is so important for you. I do down to my soul. And your grandma, I love her." I hiccupped, my emotions snowballing like I was stuck in an avalanche. "I want to be with someone who is proud to be with me, willing to go through difficult parts together. To put me first, like I matter. That means talking to Dean."

He blinked, his face paling. "What does that mean?"

"That we're done. We'll remain friends. It's the only way to prevent more hurt, I think." My voice shook, but my gut settled. This was the solution best for the future. "You can focus on football again."

"I don't want this."

"I don't want to be a secret."

We stared at each other, the air filling with a thickness that was painful. Each breath was like a little knife traveling down my lungs, poking me with the loss of Luca. No more cuddles, sneak-attack kisses, hot nights where we talked about nothing.

It was a stalemate, me not willing to sacrifice my happiness and him not sacrificing the chance of upsetting my brother.

"So, we don't... what does..." Luca said, his face crumpling. "Will I still see you?"

"We'll be friends, but I need some space. I caught feelings, Luca, even though I tried not to. I'm not cutting you out of my life, but I can't be around you when I feel the way I do."

"What if...I found another night for us to hang out? Three nights? I can move my workouts around, anything, please."

"I don't think so. We both want more but aren't willing to budge." My voice cracked. "Nothing changes with your grandma from my end. I promise." I cupped his face, hating the finality to this conversation.

There was nothing left to say, and I wanted to cry in my room when the front door opened. Oliver or Callum was there, and I used that as my opportunity to escape. Without a backward glance, I ran upstairs and shut my door.

I'd known there was a hundred percent chance I'd end up in heartbreak, but this pain was nothing compared to losing Eric. This was worse, heavier.

I'd fallen in love with Luca Monroe, the one person who couldn't afford to love me back. And the worst part was that I understood it. Nothing would change that.

CHAPTER
THIRTY

Luca

Self-loathing was a new one for me. It was easier to be mad at the world, not myself, but this time, it was all me. I shouldn't have given in to temptation, to tasting her, to imaging for a short amount of time what it'd mean to be hers. Hell, being a part of her life when she damn well knew what I had to lose had no happy ending.

She'd changed the rules on me. She didn't want to be a secret anymore, and I couldn't blame her. This was on me. I should've kept on my way, random hookups, and football.

I didn't expect to miss her.

Not like this.

It'd been a week, and Lorelei's room sat empty. Instead of hearing her sing or walk around as she FaceTimed her friend, she wasn't there. No music, no laughter, no hints of her delicious perfume. No wild hair I'd sneak a peek at just because it made me so happy. I heard her tell Dean she found a place with her friend. She'd be out in December. The thought of her leaving gutted me to my core. Every workout, study session, game tape, and conversation I had since that chat was dulled, distorted, lacking in color and joy.

People chose to do this, have relationships and develop feelings. It was messy and gross, and it distracted me from my normal life. It was a Saturday, and we had an off week, so it wasn't like I could dive into football and obsess over my last performance. Football was who I was, and without devoting every second to it, I didn't know what to do, who to be.

Be a better friend. A boyfriend. Grandson.

I could see if Dean wanted to hang. Yeah, I'd do that. But first, I called my grandma. She'd help me figure this out. I fell onto my bed, my phone already to my ear.

"Is there a reason why you're calling instead of *being* here with your frail old lady?"

My lips twitched. "No one would call you frail."

"I'm precious. On the tail end. You should be here with Lorelei, boy. It'd be fun to razz ya."

"Lorelei's there?" I asked, my stomach hollowing out. That was our thing. It was *my* grandma. She went without me and didn't even tell me. The lingering heartache doubled in size, an ache in my stomach forming like I'd worked out too hard without rest.

My grandma sucked in a breath. "She is, Luca. She told me you were stressed about an assignment and wanted to come."

Silence.

"She lied for you." Then, my grandma said, "Now, I wondered because she seemed sad. The light wasn't there in her gaze. Mm, you tell me what happened right now."

"Grandma, is she listening?" My face heated.

"No, I'm not an idiot. She's with the gang in the kitchen, wanting to know about our food for a feature idea." She coughed, lowering her voice. "I love you, but there's no way she broke your heart. That girl is too kind and genuine, and you're a tad too grumpy. What did you do?"

"What makes you think I did anything? She's the one who changed the expectations and wanted more when I don't have more to give."

"What does that even mean? I saw how you looked at her. You followed her like a lost pup. She's wonderful, so what's the problem? You either wanna be with her or not. It's not complicated."

"It is." I gritted my teeth, pushing up from my bed and pacing my room. Each step broke through more of my uncertainty. How had Lorelei gotten there? Had she driven herself? What if a deer hit her car? Had Callum taken her? Fuck. I scrubbed my face, frustrated at the world. "I can't lose sight of the goal."

"Does she make you happy?"

"Yes, but—"

"Luca. Life is too damn short to not do things that make you happy. What is this? Is it fear of someone leaving you? She clearly loves you too, so fix this. Be happy. Seeing you smile with her… you've had to grow up faster than most kids. You were the one with the old woman at home, and you've experienced heartache very few ever have had to. You've had this angry chip on your shoulder your entire life, and it was… watching that chip melt away the more you were with Lorelei made me happy." She sniffed.

Worst sound in the world. I made my hero cry. "Grandma, no."

"I want you happy. Please. It's the point of life. What were the reasons for those sacrifices if you're not happy? That's what I want." Her shaky voice was barely above a whisper, yet the impact was like she shouted.

My eyes stung.

"And I want you taken care of. Getting drafted early gets me more money, so I can pay for your—"

"Excuse me? *Excuse me*?" Her tone went nuclear. "If you finish this sentence, be very, very careful. It is not your damn job to ruin your life to take care of me. It is to enjoy life, figure out what you want to do. This place is fine. Perfect, even. I expect visits and phone calls. That is it. Nothing more fancy than here. I swear, Luca James Monroe, if you're using *me* as an excuse, I will kill you. I'll make it look like an accident too. I've been watching some shows."

A horrible, snort-laugh sound escaped me. Not quite joy, not tears. "I need you healthy and safe. I owe you my life."

"As noble as you are, I'm doing fine. Better than fine, actually. We agreed on a budget for me and we're sticking to it. You should never worry about me. You already do so much for me, I'd never forgive myself if you sacrificed a shot at happiness. Now, here's a real hard question. Do you want to leave school early and not graduate?"

No. "My plan was always—"

"Is that what I asked? Yes or no."

I chewed the inside of my cheek. "No."

"Then it's settled. Now, do you want to be with Lorelei?"

"Yes."

"Then fix whatever happened. Shit, she's coming back. I hear her. She made Bob laugh. The grumpiest man I've ever known. She's got a heart of gold, Luca, and I can't think of anyone better suited to take yours." She covered the phone, yelling. "Be right there, Lorelei! Okay, gotta go. Love you! Fix this! Or murder!"

She hung up, leaving me with my mind spiraling. Admitting the truth about staying here, being with Lorelei felt like a mammoth-sized weight had been lifted off my shoulders. I wanted to fight my grandma, but her words kept repeating in my head, so much that they started to make sense.

She wanted me happy.

Finishing out my senior year with Dean would make me happy. Being with Lorelei, for real, would make me happy. Losing my strict routine and finding ways to enjoy life would make me happy.

I'm going to tell Dean.

That was a bolt of adrenaline, causing my knees to bounce with energy. I'd have to tell him the truth, but first… I had to talk to Lorelei.

Thank goodness I lived across from her.

She never came home, and if it weren't for Dean casually mentioning the fact she was staying at her friend's place, I would've lost my shit. She didn't respond to my texts to call me, and each minute that passed without seeing her set my blood on fire. A painful burn. I wanted her, and now that I'd let go of my fear, my restraint, I couldn't tell her fast enough.

Dean sat in the kitchen Sunday afternoon wearing a soccer sweatshirt and a beanie with Lorelei's number on it. He nodded at me as I stopped in the doorway. "Hey, Monroe."

The game! Yes! I could go watch her play!

"When are you leaving for the game?" I checked my watch. This was a way better plan than stalking her bedroom until she returned. I could watch her play and cheer her on. Maybe even tell Dean the truth while we were there. "I'm coming too."

"In like five minutes." Dean took a huge bite of a protein bar and frowned at me. "Why do you want to go?"

"Support your sister."

"Fair. I like that you two are friends." He held out a fist for a bump and finished the rest of his snack. "I'm driving cause it's cold. Meet me outside in five."

I did, and my nerves were frayed. Torn to little bits at the thought of telling him the truth. He tapped his fingers on the wheel, whistling and in an entirely better mood than he'd been the last few weeks. I could destroy his happiness and our friendship, with one sentence. *I want to date your sister.*

My lips cracked from my constant chewing. I would wait for the right time. Yes, I'd wait it out. I didn't have to do it right now. Content with postponing, we parked and headed toward the stands as we chatted about the football team.

Once we got to the seats, my gaze went directly to Lorelei. She stood on the sidelines, hands on her hips and her hair in a big ponytail. She smiled and did a leg kick handshake with her friend before spinning in a circle. Her shorts showcased her muscles, and *fuck,* she took my breath away.

"So, you thinking about staying then or unsure?" Dean asked, his brows coming together as he followed my gaze.

"I'm staying."

"Dude, that's huge. Fuck yes!" He pulled me into a side hug. "We can make ourselves legends next year. Legends."

I nodded, barely paying attention when the game started. The weather was terrible, almost freezing and overcast. I shivered in my winter coat, but the girls wore shorts and Under Armour. That was it. Lorelei sprinted down the field, the ball near her feet when *thud.* An opponent slammed into her, the yellow jersey clashing with our navy ones, and Lorelei hit the ground. The sound of their bodies hitting echoed in the air. That couldn't have been a legal hit. Their heads clashed.

My vision blurred, my stomach clenching. She remained lying down, unmoving. Her teammates swarmed her, the crowd going silent as my pulse blared in my ears like a siren.

Is she moving?

Why wasn't she getting up?

Without thinking, I walked down the stairs and closer to the field. Her friend Mack stood by her, her face pale. The coach and team trainer ran toward her, someone shouting in the distance.

"Get up," I mumbled, fear paralyzing me as I stood against the fence. "Get up, Lo. Get up."

I gripped the edge of the railing, damn near ready to break it off when Lorelei sat up. The trainer lifted her and supported her weight. People in the stands clapped. I tuned it all out and stared at the girl I loved.

How could I have been so stupid? She owned my heart, and I was gonna pretend she didn't? She seemed dazed, hazy even. She moved from one person to the next, her legs wobbly. She had to be scared. Fuck, I wanted to be there to comfort her. Would they let me go back there? Hold her hand? Tell her I'd be there no matter what?

I could jump the fence. Yeah, they wouldn't stop me. I hoisted myself up right as Dean approached, his face twisted with worry. "What are you doing?"

"Going back there. She must be terrified, and I want to be there for her. She needs me."

"The fuck you mean by that?" He stilled, his gaze moving from my face to his sister, then back. "I'm here. I can be there for her."

"Romano!" Someone yelled.

Dean glared at me, suspicion and hurt in his eyes before he hopped the fence. With one scathing look, he jogged toward the trainer and disappeared into the locker room with his sister.

I had no idea what to do. My girl was hurt, and she had no idea I was completely hers. She had her brother, who was probably going to kill me, and I just needed to know she was okay. Was it a concussion? A strained ligament? Would she be able to play again soon?

The game continued, and Dean and Lorelei were gone. I'd find a way home and wait for them there, desperate and hopeful that they'd both still speak to me. In my plan to win Lorelei back and talk to Dean, it backfired.

And for the first time in my life, I wasn't worried about *football.*

CHAPTER
THIRTY-ONE

Lorelei

Statistically, it was common to get a concussion playing soccer. I knew of the chances, but holy macaroni salad, it hurt like a mofo. I groaned, covering my eyes from the light of the training room. I wanted my bedroom, my fuzzy blanket, and zero lights.

They kept me in the training room until they did the CT scan and confirmed that I had a big whopper of a concussion. My first one, oddly. I'd been playing soccer my whole life, and today was winning bingo on the card for pain.

"Rest. Mental and physical, Romano." The trainer squeezed my leg. "No practice for ten days. We'll check then and *maybe* bring you back."

"Ten days?" I groaned. "For real?"

"That's an order. Nothing physical." Something clicked, and I imagined she held a clipboard. I put my arm over my eyes to block the light so I couldn't see what she was doing. "Your brother is outside, waiting to take you home. I have a list of recommendations for your care the next ten days. I'll go over it with him too. You have someone who can watch over you tonight to ensure you don't get worse?"

"Yes." My fuzzy brain thought of Luca, his strong hands and heated gaze. But that made the pounding worse. No. I thought of Dean instead. "My brother. I live with him."

"Excellent."

She helped me sit up, and I winced at the brightness.

"Lorelei." Dean came in the room, his hand going toward my shoulder. "Are you okay? They didn't tell me shit."

"Concussion." Our trainer clicked her tongue. "I'm going to go over care instructions with you. She said she lives with you?"

"Yes. Tell me what you need."

I tuned them out, my brain on a hiatus. She was tired. Their voices faded to cartoonish ones, and I swayed, dreaming of my bed and my pillows. Yes, they were feathers. Weightless. So comfy. Sighing, I rested my head on my brother's shoulder. He'd get me home. Safe. I was grateful. My brother was the best. "Thanks, Dean. I love you."

He patted my hand, and the rest of the night was hazy. I somehow got into his car. Someone strong carried me to my room. They smelled like home, but that couldn't be Dean. He always smelled like too much cologne, but my brain wasn't right.

"Mm." I snuggled into the shoulders of whoever carried me. Their fabric was soft. It reminded me of Luca, but he wouldn't do that. Dean would see us. Luca and I were done. "Pillow."

"Almost to your room, Lo."

God, my brain was playing tricks on me. Why did it want me to think of him when it hurt so much?

"So much light." My headache throbbed from the brightness.

"I'm so sorry," a deep voice said. Something soft touched

my temple, like a kiss. Would Dean do that? No. That'd be strange as hell. "I'm going to set you in your bed, but we should change you out of your clothes. You don't want to wear your jersey, do you?"

My face touched my bedsheets, and I sighed, so happy to be here. "Dean, why do you smell like Luca? Is my mind playing tricks on me?"

"No, baby, it's me. I begged him to let me help you. I needed to make sure you were okay." The voice grew soft, warm, and breath hit my face. "I'm going to take care of you tonight, okay?"

He cupped my face, running his fingers over my jaw and lips. I leaned into it, a purr coming out of me. "God, I fucking missed you."

I smiled, hoping he'd see that in the dark. There was no way this was happening. It was a lucid dream or something. My Luca wouldn't be this open with me.

"Can you sit up for a bit to take off your shirt?"

"No. Tired. Want sleep."

"Okay. I'll wake you up in a bit, and we'll change you then."

I briefly recalled him sliding into my bed with me, wrapping his arms around my waist and pulling me against him. He was like my favorite sweatshirt, my favorite season, and favorite song all rolled into one. He was comfort and love, and I fell asleep within seconds, feeling safe in his arms.

"Hey."

A gentle touch moved up and down my face, then around my ear. Goose bumps exploded down my body, and I opened my eyes. I was in my room, it was dark, and my head hurt like I had a migraine on steroids. "Ugh."

"Can you sit up for me, please?"

"Luca."

"Yeah, baby?"

His voice washed over me, warming me. "You're in my bed."

"Yes. I'm helping you tonight, and I need to make sure you're safe. Could you sit up, and we'll take your jersey off?"

"Uh, sure."

He helped me sit up, his touch gentle, like I mattered to him. My thoughts were fuzzy, and my heart ached. We were broken up, yet we never dated. Why would he be here?

"Good girl. Okay, arms up, slowly."

I obeyed, my head hurting as more questions filled it. "Why are you... what's..."

"Hey, *hey.*" He took off my shirt and tossed it on the ground before tilting my head toward him. "I will answer every question after you sleep. The first two days after a concussion are hard, so I don't want you to worry about anything except resting. Can you do that for me?"

I frowned, something nagging me, but I couldn't place it. It was like trying to catch smoke from a burning match. It disappeared as soon as I saw it.

Luca caressed my face, his lips curving up on the side. "I can hear you thinking. Relax. I'm not going anywhere."

"Okay."

"Do you want your sports bra off or on?"

"Off."

"I'm going to remove it, okay? Then we'll get you comfy, and you can sleep more." Luca dipped a finger under the band and pulled the fabric over my breasts and head.

I never thought we'd be in this position again, but Luca

didn't stare at my chest at all. He tossed the bra on the floor and quickly put a shirt over my head. It was large and warm and smelled amazing. "It smells like you."

"It's my shirt. It's comfy, and I figured it'd be easy to get on without pain."

"Mm." I burrowed into it, inhaling the detergent scent. "Thank you."

"Of course, anything." He pulled me to him again, wrapping his arms around me and nuzzling his nose along my neck. "Rest, and tomorrow we can chat more."

I woke up with my hands inside Luca's shirt. He wore sweats that sat low on his hips, and in the morning fog, I forgot what day it was. I just wanted to feel his skin on mine. I crawled onto him so I lay on top of him, like I was his personal blanket, and he laughed.

"Good morning to you too." He kissed my temple and ran his hands down my back. "How's the head?"

"Bad. But not like jackhammers." I snuggled into his neck, not caring that this wasn't appropriate. "No lights though."

"You got it. No lights, no thinking, no screen time. Those are the rules." He held me against him, one hand on the back of my head and the other on the lower part of my back. His grip tightened, like he didn't want to let go. "What do you prefer to eat? Toast? Eggs? Bacon?"

"Mm, bacon."

"I'll run to the store and get some. You stay here and rest, okay?" He patted my butt and moved me to the side.

I wanted to protest the loss of his heat, but bacon sounded good. "You'll cook it for me?"

"Yes, baby, I'll cook it for you. Anything you need."

"Mm. I like that." I smiled into my pillow, the gesture hurting a few seconds later. "I might nap again."

"Good. Now, I'm going to leave your phone in my room so

you're not tempted to use it. Screen time can hurt, so if you need anything, just ring this bell. Callum or Dean will get you whatever you want. I won't be gone long, an hour max, but I don't want you worrying."

"You're fretting over me."

"Yes, I am. Now let me." He bent down and kissed my forehead. "Be right back, baby, keep the bed warm for me."

"Luca." I peeked one eye open and found him staring at me with so much love my throat hitched. He had a sheet of paper in his hands and a pen behind his ear, like he wrote a list of things to get me. My heart swelled. "Did you change your mind?" I whispered, not clarifying what I meant.

He knew.

His eyes softened, the lines around his mouth loosening as he smiled. "More like I got my head out of my ass, but that's a conversation for when you're better."

Hope burst through my body, making me feel like flying.

"Okay."

"Sleep, pretty girl. Let me take care of you."

He left my room, shutting the door behind him, and I sighed, content despite the pain. We'd talk later, when I was better, and that sounded optimistic. Good even. I flipped to my other side just as deep voices came from the hall.

Dean. Luca.

My pulse raced, causing my head to ache, but I had to hear. They said my name, and that was what caught my attention. The fog settling over my mind faded enough for me to eavesdrop. I was still me, so obviously I'd listen in on their chat. I had questions, ones that weren't quite able to form yet, but I tensed. Luca had just left my bedroom, and Dean was outside.

Does he... know?

"I'm heading to the store to get some food for her, then I'll make breakfast," Luca said. There wasn't any meanness to his tone.

"And she slept okay? You were there all night?"

"Yes and yes. She's groggy but doing better. I stayed by her side the entire time."

Dean cleared his throat. "Thanks, man. Uh, you really don't have to do this."

"Dean." Luca's voice dropped. "You wouldn't have been able to stop me. I told you how I felt, and nothing's changing. Now, if you want to see her, wait an hour. She needs to rest again."

"You really care for her," Dean said.

They spoke quiet now, in whispers. I strained my ears, but there was no way to be sure what they said. My pulse sped up, the zing of hope coursing through my veins. It sounded like Luca had told Dean about me… but there was no way.

Football. His grandma.

He wouldn't.

I faded, my mind shutting down just as the phrase *I love her* carried through the door. It had to be my injury. Just because I wanted to hear those words didn't mean Luca said them. He definitely cared about me, but he'd never veer off course.

CHAPTER
THIRTY-TWO

Luca

Grandma: how's our girl doing?

Luca: better. It's taking all my strength to keep her phone from her. Giving me attitude about it.

Grandma: you have your chat yet?

Luca: not yet. Soon. It's only been a few days since her concussion.

Grandma: stop finding excuses. She's well enough to talk. Fix it, then call me to celebrate.

She was right. I hated it. It had been four days since the injury, and tomorrow, we had a football game. Not telling her how I felt ate at me all week. I wasn't excited about the game. It'd mean I'd have to spend even more hours away from her. I ran my fingers through my hair, pulling on the ends as I stared at the snack tray I'd prepared for Lorelei. She was in our living room, away from the TV, but there was so much sunlight. She said she was sick of her bedroom and demanded she come down here. I didn't blame her.

Callum and Oliver had been talking her ear off, annoying

me to no end. They offered to make posts for her project, and she ate it up. I could've done that too. I wanted her to need me for everything, as selfish as that was.

"Monroe." Dean walked into the kitchen, his expression neutral. He jutted his chin toward the table. "Sit with me a minute."

It's time.

"Let me drop off the food to your sister first."

"She can wait ten minutes. She also can walk." He pulled out a chair and plopped down, holding his hands together so it looked like he was praying. I joined him, my stomach churning with unease.

He knew I loved his sister and wanted to be with her. I'd laid it all out Sunday night after her injury. Told him how I didn't plan for this, how I'd hurt her, how I'd fucked it up but planned to earn her back. Told him I'd always be his teammate and football was a priority, but I couldn't have just football as my entire life.

He never punched me, which was a good sign. He said me he needed time to adjust to this, then we'd talk. We agreed to take care of Lo and then hash it out.

Seemed like he was ready.

"I don't say this lightly." Dean closed his eyes, exhaled, and glared at me. "I trust you. You're loyal, intense, hardworking. I love you like a brother, on and off the field.

I nodded, swallowing the ball in my throat. There had to be a *but* coming.

He winced, glanced over my shoulder before meeting my gaze. "I also know you're stubborn and can lose sight of others when you're focused. You say you love my sister, but what—"

"There is no but what. I love her."

Dean's eye twitched. "When you hurt her—"

"Then I'll apologize, learn from it, and never do it again."

My body raced with my pulse, the intensity of this conversation like a Big Ten game. Oxygen flowed through me, fueling me with each breath. This was a defensive play, and I had to react the right way. Instead of bodies on the field, it was words. "This isn't temporary for me, this is…Christ, how do I say this?"

Dean crossed his arms and leaned back.

"Her and I need to chat still, so all of this depends on her. If she doesn't want this, then I'll respect her and be whatever she needs. I can't not have her in my life. But if she'll give this a real chance, I'll put her first. I don't care if you approve or don't like it, Dean, that won't stop me. I know you won't let this affect us on the field because that's not who we are as athletes, but I want Lorelei as long as she'll have me, in any capacity. Now, if that affects our friendship, it sucks, but I hurt her by wanting to hide her. I can't… I refuse to upset her again." I stood up, the urge to hold her even stronger than a few minutes ago. "I want a life with her."

Dean nodded, tapped the table with his fingers, then held out his hand. "Every time you make her cry, I punch you in the face."

"How long does this stipulation last?"

"Forever. I don't care if you're fucking sixty. You hurt her, I punch you."

My lips twitched. "You're assuming she won't hand me my ass first."

"I expect her to. Romano twins are tough."

I shook his hand, and he pulled me for an unexpected hug. "You two make sense together, and it'll get easier to accept. Just, no excessive PDA around me, alright?"

I squeezed him hard. "You got it."

He patted me twice before walking away, and I jogged toward the snack tray. Lo and hunger didn't mix well together, and I loved how her face lit up when she saw me. If I made her even half as happy as she made me, then that'd be enough. My teammates had left her, thankfully, so it was just her in the living room. "Hungry?"

She licked her lips. "Is that cheese?"

"Lots of it."

"God, I love you." She clapped before her eyes widened. "Wait, I mean, I love cheese. I love cheese, yes." She blinked a lot and tilted her head. "You're fine too."

I smiled and sat on the couch next to her. I placed the tray on the coffee table and pulled one of her feet into my lap. She always moaned a sexy little sound when I massaged her foot. Even now, she closed her eyes and sighed.

"Relax, eat. Then we can talk."

"Mm, how about we talk while I eat?" She leaned forward and snatched four pieces from the tray. She crossed her eyes as she bit into them. "Mild cheddar gives me a stomach boner."

I snorted. "You're feeling better."

"I am, yeah. I want to start getting on my computer for an hour at a time tomorrow, see how it feels. That is… if my keeper lets me." She glared at me and pinched my side. "You're a real mother hen, Luca."

This is my moment.

"Lorelei." Shit. My voice cracked and got all deep. My face heated, and my blip of confidence faded into nothing. She could want me as just a friend again, as nothing. She could've realized I wasn't good enough for her. Hell, she could tell me to fuck off.

This was hard.

"Luca." She smiled and bit into another bite of cheese. She nudged my side with her foot. "Are we finally having *the talk?*"

Narrowing my eyes, I stilled my hand on her foot. "Are you mocking me?"

"Yes." She laughed and scooted closer to me. "It's so easy."

"This is serious." I gulped, the back of my neck sweating at this point.

"So serious." She scrunched her nose.

"Would you stop it?" My lips twitched.

Lorelei grinned so hard her smile covered her entire face, and joy radiated from her like physical waves. She pushed her hair behind her ears and sighed, shaking her head at me as her gaze softened. "I'll behave and listen. Have your speech."

"God." I laughed. "You're the worst."

"Yeah, but you love me anyway."

"See, that's the thing." I cupped her jaw, running my thumb over her cheek. She leaned into my touch and placed her hand over mine. My chest tightened with a gooey, warm sense of peace. "I love you, Lorelei. I want your smiles, your laughter, your attitude, and your hanger attacks. I want to wipe away your tears when you cry out of joy, fear, or even if you're sad. I —" My voice shook, and I blinked away emotion. "You want someone to put you first, and I'll be that person. You deserve the world, and I can try to give you that. I'm done being afraid of all the what-ifs in my life and want to focus on the what-I-haves, and that's you. So, can you forgive me?"

"Forgive you?" She sniffed.

Tears fell down her cheeks, and I wiped them away. She smiled, so could they be happy tears? I pulled her closer so she sat on my lap now. Her warmth spread through me and her scent—God, she smelled so damn good. I kissed her temple, pulling her in a hug. "For not being what you needed before. No secrets, no hiding. We do this thing for real. A relationship. I show you every day how much I love you, and you continue being the light in my world. Football is important, and so is my grandma, but you…I need you to be mine. To be my person."

She glanced up at me, a watery smile on her lips as she said, "You want me to be your goddess?"

I snorted. "Yes, be my goddess. Love me back."

"Okay." She hummed, rested her head against my chest and hugged me hard. "I will."

"That's all you have to say? *I will?*" I cupped the back of her head, gently kneading her scalp with one hand and rubbing her lower back with the other. I'd never tire of holding her like this, our chests pressed together and her scent enveloping me. Yet, I expected more from her. More words.

"Four days." She pinched my side. "You can wait to hear me say I love you back for four days, Monroe."

"Is there any reason why you're being sassy right now?"

"You and Dean talked outside my door Monday, and I heard you. You told him you loved me, and I had to wait four fucking days for you to tell me. So yes, Luca, there is a reason I'm being sassy."

"Fuck, I missed you." I cupped her face, staring down at her until I couldn't take it anymore. I kissed her. She tasted like cheese and coffee, and she groaned into my mouth, sliding her tongue into the kiss and stealing all my rational thoughts. "Baby, I have more to say."

"Mm, can you kiss and talk?" She pulled back, grinning at me with red cheeks and flushed skin.

"You're fucking gorgeous." My breath hitched in my throat. "There's nothing I wouldn't do for you. You know that, right?"

"I do." She cupped my chin, a glint of mischief entering her eyes. "You submitted my assignments, did multiple grocery runs, held my hand, and told my brother the truth. I can *feel* how much you care for me."

"I sense a but coming..." I gripped her waist, letting my fingers tease the skin above her pants.

"But if you truly want to be my boyfriend, you'll meet every need, yes?"

"Anything. Ask me anything and I'll do it."

She licked her lips, bent low until her teeth grazed the shell of my ear. "Anything?"

"Baby, yes."

"Then I want you to take me upstairs and use your mouth to make me come."

I coughed into her neck, the image of my fantasy already coming to my mind. I'd been super careful because of her injury but… "You can't move or strain yourself."

"I don't plan to. My boyfriend's mouth is really talented."

She looked so smug, so pretty sitting on me. I laughed. "Fine. *Fine.* I guess I'll eat you out until you come. I'm giving like that."

Her winning smile felt like a punch to the chest, and her joy knocked me off-balance. I picked her up, held her tight against my chest when she mumbled something quiet. "What was that?"

"I love you."

I stopped, waited for her to look at me. "Say it again. Slower."

"I love you." She chewed the side of her lip. "I teased you before, but I wanted you to know for sure. I'm in this. Whatever we do, its together. You and me. Luca and Lo."

"Fucking love the sound of that." I kissed her forehead and continued upstairs, where I'd show her over and over how much I loved her.

I might've almost missed my chance with her by being too afraid, but she got me out of my shell. She pushed me to be better, to realize there was more to life than just football. Lorelei Romano entered my life as a forbidden distraction, but she taught me life was about joy, laughter, and letting people in. My world changed for her, and I'd make sure I showed her how much she meant to me every single day.

EPILOGUE

Seven months later…
Lorelei

P leasure danced along my skin, making me squirm. It was that time of the day where it wasn't quite sunlight yet, but night fell into the next day. My normally pitch-black room had a trickle of light dancing through the curtains, and I squirmed against my sheets.

"Mm." A deep, gravelly voice hummed against my neck.

Luca's breath tickled the spot where my neck met my shoulder, and goose bumps exploded down my arm and to my legs. I rocked against him, his erection digging into my ass.

He sighed as his hand moved from my hip, going underneath my shirt and right to my nipples. He tweaked them, pulling on the ends before repeating the process to the other. I moaned, the pain and pleasure combination already making me wet. His warm mouth sucked on my skin as his other hand slid my panties down my legs. I loved morning sex. It was my favorite thing, where we were sleepy and not in a hurry. It was soft touches and gentle kisses, slow teasing and long strokes.

Sex with Luca never got old, ever. If anything, since deciding to be together, it had improved if that was even possible. With our feelings out in the open and us *choosing* each other, each touch heightened the experience.

"I'm so proud of you," he whispered, kissing along my neck and over my shoulder. He placed his fingers between my thighs, taking his time playing with me. He knew where to touch, where to tease, and he did it well.

I arched to my side, meeting his heated gaze. He was so handsome. His dark eyes and long lashes, his messy hair and jawline... he still made my heart beat faster even though it had been months together. Best half a year of my life if I was being honest. He smiled, his signature half grin that was meant just for me before he kissed me.

"Luca, morning breath!" I shoved him away, but he wouldn't have it.

"I don't care." He kissed me again, deeper, like kissing me was his favorite thing in the world. "My girl is a working woman. I'm gonna steal kisses when I can."

He rolled on top of me, pressing his lips along my collarbone, chest, and stomach. He lifted my shirt up and flicked my nipple with his tongue before sucking the tip into his mouth with a loud groan.

My skin lit up, the urge to have him overtaking me. "Luca," I moaned.

"Yes, baby, I know." He cupped my breasts, sucking and biting them before reaching over me toward the side table. He grabbed a condom we left out last night and quickly put it on. He cupped my face, his thumb tracing my lip before he slid into me. He rested his forehead on me as he thrust, his hand moving to arch my hip up.

Each movement sent a flurry of current through me, my body coming alive with pleasure from his touch. There were no rushed movements, all lingering touches and a slow burn. He knew what angle I needed to get me to release. I knew to wrap my legs around him, letting him go deeper.

"*Yes,* that's it Lo." He nipped my earlobe, tugging on it. "Need you closer."

There wasn't an inch between us, but I felt the neediness, desperation in his voice. Adjusting to me working was hard on us. I was gone most the time, and this right here, our bodies melding together all sweaty made everything else disappear. Digging my fingers into his ass, I sucked his neck, and he went harder.

Unhinged Luca was my favorite Luca.

"You taste so good," I said, dragging my tongue along every part of him I could reach. His neck, his shoulder, the spot behind his ear. His breathing picked up, his grunts louder. Pleasure built at the base of my spine, dancing up to my neck as he adjusted his angle.

"Come for me." He ground into me, pushing up as he studied my face. "Eyes open."

Even now, after months of this, seeing his pupils dilated as he watched me come made me shudder. I chewed my lip, welcoming the orgasm as it took me hard. He continued fucking me, his eyes never leaving mine as his legs shook. I gasped for air, the pleasure blinding me as Luca stroked me in all the right places. "Yes, Luca." I gripped him hard, never wanting this to end.

He quickened his pace, his breath coming out in pants as he went even faster. His grip tightened, his face twisted and then he was coming. "*Fuck,*" he moaned, his head dropping onto my shoulder. "Never gets old with you."

I rubbed his back, kissing the side of his neck and breathing him in. "Never."

"You're perfect for me, Lo. In every way." He kissed my

ear, then pulled out, staring down at me with the same tender expression he wore the last few months. The depth of his dark eyes made me feel special, loved, alive.

"Remember how we thought we could keep this to one night?" I whispered.

"Idiots." He chuckled, pushing up and tossing the condom into the trash. His back muscles rippled with the movement, and I traced along his spine. He shivered and quickly rolled back to face me.

"I love you." He kissed the center of my chest, right above my heart. "I'll cook you breakfast while you shower."

"Mm, you're sexy when you fret over me." I pushed up onto my elbows, my pulse still racing from the orgasms. "You don't have to make me anything, Monroe. I can eat a protein bar on my way to work."

"My girl needs a full breakfast before her fancy job." He pushed my hair behind my ear, his smile gooey and soft. He held me there for a beat before getting up and slipping on a pair of gray sweats.

Those sweats made me do stupid, silly little things like demand he model for me or flex his ass or promise me he'll never leave me. He wiggled his ass at me, making me laugh as I slid my legs onto the floor. "Get over here, let me feel you."

He backed up, and I dug my fingers into his glutes. I even bent down and bit one. "I might be obsessed with your ass."

"As long as it's just mine, Lorelei."

I snorted. "You can't be mad I said Chris Evans was hot."

"I can and will be."

I rolled my eyes, heading into my bathroom and showering. It wasn't a hair wash day, so I was out and ready for work in twenty minutes. Earning the internship with Mrs. Gravestone was my proudest moment. The work I did for Luca's grandma and the living center had only increased. They raised thousands of dollars and had a continual stream of donations now. They had social media and partnerships with schools, churches, and rotary clubs. Seeing his grandma become a local star still made me cry. She'd reconnected with an old flame after ending things with Sebastian, much to Luca's dismay. I interviewed three rounds for the marketing specialist position for a nonprofit that helped underprivileged youth, and while it was only the first week, I fucking loved it. It made me dream big, like what I wanted to do after graduation.

"Damn girl." Mack whistled at me as I walked out of my room and toward our kitchen. We finally got our place together, just two blocks away from the boys' house. Luca spent almost every night here, but two nights a week were for me and Mack. "You're wearing the hell out of that skirt."

"Thanks." I beamed. For a girl who spent most of my life in workout clothes, it felt fun to dress in skirts and professional shirts. I loved this new version of myself, and it was cool to have everyone's support. Mack, Luca, my brother… "Oh, I saw Dean last night, and he mentioned he was coming to get you today. What are you doing?"

"Oh, uh, this volunteer thing." She avoided my gaze and walked into her room. "Have a great day at work, hun."

I narrowed my eyes, almost ready to confront her. Was she seeing my brother on the side? Probably. Did I care? Not at all except for the lies. But… I couldn't really talk. Not after what Luca and I did. If they were together, they'd tell me when they were ready.

"Fuck, Lo." Luca stared at me as I entered the kitchen, his brows furrowed. "I want to eat you in that skirt."

"Monroe." I blushed. "You just got some, settle down."

"You are a goddess." He stalked toward me, picked me up, and set me on the counter. He kissed me right on the mouth. "Mine."

Laughing, I placed a hand on his chest. "You're wearing my lipstick."

"Don't care." He kissed me again, softer. "I can't get enough of you. It's been months, and I need *more*. Can I move in with you? Propose? Demand you live with me?"

When he joked about moving in or eloping, it always made me smile. I knew how Luca felt about me. He was a protector, a caregiver. He was an all-in, give one thousand percent to something no matter what. He was like that with football, the team, his grandma, and now me. To be on the end of his focus was special. I never took it for granted. I ran my hands down his large chest, loving the strength of him. He was working his ass off to have the best senior year ever, hoping his stats would help propel him in the NFL draft next year. And after all the worry he had about him and Dean? If anything, they played even better together on the field.

"I'll follow you wherever you sign, but senior year is for me. I love you, want to marry you and have babies and live with you even though you're really messy. But this is my final year. I have a plan, you know. Things I gotta do."

"Like what?"

"Adventures with Mack. Find the hidden tunnels I've heard about. Stay up way too late and regret it the next day." I traced his bicep.

Lines formed around his eyes, a flash of worry sparking behind them. "You'd tell me if you were unhappy, right, like I was holding you back?"

"Luca." I swiped my lipstick of his lips. "You make me the happiest. I'm telling you I want the rest of my life with you, but I don't want to rush this year. That's all."

"You're sure?"

I rolled my eyes. "Am I some shy broad who doesn't speak her mind? No. I told you when you pissed me off last month when you thought texting ok, with two letters, was fine. I'm better with you. We're better together."

He sighed and rested his forehead against me. "I like the sound of that."

"Good, now I should eat before I'm late."

"Right." He ran his hands down my body and lifted me off the counter. "Can I drop you off this morning, so that way I can swing by later to get you before meeting my grandma for dinner? Her boyfriend can still drive, so they're heading this way."

"Oh, I'd love that." I beamed at him, so damn happy life worked out the way it had. "I think she wanted Dean to come this time too. Want to invite him?"

"Absolutely." He pointed to the island. "Now sit, so I can feed you."

It's funny how you could plan exactly what you thought would happen. I had *plans* this past year, ones that I swore I'd do. Yet they all veered in different directions, and it was amazing. I got Luca, his grandma, and this internship. I learned about what motivated me and what I wanted to do in the world, all while having Luca by my side. I was a lucky girl, and while he joked about getting married, I couldn't wait.

Lorelei Monroe had a great ring to it after all.

THE END

CRAVING MORE?

Want an extra scene between Luca and Lo? Click the link below to receive a bonus scene one year later.

https://landing.mailerlite.com/webforms/landing/l7e7t3

SNOWED IN FOR CHRISTMAS

Want to read the first chapter of my October steamy holiday
romantic comedy? Flip the page to the first chapter of
SNOWED IN FOR CHRISTMAS!

CHAPTER ONE
BECCA

HGTV had to be created with magic—it sucked me in within the first second, and I hadn't moved in three hours. *Love It or List It* was my catnip. Three entire hours of sprawling out on the massive leather couch when I had shit to do. Lots of shit. As the house mom for Betas, I had to make sure the chef was paid, and since the cleaning service had two weeks off for the holidays, that had become my responsibility too. And considering the fun fact that there was a blizzard coming, I had to make sure I had enough food to shelter in place for a week. If I wanted to get into specifics, I needed to make sure I had enough sugar, chocolate, and wine to survive the holidays alone. *Again.*

"Becs? My mom wants to know when the doors are officially locked for winter break." Marissa Kelly patted my shoulder as she came to a stop behind the couch. I would never rank students in the Beta house in order of favorites, but if I was forced at gunpoint, Marissa would be in the top three.

"Friday, girlfriend."

I looked away from the TV and cringed at my outfit: hot

pink pajamas covered with little suns wearing sunglasses tucked into purple-and-green fuzzy socks, with a stain on my chest from either chocolate or coffee and a clear view of my stomach because I forgot a button. *It's no wonder I'm single.*

"Is it sad I wish I didn't have to leave for two weeks?" Marissa joined me on the couch and sighed with as much angst as a nineteen-year-old could.

"You have a home here waiting for you when you get back. Trust me, enjoy the time you have with your family while you can, because adulthood comes fast and hard." I adjusted my position, moving so we sat shoulder-to-shoulder, and snuck a look at her. Her typical smile disappeared. A deep frown that made her look years older replaced it. I nudged her shoulder with my own. "Hey, talk to me. I haven't seen you this sad since the infamous breakup freshman year."

She shrugged. "My parents are going through a rough time, and it's hard seeing them fight. It never used to be like that."

Poor Marissa. My soul hurt for her. "I'm sorry. I really am. I wish I had some profound advice for you to help or make it better, but that is out of my realm. Just…maybe try to find things to do with your parents separately. Offer to help with dinner or cleaning. You can always text me if you want."

"You're the best, Becs." She leaned her head against me.

A rush of *this-is-why-I-love-my-job* bloomed over me in a full-body hum of happiness, and I couldn't stop my smile. "I *am* your house mom, and yeah, I can be the best."

She laughed, and I put my arm around her shoulders for a half-hug. She leaned into it, and a lightness filled my chest.

No one in my education-focused family understood why I did what I did. They always asked how it was going and what I actually did, but it was so foreign to them that their eyes would gloss over and they'd nod a lot. They appreciated the fact that I helped college students, sure, but it wasn't the same as teaching in their eyes. Yeah, I loved my parents, and I knew they loved me, but they didn't understand me. None of my endless stream of first dates ever understood me. Very few people did. *Except these girls.*

"I guess I better start packing since it'll take me forever to clean my room."

"Yeah, honestly, you're a great human but a slob, Issa." I earned another smile from her.

I was about to offer to help when Amanda Lee rushed down the spiral staircase to my right, face flushed and eyes the size of saucers. "Becs."

"Yes?" I sat up straighter, already imagining the crisis I would have to deal with. Was it her creepy boyfriend? Her slipping grades? Her secret stash of vodka I knew she kept behind her desk but we never talked about?

"I tried opening the window and it wouldn't work, so I forced it, you know, to get fresh air into the room. I do live on the highest floor so it gets stuffy, yeah? So I shoved it and the window shattered and I tried cleaning it up but then the wind picked up, and anyway…my clothes are on the roof, and you know how my mom feels about me losing *anything*," she rambled, slurring words and syllables in an almost incomprehensible way. But I knew her well and pieced it together.

"Your clothes are on the roof?"

"And all over the yard." Her bottom lip trembled. "My mom will kill me if I lose those blouses. My grandma made them for me."

Save the clothes and then look at the glass. "Okay girls, get your coats. We're going on a recovery mission."

I marched from our huge living room to the closet, shoving

my feet into my favorite pair of sequined Uggs, bundling up with a head-to-toe hot pink parka and ridiculous yellow hat I'd knitted myself two years ago. Not my best-stitched work, but it was warm and that was all that mattered in winter. Marissa, Amanda, and another pair of girls joined us and bundled up, and we set out the back door. Sure enough, colored shirts decorated the dull landscape. It had been a brutal December in the Midwest. Poor central Illinois was already prepared for a blizzard before Christmas, and the wind burned the exposed parts of my face. I didn't complain though—we had a mission to complete.

We each took off in different directions, grabbing shirts before they blew away, and a bright red something caught my eye next door. Damn it, Amanda. It landed in *his* front yard. Of course, I'd be wearing something totally uncool as I trekked around Harrison's property in search of a runaway shirt. He probably wasn't home anyway. He had family in state—a niece and nephews, if I remembered correctly—and it was Thursday before break. Yeah, he wouldn't be home, and I'd be fine. *No need to panic.*

With a quick glance at Harrison's front window, I blew out a relieved breath at the dark stillness within. Yes! He's not even home!

I sprinted toward the yard and snatched the shirt. Unfortunately, whoever was in charge of my life thought it'd be hysterical to increase the wind and send the shirt flying onto his front porch.

Rats.

Okay, I can do this. He wasn't home, and even if he was, I had nothing to be embarrassed about—even if he did ghost me on the after-date call he'd promised.

Ten steps. That's all it'd take. I scanned the house once

more, and then I moved stealthily in case I was wrong. The last thing I needed was to come face-to-face with that man.

Each crunch of the ground beneath my boots echoed, and my heart raced. Tiptoeing on the bottom step, I winced as it creaked. My eyes shot to the window, hoping his handsome face and infamous frown wouldn't appear.

A long moment passed before I moved again. Then, blowing out a breath, I snatched the shirt off the railing. Thinking I was home free, I almost did a victory dance. But before I could stop myself, my right foot slid out from beneath me on a patch of wet leaves, and I crashed onto my butt on his porch. Hard. With enough noise to wake the dead. Fate was seriously messing with my life.

"Shit, shit, shit!" I yelled, my lower back hurting more than I'd like to admit. I lay there for several seconds before heaving myself upright, and as I stood, the front door flew open. I tried to never let the girls hear me curse. But the pain caused it to slip out.

It was like a movie, a slow-motion action scene where my heart crept up my throat and my palms sweated despite the freezing temperature. I took one deep breath and met the intimidating and perfect green eyes of Harrison. "Hello, Harrison."

"Becca," he grumbled. His rough, deep voice was way too sexy and commanding for his own good. And oh, baby, I hated how he affected me.

"Great porch you have here. Just wanted to say have a nice holiday." I marched down the stairs with more trepidation than before. I winced, but my back was to him so he wouldn't see. *Just let me escape, please.*

"Why are you on my porch?"

"You wouldn't believe me if I told you," I said into the wind, still not turning back.

"Try me."

I snuck a glance at him again, hating how his gray Henley showcased his sculpted arms and strong chest—broad shoulders were my weakness—and the shirt paired well with his black jeans hugging his massive thighs. It wasn't fair he looked like that when my pink, girly pajamas peaked out from under my coat. Channeling my tiny inner badass, I gave him my best smile.

"Okay." I held up the red shirt and motioned to the sorority house with my chin. "One of the girls broke a window on the top floor, and her clothes escaped her room. She blamed the wind, but now that I think about it, it's a bit suspicious. Was she waving clothes out to signal someone? Smoking a doobie? Airing out a fart? I just don't know." I frowned for a beat before chewing on my chapped bottom lip in the awkward silence. "Anyway. So, yeah. We're on a dangerous recovery mission before the elements destroy her clothes."

His expression never changed beyond a slight lift on the side of his mouth. "Recovery mission?"

"Yes. For the clothes." I held the shirt up like I was wearing it, pretending to be a model. "See?"

"Yeah, I see. You expect me to believe it just *landed* on my porch?" He arched one disbelieving brow.

"Yes." I gave him a firm nod.

"What was the crash I heard?"

"Oh, that." I tried thinking of something that would explain the sound of my tush hitting his stairs, but the longer the silence grew between us, the more I felt the need to ramble. "A raccoon. I saw a raccoon, and we fought over the shirt."

His nostrils flared for a second before he tilted his head to the side. "You fell."

"Okay, fine. Yeah. I fell. Happy?"

"Not particularly. Are you okay?"

Did his face look like he was actually concerned? My heart skipped a beat at the thought, but it settled down just as quickly. No, he must be cold.

"The diagnosis is that I will survive. It'll take a couple of hot baths, but nothing more than my ego and butt is bruised."

"Glad you're alright."

Those simple words should not have caused me to blush like a teenager around her crush, but they did. I had to get out of there, like five seconds ago. "See you around, Harrison."

I took a couple steps back toward the sorority house when he spoke again. This was the most words we'd exchanged in over two years…since that night. Since that *kiss*. Weird didn't cover how I felt about it.

"Are you staying in the house alone over break?"

"Yes." I didn't stop walking.

"That's a huge house for one person."

I spun around and narrowed my eyes, giving him my *no bullshit* look I always gave the girls. My mom referred to me as a tough marshmallow when I tried to be mean, but it was all I had. "I'm a big girl, and I've done it before. I'll be fine. It's my job."

"Make sure you fix the broken window. You shouldn't wait too long to repair it with the blizzard coming."

I squeezed my eyes shut. He was right. *Ugh.* I had to call someone to come out today or tomorrow or I'd have an open portal into the frigid negative temperatures that would last for an entire week. My heart rate sped up like I was running.

"I gotta go." I waved over my shoulder, still too humiliated to face him again.

"Have a nice holiday, Becca."

I didn't respond to him. The window was my priority. I had

never had to get one repaired before. Did I just call a window guy and beg? Were there window guys? Oh my gosh, how could I be a house mom and not know how to fix a broken window?

I rushed by the girls carrying various shirts and waved at the few sitting in the front parlor with their suitcases. Parents started picking up their girls today after finals, and I doubled back to say goodbye. They couldn't see me with anything but a smile. No one ever saw my panic. *Remain calm, stay positive, and always have a plan.* That was my motto for life.

"Ladies, have a wonderful time at home. I'll miss you."

"We'll miss you too, Becs." Ashley, Beatrice, and Maria all hugged me, and I squeezed them back. "We left you presents under the tree. You can't open them until Christmas, though."

"You did?" I almost cried at their genuine expressions. "I said no gifts!"

"We know, but you're unlike other sorority moms. You invest yourself in us, and believe in us, and well, you deserve a nice holiday."

My eyes watered. "I told myself no tears when you all left but look at me, already weepy."

"You cry at animal rescue commercials, every rerun of *Friends*, and when we get good grades. Never change, Becca Fairfield."

"Don't forget every single Hallmark movie," Beatrice added.

"Okay, leave already." I gently pushed her away, causing the three of them to giggle.

I peeled off my coat, refilled my cup of coffee with the newest hazelnut roast and coconut creamer, and sat. I had a crisis to deal with, and I had no idea how. But the first step: clean up the mess.

That I could do. I grabbed the broom, a trash bin, and

heavy-duty gloves I still had from an intense scarecrow costume for Halloween and marched up to the third floor still wearing my puffy coat. Amanda's room faced north—the exact direction of Harrison's house—and sure enough, the wind whipped around her room. Pieces of glass decorated the floor, the windowsill, and the roof.

I am their house mom. It is my job to take care of them when they are away from home. I can do this. I will do this.

"Becs, do you need help?" Kristin Garrison, the president of the Betas with enough potential to run the world—despite her terrible taste in men—entered the room.

A rush of happiness flooded through me at her offer. "I'd rather you don't cut yourself. But could you find me a tarp and lots of duct tape? We should have some in storage outside."

"You got it. Be careful."

"You too. That shed is a piece of work out there."

Kristin left, her face set in determined lines, and I scanned the damage. It took ten minutes to sweep up the floor, the desk area, and the windowsill. So far, no cuts.

Outside the window, there were huge pieces. I stepped onto the roof—just one foot—and balanced, picking up the broken glass and tossing it into the bin. The wind blasted and I stumbled, slamming my shoulder into the window frame—right where a minor shard stuck out.

"Balderdash!" The cut hurt. The sharp sting stole my breath for a second, and I maneuvered myself back into the room. I unbuttoned my top and surveyed the damage. Yup. A small shard impaled my arm, leaving a trail of blood dripping down my pale skin.

My head spun...oh no. I hated blood. I did. It was the worst.

I needed to sit. Yeah, just for a second. I found my way to Amanda's twin bed and put my head between my knees. Everything turned fuzzy, and I focused on my tasks.

Clean up damage.

Repair area with tarp.

Make insurance claim.

Call repairman.

I repeated it three more times as everything went black.

You can pre-order it now! Snowed in for Christmas

ALSO BY JAQUELINE SNOWE

CENTRAL STATE FOOTBALL SERIES

First Meet Foul

Book 2 (January 2024!)

Snowed in for Christmas

CENTRAL STATE SERIES

The Puck Drop

From the Top

Take the Lead

Off the Ice

CLEAT CHASERS SERIES

Challenge Accepted

The Game Changer

Best Player

No Easy Catch

OUT OF THE PARK SERIES

Evening the Score

Sliding Home

Rounding the Bases

SHUT UP AND KISS ME SERIES

Internship with the Devil

Teaching with the Enemy

Nightmare Next Door

STANDALONES

Holdout

Take a Chance on Me

The Weekend Deal

ABOUT THE AUTHOR

Jaqueline Snowe lives in Arizona where the "dry heat" really isn't that bad. She prefers drinking coffee all hours of the day and snacking on anything that has peanut butter or chocolate. She is the mother to two fur-babies who don't realize they aren't humans and two amazing kiddos. She is an avid reader and writer of romances and tends to write about athletes. Her husband works for an MLB team (not a player, lol) so she knows more about baseball than any human ever should.

To sign up for her review team, or blogger list, please visit her website www.jaquelinesnowe.com for more information. If you want updates on her latest releases, join her newsletter here!

Made in the USA
Las Vegas, NV
02 June 2024

90635879R00193